Wild Hunt

Wild Hunt

The Witch's Odyssey

Book Two

Alison Levy

SPARKPRESS

Published in 2026 by
SparkPress, an imprint of The Stable Book Group

1569 Solano Ave #546
Berkeley, CA 94707
https://shewritespress.com
Library of Congress Control Number: 2026932720
ISBN: 979-8-89636-378-1
eISBN: 979-8-89636-379-8

Printed in the United States

For Matt and Eric

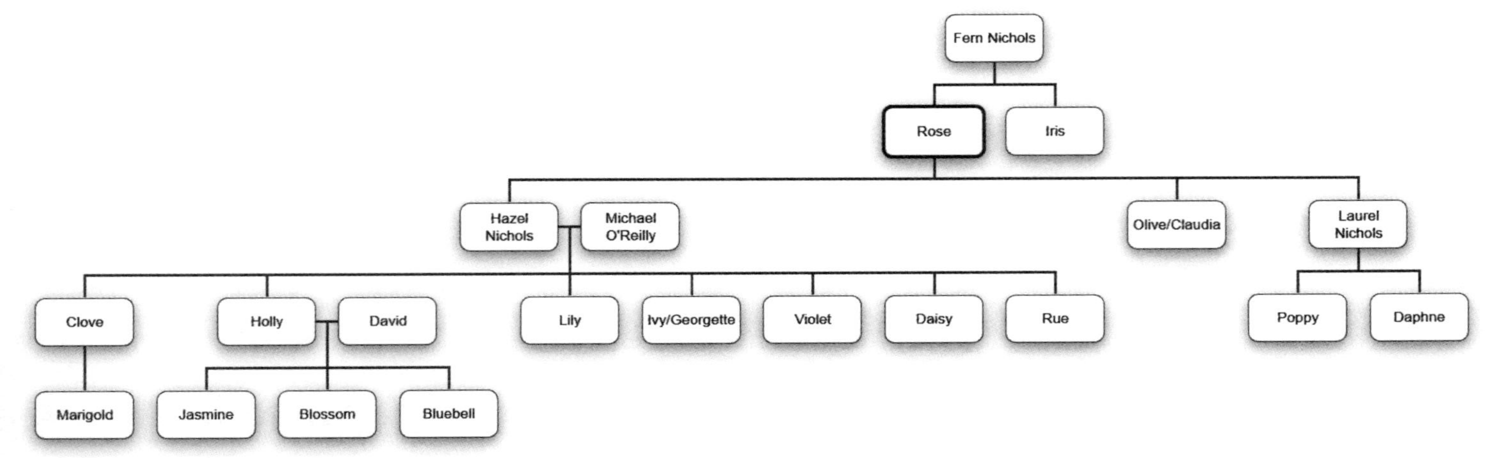
Fern Nichols
Rose
Iris
Hazel Nichols
Michael O'Reilly
Olive/Claudia
Laurel Nichols
Clove
Holly
David
Lily
Ivy/Georgette
Violet
Daisy
Rue
Poppy
Daphne
Marigold
Jasmine
Blossom
Bluebell

Kazimiera

"NO!"

Georgette shrank a little at Kazimiera's harsh tone but, to the Vampire's annoyance, recovered quickly. The skinny little blonde flicked her bouncy curls out of her face and met her boss's intense stare with a smile—which had the effect of water on a grease fire.

Six months after signing their renegotiated contract, the witch was getting bold. More and more, she questioned her boss's decisions, insisted upon debate. Kazimiera huffed. This argument was a headache she didn't need.

"I know the ingredients are a little pricey," said Georgette, gesturing to the list she had compiled, "but they should be easy to find."

"Absolutely not!"

"The spells are time-consuming, but I think I can cast them in stages. You know, one spell a week for a couple of months—"

"What part of 'no' is confusing you?" Kazimiera flashed her teeth.

"Well," the witch said, eyes wide behind her glasses, "what part is holding you up?"

"Every part!" Kazimiera held up one hand, ticking off three fingers as she spoke. "I will not pay for the ingredients,

I will not make time in your schedule for the spellcasting, and I will not sanction this project under my roof!"

"But Kairos—"

"You mean Demetra."

"He wants to be called Kairos."

Kazimiera crossed her arms over her chest. "I'm not calling her that."

"Look." Georgette sighed, avoiding Kazimiera's eyes. "I get why you would refuse funds for Kairos's gender reassignment, but you won't make time in my schedule? Helping the Fae in this club is my job—it *is* my schedule. Also," she added after a tense pause, "you refusing to use Kairos's name or correct pronouns is upsetting a lot of the staff. They say it takes minimal effort to use the right name, and they don't like that you won't do it."

"Quiet!" Kazimiera snapped. The witch's voice was like a gnat in her ear, distracting her from important work and aggravating the tension in her head. "I've done enough! I looked the other way when she started using a binder. Do you have the slightest idea how absurd it is for a Sphinx to bind her breasts? Sphinx breasts are supposed to be out and proud. It's what my VIPs expect! Even so, I ignored the damn binder. But then she started wearing that nasty lion mane. God." She cringed. "It's not even realistic, it's just a rag wig."

"He wanted to buy a good one, but you wouldn't authorize the funds."

A knock on the office door drew the witch's gaze, but Kazimiera ignored it and slammed her palms down on her desk. The loud bang made Georgette jump.

"I can't have her parading around in front of my VIPs looking like some lion rag doll! No one will pay money to see that!"

"But if I do the spells," the witch pushed, "he won't need the wig or the binder anymore. Won't that solve the problem?"

A second knock, louder than the first, broke the air. Kazimiera hissed at the sound but stayed focused on Georgette. "Shoveling money at her identity crisis creates more problems than it solves! Everything in this club costs money—money she's no longer making for me. If I let her keep draining funds without contributing, it puts me in debt and it sets a bad precedent."

"What precedent?"

"I'm not running a charity!" Kazi shouted, throwing up her hands. "I don't need half the Fae in the city coming to me for handouts. If you're determined to use magic to give Demetra a dick, do it on your own time and your own dime."

A thunderous knock shook the walls of Kazimiera's office. Fists balled in frustration, she snapped her gaze to the door and roared, "*WHAT?*"

The door swung open, allowing the light from the hallway to sweep into the dimly lit office. Kazimiera squinted, willing her nocturnal vision to adapt.

Silhouetted in the doorway was a tall, broad-shouldered man dressed in a long black coat. There was only one Fae in her building who carried his head under his arm: the Dullahan.

"What do you want?" Kazimiera demanded, glaring.

"We have a new arrival," said the Dullahan, his deep, echoey voice emanating from his neck hole rather than his decayed head.

"It can wait!"

The Dullahan shifted his weight and switched his head to his other arm. A sliver of light leaked over the head's yellowish skin and one milky eye. "There's a problem."

Eyes squeezed shut, Kazimiera pinched the bridge of her nose. "Of course there is," she muttered.

"I'll handle it," Georgette said, jumping up from her seat. "You've got other work to do."

"*I'll* deal with it," Kazimiera said, throwing her hands into the air as she brushed past Georgette on her way out the door. "This is my business, dammit."

On the ground floor of the building, Club Nocturne was enjoying a quiet Wednesday night. There was a handful of patrons at the bar, and there were a few more in the lounge areas, but the dance floor, despite the lively recorded music on the sound system, was empty. No lights illuminated the vacant stage; the Siren whose songs lured crowds on weekends was upstairs in her room, resting her magical voice.

Kazimiera wasn't bothered by the low numbers; she never expected much profit Tuesdays through Thursdays. She kept the club open those days mostly to keep her live-in staff occupied. Idle hands were the devil's workshop—a dangerous prospect for an enterprise that relied on secrecy—so a steady routine was vital. It also kept *her* busy, which was the very reason she'd opened the club in the first place.

A faint silver glow emanated from beneath the overhang of the bar's indigo top. Mirrored shelves full of liquor bottles stretched out behind it, tiny lights sparkling amongst them like bashful stars. Purple-cushioned bar chairs stood in a neat row all down the bar's length, only a few of them occupied by patrons.

Slipping past the bar itself and stepping into the stock room behind it, Kazimiera found two of her bartenders—an Incubus and a Succubus—tending to an unfamiliar woman.

"Keep those men distracted while we're in here," Kazimiera said, jabbing a thumb toward the bar behind her. She pointed at the Succubus's frilly top. "Show some more cleavage and be sure to smile."

The Succubus shimmied her top a little lower and trotted off. Once she was gone, Kazimiera put her hands on her hips and stood over the newly arrived girl, sizing her up.

The woman was probably in her late twenties, curvy, with smudges all over her brown skin. Though the brands she wore suggested she could afford a good wardrobe, her clothes were dirty and torn and smelled of several days' worth of wear. The cloth she had used to wrap her head didn't properly hide her erupting frizz.

The Incubus had given the girl a plate of food from Nocturne's second-floor restaurant that she was actively devouring.

After staring at her for a long minute, Kazimiera realized why the Dullahan had labeled the girl "a problem." She narrowed her eyes. "What are you?"

The girl froze, a chunk of roasted potato between her fingers and halfway to her lips. "I'm sorry?" she asked, her voice a bit hoarse.

"What *are* you?" Kazimiera repeated.

"I'm, uh, Audrey Collins."

"That's *who* you are. I'm asking *what* you are."

Visibly confused by the question, Audrey's eyes darted from Kazimiera to the Incubus and back again. Annoyed, Kazimiera leaned in close, putting her nose within inches of the young woman. Her heartbeat raced, drumming wildly in Kazimiera's sensitive ears, but she didn't try to move away. The bite of potato was still halfway to her mouth, frozen by her fear and disorientation. Kazimiera inhaled deeply and took a long moment to analyze the newcomer's scent. Healthy, tired, sweaty . . . and human.

"You took in a human?" Kazimiera snarled at the Incubus. "What were you thinking?"

The bartender drew back, his handsome features painted with surprise. He squinted at Audrey as if trying to pierce a disguise. "That can't be right," he said in a lyrical voice. "She came to the door knowing all the right things to say."

"She's human, you twit!" Kazimiera snapped.

"But then why would she come here?"

An unexpected footstep made the Vampire whirl around. Standing in the stockroom doorway, pale, freckle-faced Georgette stared past Kazimiera at the intruder.

"Do I not give you enough to do?" Kazimiera said to Georgette, feeling a sheen of red creep into her eyes. "You seem to be looking for extra work!"

Georgette spread her hands in a gesture of futility. "This is what you hired me for. I'm supposed to meet all incoming Fae so I can link them into the cloaking spells on the building."

Kazimiera wanted to lash out, but the witch was technically correct. Biting back her irritation, she said, "Well, this one's not Fae. Wipe her memory and throw her out."

"Wait!" Audrey exclaimed, jumping up from her chair with the plate still clutched in her hands. "I need help!"

"You don't belong here," said Kazimiera.

"But I can't go anywhere else," Audrey said. "Please!"

All set to order the young woman off her property, Kazimiera was caught off guard when Georgette moved between them. Eyes glued to the girl, the witch tilted her head back and forth like a dog hearing a high-pitched sound.

"Are you okay?" she asked Audrey, her voice vibrating with compassion and curiosity. "What happened?"

Under the witch's kindly interrogation, Audrey began to tremble. Tears welled up in her eyes, but blinking rapidly and inhaling sharply, she stifled them. The plate of food shook in her hands until the Incubus carefully took it from her. The moment it was out of her grasp, she began fidgeting with her hands, smoothing her loose strands of hair and tugging on her torn clothes. After swallowing hard and sniffing, she managed to meet Georgette's gaze.

"I got bit," she said quietly. She rolled up her sleeve and showed them her right forearm. "Can't see it much anymore. It healed fast. Really fast."

Kazimiera looked at the scars. They were small, almost pockmarks, half a shade lighter than her skin. "What bit you?" she asked, already suspecting the answer.

"I thought it was a dog," answered Audrey. "A big dog. But then"—fresh tears appeared in her eyes—"a few nights ago . . ."

"Full moon," said Georgette.

Audrey nodded.

"Did you change all the way?" the witch asked. "Sometimes the first transformation isn't complete."

The first tears broke free and rolled down Audrey's cheeks. "My arms and legs stretched," she croaked. "I sprouted fur. And a damn tail. God, it hurt so bad." She looked back and forth between Kazimiera and Georgette. "I started having this . . . hunger."

A sudden sob racked her body, and she slapped a hand across her mouth. Georgette reached out and put a hand on her shoulder.

"I was at my cousin's house for dinner," Audrey continued, voice muffled by her fingers. "Her kids were there. I locked myself in the bathroom, but I could hear them while my body was changing. Then I could . . . I could . . ." She drew a deep, ragged breath. "I could smell them." Tears flowed freely from her bloodshot eyes, leaving clean tracks in the dirt on her cheeks. "They smelled like meat, like barbecue. The thing inside me wanted to . . ." Her voice dropped to a whisper. "To taste them." Sniffling, she swiped at her eyes and face. "I texted my cousin in the kitchen that I was sick, snuck out the back, and ran." A tired sob leaked from her lips. "I didn't dare go home because I knew my family would come looking for me and I didn't want to hurt them. I've missed so many days at work that I'm worried I'll get fired. I'm not even sure where I've been all this time; I just kept moving."

"Who the hell," Kazimiera interrupted, "told you to come to Nocturne?"

For a moment, the young woman just stared at her, mouth agape. Then, shakily wiping at her tears, she swallowed hard and answered, "I've heard rumors about this place. People at work say it's haunted or owned by a witch or something. I never believed any of it, but after what happened to me, I thought . . . if it was true . . ." Tearing up again, she looked pleadingly at Georgette. "I wanna go home but I'm afraid. Please, can you help me?"

Kazimiera curled her lip. Georgette would say yes. However expensive, time-consuming, or pointless, the witch would offer to help. So, before she could speak, Kazimiera issued her edict.

"No. I can't have a Werewolf in this establishment. It's too dangerous."

The hope in Audrey's eyes flickered out.

Unmoved, Kazimiera turned her back on the scene and headed for the door. "You need to leave."

Kazimiera was almost to the door when she heard the click of a tongue. Pausing, she looked at the Incubus, only to see him frowning at her and shaking his head. She scowled. *This damn witch. She's got my staff thinking that I'm supposed to be Mother-freaking Theresa.*

"Kazi, wait."

Closing her eyes, Kazimiera gritted her teeth. That probing, pesky little voice! "No Werewolves," she said to Georgette, emphasizing each syllable.

With that, she turned and left.

All the way back to her third-floor office, Kazimiera seethed. The witch made her life more difficult at every opportunity. And yet . . . she needed her. After the death of Martin, her last witch, she'd had a terrible time attracting candidates for the position. After months of advertising, only Georgette had eventually applied—and without a witch to keep the building cloaked from the magic community and to conceal her inhuman staff with glamours, the entire business would fall apart. Kazimiera was stuck with her.

Six months ago, they had agreed upon a month-to-month contract: Georgette would work without a salary—and pay her bills with money won via magic at casinos—so long as Kazimiera allowed her Bultungin friend and his infant daughter to stay in the building rent free. Kazimiera had not had occasion to interact with the hyena-man since then. As far as she knew, he was content, and that meant her agreement with Georgette could continue. If only the witch wasn't such a nuisance.

Kazimiera dropped into her desk chair and began thumbing through a stack of papers on her desk: orders, invoices, estimates, and dozens of other drains on her bank accounts. The sight of them usually assured her that she would be sufficiently busy for the day, but today seeing them just tightened the vise around her head. This was happening with increasing regularity. Her day-to-day tasks were no longer serving their intended function—keeping her occupied and therefore content—and that was the sign of a potential problem in the near future, one that Kazimiera did not want to address. Instead, she put her head down and willed herself to focus.

There was a gentle knock on the door. "Kazi?"

The vise twisted a little tighter. "I'm busy," Kazimiera said, massaging her temples.

After a brief pause, Georgette opened the door and peeked inside. "Sorry," she said. "I just wanted to run something by you."

"If it has anything to do with Demetra or that Werewolf, I'm not listening."

"She works for the Consumer Protection Division."

Dropping her hands to the desktop, Kazimiera stared, weary and perplexed, at Georgette. "In as few words as possible: Who are you talking about, what does that mean, and why would I care?"

"Audrey works for the Consumer Protection Division," Georgette said. "You know, the department that performs health inspections for the county. That's where she heard the rumors about Nocturne." She raised her eyebrows. "Wouldn't it be nice to not have to turn the club and restaurant inside out every time you have an inspection?"

Kazimiera knit her fingers together on top of the desk. Inspection day was always a hassle. Try as they might, her staff could never seem to hide every irregular thing in the building. Some of the dietary needs of her residents could make even a serial killer squeamish, and those ingredients had to be kept somewhere. Inevitably, the inspector would accidentally see something that horrified him. Not trusting that a bribe could cover the shock, Kazimiera always ordered that the inspector's memory be altered. It was a useful solution, but not a perfect one. If someone else in the department asked the inspector questions about the building that he or she couldn't answer, the situation could become problematic very quickly. Having someone in the department who could keep her business up to date on required paperwork without the actual need for inspections would be advantageous. But, of course, nothing was free.

"What does she want?"

"Help with her condition."

"That's too broad," Kazimiera said. "Narrow it down."

"I knew you'd say that." Georgette nodded. "I thought we could offer her a safe room to be locked up during the full moon—maybe one of the storage areas in the basement. I could also read up on Werewolf-related magic. I know there's no cure, but that doesn't mean—"

"I'm not paying for treatment," Kazimiera snapped. "We can chain her up in the basement once a month in exchange for dodging inspections, but I'm not ponying up any cash on her behalf." She leaned back in her chair, smoothing down her corkscrew coils. "That's the deal. She can take it or leave it."

"I think she'll take it." The witch started to back out of the doorway. "I'll tell her."

"Wait," Kazimiera snapped.

Georgette stopped, her face half obscured by the door's edge.

Tired, hassled, and frustrated to her last nerve, Kazimiera needed a question answered. "Why do you do this?"

"Do what?"

"Why do you let anyone and everyone make demands on your time, when it's not your job and you're not getting paid for it?"

Georgette stared at her, blue eyes childishly large behind her glasses. In a calm, level voice, she said, "They need my help."

Kazimiera clenched her jaw. She wasn't sure what response she'd expected, but those four simple words irritated the ever-loving hell out of her. It was a response she couldn't rage against, and it was a logic she couldn't disabuse the girl of. *Of all the witches in the world, I got stuck with Little Miss Bleeding Heart.*

"Fine," she muttered. Rubbing her head again, she returned her attention to the bills. "Go."

Ishak

"LOOK, ZIYA," ISHAK SAID INTO HIS BABY DAUGHTER'S EAR. He pointed to the computer screen, trying to draw her attention to the face on the video call. "Look, *sokar*."

Chubby-cheeked Ziya made a happy gurgle, followed by a string of nonsense syllables. Smiling, she pawed at Ishak's face, running her little fingers over his scraggly beard as her topaz eyes peered up at him from his lap, bright and sparkling. He grinned at her. Her smile was absurdly contagious.

"Can she see us?" asked the woman on the computer screen. She leaned close to the camera, filling the screen with her lightly wrinkled face. "Is the picture clear?"

Ishak smiled indulgently. They had this exact interaction every time he telecommunicated with his family in the Chad Basin of Africa, in the Bultungin city of Kabultiloa. His mother was distrustful of the only computer in the town library that connected to the kobold net, the witch-created network used by the magical community. She seemed to be terrified that Ziya's first memories of her grandmother would be of a fuzzy image.

"The picture is fine, Umma," he said. "She's just distracted."

As usual, his mother appeared unconvinced. The green-and-gold scarf wrapped around her head slipped a bit, allowing him to see the gray streaks in her dark hair. There were more than he remembered.

"You must be sleeping better," his mother said, her familiar gaze piercing him straight to the core. "You look less tatty than the last time we spoke."

"Thank you, Umma." He sighed. In the months following Ziya's birth, his beard and hair had grown long and unruly, giving him a wild, unkempt look. Fortunately, when it got to the point that he hardly recognized his reflection anymore, Georgette had stepped in with help.

Ziya glanced at the screen for a moment, and her grandmother's face lit up. "Hello, Ziya!" she said, waving and smiling. "Oh, how fast she grows! I wish I could hold her!"

"Let me see, Asma," said another voice. A second woman—her face older, rounder, with a longer nose—ducked into view, getting between Ishak's mother and the camera. "Such beautiful eyes!" Sidra said, beaming. "She looks so much like Kalilah!"

Indeed, thought Ishak. The likeness was both marvelous and painful to him. Most of the time he was too busy to notice, but then, in a quiet moment, he would look at his daughter and see his late wife staring back at him. It always triggered a cycle of emotions: surprise at the resemblance, love for his wife and their child, and then grief at Kalilah's absence.

A blur of brown and gray fur entered the background of the screen as an enormous Bultungin approached the two women. In a swift, fluid motion, the Werehyena's bulk contracted, its fur withdrew into its skin, and its body reformed into a man with a bald head and full gray beard who calmly sat down at the computer. "How are you managing parenthood alone, Ishak?"

"I'm not alone, Farhan," he told his father-in-law.

He chuckled, remembering. For months, he had stubbornly tackled the challenges of fatherhood single-handed, spiraling in a maelstrom of toys, clothes, and baby bottles—but just when he was ready to break under the strain, Georgette had swept into his apartment with half a dozen of the Nocturne Fae in her wake. A Kitsune and Yuki-onna had gathered all of the dirty clothes and whisked them away to be washed. A Crane Woman had scrubbed every surface in the kitchen, lifting one foot at a time as she did to make room for the diminutive, hunchbacked Kikimora mopping the floor.

Amidst the mayhem, a rotund, shaggy Troll had approached Ishak with a wide smile half hidden under his ruddy facial hair. He'd carefully lowered himself to the floor next to the table, folded his thick legs beneath him, and held out his large hands. "Baby?" he'd asked in a deep voice.

Ishak had hesitated. He had never been entirely comfortable with the idea of being part of the Nocturne community. He found Kazimiera's business model—creating a free workforce out of Fae who needed her magically enhanced building to hide from witches who enslaved them—morally objectionable. But then Georgette's gentle hand had rested on his shoulder. "It's okay," she'd reassured him. "They just want to help."

Putting his trust in Georgette, Ishak had handed his daughter to Magnus and allowed the others to put his home in order. And ever since that day, he had gratefully welcomed a daily dose of assistance into his life. The Nocturne community had opened its arms to him, and he had learned to welcome its embrace.

"My neighbors," he told Farhan now, "have blessed me."

Ziya suddenly let loose a screechy yip and flopped her arms about like a baby bird stretching its wings.

Farhan's wide smile turned his smooth skin into a roadmap of wrinkles. "Already sounding like a hyena," he said.

"Yes." Ishak laughed. "She chatters and snorts in her sleep as if dreaming of the hunt."

"Quite the fierce little thing! We can't wait to meet her in person."

Ishak nodded. As desperately as he wanted to go home, to introduce his daughter to her family, her people, and her homeland, there was simply no way to do so. Since he'd been brought to America against his will, he had no identification with which he might secure a ticket home. He knew of some illegal options, but they worried him. Should he be discovered boarding a plane with forged documents, the authorities might take Ziya away from him. That was unthinkable. He felt safer waiting for Georgette to find a magical way to get them home.

"I promise I will find a way home," Ishak said. "One way or another, someday soon I will present Ziya to the elders, and we will celebrate her birth in a fitting manner."

Though Farhan nodded, Ishak saw doubt in his eyes. It was a doubt Ishak shared.

Georgette

GEORGETTE FUMBLED WITH HER BLONDE CURLS, TRYING to twist her cloud of hair into a ponytail, as she continued to skim her laptop screen. It was upsetting, though not surprising, that she couldn't find much research on Werewolves. Witches generally only studied subjects that were beneficial to them personally, usually in terms of gaining magic and power. Hybrid creatures like Werewolves and Vampires had nothing to offer. Born human, their powers were not innate but rather the product of infection, and thus they did not make good familiars. Consequently, official Werewolf research was sparse and outdated.

"Sup, babe?" asked Neil, startling her.

She smiled as he approached. Dressed in gray slacks and a white button-down shirt, her boyfriend had obviously come to her apartment straight from the office. Though she hadn't checked her watch in a while, his arrival meant that she had about an hour until she was due at work. That was how it was most days.

"Hey!" she said, pulling him down for a kiss. "I didn't hear you come in."

"Mei-Xing was just leaving when I came up the stairs, so she let me in." His smile faded as he glanced over his shoulder. "Is she okay?" he asked. "She seems kinda off."

Usually quiet and polite, Mei-Xing *had* become snippy and easily distracted lately. Georgette would have found the behavior strange as well if she hadn't seen it before.

"She's budding," she explained.

Brow furrowed, Neil asked, "Budding?"

"Yeah. You know, like how trees bud before they blossom? It's a springtime thing for Wood Nymphs. They get hormonal for a couple months. It'll pass."

Brown eyes alight with fascination, Neil sat down next to her on the sofa. "Is it just a name or does she actually grow buds on her body?"

Neil's curiosity about the Fae community and witch culture absolutely delighted Georgette. Bit by bit, the otherworldly aspects of a witch's life were becoming as ordinary for him as they were for her.

"She does," she said. "The glamour hides it, but she sprouts buds on her chest."

"Wow," he marveled. "That's wild."

"It is," she agreed. "How was work today?"

"Exhausting," he said with a grunt. "But I got a chance to talk to Danny during lunch about staying with me this summer."

"Oh good!" Though she had never met Neil's nephew, Georgette felt a bond with Danny. Like him, she had used summers to escape a miserable home life by spending time with less problematic family members. "Did he apply to some San Jose summer camps?"

"A lot of them, actually," Neil said. "But Liam and Bethany told him he could only pick one program. He'll have to decide soon." His gaze shifted to her laptop screen. "What are you reading about today?" He squinted. "Werewolves?" He put an arm around her, and the scent of his body spray drifted into her nose, sending a tingle through her. "Full moon and claws, like in movies?"

"Kind of," she said. "A Werewolf woman came to the club last night asking for help. I'm trying to compile some info for her. It's disappointing, though. Her options are limited."

"How so?"

"Lycanthropy is basically a virus." Georgette toggled over to a scanned copy of a handwritten study on her laptop screen. "It lays dormant for most of the month and then becomes active during the full moon. When that happens, it asserts its own DNA over the host's and remakes their body into what it thinks is the 'correct' form. It burns itself out in a matter of hours and then goes dormant again."

"Hell of a disease," Neil said.

"Believe it or not, it's really hard to catch. It's only transmitted through bodily fluids, and only a handful of the people exposed will actually be infected." She scrolled to a particular page of the study. "This witch has a theory that the reason the virus makes its hosts go crazy when it's active is because most victims only live a year or two post-infection. The virus forcing the victim to bite as many people as possible is the surest way for it to reproduce."

"So," said Neil, frowning, "the woman you met only has a year to live?"

"Well," Georgette said, "this info is outdated." She toggled to another tab. "This is a website for a private island, Luna Gris, off the coast of Baja California. It's a Werewolf colony. According to their website, living in a place without uninfected humans has a calming effect and makes the monthly transformations less violent. That can mean a longer life expectancy. One of their residents who recently passed away lived there for twenty years."

"Longer life expectancy, less violence . . ." Neil pursed his lips, considering it. "Sounds like a win-win."

"Except it means uprooting your entire life to go live on an island with strangers. And," she added, "sterilization."

Neil pulled back, eyes wide. "Why?"

"Safety. If a Werewolf were to carry a pregnancy to term and if the baby were to inherit the virus, it wouldn't survive the first transformation. If it didn't inherit the virus, the presence of an uninfected human on the island could make the Werewolves violent. The baby would have to be sent away immediately." Georgette sighed and gently tugged at one of her curls. "Tough choices all around."

Neil leaned back on the sofa, his gaze distant as he processed the information she'd just shared with him. While he mulled it over, she considered how she was going to give all this information to Audrey. There was really no way to soften the blow; no matter what she decided to do, she was going to have to make some major lifestyle changes. Georgette did have some alternative ideas to try if she was willing, though.

"How'd the lady who came to Nocturne get the virus?" asked Neil.

"She was bitten by a Werewolf."

"What Werewolf? Just some random Werewolf running around the South Bay Area?"

Georgette stared blankly at the computer. Seconds ticked by. She felt like she had just sat down for a test only to realize that she had studied the wrong chapter.

"You're right," Georgette whispered. "There must be another Werewolf."

Her mind raced. Had the other Werewolf been taking precautions to isolate themself during the full moon? The night Audrey was bitten—was that a one-time slipup? Or were they just running loose every month?

An arm slowly encircled her shoulders and applied gentle pressure. Only then did Georgette realize she was holding her breath.

"Breathe," Neil said softly into her ear.

She drew several deep breaths and then looked at him, feeling a rush of gratitude for his support. "I'm okay."

He nodded. "Good. So, what's our next step?"

"I don't know." She paused for a moment as her brain rattled off possibilities. Thinking quickly, she tried to weed out the absurd ideas to find something practical. "I can go to Kazi, but she probably won't do anything. Maybe Delia and Senji can help. Valkyries are supposed to report anything unusual in their territory to Valhalla anyway. And I should check hospital records for animal bites."

"Can you do that?"

"Not legally . . . but yeah. It just takes a basic scrying spell superimposed over a Google search."

Smiling proudly, Neil leaned his head toward hers. "You got this."

Yeah. I've got this. After one last cleansing breath, she kissed him and then nuzzled her face against his shoulder. "Thanks."

He kissed the top of her head. "Anytime."

Delia & Senji

Golden Valhalla—roof thatched with shields, rafters made of spear shafts—echoed with the sounds of battle. The war was not visible, but the clash of weapons and cries of soldiers were ever-present.

Soaring above, Senji saw numerous creatures. Gray wolves stalked the grounds. Ravens, like himself, perched in the ancient red-gold trees. Horses—white, black, dappled—drank from the immense crystal river. They were all like Senji: former humans transformed into animals after death to assist the Valkyries.

Delia's gaze passed over warrior souls, the chosen slain not on the front lines, who were gathered within the hall. Some feasted, partaking of the unending food piled on the tables. Others lounged, resting on the benches covered in coats of mail, while drinking and playing games. More still, too many, were recovering from wounds.

The dead could not be killed, but they could be grievously wounded. And while Valhalla made spectral bodies whole, it could not always heal a soldier's mind. Too much strain could break a warrior, shattering their soul into irreparable pieces.

Every Valkyrie was a murdered woman. Every animal partner was the man responsible for his Valkyrie's death. Once dead, Valhalla united them, pouring a lifetime of the other's memories into each and linking them into a single consciousness.

They are not all like me.

What's that? asked Delia, walking through a recovery room, her eyes lingering on a cluster of badly burned souls.

The partners, Senji said. He swooped down into the courtyard and alighted upon the largest tree, its metallic leaves shimmering in the light. *Many of them are like servants to the Valkyries, little more than tools to be used, never to be treated with respect and friendship. We are unusual.*

Yes, she agreed after some thought, *I suppose so.* An injured soul wailed, drawing her attention. The Idisi, elfish attendants of the chosen, knelt by him, magically healing his wounds. He still howled. *Many of the sisters resent the men who killed them. Understandably. Even after death, it's hard not to carry a grudge.*

You do not.

Most were killed by men who should have loved them—brothers, fathers, lovers. You and I never met until after we were dead. And we were at war; you were just a kid serving his country. What's to hate?

Senji smiled. Delia had a way of cutting through life's ambiguities.

Delia watched the warrior soul reject all comfort offered by the Idisi. He continued to scream, limbs flailing, head shaking wildly. The Idisi, their large, multicolored eyes flashing, exchanged glances.

Not good.

What's that?

Look.

Through her eyes, he saw the Idisi place their spindly fingers on the spirit. Senji realized what was about to happen.

No, not another one.

The Idisi gently pushed. Slowly, the soul compressed, shrinking and distorting. The cries of the dead man gradually faded as his spectral body condensed from human form into a ball of glowing silver energy. One Idisi held the ball—ghostly and swirling—between her thin hands. With the other Idisi in a procession behind her, she carried the now silent soul across the room.

May they deliver him safely.

May he find eternal rest beyond the veil.

That's the third one this month. Delia watched the attendants fade into transparency. *Our army needs a win.*

So I've heard. He cocked his head upward at a flock of passing ravens, listening to their chatter. *Rumor has it that the tide has turned against us and we are slowly losing ground to Muspelheim.*

I've heard the same. The Idisi vanished into light and shadow; the silver glow of the soul lingered a few seconds longer before disappearing forever. *We had all but taken the Ginnungagap, but now the enemy is advancing and pushing us back.*

Is that why we have been ordered to deliver chosen who are . . . not ideal?

Their last few targets had been far from battle-ready. Some of the recent chosen struck him as quite bookish, unlikely to have ever thrown a punch.

Walking through many rooms, passing the rows of wounded, Delia felt a crawling sense of unease. They were losing warriors and replacing them with clerks and stockboys. That was no path to victory.

An internal tug caught her attention. The brand she and Senji shared with Georgette, Mei-Xing, and Ishak was pulling at her.

Georgette wants us.

So I gather.

It doesn't feel urgent, so I'm guessing it doesn't involve her mother.

Georgette feared her mother, a powerful and intimidating witch. Ever since Hazel Nichols O'Reilly had tracked down her runaway daughter, Georgette flew into a panic every time they interacted. More than once, Georgette had frantically yanked at the *Hathiya* link when getting a mere phone call from Hazel.

Delia smirked. For all her power, Hazel feared the Valkyries. And Georgette knew it.

I don't feel she needs us now.

Not at present. We will have to wait for another chance to intimidate the old bitch again.

The moan of another wounded soul melted her smirk.

A squawk seized Senji's attention. Another raven passed overhead, swooped down out of sight, and then rose again with a Valkyrie in tow. The bird and shieldmaiden flew off, vanishing from view. Soon afterward, a Valkyrie astride a wolf cloud-hopped over the horizon.

Senji watched more Valkyries fly from the Great Hall. *The sisters are leaving. Have they received their new orders?*

Yes. She turned and strode toward the nearest exit. *So have we.*

He stretched his wings. *Is there a chosen to fetch?*

There is always a chosen to fetch. She sighed. *But the first on our list will not die today.*

We can check on Georgette, then. Senji took flight, soaring over the shield-tiled roof with the brisk wind in his feathers. *I'll meet you out front.*

Be right there.

Walking more quickly and averting her eyes, Delia hastened to leave the hall, closing her ears to the wails of the felled chosen.

Mei-Xing

SEATED ON THE APARTMENT BALCONY, MEI-XING SOAKED up the cloud-filtered sunlight. A gentle wind flowed through the air, rustling her many potted plants and painting her body with scents from all over the city. There was a delicious warmth to the breeze. Spring was shifting into summer.

Mei-Xing had felt the onset of spring long before Georgette noticed, her photosensitive skin taking note of how the days gradually lengthened. Soon after, she'd felt buds beginning to grow from her chest and shoulders. Though expected, she disliked the sight of them.

Peering through her glamour, her human disguise, Mei-Xing examined the tightly closed little pink-and-white buds that dotted her breast. She'd felt herself becoming irritable and restless since their appearance. That was common enough, but accompanying the agitation she was also experiencing a strange sense of loneliness.

Spring was meant to be a social time. Before fleeing China, Mei-Xing had spent every spring in her grove preening with the Nymphs and Spirits of her family. After stirring from winter lethargy, her family would gather together while the elders shared their stories with the young ones, spreading wisdom and nonsense in equal measure. She'd lay her head on her mother's lap while an auntie or a cousin groomed away the brown grasses on her body to encourage fresh green growth. Her father and uncles would mill about the ripening grounds, calling out in singsong voices to lure the new seedlings to the surface. All the while, the entire grove would try to coax the buds on the adult Nymphs to blossom. It was always a cause for celebration when the buds opened into flowers, signaling a rare time of Nymph fertility. Mei-Xing's had opened only twice in her life: the first time marked her transition from adolescence to maturity, and the second . . .

She closed her eyes and willed the long-repressed memory to sink back into the hidden areas of her mind.

Since coming to America, Mei-Xing had rarely missed her grove. She had made a conscious decision to run, to save herself from an abusive marriage that her family wouldn't let her leave. The grove had needed the water her husband had provided, and if that arrangement cost Mei-Xing her health, her freedom, or even her life, they were willing to pay the price. Mei-Xing was not.

Now she and Georgette had become their own little grove, a cozy knot of kith-kin. But close as they were, Georgette simply could not provide the type of companionship Mei-Xing's Nymph senses craved in the spring.

Behind her, inside the apartment, Mei-Xing heard Georgette talking on the phone. Through the *Hathiya* link they shared, the Nymph could feel her friend's distress. Georgette was talking to her mother.

Despite the fact that she had once almost dragged her runaway daughter back to Boston by force, Hazel had lately been suspiciously polite, calling Georgette as regularly and casually as any mother checking in on her adult child. The two friends agreed that this was a ploy Hazel was using to worm her way back into her daughter's life, and yet Georgette continued to allow the phone calls. Though she had once uprooted her entire life to flee from her mother, Georgette didn't seem willing or able to cut contact a second time. Mei-Xing tried to be supportive, but she feared it would all end badly.

Inside the apartment, Mei-Xing heard another voice. Neil. Without turning to look, the Nymph could picture them clearly. Georgette would be seated and Neil would be next to her, probably holding her hand. Periodically, a flash of panic would come over Georgette's face, and she would look to Neil. He would offer her reassuring smiles, a squeeze of his hand, or a few murmured words of encouragement.

This was how things had been for the last six months. Where Georgette once had only Mei-Xing to lean on, she now also had Neil. So at a time when Mei-Xing craved companionship more than ever, she found herself alone on the balcony while the loving couple kept their own company.

I haven't lost my connection to Georgette, she told herself, wrapping her arms around her knees. Staring vacantly at the many windows across the way, she let the breeze ruffle the hidden buds on her shoulders. *A lotus may be cut, but its fibered threads remain connected.*

An unwelcome wash of homesickness came over her as instincts urged her to seek out her own kind. Mei-Xing gripped her knees tighter to her chest. *I cannot risk seeking my own kind, or my birth grove might learn that I'm alive*, she reminded herself, and the instinct shifted its focus, urging her to seek out Georgette.

She was on the verge of emotionally tugging at her *Hathiya* mark to alert her friend to her distress when she heard Georgette and Neil talking to each other in that conspiratorial tone used only by thieves and lovers. Her loneliness intensified; she hugged her knees tight as shaded sunlight spread over her skin without providing warmth.

My grove has no room for me.

Nicolás

NICO KNEW THAT CLUB NOCTURNE, ITS RESTAURANT, AND the residential floors above were populated by creatures of folklore. But knowing and seeing were not the same.

Six months ago, Nico's otherworldly vision had expanded wildly; in an instant, he'd found himself able to see beyond the ethereal curtain that separated humanity from the Fae. Previously, in the course of his *curandero* training, he had progressed in short bursts—connecting to his spirit allies, gaining greater command over his dreams—but this had been a much bigger leap. He now had the ability to see Fae beings not through a haze but as perfectly as he saw the customers who entered his aunt's Botanica. After seeing beyond the curtain once, he now found that he could pierce it at will.

Entering the club now with a box of herbs and other products clutched to his chest, Nico initially only saw humans, or rather beings that appeared human—but a tickling in his soul told him he wasn't seeing these people for what they really were. He flexed his new ability and pierced the glamours, allowing him to see the fairy-tale beings beneath.

Though he knew it was rude to stare, he couldn't look away.

Once he entered the stairwell, he found that his extrasensory vision was no longer necessary. Away from the eyes of human customers, most of the upper-floor beings didn't bother disguising themselves with glamours, and the heavy magic encompassing the building made them openly visible. Climbing the stairs to Nocturne's upper floors, Nico caught sight of a misty Air Elemental floating up the stairwell, two chattering Harpies hopping along the rail with their wings partially extended for balance, and a Sarangay—a bull-headed man with gemstones in his ears—shuffling down the steps with his head stooped.

On the sixth floor, Nico slipped out of the stairwell and into a long hallway lined with doors, one of which was open. Upon peering into it, he saw Georgette.

"Hey," she said, waving him in. "Good timing."

Nico's jaw fell open. The room was bustling with otherworldly activity. Kneeling on the floor in a tight circle, a group of four Elves—thin and glittery, as if made of starlight thread—drew on sheets of printer paper with the intensity of preschoolers, reaching across one another to touch up or add to each other's pictures without uttering a word. Near the window stood a Chalkydri, its lion body bathed in a sun-and-shadow-striped pattern from the blinds and its crocodile head shaded by its rainbow-feather wings. In the tiny kitchen, two Water Nymphs bent over a line of cutting boards. A strange mélange of scents filled the air from whatever they were chopping and grinding. One of the Nymphs—a saltwater variety, he guessed, given her extraordinary parrotfish coloration—spotted him standing by the entrance and immediately darted in his direction. He started to greet her, but she silently snatched the box out of his hands and went back to work.

"Thanks for bringing this stuff on such short notice," said Georgette, breaking him out of his thoughts.

"Yeah," he murmured, still taking it all in, "no problem. Where's the patient?"

"In the bathroom, getting changed."

The Werewolf is getting changed in the bathroom, he thought in amazement.

When Georgette had come to him with a list of odd ingredients and a story about B-movie monsters, he'd been flabbergasted. Even after everything he'd seen, he'd never imagined that Werewolves were real. But when he'd presented the list to Tía Mariana, she'd read it and calmly asked, "*¿Hombre-lobo?*"

Nico had sputtered, so many questions jumping to his lips at once that all he could manage was, "Huh?"

Chuckling, she'd dismissed his confusion with a wave of her hand. "What else could this"—she nodded at the list—"be for? If I had to guess, I would say your *bruja* friend is assembling ingredients for a full moon charm." Staring thoughtfully at the sheet of paper in her hand, she'd tapped her front teeth with one fingernail. "I hadn't heard about a lycanthropy outbreak. I should stock extra of these things, just in case." She'd returned the list to him. "Does the *bruja* have enough silver?"

"My aunt says if you need silver," Nico told Georgette, "she can hook you up."

"I'm good," Georgette said. She leaned across the kitchen counter and looked into the Nymphs' mixing bowl. "My new recipe doesn't use as much as the old one."

"Are you not making a full moon charm?"

"No. I talked to Audrey about charms, but she didn't like the idea."

The bathroom door swung open with a bang, startling Nico. A woman in her mid to late twenties strode into the living room wearing a yellow bikini. The shock of seeing a woman wearing something so out of place did nothing to ease Nico's disorientation. Without thinking, he scanned her up and down before catching himself and jerking his gaze aside.

"A charm doesn't sound safe to me," said Audrey. "Seems like it's too easy for a charm to fall off and get lost."

"Nico," said Georgette, "this is Audrey Collins. Audrey, Nico García. He and his aunt run a local shop that supplies things you'll need on a regular basis from now on."

Immediately slipping into customer service mode, Nico smiled and held out a hand. Audrey shook it but did not return his smile. Exhaustion and defeat radiated from her every pore.

"My aunt will make sure we have a ready stock of ingredients for the daily tonic you'll need," he said. "I suggest buying in bulk and keeping a standing order with us to make sure you never run out."

"What's in the tonic," Audrey asked with a resigned sigh, "and how do I make it?"

"Rowan berries, angelica, agrimony, and the activating incantation that Georgette will provide. To make it, you basically brew the mix like coffee. Depending on your preference, we can add flavors to make it more palatable."

"I'm not worried about taste," she said, walking into the kitchen. "I just want whatever will be most effective. That's why I said no to the charm. I don't wanna take any chances."

"The representative I talked to at the Werewolf colony did admit the charms can be problematic," said Georgette. She followed Audrey into the kitchen and gestured for Nico to come along. "The charm only works if it's in direct contact with skin at the start of transformation. If it slips off or gets caught up in the wearer's clothes, the virus won't react to the silver, and without that severe allergic reaction, the magic in the charm never activates."

"And then it doesn't stop the change?" asked Nico.

"It won't stop the change regardless," huffed Audrey. "Apparently, nothing can stop it." She plopped down at the breakfast table, put her elbows on the tabletop, and dropped her chin into her hands. "I'm stuck like this for the rest of my shorter-than-average life."

"Don't think like that," said Georgette, smiling kindly. "Modern Werewolves are living much longer."

"Only if they're on that island colony," Audrey grumbled.

"If they can do it, so can we," Georgette said. "But," she reluctantly added, "you're right that we can't stop the transformation." Turning to Nico, she shrugged. "The charm, if used properly, keeps the Werewolf's mind intact after the change so he or she doesn't go berserk. The daily tonic eases the pain of transformation and helps prevent the virus from overextending the body's resources. They're not a cure, but they help."

A Water Nymph—algae green with white snail shell swirls covering her body—held out a large mixing bowl to her colorful companion. The saltwater Nymph peered into the bowl a moment, grabbed two handfuls of the greenery she'd cut up, and dumped it into the mix. The first Nymph transformed her hand from flesh into pure liquid and plunged it into the bowl, soaking and stirring the contents, then withdrew and solidified her hand. She extended her arm toward Georgette, her fingers dripping purplish goo.

Georgette dipped one finger in the glop and brought it close to her face, smelling and inspecting it. "Let's add more monkshood," she said to the Water Nymphs, who nodded in unison. She looked across the living room at the Chalkydri. "We'll be ready for you in a minute, okay?"

Staring at her from under its vibrant wings, the creature emitted a melodious, twirling purr.

Georgette nodded. "I know you're busy. It won't be much longer, I promise."

Chalkydri are heralds of sunlight, thought Nico. *Mariana said the Werewolf virus goes dormant in sunlight. Can't be a coincidence.*

Rising from the floor, the shimmering Elves glided up to the witch with their drawings outstretched, large eyes wide and eager. Georgette scanned the papers as she chewed on her lower lip. Then she pointed at one of the designs. "Not that one," she said. "Or those two," she continued, pointing. "The rest look great. You guys are talented."

The Elves beamed with delight, their happiness causing a cascade of sparkles to flutter through their skin.

"Audrey," Georgette said over her shoulder, "take a look at these, okay? You've got a bunch of options to choose from."

"Whatever," Audrey mumbled, but she accepted the papers from the smiling Elves.

"If you're not making a charm," asked Nico, "what *are* you doing?"

"I'm adapting the same principle as the full moon charm to make a more permanent solution," Georgette said. "After doing research, I had the idea to use similar ingredients and magics but apply them directly to Audrey's skin instead of putting them in a piece of jewelry."

Nico's years of *curandero* training brought all the facts into focus. "A tattoo."

"Multiple tattoos," Georgette said. "Biceps, thighs, stomach, lower back, shoulder blades, and pectorals. The same spell ingredients that go into the charm will be in the tattoo ink, except the tattoos don't require as much silver." The glow of her self-confidence dimmed a bit, her smile faltering. "What do you think?"

I think your reasoning is solid, he thought, his counselor mode kicking in, *but that's not what you need to hear.* "What do *you* think?"

"I think it'll work."

Despite her qualifying tone, Georgette sounded quite positive. Nico felt a touch of professional pride that their therapy sessions had helped develop her self-confidence.

"The mechanics are the same: when the virus becomes active at the full moon, the silver we've put in the ink will produce an allergic reaction that triggers the magic. The only thing that's different is the tattoos can't be separated from Audrey, so there's no chance of them getting lost."

"Even if it works," Audrey grumbled, "I'll still have to be isolated two or three nights a month. 'Cause one day isn't bad enough."

"It depends which strain of the virus you got," the witch told her. "You might transform only on the night of the full moon or you might also transform on the night before or after. We'll know after this next full moon."

Audrey shifted in her seat, fiddling with the ends of her hair. "This sucks."

"Yeah," Georgette agreed, "it does. But since there's no cure, you have to—"

"Protect innocent people from ending up like me," Audrey said bitterly.

Georgette sighed. "I was going to say that you have to protect yourself. If you run through the streets looking like a big, violent dog, somebody will shoot you. And forget what you've seen in movies—silver isn't the only thing that can kill a Werewolf. A regular bullet does the job."

Audrey flinched, her lower lip trembling. Georgette glanced at Nico, and he thought he saw a flash of guilt in her eyes for having upset the poor woman. He offered a half smile, trying to convey that she had done nothing wrong and it was just a bad situation all around.

"Which designs will you use for your tattoos?" he asked Audrey in a tone he hoped sounded conversational.

Sniffling, she looked at the papers on the table. "They all look similar. Honestly, I never wanted a tattoo at all. Now I'm getting ten at once."

"Well," Georgette said, "it's not too late to make the charm instead."

"No," Audrey said firmly, swiping at her eyes. "No charms, no island colony." She stared at the papers for a moment, then pointed at one. "Let's use these."

She had chosen a cluster of three designs: one of abstract flowers, one of simple arrows, and the last of petite shooting stars. The Elves took the paper from her, huddled together in a circle, and chirped to each other like gossiping birds.

The freshwater Nymph handed the mixing bowl to Georgette, who carried it across the living room toward the Chalkydri. Without a sound, the creature stretched its rainbow wings over the mix and showered droplets of gold into the concoction. The beauty of that liquid sunlight lifted Nico's heart into his throat, and he sent up a silent prayer of thanks that he was blessed enough to see this miracle.

Rustling through a pile of dried leaves on the countertop, the saltwater Nymph produced four long, thin white needles and held them out to the Elves in her open palm.

Are those bone? Nico wondered.

One Elf took the bowl of ink, another took the needles, and the other two ushered Audrey into the middle of the living room, where they settled her onto a cushioned stool.

Why use bone needles? thought Nico. *There are more efficient tattoo methods.*

As if reading his mind, Georgette said, "The needles are made from the bones of a Bakunawa. They eat moonlight. I thought a little anti-moon addition to the tattoo process might help."

"But won't it take a long time to finish with—"

The Elves began tattooing Audrey's arms and legs with the speed of caffeine-addicted cheetahs. Audrey's jaw clenched and her face scrunched up as pinprick tears appeared in the corners of her eyes.

With movements too fast for Nico's eyes to follow, the Elves completed tattooing their artwork in rings around Audrey's thighs and biceps in mere minutes. As the four artists stepped back, Audrey gasped as if she'd held her breath through the entire procedure. Georgette grabbed a tall glass and held it out to the freshwater Nymph, who poured crystal clear water into it from her fingertip.

As Audrey sipped from the glass, Nico looked at the Elves' work. Crisscrossing arrows girdled her thighs, and intersecting shooting stars encircled her upper arms. They were actually quite lovely—delicate black designs with a silvery-purple sheen.

Audrey noticed him looking and raised an eyebrow. "How do they look?"

"Good," he said honestly. "They look artistic and professional."

"Yes," came a voice from behind him, "impressive work."

Turning around, Nico saw the Valkyrie Delia standing just inside the window, her raven partner perched on her shoulder. Despite his best efforts to suppress it, Nico felt a rush of excitement at the sight of her. Tall, regal, and classically beautiful, she was the most stunning woman he had ever laid eyes on. Every time he saw her, he was absolutely taken aback by her grace and loveliness. *Not healthy, Nico,* he scolded himself, not for the first time. *She's dead. Not like you can ask her out for dinner.*

"Delia," said Georgette. "Anything?"

"We didn't find any recent signs of a Werewolf," she reported, the ghost of a Louisiana drawl dancing through her voice, "but there are some old trails. I'd guess they were made over a month ago."

"That tracks with reports I've seen from local hospitals," said Georgette. "There were a handful of dog bites around the time Audrey was attacked, but nothing since. It's possible that Werewolf died or moved on."

"Regardless, I will report the matter to Valhalla."

Eager to join the conversation, Nico asked, "Will Valhalla respond to the situation?"

Delia looked at him, and his soul lit up with crackling fireworks. "Possibly," she answered. "It's irregular and has the potential to disrupt official duties." Exchanging a glance with her raven, she sighed. "Now more than ever, Valhalla cannot afford a disruption."

He wanted to ask what she meant. He wanted to hear every detail about her post-life work. He wanted to listen to her talk all day and night while staring into her eyes. But that wasn't possible. Or advisable. Or the reason he was here.

Forcing himself to return his attention to Audrey, he saw

the Elves brushing her hair off her shoulders and pulling aside her bikini straps in preparation to tattoo her back.

"I gotta go," he told Georgette.

She nodded. "Thanks again."

As she went back to helping the Nymphs with kitchen cleanup, Nico turned to Audrey. "Come by the Botanica later," he told her. "I'll have the first batch of the tonic ready, and my aunt can show you how to brew it at home."

Audrey nodded, and for the first time since he'd arrived, she smiled a little. It was an unhappy, overtired smile, but it softened her expression nonetheless. For one moment, all the bitterness, anger, and fear he'd seen from her since arriving faded and left in its wake a young woman who was struggling to find her footing in this terrifying, inhuman world.

Nico offered her a reassuring smile. "It's a lot right now, but it won't feel this big forever. You'll get a handle on it."

"Maybe," she said wearily, "but I had a lot of plans for my life that aren't going to happen now."

The manic tattooing began again, one Elf holding the ink bowl while the other three marked her shoulder blades and lower back with intricate flowers. Through lips drawn up tight against the pain, she said, "I'm not ready to cope with it yet."

"Then don't," he said. "Take it slow and cope with things as you get to them. My aunt always says, 'I can tackle just one crisis at a time. All the others will have to wait their turn.'"

Despite the pain, Audrey chuckled, giving Nico a sense of accomplishment. Then, just beyond where Audrey sat, he saw Delia favor him with a slight smile. The feeling it gave him was a pure, perfect triumph.

Yanking his gaze away, he headed for the door. *The rest of today can suck balls and I'll still be great.*

Neil

"UGH."

Looking up from his desk, Neil tried not to glare. Jin Li, the boss's son, was leaning back in his executive chair, twirling a pen between two fingers. Though he had been in a meeting that morning, he was wearing running pants, a T-shirt, and sandals. His computer was on, but his gaze had drifted to the bright, sunny day outside his window.

"So much paperwork," said Jin, still looking out the window. "Commercial invoices, customs duties . . . taxes . . ." He gave the pen another twirl with one hand while brushing his short black hair off his forehead with the other. "Paperwork is ridiculous."

Neil returned his eyes to his work, quietly grinding his teeth. For Neil, the paperwork for Li International's imports was time-consuming but rarely required him to work outside of automatic-pilot mode. For Jin, it seemed to be a painful endeavor, as were office meetings, client interactions, and business calls. And whenever Jin found an activity onerous, he pawned it off on someone else. Just like he was trying to do now.

"There's a million things I could do with my day other than this," Jin groaned. Though he didn't look up, Neil felt his probing eyes on him. "A day like this . . . everyone who's anyone will be at the club."

Closing his eyes, Neil let out a soft exhale. Silver Oaks Country Club: fine dining, tennis, golf, and fun for the whole family at a price guaranteed to keep out the riffraff. Given the option, Jin would spend all day every day at the pool, the fitness center, or the bar, all under the guise of "networking" for the company. He heard Jin's chair creak and looked up to see him walking over to the window.

Eager as he was to tell the guy to suck it up, he bit his tongue. Instead, he adopted a tried-and-true tactic: redirection. "How are things looking for the corporate party?" he asked.

"Looking good," said Jin, grinning. "I booked the club's main event hall. We'll have hors d'oeuvres on the patio, then come inside to a plated dinner, live entertainment, and an open bar." He chuckled. "Even my old man won't be able to complain."

Pride radiated from Jin's face as he related his plans, the paperwork obviously forgotten.

"Is your mom coming this time?" Neil asked. An image of the boss's wife flashed through his mind: a short, mannequin-thin lady with block bangs and designer clothes.

"Yeah, she'll be there." Jin's smile became strained. He plopped down in his chair with a huff. "She's insisting that I bring a date."

"She *wants* you to bring a date?" Neil asked, surprised. At the Christmas party, Jin had brought a date, and his mother had spent the entire event scowling at the pretty blonde girl. Of course, by the end of the party most of the office had been scowling at her too, since she'd overindulged and gotten into a slurred argument with the catering staff.

"An *appropriate* date."

"And by appropriate she means . . . ?"

"Chinese."

"Did she have someone specific in mind?"

"Several." Jin rolled his eyes. "She brought me photos and profiles like she's running a frickin' dating service."

"Any appealing options?"

Jin groaned and let his head roll to the side. "All of 'em are daughters of her friends and associates." Raising one hand, he counted off on his fingers. "One is a horse-faced law student, one is a nurse who's obsessed with boy bands, and one is a secretary who's a total gold digger. Hard pass."

Though he nodded along, Neil suspected Jin would reject any girl championed by his mother, regardless of her looks or personality. "Going stag, then?"

Jin sighed. "I'd rather just bring a Chinese girl with me, if only to shut her up." He leaned over the arm of his chair. "But most of the girls I meet are at the club. A handful of Chinese families are members, but none of their girls are my age and single."

"Really?" asked Neil, brow furrowed. "Every time I've been there, I've seen a lot of young Asian women."

"Staff," Jin said. "Mom would lose her shit if I dated the help." Eyebrows climbing his forehead, he asked, "Could you find someone for me?"

The question startled Neil. He was used to the Li family asking him for things—sales, opinions, overtime—but this was a first. "No," he replied with an awkward laugh. "No way. The only Chinese girl I know is my girlfriend's roommate."

"Yeah?" Jin leaned forward. "Got a picture?"

Crap.

"I-I don't think she'd want to be set up," Neil stammered.

"Come on," Jin urged, "you got a picture?"

Crap crap crap crap.

Neil's mind stalled out from panic. Dazed, he pulled out his phone and scrolled through photos. Mei-Xing avoided cameras whenever possible because the glamour that made her look human didn't photograph reliably. Sometimes a picture perfectly captured her facade, but other times, the image was checkered with glimpses of her true form. Still, he knew he had one good photo of her—one where she was sitting next to Georgette on their sofa, smiling politely.

Jin gave Mei-Xing a thorough examination. "Thin," he murmured, "kinda plain . . . skin's a little dark." He stared at the phone screen a moment longer and then gave a nod of approval. "She's cute," he concluded. "Hook me up."

CRAP.

"I mean . . . I can ask her, I guess," Neil fumbled, "but—"

"What? She have a boyfriend?"

"N-no. She's, uh . . ." *She's a Wood Nymph who faked her death and ran away from China to escape a bad marriage.* "She's divorced."

An expression crossed Jin's face like he had tasted something bitter. "Mom'll hate that," he said, and for a moment, Neil felt relieved. He wasn't going to have to discuss this with Mei-Xing after all. But his relief was dashed when Jin smirked. "Good," he said. "Mom won't pressure me to keep seeing her. She's perfect. What's her name?"

Neil felt his heart sinking into his guts like a bowling ball into Jell-O. He'd only brought up the party to avoid having to do Jin's paperwork, and now his options were to upset Jin, who had the power to make his professional life difficult, or to upset Mei-Xing, who had once drugged him when she lost her temper. Either option ended badly for him.

Delia & Senji

Skogul sat at the head of the table, helmet on the arm of her chair. Tight black braids damp with sweat covered her scalp and draped over her shoulders. A long scar crossed her throat in a jagged smile, the mark of her last moments alive. Eyes closed, the commander looked pensive.

To her side stood Olrun, a long spear in her three-fingered hand. Other Valkyries sat at the table, quietly digesting Delia's report.

Standing at the foot of the table, her helmet under her arm, Delia waited. She struggled not to fidget.

So many are here, she thought, furtively scanning the room. *I didn't expect a Werewolf to attract so much attention.*

More than you realize. Given the number of partners here, there are far more Valkyries you've not yet seen.

The animal partners of the assembled Valkyries waited outside in a red-gold copse. Most of them twitched or paced the area. Senji knew why. Through Delia, Senji felt a constant crackle of anxiety that compelled him to fidget. The beasts, like him, were experiencing the tension of their other halves.

"Sister Svanhild," Skogul finally said, eyes sliding open, "your news is disturbing."

"Yes, Sister Skogul," Delia agreed, though perplexed. The commander's manner was deadly serious, which she had not expected.

"I must discuss this with the other officers," Skogul said. She nodded to Olrun, who, tightening her grip on the spear, walked to the nearest door. Skogul rose from her seat and followed. "Wait here," she said without looking back. "I will return shortly."

Delia sat down, obedient but confused. *Wait here? There's a list of chosen to fetch. I must return to work soon. And why are other officers here? Did Skogul call them in ahead of this meeting?*

Senji's gaze swept the copse. *This gathering smells of a deeper purpose.*

His tone increased her suspicion. *Have you learned something at your end?*

No. They are uncommonly quiet. Except, he added irritably, casting a sharp eye to a wolf who was incessantly mumbling prayers, *for Giovanni, the blathering fool.*

Rota's here? she thought in surprise. *Do you recognize anyone else? Can you tell me what other officers are here?*

Senji scanned the gathering to identify Valkyries by their partners. *Skuld . . . Gunnr . . . Perchta . . . Holle . . . and Lussi.*

Delia glanced nervously around the table, wondering if any of the others who waited for Skogul were as baffled and concerned as she was. One by one, each met her questioning gaze and replied with a shrug or shake of her head. *What the hell is going on?*

Valhalla must have been expecting this. It's the only explanation.

Valhalla was expecting a Werewolf?

They were expecting something. *Valhalla either had the officers on notice so they could get here quickly—*

Or Valhalla called them in a while ago to wait for this.

Exactly.

The ramifications churned in her mind like a rancid meal in an unsteady gut.

Could they be on to us? Could they know about the brand and our deal with the witch?

Senji ducked his head as if to scratch an itch on his leg so he could check his brand. It was well hidden under a smear of mud. *Surely not. This hardly seems like the way Valhalla would address a . . . situation like ours.*

A borderline treasonous situation?

Yes. The sisters would arrest and detain us indefinitely.

If they knew, I would agree. But what if they don't know? What if they suspect but have no proof?

I don't know. Senji glanced around at the partners—ravens, wolves, and one mustang. Were they here to trap him? *Should we run?*

Run? There were Valkyries everywhere. *I can't. And what if we're wrong? We'd tip our hand.*

This could be our last chance.

Senji. She sighed quietly. *Where could we go where they couldn't track us?*

Their power had been forged in Valhalla. They could no more hide from their maker than a finger could hide from the hand that wielded it. Even the witch's brand, which could temporarily mask them from Valhalla by allowing Georgette to hold some of their power, would not protect them from a manhunt.

Weary, worried, Senji hung his head. *What can we do?*

We can wait. Clutching her helmet, she leaned back in her chair. *We can wait.*

The silence that stretched between them was filled by the whispered chatter of the waiting Valkyries.

The silence that stretched between them was filled by the eternally muttered prayers of the wolf Giovanni.

None of the sisters showed undo concern about the meeting, though many complained that they were behind schedule. Two were discussing their recent chosen—a campaign manager and a civil engineer, neither of whom had ever seen combat. Another hummed while winding a lock of hair around her finger.

None of the other animals seemed unduly bothered by the long wait, though many of them fidgeted from annoyance. The leaves rustled in the wind. Bright red blossom petals fluttered on the air and rained down over the gathered animals.

My only regret is not getting to greet my sister at her death. I will never regret what we've done.

Nor I. Seeing my brother one last time was worth any punishment they could give us. Whatever comes, we stand together.

Delia's nerves grew still. Resigned and calm, she closed her eyes.

Senji's nerves grew still. Resigned and calm, he preened his wings.

Ganbatte kudasai, *Senji.*

Lâche pas la patate, *Delia.*

Set in their mutual resolve,
they waited.

Set in their mutual resolve,
they waited.

Ishak

ISHAK STARTLED AWAKE AND BOLTED UPRIGHT. INITIALLY caught between dream and reality, he quickly realized that he had fallen asleep sitting on the floor of his living room with his head on the coffee table.

Obeying his heightened instincts, he swung his head back and forth to find Ziya, whose tiny cry he was sure had invaded his dreams.

"You okay?"

He whipped his head around and felt his fatherly alarm diminish. Georgette sat at his kitchen table with Ziya cuddled in her arms. Ziya was pulling the witch's blonde curls straight and then watching them spring away when released.

Ishak sighed and ran a hand over his face. For a moment, he had forgotten that Georgette had come to visit. "Did I sleep long?"

"Half an hour." Georgette chuckled. "I didn't want to wake you. You're a new dad. Gotta sleep when you can."

Ishak hauled himself up, sending a cascade of soft toys tumbling from his lap. He slid into the chair next to Georgette and saw a hardy meal laid out on the table: for her, a thick sandwich and homemade potato chips; for him, a juicy steak and roasted red potatoes.

"Courtesy of the kitchen," Georgette said as she lifted a spoonful of applesauce to Ziya's mouth.

Smiling, Ishak picked up a knife and fork and dove in.

He was halfway through his meal when Ziya suddenly whined, turning her twisted-up face away from the newest spoonful of applesauce as if she hated the sight of it. Shifting the baby on her lap, Georgette dropped the spoon back into the bowl, snatched a toy panda off the floor, and thrust it into Ziya's hands. Instantly distracted, the baby girl's eyes widened as she discovered that the soft toy made crinkly sounds when she squeezed it. While she played, Georgette grabbed her sandwich and ate it with impressive speed.

Ishak chuckled. It was the same way he'd learned to eat ever since becoming a parent.

"You have experience feeding small children," he said.

"My niece," she replied, her mouth full. "Well," she added after swallowing, "my oldest niece. I've got more I haven't met."

Born after she fled from her family, he assumed. He forked a slice of steak. "How many do you have now?"

"Four, with another on the way." She took another hurried bite. "When I left, Holly was pregnant with twins—Blossom and Bluebell—so with her oldest, Jasmine, she's got three now. My fourth niece is Marigold. She's the daughter of my eldest sister, Clove. Apparently, Mom was pissed that Clove got pregnant by some"—she briefly dropped her sandwich to make air quotations with her fingers—"'random boyfriend' instead of through an arranged relationship that could benefit the family." Georgette's lips twitched as if she was trying not to smile with guilty amusement. "Clove's chances for becoming the next Nichols matriarch are sinking fast."

"Witches," muttered Ishak as he ate another piece of steak. "Born with magic in one hand and knives in the other."

Far from showing offense, Georgette nodded. "You don't know the half of it." She looked at Ziya, happily playing with her toy, and then back at him. "Speaking of witches. I wanted to update you on the progress I've made since we last spoke."

Ishak nodded. Every time Georgette visited, she made a point of telling him what possible means of magical transportation she was exploring in order to get him and Ziya home.

"What have you found?" he asked.

"Well"—she sighed—"nothing new at this point. I've had some new ideas," she quickly added, "and I'm following up on some others, but . . ." She shook her head, her eyes filled with sorrow. "You may be stuck here a while."

Ishak nodded. This news was expected and he did not fault Georgette for it, but nevertheless, it was disappointing. With every call to his family, he was reminded of how much he was missing back home. Aside from their loving relatives, there were things in Kabultiloa that he could not duplicate for his daughter in America: seasonal festivals rich in Bultungin culture, a unique blend of languages spoken on every corner, and four-legged excursions into the night in search of prey. He wanted to raise Ziya on the same diet of ochre sunsets and windswept savannas that had nourished him. Nothing less was suitable for his precious girl.

Delia & Senji

The fire in the massive hearth blazed and crackled, heating the dining hall to sauna temperatures. Delia swiped the back of her hand across her forehead to keep the sweat out of her eyes.

The officers' meeting still had not adjourned, so the Valkyries decided to pass the time with a feast. While in Valhalla, their ethereal bodies became more substantial, enough so that they could eat; however, the taste was always nebulous, like soup severely watered down. Given the choice of ghostly food or nothing, Delia opted for the latter. While the others ate, she restlessly paced the floor.

Perched in a tree outside, Senji slept a perfunctory sleep. While necessary for his post-death body, he did not enjoy sleep, given his link to Delia. She was always in his head, making true rest impossible.

A hand on her shoulder made Delia jump. She whirled around as a voice asked, "Won't you have some?"

He felt the touch on her shoulder, and it roused him.

The girl had long, dark hair framing a heart-shaped face. Bands of color—red and black—were painted across her nose and almond eyes. Delia knew they had met before but could not recall a name. She'd never noticed how young this Valkyrie must have been at her death. Without her armor, the girl looked pitifully small and delicate.

"No, but thank you, Sister . . . um . . . "

"Sister Gondol." Looking at the offered plate piled high with steaming meat, she asked, "What is it?"

"*Sæhrímnir*, I imagine," Gondol said. "Most of what the Idisi serve comes from the sooty sea-beast."

"I see."

Smiling, Gondol offered Delia the plate again. "Ever had it?"

"Many years ago." Delia remembered the weak flavor of the chewy meat. "I prefer my memories of real food."

Nodding, Gondol said, "If I was young enough to remember the taste of real food, I would feel the same." Chuckling, she said, "I'm a few centuries separated from those memories."

Another Valkyrie—Hlokk—got up from her seat and approached. Her long black hair was split along the side of her skull by a pronounced scar. *She told me once how that happened. I've forgotten.*

Gondol.

Ax. From a missionary priest.

Delia nodded politely, and Hlokk returned the gesture.

"Sisters," she said, "do you think we'll be here long? My next chosen is nearing his end."

"True for us all," said Gondol, her eyes scanning the dozen or so Valkyries eating the *Sæhrímnir.* "Valhalla has made such a fuss about us fetching more chosen, I can't imagine that this Werewolf business should be more important."

"It does seem questionable," said Hlokk. "Werewolves. Bah! Since when does Valhalla concern itself with Werewolves?"

Despite her worry, Delia was pleased that her assessment of the situation was shared by others.

Her gentle relief eased Senji's agitation and allowed him to slip back into sleep.

"I had no idea my report would garner this much attention," said Delia, feeling more at ease.

"Of course not!" exclaimed Hlokk. "Werewolves . . . It's madness!" Hissing through her teeth, she shook her head. "It's a waste of everyone's time."

The tree shook, waking Senji. He spotted a mustang scratching his side against the trunk. Annoyed, Senji squawked until the horse stopped and looked up. They stared at each other a moment before the mustang snorted a "*lo siento*" and walked on. This was Alonzo, who, circa 1650, had split Hlokk's head open for the crime of having a relationship with a woman.

"Who's to say what's a waste of our time?" said Gondol. She offered her plate to Hlokk, who plucked a strip of meat from it. "All we've done for months is bring chemists and professors to serve Valhalla."

"I suppose," said Delia, "there's a shortage of soldiers."

Is there? asked Senji.

Hell if I know.

"Yet another reason," muttered Hlokk, "why this meeting is nonsense. Why be concerned with a Werewolf when the enemy is advancing?"

"I think," Gondol said in a conspiratorial tone, "they've been waiting for an upset like this to distract us."

We speculated something similar.

True.

"From what?" asked Delia.

Gondol leaned closer. "The fact that we're losing the war."

She drew a sharp breath. Neither of them had considered this possibility.

He drew a sharp breath. Neither of them had considered this possibility.

"Losing?" exclaimed Hlokk, shaking her head. "No. It's a setback. We've had setbacks before."

"Not like this," said Gondol.

Delia noted that the other Valkyries were listening in on their conversation.

Senji looked around at the other partners in the grove. Many seemed to grow increasingly alert as the talk went on.

"I've been at this job for five hundred years," Gondol said. "I've never seen Valhalla lose so much ground so quickly." She turned to address the entire room. "Those of you who have served as long as me: Has our army ever experienced anything like this before?"

Senji scanned the partners in the copse. They stood eerily still, mentally listening to the Valkyries' conversation. Even Giovanni fell silent.

Delia scanned the Valkyries at the tables. Aside from Gondol, she guessed that the eldest was Randgrid—killed during the Miao rebellion—or Thrima, who was sacrificed on a god's altar in Tenochtitlan. Both of them shook their heads.

Nearby, Senji spotted Gondol's partner, Fernão. He alone seemed inattentive to the conversation, his wolf face turned up to the starry sky with a wistful expression.

What she says . . . there's a logic to it.

There's no proof. Until we hear otherwise, it's speculation.

But could the war be as far gone as they say? Delia nervously looked around at her sister Valkyries. Each worried expression she saw amplified her fears. *Has it really never been this bad?*

I don't know. He looked around at his fellow partners. Each clueless expression amplified his confusion. *If it's true, what does it mean for Valhalla?*

What does it mean for us?

The blast of a horn sounded through the dining hall, cutting off her worries. Each Valkyrie leapt to her feet.

Every beast in the copse jolted at the secondhand sound. The partners roused, getting to their feet and standing at attention.

Delia watched as a posse of Idisi, identical from their pointed ears to their multi-jointed toes, entered the hall and gestured for the Valkyries to follow.

We're being ushered back to the meeting room.

They must have come to a decision.

Senji. Her unbeating heart was in her throat as she fell into step with her sisters. *I'm so nervous.*

Be strong. He flew to a lower branch and fixed his gaze on the towering twin giant doors of Valhalla. *Show them nothing.*

One foot in front of the other, Delia walked the halls of Valhalla in a procession of Valkyries flanked by Idisi. In that moment, the echoes of ever-present battle sounded louder and closer to her than ever before. It was as if the war might crash through the cathedral ceiling at any moment, burying her in death and defeat.

Passing through a door, she saw a cluster of officers at the far end of the room. Their faces, scarred from murder, hardened by centuries, were stern and somber. Delia licked her dry lips.

Stay with me.

Always.

"Sisters," announced Skogul, her voice booming through the room, "we have reached a decision."

Georgette

THE SHRILL RINGTONE OF HER PHONE IMMEDIATELY SHOT adrenaline through Georgette's body. Without looking at the screen, she knew it was her mother. She wanted to hurl the phone out the window, but she felt compelled to answer. She hated that feeling but couldn't shake it. Nico called it "FOG": fear, obligation, and guilt. Though she fought to break through the FOG, a thousand memories of her mother's disapproving sneer kept flooding her brain.

"Hi, Mom," she said into the phone, sitting down on the edge of her bed.

"Hello, Ivy," said the familiar voice. "Goodness, it took you so long to answer I thought you lost your phone."

Georgette grimaced. The subtle reproach in her mother's tone was just noticeable enough to annoy her. "My name's Georgette now, Mom," she said.

A dismissive tsk filled her ear, instantly conjuring an image in Georgette's mind of her mother tossing her hair.

"That's not the name I gave you," said Hazel.

Rolling her eyes, Georgette opted to change the subject rather than rehash this argument. "How are Holly's twins doing?"

"Oh, they are the cutest babies!" Hazel cooed. "Chubby arms, dark hair, dimpled cheeks!"

"How's Marigold?" Georgette asked.

"Goldie is doing well," Hazel said. "She's not yet six months old but already shows an ability to see through glamours."

"You gave her the apple test?" asked Georgette in surprise. "At six months?"

It was a simple test that Hazel performed on all Nichols children. She would take a decorative crystal orb in her hand, glamour it to look like an apple, and tell the child to take a bite. Georgette vividly remembered watching Hazel give the test to Rue, the youngest Nichols O'Reilly sister. Toddler Rue obviously saw through the glamour—her eyes filled with confusion when presented with the rock-hard orb—but, trusting her mother, she lunged forward, mouth open. Hazel snatched it away before Rue could break a tooth and laughed uproariously. It wasn't until Georgette shared the story in a counseling session with Nico and saw his horrified reaction that she realized how messed up it was for a mother to order her child to do something that would hurt her.

"A version of it," Hazel said casually. "Quite impressive to pass so young."

Wanting to end the conversation as soon as possible, Georgette plowed ahead. "How's Lily? How far along is she now?"

"Nearly four months." Hazel made a happy sort of purring sound. "Lily carries herself with such grace! It's so nostalgic to see that perfect baby bump! Why, when I was pregnant with Clove, I—"

Georgette tapped the speaker button and put her phone on the end table. She had to get ready for work, and since her mother was prattling on, she might as well get dressed.

Though most of Georgette's job involved working behind the scenes, Kazimiera insisted that she dress in club attire. She didn't mind. Before she'd struck out on her own, most of her clothes had been hand-me-downs or picked by Hazel. It was nice to wear clothes that fit and flattered her.

Hazel was still talking when Georgette finished her makeup and zipped up her dress. She looked in the mirror at the thigh-length teal sheath hugging her thin frame under a long, sheer, glittery overlay. It gave her a soft elegance that none of her old clothes ever had. She put on sparkly chandelier earrings, then combed her fingers through her hair to separate her curls. *I look nice.*

". . . preparing for the Mediterranean cruise I'm taking in August," Hazel plowed on. "I thought your Aunt Laurel might come with me, but she'll be traveling with your cousin Poppy *again*. At least she'll be home for July fourth. I'm sure she's looking forward to seeing you then."

Seeing me?

"Mom," Georgette interrupted, "what are you talking about?"

"The cruise will stop at several Greek islands and then—"

"Mom," Georgette said louder, "why would Aunt Laurel be looking forward to seeing me?"

"At the party, of course."

"Party?"

"Ivy," Hazel said in a scolding voice, "we have a Fourth of July party every year. It's an important family function. You know that."

Family function. Yes, the family would be at the party, but only as window dressing for her father's business associates and the Boston socialites her mother wanted to impress. At last year's party, her parents had announced Georgette's engagement to Zachary Thayer—an engagement no one had discussed with Georgette first. Then they had all avoided her for the rest of the night while strangers offered their congratulations.

"I won't be at the party," Georgette said.

There was a pause, broken only by the sound of her heart hammering in her ears.

"All of your sisters will be there," Hazel said, her icy tone making Georgette shiver. "Your cousins will be there. Two of *my* cousins are flying in to present their baby granddaughters to receive the family signet. You will be there."

Georgette took a breath. "No. I'll be working."

"Excuse me?" Hazel snapped. "You are choosing to disregard family tradition for a job in a strip club?"

All blood drained from Georgette's face. Hazel's "public" voice was rapidly degenerating. It wouldn't be long before her mother lost any pretext of civility. Hazel Nichols O'Reilly was never so dangerous as when she dropped her public mask.

"It's not a strip club," Georgette said carefully. "I like my job. I'm not going to the party."

"How will it look if one member of the family doesn't come?" Hazel asked sharply. "What am I supposed to tell my guests?"

Guests, thought Georgette. *Of course that's what matters.* Michael and Hazel loved to trot out their daughters at formal occasions. The importance of the family image was hammered into the girls from the day they were born. But that wasn't Georgette's problem anymore.

"Well," Georgette said, remembering sessions with Nico, "I have no control over what other people think, and I don't owe those people an explanation."

"Ivy!" Hazel shouted, startling Georgette. "If you're going to be like this, then I don't care to speak to you!"

The phone beeped. Slack-jawed, Georgette stared at the screen—CALL ENDED.

For a second, she felt a frantic need to analyze the conversation word for word to identify her mistake, but then her inner voice, made stronger by months of counseling, asserted itself. *I didn't mess up. She just didn't like that I disobeyed her.* Eyes still on the phone, she smiled. *Maybe she really won't call for a while.* Her smile widened. *She thinks that's a punishment.*

Georgette took another look at herself in the mirror. She wondered if this teal dress would be appropriate for Neil's upcoming corporate party. It would be her first time meeting his employer and colleagues, so she needed to make a good impression. Maybe she should buy something new. A shopping trip would be a great excuse to hang out with Mei-Xing. Between how much time she'd been spending with Neil and Mei-Xing's springtime funk, they hadn't seen much of each other lately. It would be great to have some bestie time.

"Lovely dress."

Georgette nearly jumped out of her skin. In the mirror, she was alone, but when she whirled around, she found Delia standing mere feet behind her in full Valkyrie regalia—silver armor atop flowing white robes. She looked like an avenging angel.

"Please," Georgette exhaled. "Knock or something."

Ignoring her, Delia removed her helmet and slowly set it on the bed. Waves of long brown hair fell down over her shoulders as she turned to glance out the bedroom window.

Following her gaze, Georgette saw Senji perched on the windowsill, his head turning back and forth. *Keeping watch,* she thought nervously. *They're being weirdly cautious.* "Is something wrong?"

Pinching the bridge of her nose with two fingers, Delia let out a slow breath. Though eternally young in her ghostly state, her fatigued expression made her look older. "I reported the Werewolf to my superiors. They were far more concerned than I anticipated."

Georgette's stomach fluttered, and a tiny chill zipped up her spine. "What happened?"

Delia straightened up, squared her shoulders, and met her gaze with weary resolve. "At the next full moon," she said, "the Valkyrie Sisterhood will engage in a Wild Hunt."

Mei-Xing

AS SHE WALKED THROUGH THE NEIGHBORHOOD, TURNING at random with her hands in her coat pockets, Mei-Xing's eyes bounced between the sky and the sidewalk. The late-afternoon sun painted her face, providing the photosynthesis fuel she needed to keep herself fed—but even so, she felt empty. Under her coat and pink, gauzy scarf, she could feel the tiny buds on her chest and shoulders straining to stand upright. It was uncomfortable, like bending an ear the wrong way, but twisting them off was painful, and they always grew back within days. Eventually they would wither and fall off on their own, but in the meantime, she was stuck with them.

Her gaze drifted up the street to a flush of greenery just beyond the buildings. Her shuffling feet slowed to a halt. It was the Plaza de Cesar Chavez, a downtown park with trees in bloom. There would be Nymphs gathered there, talking, giggling, and preening. Her ever-lurking feeling of loneliness swelled, attached to the knowledge that she had no place with them. She put her back to the plaza and walked on.

Across the street, she saw a digital sign displaying the time and temperature: 4:31 p.m., 68 degrees. Neil would be on his way to the apartment about now. He would hang out with Georgette for a while, and then the two of them would walk to Nocturne together.

These days, Mei-Xing tried to avoid being in the apartment while he was there. Their couple-closeness made her feel out of place in her own home, like a small flower struggling for sunlight in the shadow of trees. *It's just springtime hormones*, she told herself for the hundredth time. *This will pass.*

Wandering aimlessly, she didn't realize where she was until she rounded a corner and saw the front door of her apartment building. There, standing near the entrance, she spotted Neil.

Mildly annoyed, she removed a hand from her pocket to wave and continue up the street—but to her puzzlement, he hurried in her direction wearing a deeply troubled expression.

Once they were face-to-face, he started to speak, paused, put his hands together in a prayer-like gesture, and flashed a nervous smile.

"Please don't drug me again, okay?"

"Why, why, why?" ranted Georgette. "Why would you do this?"

Standing near the sliding balcony door, Mei-Xing watched the couple's reflection in the glass. Georgette, dolled up for work, was pacing the living room with her shoes in her hand.

"I'm sorry," Neil mumbled. "It got out of hand so fast. Jin put me on the spot, and I couldn't think of an excuse. But," he added, lifting his head a bit, "if Mei-Xing says no, then that's it. Problem solved."

"Problem solved," Mei-Xing muttered darkly, ill memories stirring of her forced marriage so many years earlier. "He should not even know I exist."

"You're right," Neil said. "I'm sorry."

She shifted her perspective, blurring her view of the couple so she could look at her own reflection. It was strange how the human glamour reflected so clearly in glass when it photographed so poorly. If only it couldn't be photographed at all, Neil would not have had a picture on his phone to show his impertinent colleague.

"This man sounds like my ex-husband," she said. "Entitled. I do not want another man like that."

"And I don't need this right now." Georgette groaned, pressing one hand to her forehead. "I've got work, I've got a Werewolf running loose, I've got an incoming Wild Hunt—"

With a loud gasp, Mei-Xing whirled around and stared intently at her friend. This was alarming news! Individual Valkyries kept to their assigned regions not just for efficiency but as a way of preventing excessive Valhallan magic from accumulating in an area. One Valkyrie was indetectable to human senses, but a group of them, while still hidden from eyes and ears, was a force of nature. A Wild Hunt could set off storms, floods, earthquakes, and, worst of all, violence. The energy from a Wild Hunt stirred something in the blood that made humans skittish and impulsive. Though Mei-Xing had never experienced a Wild Hunt, her uncle had lived through one during the Manchu Qing Dynasty. He'd told her it lasted less than an hour, but the resulting human violence had left thousands dead throughout Inner Mongolia.

"Wild Hunt?" she repeated. She locked eyes with Georgette and felt a momentary connection. The familiar feeling warmed her, easing her tension.

"The loose Werewolf," said Georgette. "Delia says they're going to hunt for it at the full moon."

Two chaotic forces running loose in the city. Mei-Xing shuddered. "Madness."

"Yeah."

"I'm confused," said Neil, looking back and forth between them.

As Georgette rattled off an abbreviated explanation, Mei-Xing tried to sort through her jumbled thoughts. Wild Hunt, springtime, country club . . . there was too much in her head. The only thing that calmed her was feeling that grove-like connection with her friend. And this conversation was the first time she'd felt that emotional bond since spring began. The longing for grove comfort seized her once again and washed away every other feeling.

"I will go," she said.

Neil and Georgette stared at her with twin expressions of surprise.

"You will be at this party, right?" she said, looking at Georgette. "We can hang out together."

After a pause, Georgette flashed a joyful look that warmed Mei-Xing to the core. "Yeah," she agreed. "And we can go shopping for dresses together. But"—her expression turned sober—"we'll have to do some prepping with the glamour and energy flow to make sure we don't slip up at the party."

Mei-Xing smiled back at her.

A brief silence filled the apartment, during which the two women looked into each other's eyes, their *Hathiya* marks conveying their emotions between them. They both worried, doubted, hurt, hoped, longed, and loved. Eventually, their shared mood settled into a familiar affection, a grove-like sensation that Mei-Xing treasured.

Georgette shot Neil a sly look, hugged him, and said, "I guess you're off the hook."

"Yes," Mei-Xing chimed in. "I will not drug you this time."

With a long exhale, he nodded and returned Georgette's embrace.

It will be fine, Mei-Xing told herself. But a small part of her still felt unsettled. And the longer she stood in place, watching Georgette and Neil hug and smile at each other, the more she felt her smile sag.

Kazimiera

THE RHYTHM OF MUSIC TWO FLOORS DOWN REVERBERATED in Kazimiera's ears. Though the nightclub was well insulated from the rest of the building, her hypersensitive Vampire hearing sucked up sound like a sponge absorbing water. She usually had better control of her senses—could turn them on and off like flipping a switch—but lately her grip on them was slipping. It had happened before. Every fifty years or so, in fact. It was horrid, but she always managed to power through.

With a sigh, she opened her phone's calendar. There she saw the usual clutter of appointments and notices, along with a list of VIPs expected each day that week. Though her to-do list was stuffed to the brim, she had no doubts or concerns about her ability to see it all to completion. It was a lot of work—but for her, it was routine.

Except for Friday night: "Full moon. Audrey. Wild Hunt."

Irritated, Kazimiera scraped one long magenta nail over the arm of her chair. A paper-thin wood shaving curled under her finger.

A Wild Hunt was going to ride through the Bay Area to find a Werewolf. While the witch believed there was another running loose in the city, the only Werewolf Kazimiera knew of was the one she had agreed to shelter in her building for three nights around the full moon. That meant the witch had one night only to make sure the room where Audrey changed was airtight with concealment magic. If it wasn't, Nocturne might get swarmed by Valkyries. And Valkyries on a Wild Hunt would run down anyone and anything in their path.

I can't shut down on my busiest nights, she thought, slowly scraping another wood curl from her chair, the beat of the club music quaking through her bones. *I'll be on the phone all night canceling reservations and fielding complaints.*

The sensible course of action was to renege on her deal with Audrey. Kazimiera didn't like the idea of backing out of a contract, particularly one that would eliminate her problems with the Health Department, but she had a business to protect. Refusing to help Audrey would protect the building . . . but it would create another problem: her staff.

Damn bleeding-heart witch, she thought, lips pulling back from her teeth. *The Fae in my building used to follow my rules without question. But this bitch wants to save the world. And my staff actually admire her for it.*

She'd seen the way her Fae went to Georgette with their troubles, asking for favors—which, more often than not, she granted. They liked her so much that they now went to her for matters that had previously been Kazimiera's dominion. In recent months, her day-to-day burden had lightened significantly. For a typical business manager, that might have been a welcome change. In Kazimiera's case, it was not only problematic; it was dangerous.

The pain in her head was a warning. She *needed* to be busy. That was the whole reason she had opened Nocturne in the first place. If she didn't stay busy . . . She gritted her teeth. She didn't want to think about how bad her condition could get.

This business only works because of the witch's spells. Without her magic, magic I can't do myself, this building is nothing but steel and concrete. If she leaves—a sharp pain shot through Kazimiera's head—*the whole system breaks down.* Music vibrated through her skull in a rippling pulse, causing her vision to wobble. *Unfortunately, I need her.*

The smartphone chimed, adding a new tremor to her aching head. She saw a message from the Dullahan: *Security breach.*

Fangs fully extended, their tips piercing her lower lip, she typed, *???*

4-5 human men, mid 20s, drunk, harmless.

She hmphed. Harmless. That just meant the intruders had not breached security with the intention of capturing Fae. Drunk idiots who wandered too deep into the building still had the potential to cause harm.

Kazimiera's current security team was one of the best she had ever had—from the many-eyed Ophan who watched the screens 24/7 to the Nurikabe who created invisible walls that compelled trespassers to turn back—but every once in a while, someone slipped through.

She stood up, smoothed the front of her dress, and licked her lips. After a moment's thought, she fished a flask out of her desk drawer and took a swig. There was just enough salty, metallic blood in it to coat her tongue and trickle down her throat—barely a mouthful, but enough to ease the pain in her head.

Charging out of her office and into the hallway, she homed in on some drunken laughter three rooms down. Through the open door, she spotted a pack of young men in dark jeans, T-shirts, and dirty, torn sneakers. *The bouncer should have turned them away dressed like that*, she thought irritably.

"Gentlemen," she said, projecting her voice above theirs, "this area is off-limits."

As the five men turned toward her, Kazimiera spotted the Banshee and one of the Kitsune huddled together in a corner. The fox woman's clothing was rumpled, one of her shoulders was fully exposed, and her usually upright ears were laid flat against her head. Half of the Banshee's red hair had come loose from her headband in long, messy strands, uncovering one of her pointed ears. Clutching each other tight, they both shot Kazimiera looks that told her all she needed to know.

"Whaz this room for?" slurred one of the grinning men. Pointing to the two girls, he asked, "Who're they?"

"These rooms are for special events, and they are only available by paid appointment," Kazimiera said.

"S'cool." The man dipped his hand into his back pocket and fished out a wallet. "We got money."

"But not an appointment." Regally sweeping one arm in an arc toward the door, she stepped aside. "This way, please."

"Nah," a second man said, laughing. "We wanna see them."

"Lookit!" said another, tugging at the Kitsune's robe. "Lookit those tails she's got! What'er those? Hey"—he smacked his friend's arm—"take a pic!"

Kazimiera's professional smile grew strained. The spells that coated the VIP rooms obscured memories but didn't eliminate them. These obnoxious boys would remember that they had seen something astounding, even if they couldn't recall exactly what it was. That retained sense of wonderment was what brought her VIP customers back for more week after week—but, unfortunately, it would have the same effect on these assholes.

"Unhand her," said Kazimiera, dropping her tenor of voice, but the boys continued to prod the weeping fox woman.

Fuming, Kazimiera whipped out her phone and shot off a message to the Dullahan: *You, witch, room 319, NOW.*

One guy grabbed the Kitsune, pried her away from the Banshee, and forcefully turned her teary face toward his friend's waiting camera phone. The Banshee's face began to rapidly age, shifting from a beautiful young redhead into a raging gray crone, and she let loose a window-rattling shriek. One of the boys flinched and backed away, but the others laughed as if the Banshee's supernatural display was nothing but a performance.

The hammering in her temples straining against her skin, Kazimiera held up a hand to the wailing creature, giving her a "I'll handle this" look. Hissing, the Banshee slowly backed away.

"STOP!"

Kazimiera's voice now echoed with the soulless tones of the undead. The intruders instantly fell silent. She could feel her eyes going black as her vampiric nature asserted itself. With it came a powerful thirst made all the more potent by the fierce pain in her head.

"You are trespassing on private property and you are assaulting my staff!" she hissed. "This is your final warning." She pointed at the nearby sofas. "Sit down and shut up."

Four of the boys paled, sobering up enough to quiet down, but the fifth, the one holding the Kitsune, scoffed and demanded, "Or what?"

"Austin," muttered his photo-snapping friend. "C'mon, man."

"No," Austin barked. "What the hell's this bitch gonna do? Hey, honey," he sneered, "why doncha get back to serving drinks, okay?" He let go of the trembling fox woman and, tottering slightly, stepped up to Kazimiera and glared at her. "We'll leave," he said, his rancid breath pummeling her face, "when we're ready to leave."

Against her better judgment, Kazimiera inhaled. Underneath the stink of alcohol, she smelled a man in the prime of his life. Young and juicy. She smiled, her lips sliding back as her jaw unhinged to reveal row upon row of shark-like teeth. Austin's expression changed in a blink, confused but registering that he had made a crucial mistake. He took just one step back before Kazimiera seized him by the hair, threw him to the floor, and lunged at his exposed throat.

The first mouthful of blood filled her with delicious warmth. The second diminished her music-induced headache, leaving her feeling balanced and whole. Tuning out the screams of the other four men, she focused on the delightful sound of her gurgling victim's frantic heartbeat.

Kazimiera felt a hand on her shoulder. "Kazi," said Georgette's soft voice, "please let him go."

With a growl, the Vampire disconnected from the young man's throat and leapt to her feet. She looked over her shoulder, toward the door, and saw the Dullahan's imposing form blocking the exit. Austin's four companions cowered at the headless creature's feet, their faces full of horror. Suddenly, one of them darted for the door, trying to duck under the Dullahan's arm. Smooth as water, the Dullahan swung his arm downward, clocking the young man in the face with his rotted head. The drunk boy fell backward and sprawled on his back, a red mark on his cheek.

At the sight of another bare throat, Kazimiera shoved the witch aside and dove in.

"Kazi!" she heard Georgette exclaim over the victim's gurgled screams. "Don't!"

"*Kusoyaro!*" cried the Kitsune. "Kill them!"

Rolling one eye back, Kazimiera saw the Banshee holding the Kitsune in a tight embrace while the fox woman sobbed into her shoulder. The red-haired creature stroked her fox ears while shooting their harassers a vicious glare.

"Don't kill anyone," said the Dullahan. "We're too busy to dismember and dispose of bodies."

The three remaining young men gasped in unison, and she heard one of them retch. Another started begging them all to let them go. Though her mouth was full of blood, the Vampire giggled, tickled pink by his obsequious tone.

The pounding in her head had all but vanished by the time Kazimiera dropped the second boy, blood trickling from the punctures in his neck. She rose from the floor feeling fully in control of herself for the first time all night. "When I'm done with them," she said to Georgette, "erase their memories. And their phones. You," she said to the Dullahan, "add them to the banned list." She flashed her many pointed teeth at the intruders, making them cringe and shiver. "I never want to see these little shits in my building again." With an inhumanly fast motion, she seized a boy and bent his head back until he yelped.

Of the remaining two, one was praying, tears streaming down his face, while the other had curled himself into a ball and was gently but feverishly rocking back and forth.

Kazimiera narrowed her eyes at Georgette. "When I'm finished here, we'll discuss the plan for Thursday."

"Again?" asked Georgette.

"Yes, again." The young man in Kazimiera's grasp flailed an arm in her direction. She knocked him sharply on the forehead, making him go limp. "You're going to make absolutely sure we have a contingency plan for everything that could possibly happen on Friday," she hissed at Georgette.

"Tonight's security breach proves that the club's defenses are far from perfect, and a Wild Hunt demands perfection. You hear me?"

"Okay," Georgette agreed. "We'll go over it again."

"Good." Inclining her head toward the Kitsune and Banshee, Kazimiera said, "Take them to their rooms and find someone to cover their shifts. They're off tonight."

The pair sighed heavily and thanked her. On her way to the door, still holding on to the Banshee, the Kitsune lashed out one foot to stomp on Austin's fingers. Groaning, he stirred but didn't wake. The Dullahan allowed the girls to slip past, Georgette just behind them.

"Um, e-excuse me, ma'am?" mumbled the praying boy. "I-I'm so sorry for everything." His eyes filled with tears. "Please," he sobbed, "what's gonna happen to us?"

Kazimiera laughed aloud. "You'll wake up tomorrow in a public park with the worst headache of your life and a spotty memory of being thrown out of Nocturne for getting handsy with the staff. So don't worry, honey," she purred, "you're going to live through this. But first"—she leaned closer to the woozy drunk in her grasp—"you're going to make up for your behavior by treating me to a meal."

Georgette

THIN CLOUDS DOTTED THE SKY ABOVE THE SETTING SUN, pink and orange smears on a blue canvas. Long shadows painted the streets, darkening the city in patches as the sun sank lower, light illuminating only the spaces between the buildings. Cars jerked and halted their way between stop-lights as clusters of people, shuffling and scurrying, traveled the sidewalks.

Trying to stay out of everyone's way, Georgette stood by Nocturne's front door, her back to the sign that read CLOSED THURSDAY FOR PRIVATE EVENT.

"How does it look?" she asked.

She watched as Delia inspected the spellcraft. Slowly, her eyes continually scanning Nocturne, the Valkyrie paced the front sidewalk. Several times, pedestrians walked into her personal space, sometimes passing through her spirit body and other times slipping around her, as if sensing her invisible presence. As she walked, her fingers drummed the top of the helmet in her arms. High above them, Senji flew in a tight circle over the building. Through the *Hathiya* mark that linked them, Georgette sensed that the Valkyrie and the raven were communicating with each other, though she couldn't hear their unspoken words. She waited, heart pounding, for their final verdict.

"It's well done," said Delia, eyes still inspecting the building. "It seems opaque, and Senji doesn't see any gaps. So long as you don't damage the spellcraft or draw on our *Hathiya* brand while inside the building, my sisters should pass it by without a thought. Of course"—she glanced at Georgette—"we can't be sure until there's a transformed Werewolf inside."

"Right." Georgette sighed. "Thanks for your input."

With a squawk that drew curious looks from pedestrians, Senji swooped low over their heads. Delia seized his foot with practiced ease, and he soared away with her in tow.

Georgette took a deep breath. Delia's assessment was important, but the hardest part was still ahead.

Dressed in gym shorts and a ratty T-shirt, Audrey sat on the floor with her bare arms wrapped around her legs and her toes curled up tight against her naked feet. The fresh tattoos encircling her thighs were still red and puffy. As Georgette gazed at her, a shiver rippled through the young woman's body. Georgette wondered if it meant she was cold or scared.

Looking up over the tops of her knees, Audrey murmured, "How much longer?"

"Any time now," Georgette replied.

Nestled in her oversized sweatshirt, Georgette scanned the room carefully. This cold, damp basement storage room was unpleasant, but it was all Kazimiera was willing to spare. At least she'd had the staff remove all the supplies, save for a few empty shelves. What was left was a twelve-by-twelve concrete room, its one exit protected by a heavy, triple-bolted door. Not pretty or comfortable, but sufficient for the purpose.

Muffled voices from the hallway told her the club's security team was standing guard as planned, though she hoped they wouldn't be needed. Georgette rested her fingertips against the cinder block wall and felt the pulse of her own magic. A thick, invisible tapestry of her craft, tightly woven from a dozen different spells, covered every inch of the room. In theory, it would be enough to contain a rampaging elephant.

"Ugh!" exclaimed Audrey. Slipping into a cross-legged position, she leaned back, palms on the floor. "I hate waiting!"

Georgette checked her watch. "The moon is rising right now. If you're going to change, it'll happen within minutes."

"If," Audrey repeated, her voice as bitter as horseradish. "If, if, if. All this prep might be for nothing."

"Unlikely," Georgette said, "since you were bitten the day after the full moon. The odds are pretty high that you have the three-day lycanthropy variant."

"So what's the hold-up?!" Audrey jumped up and paced the room on bare feet. "Can we just get this over with?!"

Georgette heard the locks turning on the room's metallic door. The hinges squeaked and groaned as the door slowly swung open to reveal a weary-looking Kazimiera.

Gently massaging her temples, the Vampire swept her gaze over the room. "No Werewolf," she concluded.

"No," said Georgette. "Not yet."

"Well," Kazi said with a click of her tongue, "that's . . . inconvenient."

"For who?" Audrey shouted indignantly. "Are *you* the one locked in here?"

Cocking an eyebrow, Kazi shot Georgette a stern look. "Didn't you explain to her about the Wild Hunt?"

Her disapproving stare cut deep, making the witch feel small. "I-I forgot," Georgette stammered.

"Wild Hunt?" said Audrey. "What does . . . never mind." She threw her arms into the air and turned her back to them both. "I don't care."

With a tiny shrug, Kazi slowly approached Georgette, her spike heels clicking with each step on the concrete floor. The edges of her face looked pinched, as if she was suppressing pain. "If she only transforms for one day, then we can't test the building's defenses before the Valkyries ride through. That's a problem."

"I had Delia and Senji check it out, and they think it looks solid," Georgette said.

"They *think*." Coming to a stop and crossing her arms, Kazi tsked. "That's not reassuring."

"Kazi, please," Georgette said. "I'm doing the best I can."

Placing one hand on her hip, the Vampire gestured around the room. "What if your best isn't enough? Are you willing to bet the safety of everyone here on your spellcrafting abilities?"

Georgette felt all the blood drain out of her face. She had heard similar speeches from her mother many times in her life. Hazel Nichols O'Reilly had questioned her daughter's talent, intelligence, and basic competence at every opportunity, all but eliminating her self-esteem. With Nico's counseling, Georgette had grown stronger in recent months, but Hazel's derisions were still in her brain, waiting for any chance to undermine her confidence.

You're weak, her mother's voice taunted her. *You've always been—*

Shut up.

Georgette suddenly found herself standing taller. She'd been hearing her mother's voice repeat the same insults since the day she was born, and she was sick of it. *Shut up. I'm better than this.* She crossed her arms over her chest. "I've done everything I can think of," she said in a level voice. "There's no other spell I can use."

"As if it mattered," the Vampire sneered. "I'm stuck with your spellwork no matter how subpar it is."

"Bitch," Audrey's voice filled the room, "shut the hell up."

Nostrils flaring, a hand gingerly pressed to her forehead, Kazi slowly twisted her head in Audrey's direction. "What did you say?" the Vampire asked sharply.

Audrey stepped forward until she was standing shoulder to shoulder with Georgette. "I said," she slowly enunciated, "shut the hell up."

Wide-eyed, Kazi stared at her. Twice, she opened her mouth as if to speak, only for no sound to come out.

Stunned yet secretly enjoying her employer's speechlessness, Georgette held her breath and watched.

"Who do you think you are?" Kazi finally snapped. "You're in *my* building!"

"So what?" Audrey shot back. "You're not exactly a hands-on owner, are you?" Nodding at Georgette, she said, "She taught me about this virus, she researched my options, she made the ink for my tattoos, and she prepared this nasty room in *your* building. I haven't seen you do a damn thing except complain."

Eyes gone black and fangs bared, Kazi looked posed to tear into her opponent, but Audrey pressed on undeterred.

"Doesn't matter if you don't like me. We made a deal and I kept my end. I altered department records so this place isn't due for inspection for six to twelve months. I could lose my job and probably get arrested for that." Audrey advanced on Kazi, thrusting herself into her personal space until the Vampire, to Georgette's amazement, took a step back. "You are definitely gonna uphold your end or, so help me God,

I'll tell my boss that you bribed me to alter the reports." Turning on her heel, she marched to the far side of the room. "You think dealing with one health inspector is a pain in the ass, wait until there's twenty in *your* building."

"Are you *threatening* me?" Kazi turned to Georgette, clenching her pointed teeth. "Is that . . . that *human* threatening *me*?"

With a snarl, the Vampire strode toward Audrey, fists clenched. Georgette jumped into her path with her hands held out. "Kazi—"

"NO!" bellowed the Vampire. She grabbed Georgette by the arm and flung her aside, sending her slamming into the wall shoulder-first. A sharp pain shot through Georgette's arm as bone made contact with concrete.

"I've listened to you enough!" Kazi yelled. "Why are you even here?!"

Rubbing her bruised arm, Georgette stared at the Vampire. "I'm here because you hired me, remember? According to you, I was the only one who applied for the job."

Kazi hissed, closed her eyes, and pinched the bridge of her nose. "Damn witch." She snarled and shoved a finger in Georgette's face. "You've turned everything upside down. Before you got here, I had a handle on things."

Georgette held her ground. "Then why did you hire me?"

As her boss glared at her in silence, fangs exposed, Georgette racked her brain, trying to pin down the source of her rage. For months, she had done her best to be helpful to everyone in Nocturne, especially Kazi. She had thought she was doing well—but now, caught in Kazi's fiery stare, she felt like she had failed.

Kazi suddenly winced and grabbed her head. Reflexively, Georgette reached out to help.

"You okay?" she asked. "Headache?"

"Don't touch me," Kazi hissed, yanking her arm away. She turned around and shouted at the open door, "Hey! Tell whoever's making that ungodly noise in the bar to knock it off!"

"The bar?" Georgette said in surprise. "The bar in the club?"

"The bar in the restaurant!" Kazi snapped. "We're closed for the night! There's no reason for anyone to be stocking liquor!"

"The restaurant? That's two floors up. You can hear that from down here?" Georgette started to reach out to touch Kazi's arm, thought better of it, and pulled back. "Are you okay?"

"Wine," Audrey said with a groan.

"What?" Georgette asked.

Audrey was crouched on the floor, her entire body trembling. "Somebody"—she said with difficulty—"broke a . . . wine bottle."

A grim suspicion crept over Georgette. "How do you know?"

Audrey lifted her head, and Georgette saw to her horror that the young woman's face was scrunched up in pain and her eyes had become a brilliant orange. Those eyes exuded terror and—worse—hunger.

"I," Audrey said through gritted teeth, "can smell it."

In a fluid, explosive motion, she sprang into the air and transformed. In the blink of an eye, a fully formed Werewolf was hurtling toward Georgette.

Before she could even take a breath, Kazi shoved Georgette hard, sending her sprawling. Werewolf Audrey leapt over the advancing Vampire, landed roughly, and scrambled out the wide-open door. Georgette looked up just in time to see a scruffy tail vanishing into the hallway amidst the scrape of claws on concrete.

"Stop her!" Kazi shrieked. "Stop her!"

From the hall, Georgette heard Louis scream as Odhran shouted Irish obscenities. She raised herself up, shoving her hair out of her face, as the two headless men appeared in the doorway. Odhran's bulky coat was slashed in multiple places, exposing the putrid flesh underneath. Blood oozed from a deep gouge across Louis's body—a gash that stretched between one large eye in his shoulder and the mouth covering his stomach.

"She got past us," said Odhran. "Dammit, she bowled us right over!"

"She's huge," Louis whimpered. "Werewolves are never that big."

Kazi cursed and punched the wall, leaving a dent in the cinder blocks. "Your spells failed!" she snarled at Georgette before dashing out of the room.

She was out of sight before Georgette could find her voice to say, "Only because you left the door open."

Ishak

THREE HALF-PINT, HAIRY MEN WANDERED ABOUT ISHAK'S small kitchen, cleaning the cabinets, dishes, and glasses. These gruff but kindly Hobs visited his apartment once a day to keep every inch of the kitchen spotless. Oftentimes, they also brought food from the restaurant, keeping Ishak's refrigerator stocked with essentials and leftovers from the previous day's menu. Ishak always thanked them and had even tried to make conversation with them once or twice, but they never made a sound aside from the occasional grunt.

In the adjoining living room, Ziya sat at the small table in her highchair, round cheeks splattered with vegetable puree. The Huldra sitting next to her scooped a spoonful of mash from a bowl and offered it to her. Orange goop leaked from the sides of Ziya's mouth and dribbled off her chin as she gulped it down.

Seeing her father approach, Ziya pointed one chubby hand at him and smacked her lips.

The Huldra, Sissel, glanced at him and smiled—with her lips, anyway. Her large green eyes never smiled. Those eyes were as haunted as a graveyard, making Ishak wonder what she'd seen before coming to Nocturne.

"She likes this vegetable mix," Sissel said, nodding at the bowl. As always, she spoke in a raspy whisper, as if each word formed by her damaged vocal cords had to claw its way off her tongue. "It's made of carrots and squash."

Ishak responded with a polite nod. "You are too kind, Sissel."

"Your little girl is a darling," she said as she wiped the baby's messy face. "So many of the Fae here have young ones they can't see. Little Ziya warms their aching hearts."

A low humming sound vibrated through the kitchen, drawing Ishak's gaze. Over the countertop, he saw the Hobs' three domed heads, cabinets hiding them from the cheekbones down, lined up in a row. Their watery eyes—each pair separated by an upturned, bat-like nose—looked uncharacteristically soft, almost wistful, as they gazed at Ziya. When they noticed Ishak looking at them, the humming stopped and they quickly ducked out of sight.

"Do you have children, Sissel?" asked Ishak, taking the seat across from her.

"No," she said, "but my brothers do, my little mob of nieces and nephews. I write them letters." She lowered her eyes. "Sometimes they write back."

Ishak didn't press for more information. Every Fae in Nocturne had a painful story, and they seemed to have an unspoken agreement not to share. Each carried scars; some were more visible than others, but they all bore the mark of a witch that had branded them as property. Ishak also carried a mark—the *Hathiya* Georgette had given him—but his was unique because he, unlike them, had taken his willingly and could use it to increase his power when needed.

Fussing, Ziya pointed at the bowl. Sissel obediently scooped up more mush and, babbling sweetly to the baby, slid the spoon into her mouth. As Ishak watched them, the

Huldra's hoarse voice suddenly seemed to fade out of his ears, and something else seized his attention: the brand on his inner wrist was . . . pulling.

The sensation wasn't physical, exactly, though he did feel a sort of tug under his skin. What he felt was internal, like a nagging thought.

Puzzled, he focused inward. As he cleared his mind of distractions, the pull from the mark grew stronger and he identified its source.

Georgette.

Descending the stairwell, Ishak heard shouts that grew louder and more frantic the lower he went. When he got to the first floor, he clearly heard Georgette scream, "Stop!"

Alarmed, he quickened his pace.

He burst through the stairwell door and dashed into the nightclub—and was almost flattened by a mass of fur and muscle. But instead of attacking him, the beast charged past him, slipped, and slid into the wall.

The Werewolf.

She braced against the wall, panting. Her thick gray coat rippled from her broad shoulders to the base of her spine, the fur standing on end. Tucked between her hind legs, her white-tipped tail trembled like a viper's rattle. Heavy breaths racked her body, sending violent quakes down her long limbs.

Ishak was astonished by her size. According to Georgette, most Werewolves had a scrawny, underfed look to them—they tended to be a gangly mess of hair and bone scarcely sturdy enough to withstand a gust of wind. But this Werewolf was impressively robust, so wide and tall that Ishak was surprised she had managed to climb the narrow back stairs from the basement. He wondered if she owed her size to the newness of the infection—the fact that the virus had not yet had time to burn through her bodily resources.

As Ishak took in the situation, Georgette entered his field of vision, running across the nightclub toward the beast. "Audrey, calm down!"

Kazimiera appeared at the witch's side, grabbed her roughly by the arm, and yanked her to a stop. "Stay away from that thing!" she commanded. Whirling around, she shouted back the way they'd come, "Get the rest of security down here! Bring this bitch down!"

Georgette shook her arm out of the Vampire's grip. "No! She's just overwhelmed! Give the tattoos a chance to work!"

"Shut up!" the Vampire snapped. She edged toward the Werewolf with her fingers hooked like raptor talons. "Get down on the floor," she ordered, "or you'll find out just how 'hands-on' I am."

The Werewolf swung her huge head in the Vampire's direction, her pointed snout drooping low and her long tongue lolling out of her gaping jaws. Instinctively sniffing the air, Ishak smelled panic verging on madness. He had never smelled a Werewolf before and thus could not say if this scent was appropriate, but it didn't sit well with him.

"Audrey, it's okay." Georgette walked slowly toward the Werewolf with her hands held out in a gesture of appeasement. "I think you were thrown off by how fast the transformation happened. Please, take a breath and let the spells do their work."

The beast turned her head slightly. As her face caught the streetlight leaking through the shuttered windows, Ishak thought he saw a glimmer of human comprehension.

"What's going on?" he asked Georgette softly. The Werewolf's bright orange eyes darted to him in alarm, but he made a point of not looking at her directly as he glided slowly forward. "Are you alright?"

"I'm fine," Georgette said, "but Audrey needs help."

"Kazi." The Dullahan's voice broke into the room, echoing inside the space. The headless man-creature jogged into view and positioned his substantial frame to block the hallway leading back to the basement stairwell. "I've got more security coming." He pointed at Ishak. "Don't let her get to the main stairs!"

Ishak knew no predator would voluntarily squeeze itself into a confined area like a stairwell unless it had no other exit. His Bultungin gaze immediately zeroed in on the nightclub's front doors. *That's a predator's escape route.*

Walking slowly, he moved to place himself between the Werewolf and the main entrance. He knew her wide orange eyes were tracking him, but he continued to avoid her gaze, watching her only through his peripheral vision. He stalked her as he would stalk prey: casually, deliberately, showing no interest yet seeing everything. A thrill surged through him. He had not hunted like this since before he and Kalilah were abducted out of their homeland.

From across the room, he heard a throaty snarl.

"Enough of this," said Kazimiera. She stalked toward the Werewolf, her shark-like jaw unhinged. Teeth bared, the Werewolf tried to skitter away from her, only to knock over several bar stools. The clatter made her jump and yelp. She scurried around the bar and, as Ishak knew she would, charged toward the front door.

Before the Werewolf made it two steps toward him, Ishak's Bultungin form emerged—skin sprouting fur, limbs lengthening, bones and muscles rearranging themselves into the form of a huge bipedal hyena. He flew at his "prey" with arms outstretched.

The Werewolf stopped dead in her tracks. In the instant before he made contact, the expression Ishak saw on her face was distinctly human in its surprise.

Ishak had lunged at the Werewolf with the expectation of a fight; instead, she went still under his claws. He knocked her to the floor and pinned her under his weight, thrusting his face close to hers with a sharp growl. Though she tensed up in his grip, the Werewolf didn't move.

Ishak heard Georgette's hurried footsteps approach and felt her hand on his shoulder.

"Audrey?" she said gently as she knelt down. "Can you understand me?"

The Werewolf's eyes slowly shifted from Ishak to the witch, then to her own paw. With clumsy, jerky motions, she turned over the paw, balled in the too-long fingers, and gave the room a shaky thumbs-up.

"Good." Georgette heaved a sigh. "Okay," she said, patting Ishak's shoulder, "you can let her up."

He did so, then stepped away and rested back on his haunches as Georgette gently helped the Werewolf to her feet.

Standing on four wobbly legs, the creature regarded Ishak with a strange mix of disbelief and fascination. He noted that the panic had evaporated from her scent.

"That transformation was so fast," Georgette said to the Werewolf, "I don't blame you for freaking out. At least now we know the tattoos work."

"Ha!" Kazimiera stood over them with her arms crossed over her chest. She looked wholly human and wholly infuriated.

"The magic worked, Kazi," Georgette said. "Her mind is intact."

"She's a menace!" the Vampire said. "What if there had been customers in here?"

"The basement room will work next time," Georgette insisted.

"Next time?" Kazimiera snapped. "Are you insane?"

Ishak narrowed his eyes at the Vampire. A few stools had been knocked over, but nothing was broken and no one had been bitten. Kazimiera's vitriolic tone struck him as a gross overreaction. The Werewolf seemed to share his opinion; curling her lip, she snorted and shook her head.

The Vampire's eyes went black and her fangs extended. "Don't you dare," she hissed. "You were supposed to stay in the basement. This"—she gestured all around her—"isn't covered by our deal."

The Werewolf snarled, raised her hackles, and advanced on Kazimiera. With a scoff, the Vampire looked at her as she would at a chunk of maggot-infested meat.

Ishak was ready to let the physical altercation play out, but Georgette quickly got between the two, grabbed the Werewolf's head, and leaned close to her ear. Ishak cocked an ear forward.

"Don't," the witch whispered. "However powerful you're feeling right now, that's just the virus firing you up. Go after her, and you'll burn through your body's energy and pass out long before she breaks a sweat."

A low growl rumbled in the Werewolf's throat, but she didn't move. Instead, she continued to stare at Kazimiera, who glared back with a smug look that made Ishak feel sick—and almost compelled him to take a swipe at her himself.

"Since you found your way up here," the Vampire said,

"you can find your way back to the basement. Without," she added sharply, "damaging my property." She turned and sauntered toward the Dullahan, who stood aside to let her by. "If the magic doesn't hold her in, I want that mutt banned from the building."

The moment the Dullahan closed the door behind the Vampire, Georgette muttered, "The magic would've worked if you hadn't been there."

"Are you alright?" Ishak asked her.

"Yeah." She put her arms around his neck and hugged him, leaning her cheek against his fur. "Thanks for the help. What brought you down here?"

"This," he said, holding out his left forelimb and turning it to expose the *Hathiya* brand. "I think you called for me."

"Maybe I did," she said after a moment's pause. She squeezed him again. "I'm glad you came."

Over Georgette's head, Ishak saw the Werewolf's orange eyes furtively scanning him from snout to tail. Amused, he huffed a breath through his nostrils, making her jump.

"*Ushé-ushé*," he greeted her with a bob of his head.

Georgette released his neck and gestured to the Werewolf. "Audrey," she said, "this is my friend Ishak Siad. He's a Bultungin, a Werehyena, and he's living in this building temporarily. Ishak, Audrey Collins." Smiling, she gave Ishak another quick squeeze before stepping away. "Thanks again."

Ishak nodded, enjoying her gratitude as well as a rush of post-hunt satisfaction. He had captured his prey, helped Georgette, contributed to the well-being of his adopted community, and undermined the Vampire. It wasn't a race across the savanna with his family and friends to bring home a feast for their town, but it still felt like a successful and rewarding evening.

Nicolás

THE AROMA IN THE BOTANICA, A MÉLANGE OF HERBS AND candles, embraced Nico the moment he stepped through the front door. It hadn't always been that way. When he first visited Aunt Mariana's shop as a child, the scents had overwhelmed him to the point of nausea. But at Mariana's urging, his parents had brought him back regularly. Little by little, the smell had become familiar—and eventually, over the course of many years, he had come to associate it with his aunt's strict but affectionate manner. Now he loved it like he loved her.

At a young age, Mariana had sensed potential in Nico, a latent talent for *brujería* that she wished to nourish, and his parents had agreed to let her teach him. The lessons, harsh and strange though they were, had soon uncovered a part of himself that he was delighted to find. It was as though he had unknowingly been wearing shoes a size too small, only to step out of them and feel his feet unencumbered for the first time. After that, he never wanted to restrict his growth again.

Mariana raised her head as Nico entered. Eyes lighting up as they always did, she flashed a welcoming smile from behind the cash register, then inclined her head toward the beaded curtain behind the counter that covered the entrance to the storage room.

Nico nodded and silently made for the doorway.

In the back, away from the chatter of shop patrons, he saw a box perched atop a desk piled high with books and paperwork. He stepped into the room and peeked into the open box. There he saw bundles of herbs and ingredients—the same ones he had delivered to Nocturne for Audrey's tattoos weeks before. Most of the bundles were smaller than when he had put them together, and a few were gone entirely. Atop the pile sat a note in Georgette's handwriting that read simply, "Leftovers. Thanks!"

Nico smiled, cautiously optimistic. If she'd returned unused ingredients, that suggested the tattoos had worked. After dropping his shoulder bag full of textbooks behind the desk, curious to know more, he pulled out his phone and called Georgette, who picked up on the first ring.

"Hey," she said brightly.

"Hey," he said. "Just got to the Botanica and found the box you left. Last night was the first time Audrey thought she might change, right? Did she?"

"Yep."

"And the tattoos?"

"They worked."

He grinned. "All your hard work paid off!"

He swore he could feel her face lighting up from the praise through the phone as she replied, "Yeah, Audrey can change form without losing her mind. Her transformation is, like, weirdly quick, but that might just be because she hasn't been infected long. Oh, and the spells I added to the building are working! Delia and Senji came by last night, after Audrey changed, and confirmed that for me."

The sound of the Valkyrie's name made Nico's heart skip. In his mind's eye, he saw her: rosy-brown skin, wavy hair, diamond-bright eyes, and an air of graceful strength that both humbled and enlivened him. Struggling against his own racing pulse, he tried his best to sound calm as he asked, "What exactly did Delia say?"

"That the building is as good as invisible. The Wild Hunt won't notice Audrey as long as she's inside."

Intense heat flowed into Nico's cheeks, making him extremely glad to be having this conversation via phone instead of in person.

"She also promised that if the Hunt *does* notice anything about Nocturne, she'll do her best to redirect them," Georgette added.

"She's riding with the Wild Hunt?" he asked in surprise.

"Her and every Valkyrie assigned to an area within five hundred miles of here."

For a crazed moment, Nico imagined climbing up to the roof at night and staring up at glittering Valkyries scattered through the sky. Would they ride on storm clouds? Would they fly? Would they be bellowing battle cries? The thought of seeing Delia in action was magnetically enticing. *And maybe she'll see me.*

"Is the Hunt an all-night thing," he asked, "or is there a time frame?"

"I don't know." To his chagrin, Georgette's tone had shifted. She sounded inquisitive, maybe even suspicious. "Why? Were you thinking of watching for it?"

"Yeah," he too quickly replied. "I mean, maybe. A Wild Hunt is the sort of thing people must wait a lifetime to see, right?"

"No," a third voice broke into their conversation.

Glancing over his shoulder, Nico saw Mariana striding into the room, the beaded curtain clattering in her wake.

"No one with a lick of sense would wish for a Wild Hunt," she said.

Her stern expression startled him out of his embarrassment. "Why?"

Making a *tsk!* sound, she said, "A Wild Hunt is not a parade, *mijo*. It's a tornado of madness that sweeps through an area without warning or restraint. Get in its path, and the Valkyries will cut you down without a thought." She shooed him off the desk, then yanked his phone away from his ear. "*Brujita*," she said to Georgette, "is the Wild Hunt tonight?"

"Yes," he heard her reply. "Sometime while the moon is up."

He saw calculations taking place behind his aunt's eyes. "We will close the shop early today. You must get home before moonrise. And," she added brusquely, "you will stay inside tonight." She thrust one red-nailed finger under his nose. "*All* night."

The silvery image of Delia in starlight armor disintegrated in his mind. *That's for the best*, his rational brain told his hormones. *Never forget: she's dead.*

"*Sí, Tía*," he said with a sigh.

Delia & Senji

"Sisters!" shouted Perchta. "To me!"

Dozens of Valkyries, Delia included, gathered around the captain. Each was dressed in battle regalia—black chainmail, golden armor, and red riding cloaks.

The animal partners of the Valkyries grouped together in Fólkvangr. This was an isolated location meant to be a place of rest for Valhalla's warriors in between battles. Given the current intensity of the war, it had not been in use for some time. The partners were under Perchta's orders to remain there, among the wildflowers and trees, until the end of the Hunt.

On the front steps of the Great Hall, Perchta held up a hand for silence. "The sun is down," she said. "The moon rises. The Hunt will soon begin!" She turned back to look at the Idisi in the main entrance. "We will have a toast before we leave," she said. "Bring us Heidrun's mead!"

The Idisi retreated into the hall to the appreciative whoops of the majority of the Valkyries present. Delia, however, did not make a sound. This was her first Wild Hunt, and she was not looking forward to it.

From the branch of an apple tree, Senji looked across the starlit meadow. He saw vague shapes in the darkness—horses resting in the tall grass, wolves curled up in the wildflowers, and ravens roosting in the trees. There were no crickets, no bird calls, no sound of nature at all. All he heard was Giovanni's obnoxious mumbling.

Perchta's strawberry-blonde hair shone in the faint light. The Idisi had braided it earlier, after dinner, as part of her preparation for the Hunt. Delia had been the only one to refuse food, so she was the first Valkyrie they'd prepped. Their long fingers had plaited her brown hair before decking her out in red, black, and gold. All the while, they'd pushed her to eat.

"Hunts are strenuous," they purred in her ear. "You will need the energy."

"I'm dead," Delia murmured. "I don't need food."

"*Sæhrímnir* is not mere food," they said. "It exists to nourish the dead."

"I haven't eaten in years," she'd insisted. "I'm fine."

"The recovery from the Hunt is already difficult; it will take you even longer to recover without food."

But she'd refused. Now, she was standing on the steps

to Valhalla, dressed for war, with her spectral stomach in knots.

Can't we just get this over with?

Senji wished he could have asked why the partners were being stationed in an isolated field when they could just as easily have stayed in Valhalla. But Perchta had not taken questions, only issued commands.

The Idisi sashayed among the sisters, carrying tankards of mead. Manically tapping her foot, Delia kept waving them off, getting snippier with each refusal.

Seconds away from lashing out, she suddenly felt a hand on her shoulder.

"Take the mead, Svanhild," whispered Gondol. "I think we could all use a stiff drink right now."

Take the damn drink, Delia.

I don't want it.

You need it.

Reluctantly, she took a tankard from the Idisi. The amber liquid inside reflected the light in delicate golden sparkles.

"Sisters!" bellowed Perchta. "The time has come!" She raised her tankard toward the assembled Valkyries. "*Skaal!*"

Dozens of cups were raised to the sky with eager shouts of "*Skaal!*" Delia brought hers to her lips and took a taste. Heidrun's mead was as crisp and sweet as the last time she had partaken. Pleased with its warmth, she took a deep drink.

He felt the warmth flow into her ethereal body. The effect was as he remembered.

The mead was meant to revive the chosen, but Valkyries often drank it. For them it had a pleasant, relaxing effect, not unlike being tipsy. For Delia, it stirred old memories of drinks with her fellow nurses after a shift.

Senji felt a rush go through Delia's body. Simultaneously, an electric sizzle spread through his wings and legs with such violence that his body shook as if in a seizure. His beak fell open in a soundless shriek while his body quaked.

Raw energy flowed through every inch of Delia's spirit. For a moment, she felt she was back in her human body—the body she had lost in a fiery explosion. She felt the wind tickling the tiny hairs on her arms, the weight of the chainmail on her shoulders, the pinch of her tight braids. Then she felt something she had forgotten existed: hunger.

The Valkyrie partners seized, their bodies twitching wildly: horses collapsed, wolves flailed their legs, and ravens, Senji included, fell out of the trees.

Delia downed the entire tankard and looked for the Idisi, madly craving another.

"Sisters!" bellowed Perchta. When Delia looked, she saw the captain's cheeks were flushed. "Stand ready!"

Donning her helmet, Perchta turned her face to the raging river that bordered Valhalla.

"Sea Mither!" she shouted. "Release the Nuckelavee!"

Rising from the grass, Senji saw Fernão, Gondol's partner, hunkered down in a motionless ball of fur, separate from the others.

The river Thund began to roar. Its waters darkened. Through the soles of her boots, Delia felt a rumbling so furious she thought the steps of Valhalla might shake into rubble. Suddenly, a dark stampede erupted from the water.

Senji shook out his wings. Were partner seizures part of the Wild Hunt? Once again, he felt irritated that he had not been properly briefed. *Delia, what happened?*

From the spray came a herd of horses. Galloping through the air, they raced toward the Valkyries, each with its single enormous eye blazing red.

Delia? He grew concerned. She must have felt him seize. Why wasn't she checking on him? *Can you hear me?*

The horses had no skin; every beast was bare muscle, pale sinew, and pulsating yellow veins. Though disgusted, Delia felt a wave of excitement.

Delia! Delia, answer me!

Perchta grabbed the black mane of a Nuckelavee and swung herself onto it. Without thinking, Delia seized another beast and leapt onto its back. Immediately, the creature's yellow veins sprouted tendrils that dove between the chainmail links of Delia's armor and into her legs. She tried to move but found that she was glued to the Nuckelavee's sides.

Delia! Delia, can you hear . . .

Delia saw black blood gushing through the Nuckelavee's vitreous veins and into her legs. Instant intoxication seized her. The heart she didn't have raced, and the skin she didn't have twitched. All around her, her sisters began to laugh, whoop, and bellow.

Delia's voice fell silent in his mind, and her emotions became only the thinnest of sensations. With his heart in his throat, Senji fought to reconnect without success.

He felt a powerful urge to fly to her but was still disoriented from the seizure. *Besides, I have no idea how to get to her.* It was his first time in Fólkvangr, and he didn't know which direction led to Valhalla. *That's why they left us here*, he realized. *We cannot leave until summoned. We are prisoners in our own ignorance.*

Absorbed in his thoughts, he did not immediately notice that Thrima's partner, a small wolf, had taken a seat beside Senji in the tall grass.

"This is your first Hunt?" the wolf asked, his voice woven through with authority such as Senji was unaccustomed to hearing from Valkyrie partners.

Senji nodded.

"Do not fear. Her voice will return. In the meantime, hold the thread of her in your mind."

Closing his eyes, the wolf lifted his muzzle into the air. "I feel the *ixiptla* as a faint but steady melody floating through my head." He opened his eyes. "The song will grow stronger as she returns to Valhalla." He paused. "As she returns to herself."

Raising her sword, Perchta let loose a fierce scream. She yanked her mount's mane, and the Nuckelavee reared up. Green vapor billowed from its nostrils and gaping mouth as it kicked off the ground and soared skyward.

"To the Hunt!" Perchta roared.

It took Senji a moment to recall the wolf's name—Yolotli—and his Valkyrie's story. Thrima had been an "*ixiptla*," a ritual proxy for the goddess in whose place she had been sacrificed. By a priest. By Yolotli. Long ago, he'd sawed off her head, flayed her body, and then worn her skin for ceremonies.

Despite their violent history, the pair seemed to regard each other with respect.

Delia urged her horse upward, and it obeyed. With an elation she had never felt before, she rode the beast into the air.

"What we experienced just now," asked Senji, "is it normal for a Hunt?"

"There is no 'normal,'" Yolotli said. "Every Hunt is an ordeal all its own. I have never known the drink to have such a strong effect, but the separation feels the same."

Her body thrummed with exhilaration. For the first time since before her death, she felt every nerve ending within her crackle in ecstasy.

"I worry," Senji told him. "I cannot help her if I'm not in her head."

As they rode together, she and the others became as one—one mind, one will, one force of nature.

"You will help," said Yolotli, "by grounding her in reality once the Hunt ends. Until then, we must be patient and wait."

She was madness.

Completely out of contact with Delia, he could do nothing but cling to the last strand of her in the very back of his mind.

She was frenzy.

As Yolotli advised, he
held it fast, tried to pour his
strength into her,
and waited.

Lâche pas la patate, *Delia*.

She was the Hunt.

Neil

LOUNGING ON HIS SOFA, NEIL LISTENED TO THE RAIN outside the window with a cup of hot coffee in hand. As per Georgette's firm instructions, he had taken care to be home in his apartment by sunset, with the doors locked and blinds lowered over the windows. The precautions seemed odd, but he had given his word. Ultimately, this was her world, and she knew a hell of a lot more about how to navigate it than he did.

He wished she could be with him, but Kazimiera had insisted on reopening Nocturne for Friday night. After kissing Georgette goodbye, he had tried one last time to convince her to let him spend the evening in the club with her. "Even if Kazimiera won't let me into the employee areas, I can just sit at the bar," he'd wheedled.

But Georgette had shaken her head. "I'll be too busy to hang out with you," she'd said, pressing her face into his chest. "I'd rather you stay at home. And," she added, "I'd like you to keep an eye on Nico. He's way too interested in the Hunt. I'm worried he'll try to sneak a look."

The request had taken him by surprise. He didn't know if her concerns were warranted, but he'd of course agreed. So now he sat on the couch, working on assignments for online classes while occasionally glancing at Nico's closed bedroom door.

Nico's been in his room since dinner, he texted Georgette.

Then he's definitely not chasing Valkyries! she wrote back. *Awesome! So busy over here. Wish I was with you instead.*

Grinning, Neil relaxed into the cushions, warmth spreading through his chest. With a fresh flush of energy, he returned to his work.

Then his phone began to shriek.

Georgette

GEORGETTE SILENCED HER WAILING PHONE. HER EYES darted over the words "severe storm" and "flooding" as she rushed the phone back into the armband sleeve she wore at work. The weather was an outside problem. Right now, she had inside business to deal with.

VIP entertainment was proceeding as usual; Georgette could hear the wealthy customers oohing, aahing, and laughing drunkenly through the walls. Leaving those rooms undisturbed, she ducked into the employee lounge, where she found Nocturne's Fae going about their business like it was any other Friday night . . . until they spotted her. In a sudden rush, they gathered around her and peppered her with questions about the Hunt.

Plastering a smile across her face, Georgette assured them that everything was under control and there was nothing to worry about. While they sighed with relief and thanked her, she struggled to believe her own words.

Nocturne's first-floor nightclub rocked with energy. On the stage, the Siren Lydia sang her beckoning melody to the rhythm of Veer the Gandharva's celestial guitar, both performers completely cloaked in glamours to hide their birdlike features. Also on stage was Veer's wife, a shape-shifting Apsara named Mira who needed no glamour to blend in. She zealously danced in time to the song, her seductive power lacing its way through the room as she moved, drawing more and more people to the dance floor.

Scanning the lively club, Georgette confirmed for herself that all of her spells were working at peak efficiency—and, although a few of the staff threw her worried looks, no one seemed unduly troubled.

She made her way down to the basement and let herself into Audrey's locked storage room. The transformed Werewolf lay on the floor with her chin on her paws and her eyes on her laptop. The light from the computer screen cast a soft glow over her fur-covered features as upbeat music and lively dialogue filled the room.

"How's the movie?" asked Georgette.

The large wolf shook her head slightly before letting out a slow sigh. Georgette smiled sympathetically. Though Audrey's transformation had been easier this time, she still had to face a night of sitting trapped in a basement while the Wild Hunt searched for her.

"My spells are working and everything's going well," Georgette said. "The night will be over before you know it."

Audrey grunted and shifted her weight without moving her eyes from the laptop screen.

Before Georgette could think of something else to say, the power went out.

Kazimiera

KAZIMIERA KNEW THE CURE TO THIS AILMENT BUT ALSO knew she shouldn't partake—not again, not this soon. That's why she'd shut herself into her office in the first place. But the promise of relief was proving too great a temptation.

She had started the night trying to stick to her long-established feeding schedule. There were plenty of VIPs booked for that night, and they would all be caught up in the witch's memory-altering spells, making it safe for her to sip from their veins. But her thirst had grown beyond sips.

Plagued with hunger and sensitivity to sound, Kazimiera had found herself with no patience for her employees' questions that night. Earlier in the evening, she'd snapped at each of them to go away and kept herself moving from room to room, trying to outpace her thirst with busywork. Eventually, with the slightest sound in her building assaulting her throbbing ear drums, she'd fled to her office.

Now, after an hour of battling with herself, she surrendered.

She hurried to the ground floor. Through crowds of patrons and into the back rooms, she made a beeline to the loading area and slipped out the back door into the parking lot. Her predator's eyes pierced the heavy rainfall and scanned the poorly lit area. She saw nothing. Cursing quietly, she took off her shoes and walked barefoot into the storm. The downpour engulfed her, soaking through her dress and weighing down her mane of tight coils, but her eyes remained wide, devouring everything in sight.

No homeless. They would come by later in the evening, when the kitchens threw out the leftovers. No dealers. They would be inside the club, looking for customers. No drunks. It would be hours until her staff cut anyone off and put them into cabs.

Head pounding, wet dress clinging to her skin, Kazimiera gritted her teeth and screamed with frustration into her tightly closed lips.

The sound of a car door broke through the downpour. Heavy footfalls splashed through puddles from one end of the lot to the other. Following the sound, Kazimiera saw a man jogging through the rain, adjusting his clothes as he went. She felt a momentary urge to pounce on him, but her predatory brain redirected that urge to the car he had just exited.

There in the back seat, barely visible through the rain and darkness, sat a woman—smoothing down her hair with one hand and holding on to some crumpled bills with the other.

Kazimiera's fangs tingled. She hadn't seen a prostitute this close to her building in years.

Running on her naked toes, the Vampire rushed to the woman's car. Without wasting a second, she yanked open the car door, grabbed the half-dressed girl by the hair, and yanked her onto the pavement. Caught completely off guard, the girl barely had time to yelp and flail her arms before Kazimiera struck her on the right temple and relieved her of consciousness.

Grinning, Kazimiera flung the limp woman over her shoulder and ran toward the building. The storm swallowed the kitten-soft pitter-patter of her bare feet through the puddles, erasing all evidence of her presence.

After dodging all would-be witnesses and sprinting up the back stairs, Kazimiera locked herself in her office and tore into her meal. The woman—early thirties, too thin, tasting of alcohol—never regained consciousness and uttered only soft groans before she expired. When the heart stopped beating, Kazimiera ripped open the corpse to drain the individual organs. She was sucking fluids from the liver when she finally noticed that the lights were out.

"The hell?" she muttered. She walked to the window and looked outside. Everything was black. The whole block had lost power.

Through the stormy darkness, she listened to the scream of a crazed wind blasting through the sky. Rain battered the city to the irregular drumbeat of thunder. The humid air was oppressive, even inside the building; atmospheric pressure wrapped around her head like a shroud. Despite the fresh blood in her stomach, she still felt pounding in her ears. Golden lightning forked through the rain and rattled the windowpane. If she had been alive, it would have frightened the breath from her lungs.

Underneath the storm's rage, Kazimiera could have sworn she heard a stampede of horses.

Mei-Xing

THE STAMPEDING SOUND OF THE LIGHTNING CRACKLED through Mei-Xing's body. *The Wild Hunt*, she thought with a shiver.

Curling up on the sofa, she felt a primal urge to sink deep into the earth, to huddle around her roots until the storm blew over. It would only take a moment to dissolve her body into her plants . . . but she fought off the urge. She shouldn't indulge such a sapling emotion. Still, outside on the apartment balcony, she sensed the rest of her potted garden struggling to weather the storm.

Her new party dress, the one Georgette had helped her pick out, was hanging on the nearby bathroom door. Mei-Xing stared at it as lightning flashed through the window and momentarily lit up the apartment. She sighed. It was not something she would have chosen for herself. When she wore the flapper-style dress, its sequins—shiny spangles of blue and green—reflected the light in uneven glints as she moved. Every step she took lit her up like a disco ball—which was the point, she knew. The reflective sequins on the dress and its matching iridescent wrap would make any irregularities in a photograph look like a trick of the light. No camera would catch a glimpse of her real body underneath her human glamour.

Lightly picking at the buds on her chest, Mei-Xing tried to think positively about the coming party. It was a gathering, not unlike how Nymphs gathered together in spring. Of course, Nymphs gathered not just to celebrate but to increase the likelihood of finding a suitable partner for pollination. That made Mei-Xing think of her husband . . . and the child they almost had.

Thunder rumbled outside, and she curled her body into a tight, mossy ball. A crawly prickle worked its way through her limbs, alerting her to an abrupt shift in weather conditions. Through the ether, she sensed the voice of a River Spirit breaking through the downpour. Growing louder by the second, it roared with the fury of a charging army.

Alarmed, Mei-Xing sprang up from the sofa, ran to the sliding glass door, and threw it open. She leapt out into the rain and leaned over the balcony railing.

The street below had become a canal for a rioting flood.

Nicolás

THE ROAR OF THE FLOOD COULD NOT DISTRACT NICO'S attention from the sky. Leaning out of his bedroom window into the monsoon, he strained against the wind and rain to see something, anything, in those swirling black clouds. He had promised Mariana that he would stay inside all night, and he intended to honor that promise, but he couldn't pass up the chance to see the ride of the Valkyries.

Soaked from head to waist, his ears full of shrieking wind, he tried to guard his eyes against the rain with a hand to his forehead. He glanced down at the street below and saw that the flash flood had coated the street, rising high enough to hide the tires of parked cars. For a moment, he worried about what all that water might do to the Botanica—but he pushed the thought aside. There was nothing he could do about the shop now, and even if it did sustain some damage, it would be there in the morning. The Wild Hunt would not.

Lightning electrified the dark sky, dancing through the rain, the only light in the powerless city. Nico squinted against the pelting rain and tried to shift his vision to see through layers of reality. Through the curtain of rain, he began to see a flurry of colors and motion. He strained his eyes, willing himself to look past the thunderheads—and, gradually, he began to see it clearly: horses, or something like horses, galloping through the air on long, spiderish legs, their hooves striking the clouds in hails of golden sparks as a sickly green mist billowed from their gaping mouths. Impossibly, they seemed to be running in place while also zigzagging in every direction at once. Astride the beasts, he saw shining helmets, flapping red cloaks, and golden swords that glowed and flashed when held aloft. Valkyries.

The black clouds seemed to project the riders' spectral shrieks, surrounding the city like speakers around a theater, blasting madness. What Nico heard coming out of the darkness touched a primal spot of his psyche. They were the feral cries of creatures sequestered in the night, the wails of unknown beasts circling a caveman's campfire just beyond the reach of the light. It sent a sizzle through his body, a sensation both terrible and electrifying. He felt he was in the presence of something spectacularly dangerous yet untameably majestic.

In defiance of all rationality, he found himself trying to pick Delia out of the howling company.

Delia

CRACKLE OF LIGHTNING. EXPLOSION OF THUNDER. YOWL of the wind. Weight of a sword in her hand. Screams and laughter all around her. A command flowing through her veins and echoing in her mind: *Search and destroy.*

She was drunk. There was no other way to describe the sensation. She was deliriously drunk on mead, on the ride, on power, on life! She could feel the rain on her skin and the wind on her face. The smell of mud from the river below filled her nostrils. The tiny hairs on her arms sizzled with the electrical charge in the air. Since the day of her death, she had felt only a diluted approximation of life. While in Valhalla, she could touch, taste, and smell, but never as clearly as she had with her dead-and-dust human body. Riding with the Hunt, she was as close to alive as a Valkyrie could ever be.

Encased in rain and madness, the Wild Hunt rode through the city as its asphalt veins overflowed with the river. The Valkyries rode through every inch of San Jose's airspace, stampeding over rooftops, slicing swords through power-lines, and pouring their wrath over the gutters. The insanity was magnificent.

Search and destroy.

Leys of magic, natural tracks of Fae existence, wove through the area. She sensed them all flowing through her, could read them like braille, knew what they each meant. Only one was of interest to her: Werewolf.

From every corner of the city at once, she hunted the beast. Its trail was a pockmarked series of wisps and tufts that continued for several blocks only to suddenly vanish, then restart again miles away. And the freshest of the sickly tracks seemed to be over a month old.

Perchta, eyes aflame, screeched for the company's attention, summoning them to her. Gathered together in the largest of the thunderheads, the Valkyries surrounded their captain.

"The beast is not here," she bellowed. With her sword held aloft, she reined her mount north. "We will broaden the search. Come! We ride!"

Engulfed in rumbling black clouds, the herd of Nuckelavees turned their one-eyed faces north. The Valkyries screamed a crazed battle cry and galloped on, blood-red cloaks billowing in the wind.

Georgette

THE REPORT GEORGETTE RECEIVED FROM CRISPIN, Nocturne's Incubus bartender, when she made her way to the club was calm and concise. After Club Nocturne was plunged into darkness and the music died, the club had soon echoed with drunken hollers and confused shouts. As minutes passed and the lights did not return, the rumble of noise had gotten louder and the voices had grown more frantic. Some patrons had managed to open the front doors, only to let in a gush of river water from the flooded streets. Fortunately, the servers and bartenders had quickly taken control of the situation—getting the doors safely closed again and placing battery-powered lanterns around the room—and Veer and Lydia had taken the initiative to climb up on the bar and sing a capella for the room. In this unplugged, campfire atmosphere, the club patrons—with the help of free drinks—had soon settled down. Everyone, Crispin reported, was enjoying the unconventional entertainment.

Georgette checked on the club doors. A little water was leaking through the cracks, but it was minimal. She performed some discreet spellcraft to repel the floodwater until the river retreated. That finished, she gestured at the calm room and smiled at the Incubus. "You guys are doing awesome, Crispin."

He beamed. "We've got this," he assured her.

Hurrying up the stairs, using her smartphone as a flashlight, Georgette grew concerned that she hadn't seen or heard from Kazimiera. She must know that the power was out. It wasn't like Kazi not to seize control of a situation that affected her business.

The second-floor restaurant seemed almost untouched by the disaster. Waiters had placed candles and lanterns around the dining area, brought complimentary wine to the tables, and continued to take orders as if nothing had happened. In the kitchen, Georgette found the staff hard at work as usual, except that they had placed Ignatius, the Elemental Salamander, on the dead stovetop to cook via his flaming skin. The large reptilian fire spirit looked thoroughly unamused to have skillets and saucepots on his back but, thankfully, was tolerating it. Meals were getting out of the kitchen more or less on time.

"Dinner service can continue," said Miguel, a short, hairy Pombero. "We've got light, we've got heat, it's fine. But without power, the food in the fridges will spoil."

"I'll ask Yuki to come down here to help." *A Snow Woman shouldn't have trouble keeping the fridges cold.*

"Won't Kazi want her for third-floor work?" asked Alana, the red-headed Banshee. "She's a favorite of the VIPs."

"Kazi will understand."

But where the hell is she?

A horrible smell of blood, bile, and shit immediately found Georgette's nose, making her stomach lurch, when she opened Kazimiera's office door. She cast the glow of her smartphone into the room, and there, eyes reflecting eerie green in the light, was Kazimiera—soaked to the bone, no shoes . . . and hunched over a pile of something wet and red on the floor.

"Oh my God," Georgette murmured in breathless shock. "Kazi," she asked through the hand clamped over her mouth and nose, "what is this?"

The Vampire raised her bloody face from the body, ragged chunks of flesh dangling from her gaping, fang-filled jaws, and stared at Georgette with glazed black eyes. "It's dinner," she said in a flat tone.

"Dinner?" It hit her then: the mess on the office floor was a human body. Georgette recoiled in horror, eyes widening. "Oh God," she squeaked. Her mind reeling, she quickly closed the door to hide the horrific sight from any customer who might come down the hallway. Cut off from the fresh air, the stink gave her stomach a fresh jolt. "Is that a *person?*"

Kazimiera huffed a strange, slurred laugh, spewing bloody droplets through the air. "Parking lot whore," she said.

"Oh, Kazi," Georgette murmured in a daze, "what were you thinking? This"—she gestured shakily at the mess—"puts your business in danger."

"Danger?" Kazimiera sneered. Pointing a bloody finger at her ear, she said, "I can hear everything in this building. I can *hear* the business running smoothly!" Still glaring at Georgette, she plunged both hands into the body cavity and yanked something out.

Is that an organ?

"The whole damn thing runs on autopilot," Kazimiera grumbled before biting down on the—lung? liver?—in her hands.

"Okay," Georgette whispered, feeling her stomach contents rising up to her throat again. She gulped them back. "Is that a problem?"

Kazimiera shot Georgette a vicious side-eye glare as she spat out a shriveled organ. "A problem?" she growled. "Yes, dammit! It defeats the purpose!"

"The purpose of what?" Georgette tried to find the meaning of Kazimiera's words, but in the face of this carnage, she couldn't focus. "I don't understand."

"This business exists to keep me busy!" Kazimiera shouted. "But now I can't fill my senses with my work like I used to!" She snapped off the last rib and broke it in half, but instead of consuming the marrow, she suddenly threw it to the floor. "Vampires *need* to fill their senses!" She swiped the back of her hand across her bloody mouth, and her lips rippled into a toothy snarl. "The other witches that've worked for me did what I hired them for and left well enough alone. But not you, you damned bleeding heart." The Vampire's eyes—cold black onyx—fixed onto Georgette, making the witch shiver. "You tackle their personal problems, you change the routines." She began to dig around in the corpse again, stirring up wet squishes with each movement. "Suddenly, my staff don't need me."

"Your . . . senses?"

With a shout, Kazimiera leapt up and shoved her face into Georgette's. Nose to nose with an unhinged predator, Georgette could do nothing but tremble.

"Do you have the slightest idea," Kazimiera hissed, her meaty breath blowing into Georgette's face, "how strong my senses are compared to yours? I see colors you have no words for, I hear sounds you could never identify, and I feel the vibration of the tectonic plates under your feet. No Vampire retains logic without something productive to occupy their senses. Unless I keep myself occupied, my senses will wander and fill my body with information I don't need or want. Trying to cope with that sensory input while having so little to do all night causes me pain, real pain, and the only way to stop it is to feed—even that relief is only temporary." Easing back, the Vampire groaned and pressed her hands to her head. "All this sound! The storm, the flood! It's inside my head!"

Georgette's fear and confusion shrank a bit, making room for concern. She reached out to touch Kazimiera's shoulder, but when her eye caught on the meat pile, she pulled back. "I didn't know."

"Do you really think witches know everything about magic and Fae?"

Like a punch to the gut, Kazimiera's words found their mark. Georgette had been raised to believe exactly that. She felt her cheeks go red, and she lowered her eyes. "I'm sorry."

Gripping her corkscrew coils in her fists, Kazimiera sobbed, "The sound! My head!"

Reflexively, Georgette lifted her hand to cast a quick spell. Though she had never crafted a spell of silence before, she had seen her mother cast them frequently, using them to block out the sounds of her children when she was tired of them. A sprinkle of glittering particles floated out from her fingers and encircled Kazimiera. They formed a faint, shimmery spiral, which then flattened and spread out into a paper-thin energy bubble that fully encased the Vampire's head like a deep-sea helmet.

As Georgette completed the spell, Kazimiera raised her face, her black eyes huge.

Georgette offered a questioning smile. "Does that help?"

The Vampire straightened her back and bared her teeth. "I don't want your help!"

Mortified, Georgette immediately started to babble apologies, but Kazimiera cut her off with a curt gesture.

"I may be stuck with you because I need your magic for the business, but this is my body! Your authority in this building stops at my skin!" She pointed at her head. "Undo this nonsense!"

"Yes, ma'am," Georgette said, waving her hands to disperse the magic. As soon as the spell dissolved, pain returned to Kazi's face. Fighting back tears, Georgette murmured, "I just thought—"

"Don't think," the Vampire snapped. She crouched down by her kill and unhinged her jaw again. "Get out."

Georgette bolted out of Kazimiera's office and ran to the stairwell, her eyes so clouded with tears that the glow of her smartphone did little to light her way. She climbed the steps amidst her echoing sobs, which rebounded up and down the stairwell walls as if the cinder blocks themselves were in tears. Her conversation with the Vampire replayed on a loop, driving her deeper into confusion and misery until she held no conviction at all except that she was a garbage human being.

She soon found herself at the seventh-floor entrance. Her instinct was to go to the roof, where there would be no one to see her crying, but then she remembered the Wild Hunt. The roof was out of the question, then—but she couldn't stay here, either. She couldn't stand the sound of her own voice bouncing back at her in the confined stairwell.

Tired and demoralized, she stepped out onto the seventh floor and went to Ishak's apartment.

Curled up on Ishak's sofa, Georgette released a full-blown ugly cry while her friend held her against his chest. Rain and wind battered the nearby window, and claps of thunder made the building's walls tremble, but shrouded as she was in her misery, Georgette felt miles removed from the storm. She had tried to convey to Ishak what had happened with Kazimiera, but her voice was so mangled by sobs that she wasn't sure he had understood. Nevertheless, he consoled her with soft words and a warm embrace.

When her sobs began to abate, Ishak patted her head and then gently took her by the shoulders and lifted her head from his chest. Even in the darkness, Georgette could see the kindness in his eyes.

"Do you remember," he asked, "what you told me about community?"

She had to think for a moment but then the memory came to her, and she nodded. Ishak smiled.

"You convinced me to open my door to the Fae of this building," he said. "Before that, I was exhausted and ill-kempt but"—he paused thoughtfully—"comfortable in my isolation. You changed my mind. I joined this building's community, and since then my life and Ziya's life have grown richer."

"I don't understand what you're trying to tell me," she said.

"I am trying to tell you," he said with a soft chuckle, "that being part of a community cannot be forced. It must be a choice. The Fae who live here have formed a community, but that was their choice, not the Vampire's design. They consider her their benefactor and respect her—however misplaced that respect may be—but she does not see them as anything other than items in her ledger. She gives them room and board, but she does not learn their names and remembers them only for what work they can provide." He gave Georgette's shoulder a firm squeeze as he leaned closer. "She chooses not to be part of the community."

"Right," Georgette said, still waiting for his words to make sense. "And?"

He smiled like a teacher whose student was not quite grasping the lesson. "The Vampire told you herself—she uses this business to satisfy her dietary and sensory needs. Now that the business and, by extension, the Fae are no longer fulfilling that function, she has—in her mind, at least—discarded them. It would never occur to her that the Fae she sees as commodities might be capable of helping her. Similarly, she will never accept help from you because she has already labeled you as 'part of the problem.' The Vampire has drawn a clear distinction between herself and all others in the building. In that way, she is the opposite of you."

Georgette blinked in surprise. "What do you mean?"

He chuckled. "When you began work here, you immediately set about preserving not just the function of this business, as the Vampire wished, but also the well-being of the individuals who comprise it. That's why the Fae in this building like you. You are part of their community."

Part of their community. The words warmed her heart. She loved helping the Nocturne Fae and loved that they came to her with their problems. It made her feel useful—made her feel like she was doing something to improve the world, even if only a little bit at a time.

"But what should I do about Kazi?" she asked. "She's killing people."

"And like it or not," he said firmly, "it is not within your power to prevent that."

Georgette's eyes widened. "Bu-but," she fumbled, "I have . . . I could . . ."

"You could what?" he asked gently. "Use spells to ease her pain? You tried that and she refused. Report her to the authorities and expose the secrets of this place? That would risk the life of every Fae here. Use your magic to imprison her? How will you feed her? If imprisonment fails, are you prepared to kill her to prevent further violence?" He sighed. "This is beyond your power to fix."

He was right. With each point he made, Georgette felt the reality sink in a little more deeply. Any course of action she took would fail to get positive results and could very easily put others in danger. It didn't feel right to do nothing—but realistically, doing nothing was the only option. Knowing that didn't make her feel any better about it, though.

"She says it's my fault," she said. "She says the business was enough to keep her stable until I disrupted her routine."

"This morally vague business of hers could use some disruption," Ishak replied with a snort. He squeezed her shoulder and smiled. "Despite what she may think, you are not here for *her*. You are here for the Fae."

Thoughts of Kazi's anger faded into the past as Georgette's brain summoned other memories. She remembered making a repellent charm for Crispin when he, tired of potential partners never seeing past his innate magic attraction, asked for a means to balance the effect. She remembered the series of spells she cast for Kairos, the Sphinx, to remove the female attributes of his body and give him the beard and mane he had always longed for. She remembered Tama the Ponaturi who asked for a supernaturally powerful sunblock, Guerric the Karnabo who needed a magic nebulizer to scrub his breath of paralyzing effects, Majida the Aicha Kandicha whose soft camel feet required spellcrafted shoes. She liked to be helpful, liked putting her magic to use for the benefit of others, and to hear that she was making a difference filled her distraught heart with joy.

Pressing her head onto Ishak's shoulder, she gave him a quick hug. "Thanks."

He returned her hug. "Of course, my friend."

By midnight, the rain had stopped and the flood was beginning to retreat. Once again, Georgette went floor by floor to check on the guests and residents.

Sequestered in her basement room, Audrey had fallen asleep. Curled into a furry ball, her large Werewolf body cast peculiar shadows on the walls from the faint glow of her computer. Seeing that the battery had dipped low, Georgette closed the laptop and then left Audrey in peace.

Handfuls of club patrons had braved the flooded streets since Georgette's last rounds, but most still remained, enjoying the free drinks and friendly atmosphere. Lydia invited several of them onto the stage to sing with her while Veer accompanied them on an acoustic guitar.

Satisfied that the guests were still enjoying themselves, Georgette left the club and headed upstairs.

No new restaurant patrons had been allowed into the building once the storm began, but those inside had been offered free desserts and after-dinner drinks while they waited for the weather to improve. Ailill, the Pooka chef, had even bribed the reclusive, elf-like Fossegrim with a bowl of goat curry to entertain the diners with his fiddle. Leif's songs, all magically interlaced with the sounds of wind, water, and forest life, so thoroughly enchanted the guests that most of their drinks went untouched.

The third-floor rooms stirred no worry in Georgette. The average VIP patron typically stayed in the building until the wee hours of the morning, so most of them seemed only vaguely aware that anything was amiss. The staff assured Georgette that all was well and she need not concern herself with them for now.

Despite Kazimiera's closed office door, Georgette felt content.

Until her phone dinged, alerting her to an email. From her mother. Containing e-tickets for an airplane to Boston in July.

Delia & Senji

The Nuckelavees trudged across the dispersing clouds, their heads slung low, their cyclops eyes half closed. Sweat billowed off their skinless bodies as yellow mist, mingling with their foul green breath, as they made landfall in Valhalla.

The thread of Delia grew thicker in his mind. After hours of waiting, of staring at the horizon, he could finally sense her clearly.

The Nuckelavee's veins shimmied out of Delia's legs and withdrew into its body. Black blood oozed out of Delia's spirit body where the veins had been and dripped to the ground, sizzling where it struck. As it left her, she quickly lost the drunken delirium that had driven her throughout the Hunt. In its place, she suddenly felt achy, woozy, and more tired than she ever had been in all her life—or afterlife.

. . . lia! Delia, can you hear me?

Senji?

Delia! The relief of hearing her voice made his body light. *Where are you?*

Valhalla.

Are you alright?

Am I? She slid off the horse's back. Gravity yanked her hard and she landed on her knees, her armor clanking and rattling as she threw out her arms to steady herself. *I think so. I feel . . . hungover.*

The sensations of Delia's body returned to him, filling him with queasy exhaustion. *What happened?*

I'm tired. The Nuckelavee shied away from her and headed toward the river that had spawned it. She watched it go, watched it dissolve into the water with the rest of its herd. *So tired.*

Are you safe?

She looked around. The grounds were littered with glassy-eyed Valkyries, most of them seated or prone. A few of them, to her amazement, even appeared to be asleep.

The sight startled him. While he, as a living raven, had to sleep, Valkyries, who were bodiless spirits, did not. *Delia, did the Hunt find the Werewolf?*

No. She slumped over onto her side. *The trails were old and led nowhere.*

None of the sisters saw through Georgette's spells on the club?

It took her a long moment to remember what Senji was talking about. *During the Hunt, I don't think I even noticed the club.*

Good. He sighed. *Georgette will be relieved.*

From his tree, he scanned the meadow. Every animal he saw became visibly tired as they reconnected to their partners and took on their emotions.

When will the sisters collect us?

When he got no reply, he raised his internal volume. *Delia!*

Hmm? Pulling off her helmet and cloak, she rolled onto her back and stared up at the dark sky. *I dunno.* Though her armor was uncomfortable, she was too tired to care. Slowly, her eyes slid shut.

The sensation of Delia losing consciousness was entirely new to him. It was akin to having a limb fall asleep—numb and unpleasant. Sputters of her voice continued to migrate through his brain, but nothing made sense. *The mutterings of a dreamer.*

"Yolotli," Senji called to the wolf below. "Is your partner asleep?"

"Yes." He sounded astonished. "The *ixiptla* has never slept before."

"Not even after prior Hunts?"

"No. Neither has any Valkyrie, to the best of my knowledge. After a Hunt, they often feel weak, ill-tempered, or have difficulty reconnecting, but they do not sleep."

Senji saw many beasts yawning or nodding off. He felt the appeal: after hours of stressful waiting, feeling their partners now thoroughly relaxed was the ultimate sleep aid. But the situation felt . . . twisted.

A hand shook her awake. When she opened her eyes, she saw Gondol smiling down at her. Beside her stood two Idisi, one of them holding out a goblet, the other offering a plate of roasted meat.

"On your feet, Sister." Gondol chuckled. "No rest for the weary."

"Drink," the Idisi purred. "Eat."

"Ugh," Delia grunted. "No."

"Come now, Svanhild," Gondol urged with a grin. "Look how improved I am after partaking."

Through Delia's eyes, he saw Gondol. She showed none of the exhaustion the others did.

How did she recover so quickly?

It doesn't matter. She took Gondol's hand and allowed herself to be pulled to a sitting position. *Everything's ass over elbows tonight.*

But why is Gondol waking the sisters instead of Perchta, the leader of the Hunt?

"I'll take the drink," said Delia, "but I don't want the food."

"Stubborn as ever." Gondol laughed. "Enjoy the mead!"

She downed the golden mead, tiny trickles of it leaking over the edges of her lips and down her chin. Like a cup of strong coffee, it energized her and removed the sleep from her eyes. As it took effect, her memories of the Wild Hunt faded until they became the stardust of dreams.

He felt the drink wash away the lingering sluggishness in their connection. Finally, their minds fully relinked.

Delia gave the empty cup to an Idis and reached for a full one.

Her body was . . . too real. He could feel aches in her muscles, muscles that did not exist. He could feel the mead warming a belly that should be entirely spectral. It was wrong.

"Yolotli?"

"I feel it," said the wolf. He twitched his head in a

A pair of Idisi helped her to her feet and began removing her battle gear. Soon, she stood dressed only in a white gossamer sheath. Over their heads, at the base of Valhalla's steps, she saw Perchta also being relieved of her gear.

"Sisters!" shouted Perchta. "We must report to the council! Come! Leave your armor and bring your mead!"

jerky fashion, as if trying to shake a gnat from his ear. "This is not how I remember prior Hunts."

Despite having just chugged a goblet of mead, Perchta looked as woozy as the others. Through his own eyes, Senji sought out her partner in the meadow. Pure white and bulky, he was easy to spot among the gray wolves. Senji could see how his long legs quivered from Perchta's condition. In fact, he noticed, *all* of the partners were shaky. Except one.

Laughing, the Valkyries headed toward Valhalla's towering doors. Smiling, Delia joined her sister warriors in the woozy procession up the stairs.

Gondol's partner trotted along the far end of the field, showing not even a hint of the drowsiness or aches of the others. The scrawny wolf moved confidently but casually, as if he felt no effects from the Wild Hunt. The inconsistency set off alarms in Senji's mind.

Where is Gondol now?

Huh? she replied vaguely. *Dunno.*

Something's amiss, Delia, he pressed. *Gondol and her partner are acting strangely. I think we should—*

Oh Jesus, Senji, not now. Everything tonight has been strange. I'm tired and I have to report in. Just give me a little time.

Delia, would you listen to—

NOT NOW!

With a croak of frustration, he ruffled his feathers. But the frustration passed quickly, replaced by worry. It was unlike Delia to brush him off.

On her way up the steps, an Idis handed her another cup of mead. She accepted it and brought it to her lips.

His instincts screamed at him to find a way to reach her, to convince her that this matter was serious. But the realization sank deep into his stomach that should she refuse, he was powerless. Delia was his link to Valhalla. Without her, he was just a bird.

The sweet taste soothed her aching body like a head-to-toe massage. Beside her, Thrima grabbed skewers of meat from a platter and gnawed at them. They grinned at each other with punch-drunk glee.

You must ask when the sisters will fetch us, he urged her.

Rolling her eyes, she called out to the Idisi for another mead and walked on.

He waited.

Nicolás

GOLDEN SUNLIGHT STREAMED THROUGH THE LIVING room window of Neil and Nico's apartment as the morning dawned bright and beautiful over the storm-ravaged city. With his laptop on his knees, Nico leaned back in the sofa and clicked through dozens of images of flood and storm damage from around San Jose. Lines of parked cars buried up to their bumpers in water, repair crews reattaching downed powerlines, and ordinary people squelching their way through ankle-deep mud in the middle of a city street. Multiple news outlets reported electrical problems and traffic detours all over town, while other sources shared accounts of the various crimes that had taken place during the uncommonly powerful storm. Most were limited to theft or destruction of property, but a handful had involved violence. During the storm and in the hours that followed, hospitals had experienced a noticeable uptick in stabbing and shooting victims. According to various experts, it was a fascinating example of weather-induced collective violence.

"Wild Hunt–induced," Nico mumbled to himself as he snapped his laptop closed and set it aside.

A door opened, and he glanced up to see Neil exiting his bedroom with two smartphones in his hand, dressed in gym shorts and a T-shirt with a stretched-out neck. He closed the door behind him very quietly, yawned, and ran his free hand through his brown hair before placing the two phones on the coffee table.

"Georgette's still asleep," he said softly. "She was up most of the night."

"Any problems from the Wild Hunt?"

"Not really." Neil stretched his back. "Seems like it swept through, made a mess of everything, and then just . . . left. As worried as Georgette was, I was expecting something more . . . apocalyptic."

Nico nodded but he knew Neil was dead wrong. The Wild Hunt had played out just like Georgette and Mariana had described it—like a hurricane of madness. And for a short, glorious time while he was hanging out the window in the rain, his *curandero* skills had allowed him to feel just the edge of that raw power. The memory made him shudder with excitement. It was such an intoxicating high that he knew if given the chance, he would have happily followed the Hunt.

Not healthy thinking, he thought. *What the hell's up with me?*

"But Nocturne's fine." Neil yawned, clueless about Nico's internal conflict. "The problem's her family. They're being a real pain in the ass about her refusing to go back to Boston for the Fourth of July party. She's been getting texts and calls since early this morning. Every time she blocks one relative, someone else comes out of the woodwork. She's finally asleep now, so I'm gonna keep her phone out here."

"Geez," said Nico. *Every time I get a look behind the Nichols O'Reilly curtain, I feel underqualified to be counseling her.* "How's she holding up?"

"Actually, not too bad." Neil flopped down on a chair and picked up his phone, leaving Georgette's on the table. "She's not letting them bully her. I'm proud of her."

Nico nodded, encouraged. Georgette had come a long way from the timid, easily influenced young woman she had been when the two of them first started their informal counseling sessions.

"Still"—Neil sighed—"it's wearing her down." He opened an app on his phone and began to casually scroll. "She keeps telling me, 'I just want them to stop.'"

"Based on what I know about her family," Nico said, "I think they're bombarding her with messages explicitly to wear her down so she just gives up."

"Yeah," Neil muttered. "That tracks."

The phone on the coffee table dinged. Neil shot it an accusatory glare but did not move from his seat until it dinged a second time. Only then, with a grumble, did Neil scoop up his girlfriend's phone and read the newly received messages.

"Ginger and Pepper?" Shaking his head, he put the phone back on the table. "I don't remember those names on the family tree."

"Georgette gave you a family tree?" Nico chuckled.

"I asked for one," Neil said with mild embarrassment in his eyes. "There are a lot of sisters and cousins, and they all have plant names. I was getting them mixed up." He pulled up a picture on his phone's screen and showed it to Nico. It showed a large and rather complex hand-drawn chart in Georgette's handwriting. "Georgette drew this, I snapped a pic, and I keep some notes for myself about which person is which." He scanned the image. "Looks like Ginger and Pepper are two of her mom's cousins."

Georgette's phone chimed again. Neil looked at the screen and read out loud for Nico's benefit: "*You're breaking your mother's heart.*" He scrolled down. "*I'm disappointed in you.*" It dinged again. "This one's from Heather," he said. "Another of Hazel's cousins." Casting a weary glance at Nico, he let out a weak laugh and shrugged. "They're all women. Even on the family tree she drew, the only men are the ones that married into the family."

"I noticed that too," Nico said. "I wonder what happens to the Nichols sons."

"There are no sons."

Both Nico and Neil whipped their heads around to see Georgette emerging from Neil's bedroom. Dressed in baggy sweatpants and a T-shirt, a green satin bonnet covering her curls, she yawned and shuffled her way to the couch, where she plopped down next to Nico and automatically swung her legs over Neil's knees.

"There are no sons," she repeated, "and there never will be."

Neil draped his hands across her shins. "Why's that?"

She puffed a breath through a tired frown and crossed her arms over her chest. "Three hundred years ago, two sisters in my family got into a power struggle. One of them came out on top, got the family headship, and married her sister's lover. The losing sister—disgraced, disowned, and pregnant—put a curse on the winner."

"Ooh," Nico hissed, his lips drawn back from his teeth.

Neil looked back and forth between them. "Is a curse that big of a deal?"

"A curse isn't casual magic," Georgette explained. "Curses are long-lasting, often permanent, so enacting one means paying a heavy price. In this case, she sealed the spell by . . . cutting her own throat." She grimaced in response to Neil's horrified expression. "That's the highest sacrifice a witch can offer. It makes the curse unbreakable."

Silent tension hung in the air. The moment Georgette had said the word "curse," Nico had had a pretty clear idea of what would be required to prevent any sons being born into the Nichols family—but the image of a pregnant woman cutting her own throat still gave him chills.

"That's extreme," Neil said, breaking the silence. "I mean, even if you hate your sister enough to kill yourself—which is nuts—there's nothing wrong with having daughters. Doesn't seem like much of a curse."

"It is, though." Georgette shrugged. "Knowing that my family couldn't produce sons meant that other magical families didn't want to intermarry with us. The family name and titles would die out without a son to take them, y'know? In the span of one generation, my ancestors lost their land, their money, and their social standing in witch society. By the time my grandmother came around, she could only support herself and her daughters by jumping from man to man. Even now, with our family fortune restored—thanks to my mother's schemes—most of witch society still sees us as inferior." She shook her head and rubbed her eyes underneath her glasses. "That woman chose the perfect curse, one that would rip away everything her greedy sister had torn her down to get."

Neil rubbed her leg and said, "It wouldn't be such a big deal today."

Georgette raised an eyebrow. "You sure? Aunt Laurel's long-term boyfriend—Poppy and Daphne's father—left when he found out she couldn't give him a son to take his name."

"My last name actually comes from my mom's side," said Neil. "The MacCana family has been gradually dwindling for the last hundred years, to the point that my mom and aunt were going to be the last ones. When my grandparents mentioned how bittersweet it would be to see their daughter change her name after the wedding, my dad asked to take their name instead."

Nico, who had heard this story before, watched Georgette's reaction carefully. Before his eyes, the generational trauma in her expression slowly gave ground to doubt and then to curiosity. "I didn't know that was a thing people did," she said quietly.

"Sure," Neil replied. "Dad always said it was one of the smartest moves he ever made. He said no one remembered the name 'Tim Smith' but the name 'Tim MacCana' made him stand out, personally and professionally. He even kept the name after they divorced."

Where Georgette's face just moments ago had been coated in the pain of her ancestors, she now stared at her boyfriend with stunned amazement. Nico could well imagine that it was the same expression he himself had worn the first time he was able to see Fae creatures with his naked eyes—a sheer, child-like wonder at being confronted with something fantastical.

"Was your dad's family angry?" she asked.

"Nah," Neil said with a grin. "There're plenty of Smiths out there. Besides, Mom always said Dad's parents were so happy that their introverted son brought home a girl that nothing else mattered to them."

A sweet giggle burst from Georgette's throat. Smiling from ear to ear, she launched herself forward and slid into Neil's lap. He responded by embracing her around the waist and resting his cheek against her neck.

From somewhere in the folds of the chair upholstery, her phone dinged again. Georgette let out an irritated groan as Neil fished it out to check who was texting.

"Maybe turn off the phone for a while?" suggested Nico. "Just long enough to sleep."

For a second he saw a gleam of hope in Neil's eyes—but it was quickly extinguished when Georgette shook her head.

"I would," she said, "but I'm afraid Nocturne will call. I'm waiting to hear from Delia and Senji. If they go looking for me at the club when I'm not there, I need to be reachable."

Hearing Delia's name, Nico's heart leapt. "No word about what the Wild Hunt found?"

"Not yet." Georgette's brow furrowed as she licked her lips. "Honestly, I'm concerned. I mean, if the Valkyries realized Audrey was in Nocturne, they would've come through the walls to get her, so I'm not worried about that. But I've been tugging on my brand to get Delia and Senji's attention, and they haven't responded." Restless fear danced through her blue eyes. "It's not like them."

"Well," Neil said, squeezing her knee, "you did say Delia had never been in a Wild Hunt before. Maybe being MIA for a few days is part of it."

"Maybe." She turned up the inside of her wrist and looked at the intricate brand on her skin. "I just wish I could do something other than wait."

"Well," said Neil, "how about we get dressed and go out for breakfast?" He smiled warmly at her. "That's gotta be better than stewing about it."

She sighed with relief. "Sounds great." Looking to Nico, she added, "Join us?"

"No thanks," he quickly replied, holding up a hand. "You two go ahead."

Chatting about where they should eat, the pair got up from the chair and retreated into Neil's bedroom. They had barely left Nico's earshot before his thoughts, against his will, drifted back to Delia. Tall, statuesque, soft-featured beneath the armor . . . she was a wondrous contradiction of delicate and lethal. He felt like a teenager swept up in the madness of his first hormone-fueled crush. The heart-pumping high he experienced every time he heard her name was distracting but painfully addictive.

Please help me! he hollered at his invisible spirit allies. *A grown-ass man shouldn't waste his time mooning over a dead woman. I can't be an effective* curandero *like this! Tell me how to squash these pointless feelings! Please make me stronger with your wisdom!*

His ethereal guides stayed irritatingly silent.

Delia

ALL AROUND VALHALLA'S BANQUET HALL, SERVERS CARRIED trays loaded with goblet after goblet filled to the brim with mead. The riders of the Wild Hunt drank eagerly as they staggered around in the firelight, arms around each other's shoulders and singing bawdy songs. Other Valkyries, those who had not been involved in the Hunt, gradually made their way into the hall and began to indulge as well. Before long, the place was as packed as a beehive. Echoes of shout and song boomed through the high rafters until every inch of the hall roared.

Delia downed another cup and, chortling, chucked the empty goblet across the room over the heads of her sisters. At her sides, Thrima and Hlokk laughed and hurled their own cups. One of the goblets struck the Valkyrie Geiravor in the back and splattered her pale shift with golden drink. Geiravor tried to whirl around, tripped on her own feet, and sprawled to the floor. Another sister bent down to pull her up, but instead of taking her outstretched arm, Geiravor snatched the cup from her friend's other hand and gulped down more mead.

Grabbing at a platter of steaming meat, Hlokk ripped a hunk of flesh from the roast and took a big bite.

"Hot!" she yipped. "It burns!" She laughed like a madwoman. "It actually burns!"

Thrima reached for the platter and took a handful of meat for herself. Ignoring the *Sæhrímnir*, Delia seized another cup of mead and poured it down her throat. The liquid was cool, yet it warmed her. It filled her stomach, flowed through her veins, and radiated into her skin.

You don't have a stomach, veins, or skin.

Jolting, Delia sputtered and choked on her drink. Thrima pounded her on the back as she coughed out mead, but Delia focused on the voice in her head.

Senji? But it didn't sound like her partner. *It sounds like . . . me. Am I talking to myself?* Delia could not remember ever having talked to herself since she and Senji had been joined after death. Suddenly, she realized that she had not heard Senji speak since returning to Valhalla. *Senji!* she called out inside her mind. *Senji!*

There was no response, just the weird sound of her own voice inside her brain. It felt . . . off, like looking into a funhouse mirror.

Thrima was still pounding on her back.

"M'okay," she slurred, pushing the Valkyrie away. "I'mma be back in a minute."

Lurching to her feet, she took one lopsided step—and then toppled to the floor like a wobbly toddler. Through her mead-haze, she heard Thrima and Hlokk laughing, but she ignored them. She brought one hand to a spot on her face—a wet, painful spot. When she drew her hand back, she saw something that cut through the pleasant numbness of the unearthly drink.

A tiny red drop of blood.

You don't have blood.

"Senji?" she muttered. Her eyes stayed locked on the red spot. "I don't understand."

She climbed to her feet and slowly scanned her surroundings. There were so many Valkyries in the hall—more than she had ever seen in one room before. Everyone was drinking mead, eating roast meat, and enjoying the celebration.

What are we celebrating?

With her drunk brain struggling for sober logic, she retraced the events that had occurred since her return to Valhalla. After the Hunt, the riders were supposed to make their report to the officers, but . . . there had been no report. And, she realized, her eyes narrowing, the officers were all here in the banquet hall, drinking like the others. That didn't make sense.

"Senji?" she whispered. "Senji, help me."

Silence.

Delia slowly pushed her way through the crowd. Several Idisi offered her mead, but she refused. Her eyes stayed fixed on two officers, Skogul and Olrun. She needed them to give her answers.

I don't understand, Senji, she thought. *I'm all muddled up. It's like I've grown a new body that wasn't assembled quite right. I need you.*

Despite the unending parade of drunk Valkyries crisscrossing her path, Delia kept her gaze locked on target. The two officers sat in a dimly lit corner, leaning over the tabletop in front of them to keep their whispered conversation contained. As she moved closer, Delia was encouraged to see that both of them wore somber expressions. That was good. A pair of level heads would provide welcome stability in all this madness.

One of Delia's feet snagged the other, and she toppled to the floor. The closest Valkyries calmly shuffled around her as if she was just another piece of furniture. With an effort, she managed to lift her head from the floor—but then she was struck with a wave of nausea. Just as she got to her hands and knees, she vomited. The alcohol burned her throat on its way out and hit the ground with a sickening splat. The rancid stink of it assailed her nose and made her vomit a second time.

Panting, Delia crawled away from the steaming puddle and slumped against the nearest wall. The raucous party continued uninterrupted.

"Senji," she muttered. "Help me."

No response.

Now emptied of mead, her body calmed and her mind stilled. She shifted into a sitting position and wiped her mouth with the back of her hand. Squinting at the crowd of Valkyries, she suddenly wondered who was fetching the chosen dead if so many of the Sisterhood were here. Who was supervising the battlefield to keep watch over the warriors and the enemy? What on God's green Earth was happening in Valhalla?

". . . the Hunt. Came up empty, though."

Brow furrowed, Delia turned her head toward the voice. To her surprise, she realized that in her semi-delirious state, she had unknowingly crawled close to the officers' table. Just beyond the reach of her arm sat Sigrun and Olrun, calmly sipping their mead.

Still curled in a ball, trying to get her churning stomach to behave, she listened in on their conversation.

"It's not as though we expected to find the Werewolf," said Sigrun. "That was never the objective."

"I know," said Olrun in a tone of great concern. "I wish we *were* hunting a Werewolf. Such a beast would be easier to find than a rogue Valkyrie."

Rogue Valkyrie? Delia stiffened, frozen by the words. *Are they talking about me?* Sealing her lips, she tried to block out all other sound and listened intently.

"Can't you get more details?" asked Olrun. "Vague information is useless."

"I don't think Valhalla has details," replied Sigrun. "If they knew which Valkyrie was leaving her district without permission, they would tell us her name so we could bring her in."

Leaving her district, Delia thought amid a fresh wave of nausea. *Oh God, that is me.* Not so long ago, while Senji's brother was on his deathbed, Delia and Senji had left their assigned district—the Bay Area—to go to Japan so Senji could visit with his newly dead brother before his spirit passed on. They planned to reverse roles when the final hour came for Delia's youngest sister. With all the practice they had put into properly controlling the flow of power through their *Hathiya* mark, Delia had felt confident at the time that their absence from their district would not be detected. *How did they notice we were gone?*

"But they know she's assigned to a district within five hundred miles of the Wild Hunt area?" Olrun asked.

"They *think* she is." Sigrun's words were beginning to run together; her voice was becoming slurred. "Valhalla's focus of late has been on Muspelheim, not Earth."

"Of course it has," Olrun said. "Never in thousands of years has Muspelheim taken such a leap forward. How in the ever-loving hell has everything gone so wrong?"

"Precisely the question that Valhalla was hoping to answer with a Wild Hunt," said Sigrun.

"Do they really believe our battle losses are connected to one absent Valkyrie?" Olrun took a long gulp of her mead.

"Is it even possible for one treasonous Valkyrie to bring us down?"

"Who's to say?" Sigrun chortled humorlessly. "But Valhalla wants it investigated, so . . ."

Delia strained her ears but couldn't catch any more over the drunken din of the banquet hall. Pulling her knees to her chest, she struggled to put her thoughts in order. Valhalla suspected a Valkyrie of leaving her district without permission, but they didn't know which one. Under other circumstances they might have sent officers to examine the suspects individually, but with the tide turning in Muspelheim's favor of late, Valhalla did not have available resources for a thorough investigation. Furthermore, they suspected their ill fortune was the result of treason and that the two offenders were one and the same. They'd needed some excuse to get a number of Valkyries together so they could all be covertly investigated as a group—and just in time, Delia had come to them with the report of a Werewolf. A Wild Hunt was just the excuse they'd needed to summon all the suspected Valkyries together. They'd meant to use the Hunt to root out the traitor.

I'm no traitor. But I am guilty of being temporarily AWOL. How much do they know? What should I do?

"Sister Svanhild," said a nearby voice.

Blinking rapidly, Delia turned her head and looked up at the speaker. "Sister Gondol."

Smiling, Gondol knelt beside her and held out a goblet. "You're the only one not enjoying the party, and that's probably because you're the only one without a drink in your hand. Here."

The golden drink shimmered in the firelight, sweet and inviting. Of its own volition, Delia's arm lifted, her hand reaching for the goblet. Suddenly, she remembered the last thing she'd heard Senji say: *Gondol and her partner are acting strangely.*

Her hand paused in midair and she looked closely at Gondol's face. In those almond eyes, she saw none of the mead-haze that had infected all the others. The long, dark hair framing her heart-shaped face was perfect, not a strand out of place, despite the raging atmosphere. Even the black and red decorative bands painted across her face were spotless. But the most unsettling aspect of Gondol's appearance was her smile. Her cool, cheerless, deliberate smile. Spread across the features of such a petite young woman, that smile seemed eerily out of place.

Delia dropped her hand to her side and shook her head. "I've had enough."

To her surprise, Gondol's smile widened, showing a flash of actual humor. "Who knew that you would be so stubborn?" she said. "You're more of a team player than most." She clucked her tongue. "Everyone else eats the meat. The flavor of *Sæhrímnir* is weak but it hides the taste of Eitr better than the mead, so it can take a higher dose. But you won't touch the stuff. Still"—she chuckled—"I see you're experiencing the effects."

Gondol's small fingers brushed against Delia's skin—her touch light but clammy—and came away smeared with blood. Smiling, she held up her blood-streaked fingers before Delia's stunned gaze and exhaled a heady breath. "Real life," she said. "Isn't it wonderful?"

Alarmed, Delia felt a jolt of adrenaline flood her sluggish veins. The meat and alcohol were dosed with Eitr. What did that mean? Eitr was a rare substance, born of the union of primordial ice and ethereal fire. It could be both life-giving and life-ending. Did Gondol intend to poison the sisters? To distract them? Where the hell had she even gotten Eitr?

Delia felt Gondol's clammy palm on her cheek.

"Look, Svanhild!" Gondol said. Reaching her free hand into her white shift, Gondol retrieved a small opaque bottle. "Do you know what's amazing about Eitr? It is extraordinarily potent. This little vial"—she gave the bottle a shake—"was enough to spike a month's worth of feasting, both food and drink." After gazing around the room, Gondol brought her secretive smile back to Delia. "This party's just getting started. You don't want to miss out."

Slowly sliding upward with her back pressed against the wall, Delia pushed herself to her feet. Gondol was notably shorter than Delia, but even once she had to look up to meet her eyes, the superior expression never left her small face.

"Skogul!" Delia's voice croaked. Clearing her throat, she tried again. "Olrun!"

The only response was Gondol's giggle. Glancing at the officers' table, Delia realized why she laughed. Olrun was almost unconscious, her cheek resting on the tabletop and her hand still clutching her goblet. Skogul was awake, but her eyes were glazed. She reached out to a passing Idis, demanding more mead in broken, halting words.

"They're light drinkers," said Gondol, "so I gave their round a double dose of Eitr."

Swallowing hard, Delia returned her gaze to Gondol. A million disjointed questions flooded her brain, but when she opened her mouth, all that came out was, "Why?"

Gondol drew back in surprise. "Because," she said in a tone that suggested the answer was obvious, "I want to live. Don't you?"

Before Delia could respond, Gondol popped the stopper out of the bottle, grabbed Delia by the hair, and yanked her head back. A fat drop of liquid—cold but somehow sizzling—passed over her lips and down the back of her tongue.

"That's the last of my current supply," Gondol told her, recapping the vial. "Good thing I saved it in case of an emergency."

The drop left an electric trail down Delia's throat, as if the thick liquid was throwing off sparks all the way down. Anger boiled up inside her and she opened her mouth to shout, but no sound came. Instead, she felt a painful burn in her voice box.

With a snarl, Delia lunged for Gondol's throat, but the smaller woman deftly stepped aside. Clenching her teeth, Delia whirled around and went for her again. This time, Gondol seized her arm and, using the momentum against her, threw Delia face-first into the wall, causing her a burst of pain.

"Relax," the smaller woman said, twisting Delia's arm to keep her immobilized. "You've got about ten more seconds until the effects of that Eitr hit you—and honestly, I'm not sure what they will be. I've only used it undiluted once before. Regardless, you probably won't remember this conversation."

Delia felt Gondol lean in close, almost as if to hug her from behind.

"Don't be afraid," she cooed, stroking Delia's sweaty hair. "It's going to be okay."

Gritting her teeth, Delia managed to squeak out, "Senji."

"Oh, stop it," Gondol snapped, her tone changing from comforting to spiteful. "You don't need anything from *him*. He's the one who took your life away. I'm going to give it back."

All the energy began to drain from Delia's muscles, turning her strength to mush. Gondol dropped her arm as her captive slid to the floor in a pile of floppy limbs.

Unable to control her body, Delia threw all she had left into controlling her mind. She reached for that place in her brain that held her connection to Senji, and tried with all her might to reestablish the link.

Senji! Delia screamed inside her spinning head. *Senji, please, you have to remember for me! Gondol is a traitor! Gondol has poisoned us with Eitr! Gondol! Eitr! Poison! REMEMBER!*

Her eyelids fluttered. Her mouth went slack, drool dribbling from the corner of her lips. The last thing she saw before slipping into unconsciousness was Gondol staring down at her, head tilted and smiling as she watched her sister Valkyrie succumb.

Mei-Xing

FROM THE BACK SEAT OF THE UBER, MEI-XING TRIED TO keep her thoughts on her surroundings rather than the night ahead. Her green-and-blue-sequined flapper dress glinted erratically every time the setting sun peeked between buildings along the road. Reflected in the car window, she could see imperfect blurs of the recently altered glamour that encased her. It was nearly identical to her usual glamour, except for the added cosmetics and styled hair. Mei-Xing didn't care for the look, but she supposed it was appropriate camouflage.

In the seat next to her, Georgette tapped her foot rapidly against the floormat, her manicured fingernails gripping a small clutch tightly in her lap. But despite her obvious anxiety, her expression was perfectly serene, and Mei-Xing knew why. Parties at a country club were a familiar scene to Georgette. And when it came to Hazel's beloved social events, it had never mattered how her daughters felt, only how they looked. So Georgette had painted on her makeup, styled her curly hair in an updo, zipped herself into a fuchsia-and-white cocktail dress, and frozen her face into a neutral mask that she was capable of wearing for hours.

The Uber driver turned his car off the highway, far from the flood damage of downtown. Neil looked over his shoulder and flashed both girls a smile from the front passenger seat. "Not much farther," he said. "I'll check in with you later, don't worry. Jin can be a headache."

Internally, Mei-Xing groaned. *I regret this already.*

All the way up the long entrance road, Silver Oaks Country Club looked green and vibrant. Well-tended trees and shrubs accented the pristine white buildings that dotted the enormous property. Mei-Xing found it distasteful. There was no life here. Everything she saw was as manufactured as a plastic model. There probably hadn't been a Nymph in residence on this property in decades.

The Uber veered right to follow the circular driveway just in front of the main building. The ornate fountain in the center of the roundabout—white concrete without a hint of algae—was clearly meant to be stately and opulent, but to Mei-Xing it just looked sterile.

When the car pulled up to the front entrance, a man in a tuxedo-like uniform opened Georgette's door and held out his hand. She accepted it and allowed him to gently pull her from the car. Another man, identically dressed, opened Mei-Xing's door, but she swiftly exited before he could offer his hand.

The chemical odor of the fountain immediately hit her nose. Disgusted, she moved to the far side of the car, where the chlorinated spray of the water jets wouldn't reach her.

Neil stood straight, smoothed out his blue sport jacket, and adjusted his tie. His expression seemed to subtly shift. All trace of uncertainty drained from his face, replaced by bright eyes and a smile that exuded charisma.

"Ladies," he said on an exhale. "Ready for this?"

Georgette gripped her silky white wrap tight around her as she nodded. Mei-Xing noticed how she used it to cover the freckles on her shoulders and chest that her off-shoulder dress left exposed. Though the evening was too warm for a wrap, Mei-Xing suspected Georgette, self-conscious about her skin, would cling to it all night.

With one hand on Neil's arm, the witch held out her free hand toward Mei-Xing, who took it without hesitation. Arm in arm, hand in hand, the three of them climbed the front steps and walked into the country club.

Though repulsed by the surrounding grounds, Mei-Xing was dazzled by the club's ballroom. It was tall and wide, with baroque wood designs on the floor and elegant chandelier lighting. White tablecloths over round tables, gleaming flatware, and lively music all drew the Nymph's mesmerized gaze. Most of all, she marveled at the enormous windows that seemed to draw the green lawn into the room itself. The glass was so immaculate that for a moment she forgot that she was indoors.

A lanky human male with short, carefully coiffed black hair made his way toward them. He wore a tailored gray suit that even Mei-Xing's Nymph eyes could see was expensive, and shoes so polished that they reflected the light like mirrors. As he drew close, he looked Mei-Xing up and down with a sly smile on his face.

She felt a prickle in her skin-bark. His appraising look reminded her of her first encounter with Georgette's mother. Hazel had swept her eyes over the Wood Nymph, visibly evaluating her for some unknown criteria. Whatever she had been looking for, she had not found it, and—thankfully—had never given Mei-Xing a second glance. This man, on the other hand, kept his leery gaze locked on her.

"I see you've brought my date!" he said to Neil. Without waiting for a response, he threw an arm over Mei-Xing's shoulders and grinned. "Mei-Xing, right? I'm Jin Li."

Suddenly finding herself claimed like a possession, her body locked up and she couldn't move. Two pieces of her mind collided: the present piece, which worried he would feel bark and moss where skin should be, and the past piece, which vividly remembered being claimed in such a way by her husband.

"Yes . . . hi," she finally murmured.

"Hey, Jin!" Neil said, stepping closer. His breezy laugh offset the stern light in his eyes. "We just got here. Give her some space, okay?"

Still grinning, Jin removed his arm, but the feel of it lingered on Mei-Xing's shoulders. "I just came in to lead you to the patio for hors d'oeuvres." He gave Mei-Xing an ostentatious wink. "Follow me. I'll introduce you to my mother."

He smiled as he spoke, but Mei-Xing recognized an order when she heard one. She whipped her gaze to Georgette, and the two of them locked eyes. A silent understanding passed between them.

Georgette gave Neil's arm a squeeze. "We should say hello to Mrs. Li. She's our hostess, right?"

"Sure," Neil agreed.

Relieved, Mei-Xing nodded. Still smiling, Jin waved them all to follow as he headed out a pair of glass doors toward a large cluster of people milling about on a stone patio.

The moment the group stepped outside, tuxedoed waitstaff immediately offered them drinks and food, all of which Mei-Xing declined. Georgette and Neil both accepted wine glasses, while Jin snatched up some sort of fancy cracker topped with brown mush. Mei-Xing watched in disgust as he shoved the entire thing into his mouth, chewed, and swallowed in the span of seconds.

Everything about this man struck her as disagreeable. She slowed her pace to stay close to Georgette.

Even while Neil was paying his respects and introducing Georgette to Mrs. Li, Mei-Xing could see the woman looking over their shoulders to size up her son's date. Their hostess was a small woman, short and thin like a flower stem, but she carried herself like a grand tree. One glance from her left Mei-Xing in no doubt as to who was the queen of this country club.

Mrs. Li shook Georgette's hand with a reserved smile and then turned her full attention to her son. "Who is this, Jin?" she asked bluntly, inclining her chin toward Mei-Xing. "I don't recall seeing her before."

"Her name's Mei-Xing Ma," he said, putting his arm around his date's shoulders again. "I met her through Neil."

"I see." Mrs. Li's eyes, full of fire, darted toward Neil for a second, then she leveled a stern glare at her son. Jin maintained his smile, but Mei-Xing noticed that he avoided looking into his mother's sharp eyes. "Tell me," Mrs. Li said to Mei-Xing in Mandarin, "where is your family from?"

"*Nèi Měnggǔ Zìzhìqū*," Mei-Xing replied. She wanted to shake Jin's arm off of her shoulders, but in that moment it felt too heavy to move.

"Inner Mongolia." When Mrs. Li raised an eyebrow, it nearly disappeared under her thick black bangs. "So you're Mongolian."

It was an accusation, one peppered with disdain. Confused, Mei-Xing replied, "Inner Mongolia is part of China."

"Yes, obviously," Mrs. Li said irritably, "but you speak as if your tongue is glued to the roof of your mouth. So clearly Mongolian."

Though they stood nearly eye to eye, Mei-Xing felt childishly small next to this woman. She could hardly explain to Mrs. Li that she had grown up speaking a Fae dialect and had only learned Mandarin when neighboring human villages gradually expanded and encroached on her grove's land. Hoping for help in the awkward situation, she glanced around.

Jin, though he kept his arm around her, didn't meet her gaze. Georgette was a few steps off, holding tight to Neil while he engaged in conversation with another man. Alone in the crowd, Mei-Xing felt a brief swell of fear. But then it vanished, replaced by annoyance. She had no reason to impress this rude woman or her ill-raised son.

This time when she looked at Mrs. Li, Mei-Xing felt nothing but impatience. "My ancestors came from many different places," she said. "My family lives in a fairly isolated area, and we do not often interact with government officials. Therefore, it really does not matter to us whether we are technically Chinese or Mongolian."

Mrs. Li hmphed, wrinkling her nose. "'A fairly isolated area,'" she repeated. "What manner of education did you receive in that 'fairly isolated area'? Were you properly educated in Chinese modernity, or just the backward ways of northerners?"

Mei-Xing suspected that any education she might have received would not measure up to Mrs. Li's standards for a potential daughter-in-law. *This woman is ridiculous.* Seizing Jin's wrist, she removed his arm from her shoulders. "I was married young against my will, which limited my opportunities."

"Married?" Mrs. Li exclaimed. The daggers in her eyes threatened to slice her son to ribbons. "You're *married?*"

"I was," Mei-Xing corrected her. "I left my husband."

"Why?"

Under the best of circumstances, the question would have been rude, but in the mouth of this diminutive human, it was bitingly hostile. It was the same tone she'd once heard from her grove when—as Mei-Xing dwindled away, sapped of all her strength by a husband who demanded that she grow narcotics to sell—they'd dismissed her pleas for help. *Marriage is hard work. The Water Spirit is upholding his end of the marriage contract by supplying the grove with water. How dare you neglect your wifely duties and let down the family!* Mei-Xing's suffering, even her impending death, had been less important to her loved ones than the security and comfort of the grove.

"He gambled," she said bitterly, unsure why she was sharing so much with this unpleasant stranger. "He forced me to work myself half to death to pay for his habits."

"Divorced, then," muttered Mrs. Li. "Children?"

The word stirred a deeply buried memory, rattling Mei-Xing. *Almost* . . . But thankfully she could answer, "No."

"I see." Mrs. Li reached out to a passing waiter and took a glass of wine from his tray. "Well, that's a relief."

At Mei-Xing's side, Jin was watching the interaction, hands in his pockets. His casual posture told her he was accustomed to this behavior from his mother, while his expression told her that he was enjoying the show.

Mrs. Li took a sip of red wine through equally red lips. "Now then. What exactly are your intentions toward my son and my family?"

"I have none."

The older woman's shock could not have been greater if Mei-Xing had dropped her glamour and allowed her to see her natural Wood Nymph form. Several times, she opened her mouth to speak but failed to produce any sound. Finally, she managed to say, "Excuse me?"

"Your son asked Neil to arrange this date," Mei-Xing told her. "I met him for the first time a few minutes ago, and I already find him odious. If he is a reflection of your family, then I want nothing to do with any of you."

Mrs. Li's lips sealed tight, her eyes bore fiery holes into Mei-Xing, and she straightened her backbone like a predator drawing itself to its full height—but Mei-Xing, her patience fully expended, calmly turned her back and walked away. In her wake, she heard a wordless exclamation from Mrs. Li and poorly disguised chortling from Jin as she went in search of Georgette.

The boisterous party, full of chatter and braying laughter accented by music and clinking glasses, was an oppressive maze of humans. It took minutes of active searching for Mei-Xing to spot Georgette in the crowd. When she finally did, she hurried across the room, smiling. The plan for this evening had always been for the two of them to hang out together while Neil mingled. Now that she had fulfilled her obligation by meeting Mrs. Li, they were free to step away and relax. At long last, she would have the grove bonding time that she had craved for weeks.

But before reaching her friend, she stopped short.

Georgette stood at Neil's side, looking perfectly lovely and staying perfectly quiet while he talked and laughed with others. The silky white wrap was tight around her shoulders, and the wine glass she had picked up upon entry remained full. She still wore a static smile.

Mei-Xing's briefly kindled spirits smoldered into ash.

Tonight was supposed to be a chance for her and Georgette to catch up on lost time and smooth over the frayed bonds between them, but instead Georgette was attached to Neil like algae to a rock. Mei-Xing's sole reason for coming to this absurd human gathering was now gone. Her grove was broken. She was alone.

What am I supposed to do now?

A familiar arm flopped over her shoulders. Clenching her jaw, Mei-Xing glanced to her left to see Jin grinning at her.

"That was awesome!" He laughed. "I don't think I've ever seen someone throw Mom off her game like that! Every other girl I've introduced her to has kissed her ass. She was *not* prepared for you!"

He laughed again and squeezed her close. Mei-Xing roughly shook him off and stepped out of his reach. Everything about this man made her bark crawl: his San Francisco accent, his cedarwood cologne, his casual touch, and, most of all, his sense of entitlement.

"Were you not listening?" she snapped. "I don't like you!"

"I never expected you to!" He laughed again. "Mom wanted me to bring a Chinese girl as my date, and I did. You liking me was never a factor!"

Stunned, she stared at him. There must be simpler ways for this man-child to infuriate his mother that didn't involve dragging Mei-Xing into their family drama.

Still chortling, Jin plucked two glasses of red wine from a waiter's tray and thrust one of them at Mei-Xing. "Forget about her. She'll give me an earful later, but not during the party." Flashing his toothiest smile yet, he pushed the glass into her hand and then raised his own. *"Gān bēi!"*

He took a massive swig of the wine, downing half the glass in one gulp. Revolted, Mei-Xing's first impulse was to chuck her drink at him and ruin his expensive suit. But just over his shoulder, she spotted her friend again, and her rage subsided.

Though her mouth was smiling benignly, Georgette's blue eyes were devoid of personality. Her fingers delicately clutched her glass like an actor displaying a prop as she feigned interest in whatever Neil's client was prattling on about. It was an act, Mei-Xing understood that, but there was a deeper truth at play that she could not ignore.

Neil and Georgette were a matched pair. They looked good together, they made each other happy, and . . . they were both human. This loving human couple formed a grove together, a far more natural grove than Georgette and Mei-Xing ever had. And a human grove of this type was typically limited to two. They certainly did not include one member's best friend.

Loss and grief burrowed into Mei-Xing's core. Her grove really was gone. Its only other member had formed a new connection and left her behind. She had nowhere to go.

"Alone," she absentmindedly murmured—and then raised the glass in her hand to her lips and poured the red wine inside it down her throat.

The antioxidants and rich tannins in the wine were digestible; the alcohol, however, made her floral vascular system constrict, causing her a sharp pain. She ignored it. A glass or two would put her into a dehydrated stupor and make the evening pass faster.

A waiter passed by on her right. She snatched another glass off his tray.

Georgette

FROM THE MOMENT SHE ENTERED THE SILVER OAKS grounds, Georgette immediately felt engulfed by the stress of "belonging." Back in Boston, she had seen country clubs expel, scandalize, and blacklist people who were "not our kind." Once through the doors, the "Ivy" voice in her brain, despite all her efforts to minimize it, began to assert the contradictory expectations of her childhood: *Be accomplished; don't outshine us. Be silent; speak with eloquence. Be pretty; change your appearance.* And so she smiled her best Nichols O'Reilly smile and stayed by Neil's side as he introduced her to client after client.

After several hours of tinkling glasses, society laughter, and lounge jazz, Georgette's head felt like a soup bowl filled to the very brim, like the slightest jostle would cause a hot mess to spill out. Eventually, with her cheeks sore from smiling, she politely excused herself and stepped outside.

The glass door closed behind her, sealing the music and party chatter inside. Georgette stood on the patio with the golf course stretched out before her under a blanket of stars. The painful smile at long last melted from her face. With each deep breath of cool air she inhaled, more tension passed through her skin and dissipated into the night. The

Ivy voice in her head fell silent at last, and beautiful peace spread over her, as soothing as ice on a burn.

Then she remembered Mei-Xing.

"Oh no!" she gasped. She whirled around to face the building again, her eyes frantically searching through the windows for her friend. "No, no, no!" Hurrying to the entrance, she threw open the door and felt the chaotic assault of music and laughter. "I'm so sorry," she said to no one as she started to step inside.

A loud caw cut through her panic. Startled, she turned and looked back across the patio. Her jaw fell open at the sight of a bird perched on the back of a patio chair.

"Senji?"

She trotted toward the large raven, allowing the door to swing shut again. The muffled music of the party barely registered in her awareness as she hurried over to him.

"I've been trying to contact you and Delia!" Shifting her vision to perceive any hidden Fae, she swept her gaze all around the patio and surrounding grounds. "Is she here? I don't see her."

Senji croaked, ruffling his feathers and hopping from foot to foot.

He squawked and gurgled for nearly thirty seconds before Georgette realized he was talking.

"Sorry!" she interrupted. With a shake of her head, she cleared her mind and drew on the brand that linked them to make sense of the chatter. "I missed all that. Please say it again."

"I have not seen Delia since the Wild Hunt," Senji said, his inhuman voice thick with fear. "Our connection is still there, but it is so thin that I cannot hear her voice. The brief conversation we had when she returned to Valhalla was very odd. She is not acting like herself."

A gray-and-brown mass of fur suddenly stepped out of the shadows. Georgette's heart skipped and she jumped back with a gasp. A dog-like animal with a broad face and muzzle trotted to the patio but did not approach her. Instead, it sat down on its haunches near Senji's chair and offered her a courtly bow of its head.

Perplexed, Georgette tentatively returned the gesture before raising an eyebrow at Senji.

"This is Yolotli," he explained. "He has seen his Valkyrie partner, Thrima, through past Wild Hunts. Her behavior following this most recent Hunt has him alarmed. When I made the decision to leave Fólkvangr against orders, he insisted on joining me." Senji's expressive black eyes locked on to Georgette. "I explained our deal, showed him the brand. He has no interest in exposing us. He only wishes to help his partner."

It had not even occurred to Georgette to worry about Valhalla learning of their secret. At the moment, she was far more concerned about Delia's safety than she was about exposure. "What happened?"

Speaking rapidly, Senji related what he knew—which, unfortunately, wasn't much. From the sound of it, the Wild Hunt had proceeded as expected until the Valkyries returned to Valhalla. Not one Valkyrie had come to fetch her animal partner. Despite Senji's many efforts, he had been unable to contact Delia again. However, he had briefly detected an echo of her voice calling out to him in fright. That was when he'd made the decision to seek help.

"What did you hear her say?" asked Georgette.

"Her words were . . . muffled," he said. He snapped his beak in three sharp clicks, a gesticulation that Georgette sensed stemmed from frustration. "However, I distinctly heard her say the name of the Valkyrie Gondol, as well as the word 'poison.'"

Yolotli gave a soft bark, followed by a growl. Senji bobbed his head.

"He says," Senji told her, "that Gondol's behavior was suspicious even before the Wild Hunt began. I noticed it as well. She seemed intent on sowing discord and doubt. Furthermore, her partner, Fernão, is acting peculiar. He has shown no sign of hearing or feeling anything through his link with Gondol since well before the Hunt. Whatever is happening in Valhalla, I am sure Gondol is involved."

Chewing on her lip, Georgette stared up at the starry sky. How had she gotten caught up in this state of affairs? When she'd made the deal to share the brand with Delia and Senji, she'd specifically told them she wanted to avoid landing on Valhalla's radar. *Valkyries and witches steer clear of each other,* she thought, remembering childhood lessons. *Valkyries will not suffer a witch obstructing their path and will employ all necessary force to remove her . . . permanently.* Her heartbeat sped up, turning her chest into a knot of tension. *This is bad.*

"I need your help," Senji said, breaking into her thoughts, "to contact Delia."

"Me?" she said in surprise. "Your bond with Delia is epically stronger than my *Hathiya* mark. If you can't reach her, what chance do I have?"

"I do not know how to get to Valhalla from Fólkvangr," he explained. "Fólkvangr is isolated, practically an island in the sea of nothing between realms. It is, by design, difficult to find if you do not know the way. Under normal circumstances, I could have made my way to Delia by focusing on our Valhallan link. But I could not sense her. I was, however, able to sense *you*, and thus made my way here." A shudder passed through his body. "Never before has my connection to you been stronger than my connection to Delia. I have not been so alone in my own thoughts since the day I died. I could have continued onward to Valhalla from here, but there is little I can do there without Delia. In the eyes of the other Valkyries, I am just a raven. No," he glumly corrected himself. "In the eyes of the other Valkyries, I am just a murderer. I need Delia. And to reach her, I need you."

Georgette immediately felt the swell of two incompatible urges: wanting to help her friend and wanting to avoid the wrath of Valhalla. After too long a stretch of silence, she swallowed hard and licked her lips. "What do you want me to do?" she asked quietly.

"Use the brand," he said. "You have called us through it before. Call her now. Perhaps you will reach her where I could not."

Georgette cast a glance over her shoulder to be sure they were alone, then took a deep breath and internally tugged at Delia's brand. She felt no response. Closing her eyes, she gathered her strength and yanked much more vigorously. She drew a long breath, waiting for a reply. A second breath. Third. Nothing.

"I'm sorry," she said. She lifted her head and opened her eyes. "I don't—"

Delia had appeared. Floating several yards above the golf course, her loose white garment in stark contrast to the black sky, she was drifting steadily closer to the patio.

Georgette blinked, confused. She couldn't recall ever having seen Delia without her armor. The flowy white dress would have made her look angelic if not for the mud caking its hems and the yellowish stain splattered across its front. As it was, she looked . . . spooky.

Following Georgette's gaze, Senji swiveled his head and looked at his approaching partner. He let out a loud caw. "Delia!" he called out. "At last!"

The Valkyrie descended from the heavens so quickly that when her bare feet touched the patio, she lost her balance and fell to the ground. Senji squawked and spread his wings as if to fly to her, but he stopped when Yolotli growled. The wolf cast a sharp glance first at Senji and then at Georgette. Dark hairs along his spine stood at attention, and his lips curled back to expose his teeth.

Senji cawed and clicked his beak, conversing with the wolf in a way Georgette couldn't decipher, but she got the gist. Something was very wrong.

Groaning and uttering a soft curse, Delia fumbled her way to her hands and knees. Georgette reached down to help—taking the precaution, as she did, of summoning magic into her hands so her fingers would not pass straight through the Valkyrie's spirit body. But she soon made the shocking realization that her spell was unnecessary. Her fingers gripped Delia's upper arm as if the Valkyrie was made of true flesh and bone. She braced herself to pull Delia to her feet—and was startled to find that a simple tug did the job. Delia's body, though solid, was unnaturally light, like a balloon full of helium.

"Are you okay?" Georgette asked, trying not to sound as unsettled as she felt.

With a swipe of her hand, Delia flipped her long, wavy hair out of her face and, tottering on unsteady legs, leveled a harsh glare at Georgette, making her shuffle backward. Delia's pupils were so dilated that her eyes appeared pitch black.

"I don't wanna be here," Delia slurred in a heavy Creole accent. "It's 'cause of *you*"—she pointed one long finger at

Georgette's face—"I'm missing the *fais do-do.* I was . . . I was . . ." Staring off across the golf course, her eyes enormous but empty, she seemed to lose her train of thought. Her gaze shifted and she tilted her head, squinting. "Senji? Where are we?"

"What's happened to you?" Senji asked in a breathless croak. "Is this Gondol's doing?"

"Who?" Delia stumbled forward, side-swiping a patio table. With a hiss of pain, she recoiled, a hand pressed to her bruised hip. "Why am I here?" she demanded—then, face suddenly afire with rage, lunged toward Senji, grabbed the edge of his chair, and flung it into the grass.

Senji took flight with barely a second to spare and alighted on Georgette's shoulder. She caught her breath as his gray talons scrunched up the silky material of her wrap. It was the first time the raven had perched on her; the feel of his claws pinching her skin did not surprise her so much as did the musty smell, like old books left out in the rain.

Yolotli skulked to Georgette's side with his hackles raised and his tail bristling. The wolf's movement drew Delia's eye, and she cocked her head as if noticing him for the first time.

"I dunno you," she slurred. "Who's you?"

She's drunk. The thought caught Georgette off guard; she'd had no idea before now that a spirit was capable of getting drunk. But after a lifetime of coping with her aunt's seasonal alcohol abuse, Georgette had no doubt as to what she was seeing.

"Delia," she said gently, "we were worried about you."

Delia wrinkled her nose. "I was fine till you pulled me away from the party." A blast of brassy music leaked into the night from the ballroom, and Delia turned toward it, flinching at the bright lights. "You're at a party, too," she said in surprise.

Georgette sighed. The interaction was quickly devolving into every circular conversation she'd ever had with Aunt Laurel after hours of day drinking. "Never mind that," she said. "Senji said he hasn't been able to hear you since—"

"The hell kinda party place is this?" Delia asked, pointing at the country club. "It's a guff core—a gull coos—a . . ." She closed her eyes and carefully enunciated, "A *golf course*. Ugh." She staggered off the edge of the patio and stamped the grass like a child. "My daddy hated golf. Said golf was for fat cats." Her expression turned wistful as she slowly raised her eyes toward the stars. "The last time I saw Daddy, I was a ghost and he was crying over my death." Her lower lip trembled. "I didn't get to say goodbye. He didn't know I was okay."

The Valkyrie covered her face with both hands and melted into a heap on the manicured grass.

Everything about this situation—from Delia's drunken behavior to her too-solid body—was disquieting. This was more than the result of too much booze. Something was fundamentally wrong with her.

Yolotli uttered a sharp bark. Senji stared down, listening to the wolf's guttural growls and whines, before cocking his head back toward Georgette.

"He says there's a smell on her," he said. "He says it smells of . . ." He glanced down at the wolf, who responded with a head bob and a snort. "Of volcanic ash."

"What do Valkyries normally smell like?" Georgette asked.

"They do not," Senji responded solemnly. "Smell is a by-product of life. Spirits have no scent."

Georgette looked at the woman curled into a ball and crying by the edge of the patio. Drunk, semi-solid, giving off a scent—all attributes that should not apply to Delia. *What the hell's going on?*

Senji cocked his head at Yolotli and cawed, to which the wolf responded with a sharp growl. The raven pulled his head into his body as if shrinking to escape his surroundings. "Everything about her current state is alarming."

Delia's sobs grew quiet as she wrapped her arms around her legs and fell over onto her side, her long hair splayed out around her head. Georgette nervously glanced around. "What should I do? Should I . . . I don't know, take her back to my apartment?"

Senji just stared at Delia and flexed his talons, radiating fear.

The music from the ballroom swelled. Alarmed, Georgette whipped around and saw a waiter stepping through the glass door with a tray tucked under his arm. The young man—no older than her—walked toward her as the door swung shut behind him. Wide-eyed, he slowly approached. It wasn't until he was close enough for Georgette to count the buttons on his uniform that she realized he was staring at the large bird on her shoulder.

"Holy crap," he murmured. "When I saw you, I thought the bird was, like, a shadow or something but . . . it's real!" His clear brown eyes shone in childlike wonder as he inched his way forward. "Is it, like, your pet or something? I didn't think—oh shit!"

Georgette followed his startled gaze and saw Yolotli crouched under a patio table. Senji's talons pinched deep into her skin as she held her breath and waited tensely for the waiter to freak out.

Instead, he just shook his head. "Miss," he said with practiced cool, "don't be alarmed, but there's a big-ass coyote under that table next to you."

"Coyote?" she said in genuine surprise.

She looked at Yolotli again. While he was crouched low under the table, scrawny frame cloaked in shadow, his wolfish features were obscured. A person not expecting to see a wolf could easily mistake him for a coyote.

"No worries," said the waiter. "They come around sometimes looking for garbage. I got this." Taking the serving tray from under his arm, he waved it aggressively at the wolf. "Shoo!" he said loudly. "Go on now, get!"

Yolotli shot the waiter a look, gave a dismissive grunt, and returned his eyes to Delia.

As Georgette watched the young man clap his tray on the patio stones, she silently scrolled through her mental catalogue of spells, searching for something quick and gentle to alter this poor guy's memory.

"Dang!" he muttered when the wolf refused to budge. "Big guy doesn't scare easy." Without diverting his gaze, he gestured over his shoulder. "I'll go find my manager and she'll contact the groundskeepers to . . ." The waiter's face turned slightly and his expression grew puzzled. Taking half a step to his right, he squinted at something behind her. "Is that . . . ?" he hesitantly asked. He pointed past Georgette. "Is someone in the grass?"

Georgette whirled around, alarms blaring in her mind. Delia was there, balled up just beyond the edge of the patio. No longer crying, she looked like she had fallen asleep with her face against her knees. But the waiter shouldn't be able to see her. Valkyries were invisible to the untrained eye. It had not even occurred to Georgette to put a glamour over her, because she'd taken it for granted that no one else would notice her. That this man could see Delia recast the entire situation in a far more serious light.

Georgette rushed forward with one hand held before her. The sudden motion jostled Senji, and he flew off her shoulder. Before the startled waiter could move, she planted her palm on his forehead and sent an ethereal blast through his brain. All memory of the last few minutes crumbled into dust under her spell, and the young man's brain reacted with a violent seizure. He crumpled to the ground, knocked out cold. Georgette caught him before he banged his head on the patio stone.

"He saw her," she heard Senji squawk. "He actually saw her!"

"Before he wakes up," Georgette said to the two Valkyrie partners, "we need to get Delia out of here. I-I . . . I just . . ." She paused, took a deep breath, and exhaled slowly. "Delia is drunk, she's irrational, and for some reason, she's visible. The longer she stays here, the greater the risk that either someone will see her or Valhalla will notice she's gone."

"I don't know if Valhalla is in a state to notice anything," Senji replied from the top of an unlit tiki torch. Through their *Hathiya* brand, Georgette felt a rush of frustration and fear. "Valhalla is losing ground in the war, it has become increasingly reliant on unfit soldiers, and now one of its own shieldmaidens has somehow poisoned the others! How am I to fight this?"

The waiter moaned and twitched, his eyelids fluttering. Georgette quickly sat up, turned, and cast a glamour to conceal Delia. The spell was sloppy, barely opaque, but she hoped it would be good enough.

"Senji!" she called out. "Yolotli! Get behind the glamour!"

The waiter groaned. His eyes creaked open as he raised a hand to his head. "Uh," he grunted. "What?"

"Hey," Georgette said gently, resting one hand on the young man's shoulder. "You okay?"

"Huh? Oh." Wearing a muddled expression, he allowed her to pull him to a sitting position. "Uh, yeah, I . . . I guess." He gave her a puzzled look. "Did I, like . . . fall or something?"

"Yeah," she said. "You looked kind of confused and then you just sort of . . . went down. Do you have a break room you can go to? Get a cold drink? Maybe you overheated."

"Yeah, yeah," he agreed. With her help, he got to his feet. "Hey," he said to her, "don't tell my manager, okay? If she sends me home tonight, I'm gonna come up short for rent."

"I won't say a word." She bent to pick up his dropped tray and pressed it into his arms. "Go on inside, get out of the heat."

Wobbling slightly, he headed back toward the ballroom doors. Georgette continued smiling until the door closed behind him and he disappeared into the crowd.

Yolotli let out a bark, drawing her attention. Peering through the glamour, she spotted him next to Delia, shoving his snout under her arm. The Valkyrie mumbled in her sleep but did not wake as the wolf nudged her.

"What's he doing?" Georgette asked Senji.

"We have decided," said the raven, "that he will take her back to Valhalla."

"He can do that?"

"Carrying Valkyries and the chosen to Valhalla from Earth is our purpose." Senji seized Delia's wrist in his talons, took flight, and managed to lift her arm up and over Yolotli's neck. She did not stir. "Delia's current form is too heavy for me, but not for Yolotli. He will take her to Valhalla, hopefully before she is missed, and then remain there in secret to gather intel, which he will then report back to us. Until then, I will stay with you. I need your help to figure out what is happening and how to stop it."

Georgette gaped at him. "My help?"

"Yes," he said. "Something evil is afoot in Valhalla, and it must be corrected."

He wants me *to fix a problem in Valhalla?* Georgette had already committed a potentially fatal taboo by sharing her *Hathiya* brand with Delia and Senji, and now the raven wanted her to correct the dysfunction of battle-hardened ethereal warriors? That was suicide! Blood rushed from her head until she dropped to her knees and smacked her palms to the cool patio stones to steady herself. "I can't help Valhalla!" she said breathlessly. "I'm not a Valkyrie or a warrior—"

"Please."

Senji's voice was so exhausted, so desperate, that Georgette could not bring herself to complete her objection.

Senji fluttered his wings and bobbed his head. "Delia is the one who receives orders from Valhalla, she is the one who claims the chosen, and she is the one who makes our reports to the other Valkyries. Without her, I have no standing in the hall of the slain. Without her, I am nothing but the murderer of the Valkyrie Svanhild." He gazed at Georgette with sad resignation. "There is nothing I can do or say that will raise my standing with Valhalla enough for them to hear my words when they are not spoken in Delia's voice. Please, Georgette. There is no one else I can turn to in this situation. You are all I have."

His plea made her thundering heart ache. She knew the pain of not being valued. Most of her life had been spent with a family that viewed her not as a real person with thoughts and feelings of her own but as a mismatched object that didn't fit with the aesthetic. Nothing she did, no accomplishment she achieved, was ever substantial enough to make her worthy of being heard. There was always a sister or cousin who had done better, leaving Georgette wanting by comparison. Her pleas for acknowledgment had always gone unanswered in her family, so she'd taught herself not to ask. But the pain of having no voice never completely died.

She settled into a sitting position. "I'm scared," she whispered.

"So am I," Senji replied. He hopped closer until he could place one foot on her knee. "I will help you shoulder your fear if you will help me shoulder mine."

Georgette took a deep breath and choked back her tears. Trying to mirror Senji's strength, she gave a nod. The raven returned the gesture.

Okay. Let's do this.

Rising to her feet, Georgette walked on unsteady legs to Yolotli's side. She helped drape Delia across the wolf's back and used her silky wrap to tie the Valkyrie's arms around his neck. Yolotli and Senji exchanged a few words Georgette could not understand, and then the wolf offered her another courtly head bow.

"Safe journey," Georgette said in a hoarse voice.

The small wolf crouched, sprang forward, and climbed, his feet finding invisible steps in the air that he used to bound up into the heavens. Delia's stained dress flapped gently around his running feet as he went. The higher he got, the less substantial both he and Delia appeared, as if they were fading into sky and starlight. Within seconds, they had vanished into the night.

Senji landed on Georgette's bare shoulder. "I am unsure how to proceed," he said to her, "but I will give it some thought on my way to your apartment." He brushed his wing against her cheek. The unfamiliar texture surprised her a bit, but she found it comforting nonetheless. "I am sorry to have brought you my troubles, but thank you."

He soared up into the sky and was soon swallowed up by the darkness. Georgette watched him disappear with her heart in her throat. The reality of a pending confrontation with Valhalla was so huge that her mind shrank away from it and instead settled on a simpler task: collecting Neil and Mei-Xing from the ballroom and getting a ride home.

Neil

NEIL FELT A TAP ON HIS SHOULDER AND TURNED TO FIND Georgette in his shadow. Immediately, he noticed that the wrap she had kept tight around her shoulders all evening was gone, leaving her freckled chest and arms fully exposed, which he knew she didn't like. Just for a moment, his eyes darted downward, and he spotted smudges of dirt on the front of her dress and her shoes. Her blue eyes were glazed over, as if she had been shellacked with anti-emotional varnish.

"Babe?" he said gently. "You okay?"

"I need to go home," she whispered.

A million questions flooded Neil's mind, but he silenced them. His instinct to protect Georgette was far stronger than his desire for answers. His girlfriend wasn't a person to ask for things on a whim. She needed to leave. That was all he had to know.

"Okay," he replied, squeezing her shoulder. "I'll take you home. Do you want to wait out front while I get a car?"

The glaze over her eyes faded a bit, and her features softened. She cast a nervous glance at the ongoing party. "I can't find Mei-Xing," she said in a guilty tone.

"I'll find her," he reassured her. "Wait out front. I'll take care of everything."

Clutching her purse in front of her, Georgette walked stiffly across the ballroom floor toward the main entrance.

Neil whipped out his phone, clicked the Uber app, and requested a ride. The ETA for pickup came back for fifteen minutes. *Good*, he thought. That would give him time to locate Mei-Xing, thank Mr. and Mrs. Li, say goodbye to important clients, and then make a clean getaway.

Gravity seemed to weigh especially hard on Mr. Li's wrinkled face as Neil approached him. The older man was nodding along to the angry rant being delivered by his wife while dabbing away the excessive sweat on his brow with a napkin. When he spotted Neil, he briefly locked eyes with his top salesman and gave a sharp shake of his head, a quick but clear warning to keep his distance. Neil stopped in his tracks, nodded his understanding, and quick-stepped away from the bickering couple.

Though he had not noticed Mei-Xing earlier, the moment Neil set his mind to finding her, he spotted her. She was seated at a table near one of the bars, sipping from a wine glass with a sour look on her face and Jin Li's arm around her shoulder. Jin was grinning and watching his parents across the room as he sucked down his drink. Mei-Xing never gave Jin so much as a glance; she continued to nurse her drink while staring down at the table.

Remembering how uncomfortable Mei-Xing had looked earlier when Jin put his arm around her, Neil felt terrible. He had forgotten to check on her like he had promised he would.

He marched up to the table. "Mei-Xing, are you ready to leave?"

Without lifting her head, the Nymph took another sip of wine, her eyes peering at him over the edge of her glass.

He wasn't sure what emotion he saw there. Georgette had told him that the glamour she used to make Mei-Xing look human sometimes didn't translate her inhuman expressions very well. Still, she didn't look happy.

Jin tightened his arm around Mei-Xing's shoulders. "She can't go now," he said with a chuckle, gesturing in his parents' direction with his glass. "I've never seen my mother this worked up! It's awesome!"

"Georgette and I are leaving," Neil said. Fixing Jin with a stern glare, he stepped up next to Mei-Xing.

The grin slowly melted from Jin's face and he leaned away, withdrawing his arm from around the Nymph.

"Mei-Xing." Neil placed a gentle hand on her now unoccupied shoulder. "I've got an Uber on the way. Do you want to come with us?"

Mei-Xing stared at him silently for long enough that Neil began to worry she would refuse. If she did, he genuinely would not know what to do. Georgette needed to leave and he should go with her—but he couldn't, in good conscience, leave a drunk Mei-Xing at this party with Jin. Should he put Georgette in the Uber by herself and stay with Mei-Xing? Should he drag Mei-Xing out? He didn't like either option.

Fortunately, Mei-Xing spared him the decision. Exhaling in a huff, she stood up, her glass still in hand.

"Okay," she mumbled.

Jin reached out and took her by the wrist, but she quickly shook him off.

"Stop," she hissed. "I don't like you."

The action of shaking her arm unsteadied her, and she swayed until Neil grabbed her elbow and held her upright. Closing her eyes, she seized his arm and clung to him, a strong smell of wine wafting off of her tiny frame. As she regained her balance, she dropped her glass to the table and it fell on its side, spilling its scarlet dregs on the white tablecloth. She drew a deep breath, opened her eyes, and looked up at him with that same unreadable expression.

"Ready to go?" he asked.

She nodded, pushed away from him, and slowly headed toward the door without another word or glance in Neil's direction.

Nicolás

NICO WAS HALF ASLEEP WHEN HE GOT AN URGENT MESSAGE from Neil begging him to get to Georgette's apartment for emergency counseling. Though curiosity tempted him to call for details on the situation, his professional instincts overcame that impulse, and he headed out to catch the bus.

When he walked into Georgette's place, he was caught off guard to see a big raven perched on the back of the sofa. *Senji.* When they met each other's gazes, Senji squawked and began to chatter while shaking his wings. *Is he talking?*

It was on the tip of Nico's tongue to ask Georgette, but he stopped himself when he saw her. She was curled in a ball on the sofa, eyes closed, her head on Neil's knee. She looked exhausted, clearly not prepared to translate for the raven, but at least she was calm.

While Georgette collected herself, Nico looked around the room to find the only other person who he knew was capable of understanding the bird.

"Mei-Xing?" he said, sweeping his gaze about. He didn't see the Nymph anywhere. "Hey," he addressed Neil, "is Mei-Xing here?"

A cloud passed over Neil's expression, and he used his chin to point toward the small balcony. Nico squinted to see past the indoor lights reflected in the glass door to get a glimpse of the night outside. There, surrounded by plants, their leaves swaying in the breeze, Mei-Xing's prone form was completely still but for the slight flutter of her sequin dress. Was she asleep or deliberately ignoring her best friend's anxiety attack?

Perplexed, Nico looked back at Neil, who held up one hand, thumb and pinky outstretched and the other three fingers balled up, and tilted it at his mouth. Mei-Xing was drunk. *Odd.* But not the most pressing issue at hand.

The urge to be useful prodded at him like a fire poker at a smoldering log. *If I could understand Senji, I might get some answers. What can I do?*

Instinctively, he reached within himself, attuning his mind to the voices of his spirit guides. Though they had been inconsistent with their help of late, he soon felt them respond and weave their senses around his mind. Empowered by their touch, he looked at the raven again, this time through eyes coated in spectral essence.

Standing on the back of the sofa, Senji's raven form resided in the middle of a cloud of faint blue mist that casually rotated around him like the arms of a spiral galaxy. The mist, lovely and delicate, appealed to Nico visually—but deep inside, the sight of it caused him disquiet. The various whispers of his spirit guides plaited together an explanation: This was not a real bird. This was the soul of a dead man that had been poured into a creature that resembled a living raven but was in fact a functional extension of a Valkyrie. The blue mist that surrounded the bird was Valhalla's magic, binding the soul to its living creation like ethereal glue.

At his guides' urging, Nico nodded to Senji. "Please," he said, "start from the beginning and tell me what's happened."

Nico sat with his arms crossed over his chest as the raven completed his tale. The thought of Delia drunkenly accosting her partner and Georgette at the country club was a peculiar image. In Nico's mind, Delia was the epitome of class, strength, and dignity. The idea of that stately beauty slurring her words and stumbling like a common drunk just didn't fit with his idealization of her. He shoved the feeling of disconnect away and refocused his attention.

Senji's story of the Valkyries' descent into hedonistic madness gave Nico some sense of the cause of Georgette's anxiety. For the raven to tell her that she was the only hope he had must have been overwhelming for her. Valhalla was, so Nico had been told, a powerhouse of magic in the Fae world that made and enforced its own laws at the tips of a million swords. For one young woman to be handed the burden of saving it from upheaval was unthinkable.

As Nico relayed Senji's words, Neil had gently brought Georgette into a sitting position. Now they sat in silence, side by side on the sofa in their formal wear.

Just beyond the living room, on the far side of the balcony door, Mei-Xing never budged.

"Georgette," Nico said gently, "what do you want to do right now?"

She lifted her head until the overhead light glowed across her fatigued face. "I have no clue," she croaked. "I'm so tired. I only cast two spells tonight, not counting Mei-Xing's glamour, but I'm completely drained. Just thinking about Valhalla, I . . . I can't even—"

"I don't mean about that," Nico said. "Right now, in this moment, what do you want?"

Staring at her hands in her lap, she seemed to think about his question carefully before answering. "I want a drink," she finally said. "My throat's sore and I want a drink." She rubbed her eyes, smearing her makeup. "Something with bubbles."

Nico smiled. "I'll go get it."

He headed into the kitchen and went to the fridge to find something carbonated to soothe Georgette's throat. As he scanned the chilled contents, Senji landed atop the fridge in a rustle of feathers. Nico glanced up to see a pair of small, dark eyes peering down at him.

"What do you expect from her?" he whispered to the raven. "She's one woman. Being a witch doesn't make her ready for this."

Senji clicked his beak. "I have no one else to ask," he said. "Without Delia, I am powerless."

Nico heard Neil and Georgette talking in hushed tones in the living room. He clenched his jaw. She was his friend, his patient, his magical colleague, and he hated like hell that she was in this situation.

"Does the fate of the world," he asked, choosing his words with care, "really hang in the balance because Valkyries are throwing a party?"

To his shock, Senji's immediate response was, "Yes. Without the Valkyries, this world is racing toward apocalypse."

Nico blinked in surprise. "How so?"

"Valhalla is the sole line of defense between this world and Muspelheim," Senji explained, "the realm of fire. The warriors the Valkyries recruit for this war are the souls of the dead and thus immortal; injuries to ethereal bodies can be healed. However, no soldier is mentally equipped to endure endless battle. Without rest, they eventually become unfit for duty. Recently, Muspelheim has drastically increased the frequency and ferocity of its attacks. More battles lead to less rest, and less rest leads to greater mental stress on the soldiers, which in turn leads to fewer soldiers who are fit for battle. Because of this, Valhalla has resorted to gathering the souls of people whom no general would want in his army—bookkeepers, professors, people who have never wielded a weapon in their life. Valhalla is increasingly relying on these unfit souls, both the non-soldiers and the seasoned warriors who have endured too much. Both types are breaking under the strain and dropping out of the army. If the Valkyries continue to neglect their duties, there will be no new recruits, and Valhalla's army will continue to shrink. Muspelheim will gain more ground until Valhalla falls and nothing stands between the Fire Giants and the rest of creation."

Senji shook his body, fluffing up his feathers. It put Nico in mind of a dog raising its hackles.

"The destruction of Earth may not occur immediately—but make no mistake, it *will* happen," the raven continued. "The 'party' must end and the Valkyries must be brought in line. Right now, Georgette is the only option I have." He flexed his talons and lowered his head closer to Nico's. "If you can suggest an alternative solution, then I desperately wish to hear it."

For several long seconds, they stared at each other without a word. Then Nico yanked his gaze away, snatched a Diet Coke from the open fridge, and returned to the living room.

"Here," he said, smiling, as he held the can out to Georgette.

She pulled the tab, releasing a hiss of air from the can, and began taking small sips. Soon, she was downing the soda in big gulps, her face suffused with relief.

Senji chattered, drawing all eyes in the room. When he fell silent, Nico nodded and translated for him.

"He says that we won't know enough to act until Yolotli comes back with information. Once he does, we can brainstorm some ideas."

"We?" Georgette asked softly, hopefully.

"Hell yeah," Neil jumped in. "We."

"All of us," Nico said. "You, me, Neil, Senji . . . and Mei-Xing, too, when she wakes up."

Georgette cast a mournful glance toward the balcony, where the Wood Nymph lay with her back toward them. Nico wondered what had happened between them. Whatever it was, it wouldn't be dealt with tonight.

"We'll tackle the problem as a group," he promised Georgette, "but not until the wolf comes back. More to the point, you need to sleep."

As Neil led Georgette to her bedroom, all Nico could think of was the word Senji had used: apocalypse. It summoned terrifying images of cities in flames, chaos in the streets, and charred corpses stacked to the ceilings. He thought of his aunt, his parents, all of his family screaming in pain as sulfur rained from the sky. It was hard to suppress the shudder that image conjured. It was harder still to believe that the world's best chance to avoid such a fate was one weary, traumatized young witch.

Mei-Xing

THE FLIP PHONE BUZZED AND VIBRATED. ROLLING HER eyes, Mei-Xing snatched it up, flipped it open and shut, and then slid it to the far side of the balcony.

She ran her fingers over the slightly wilted leaves of her potted plants. On a day like this—temperate and sunny—she should be urging them to grow, but instead she was devoting the last of her energy to filtering last night's alcohol out of her system.

The phone dinged, signaling a text message. Mei-Xing let out a hiss of annoyance and deliberately fixed her gaze on the blue sky. Knowing who the message was from soured the beautiful day.

The day after the Silver Oaks party, while Georgette was out of the apartment, the phone had arrived in a package addressed to Mei-Xing. The Nymph, who had never received mail before, had found the process of opening the large envelope to be both thrilling and perplexing. Who could be sending her something?

When she opened the phone for the first time, there was only one name in the contacts list: Jin Li.

The first time he called, she answered out of pure confusion, only to learn that he wanted her to join him for lunch with his parents solely for the purpose of aggravating his mother. Disgusted, Mei-Xing hung up and dropped the phone into the garbage. But he kept calling; the ringtone and message notifications blasted their way out of the trash can with the force of an airhorn.

She'd been on the verge of hurling the phone into the street when Georgette came home, full of remorse for her behavior at the party.

Georgette's sincere apology should have been the end of it. With a hug and a few tears, they should have been best friends again. But instead, her friend's words had left her hollow. It wasn't that she doubted Georgette's sincerity, only that her apology was not the fix she needed. The trouble was, Mei-Xing couldn't say what the proper fix might be.

She and Georgette had been inseparable for years—a grove unto themselves, a family of two. Then Neil had entered Georgette's life, and ever since then Georgette had been spending most of her time with him instead. That wasn't the way a grove should be; the newcomer was supposed to adapt to the existing grove, not take the place of another member. But Georgette and Neil were human, and they were doing what human couples naturally did: making a life together, forming their own grove. Never before had Mei-Xing been made so acutely aware of the fact that she was a Wood Nymph among humans. Here, instead of being part of a grove—connected to a system of interlocking roots gathering nutrients and sharing space for optimal sunlight—she was alone.

So, with nothing else to do, she went to lunch with Jin Li.

It was the first of a series of regular outings with that odious man. Mei-Xing never said more than a few words to him at these get-togethers, and he never pressed her for more. He didn't care to hear her thoughts or to know anything about her; to him, she was nothing but a means of upsetting his family for his entertainment. Mei-Xing hated playing his sick game, but she no longer had any other role to play. And at least the free booze numbed her despair.

The phone dinged again. Casting a scathing glare in its direction, Mei-Xing picked it up and read the messages.

Pick up, MX, said the first. "MX." The nickname made her bark crawl.

The second text said, *Mom's setting me up on another blind date. I'm gonna bring you along. Pick u up at 6.*

No request, no offer, just a statement, practically an order. *Damn that vile man.* But even as she cursed him, she knew she would go. She would stand next to him with his arm flopped over her shoulders, stare into the middle distance, and drink herself senseless.

Ishak

ISHAK WATCHED THE LADIES IN THE THIRD-FLOOR LOUNGE coo over Ziya as his little girl's bright, curious eyes drifted all around. Dhara, the Nagini, held the baby within her scaly coils, rippling her long lower body around the girl in a wave-like rhythm. Ziya excitedly smacked her small hands on Dhara's scaly skin while making yipping noises. Two Kitsunes, Chiyo and Kiku, crouched on either side and made goofy faces at the baby while one of the silvery Elves—her unpronounceable name sounded a bit like "Goose"—tickled her exposed feet. Ishak smiled at the scene, wishing he could watch it all day.

"This way," said a voice in his ear. Tearing his eyes away from his girl, Ishak saw Erskine, the Selkie, one of the few male beings who regularly worked the third-floor VIP rooms. Erskine nodded toward the door, his long hair bobbing with the movement. "Security office."

Ishak followed Erskine out of the lounge and down the hallway. The club on the first floor was just getting started on the night's activities, the beat of the music faintly vibrating up through his feet, and the VIPs had yet to arrive for the earliest appointments of the evenings. The third floor was, for the moment, quiet.

Erskine led him to an open door and waved him inside. The spherical Ophan floated back and forth in front of the many security screens that lined the walls, the nested wheels that made up their body spinning steadily and their countless eyes never blinking. Ishak had never learned the unusual creature's name, if they even had one.

Erskine pointed to the opposite corner. "There."

On the floor, Ishak saw Georgette lying on her side, her knees pulled up to her chest and one arm cradling her head. She was curled into such a tight ball that he could barely see her face, but he could hear breath passing through her nostrils in soft whistles.

He shook his head. For Georgette to fall asleep on a hard floor in a cocktail dress and high heels, she must be utterly exhausted. He removed his hoodie and laid it over her bare shoulders.

"Let her be," he said to Erskine. "She needs rest."

"But we have deliveries coming," the Selkie told him, his watery blue eyes darting to the witch. "Only she can exit the building to sign for them. If any of us do it, we'll be stepping outside the protection of the concealment spells. And the VIPs need someone who can negotiate prices and schedule future events. They won't deal with us; they see us as 'the help.' Georgette's been handling it for the last month."

"That long?" Ishak said in surprise.

"Well, Kazi normally does it but . . ." Erskine shrugged.

A low grumble rolled around Ishak's throat. When he'd first moved in, Kazimiera had been as omnipresent in the building as the magic that held it together. But lately, she was absent more often than not—and when she was present, she was not the same. Once a fierce businesswoman in sexy clothes and spiked heels, she had now devolved into a barefooted rag doll that moved in uneven creeps and jerks, her eyes glowing from behind a mass of tangled hair. Erskine's discomfort told Ishak that he was not the only one to have noticed her transformation.

"I am not restricted by the concealment spell," Ishak said. "I'll deal with the deliveries. It's the least I can do."

"But what about the VIPs?" Erskine protested. "Kazi says the building can't function without their money."

"Surely someone other than Georgette can handle them."

"Yes," the Selkie said quietly. "Kazi."

Ishak sighed. He didn't have the heart to wake Georgette, so there was only one other option. "Where is Kazimiera?"

"No one knows."

"I'll find her and bring her back," Ishak said, brushing past him as he strode toward the stairwell. "Please make sure Ziya is taken care of while I'm gone."

He didn't wait for a response; he knew Erskine would do as he was asked. He strode out of the room, and within seconds, he was bursting through the employee exit into the back parking lot and putting his nose to the wind.

Immediately, he picked up the Vampire's scent.

Kazimiera

KAZIMIERA SAT ON A CURB STOP WITH HER ARMS WRAPPED tight around her head. The thrum of the city rattled through her bones, booming inside her skull. Every vehicle rumbling down a street, every casual conversation between passing pedestrians, every ringtone, every car radio, every whistle of wind . . . There was so much noise that it no longer registered as sound. It was just pain.

Lifting her head, she cracked open her eyes. She was in an empty parking lot. When she turned her head to scan the nearest buildings, she had to grit her teeth against the sound of her neck bones creaking. It took a long minute of staring at the signs above the doors before her brain remembered how to read. A law office, a barber shop, a nail salon, and a chiropractor. Gradually, she managed to wrestle some logic from her situation. There were no cars because it was long past the closing times for businesses like these. She was alone.

It wasn't until she brushed her hair off her cheeks that she caught the scent of dried blood. She brought her hands close to her face to examine her fingers, and she saw blood caught under her nails. The sight did not surprise her, but her memory did not offer an explanation for it.

I am relatively lucid right now, she thought sluggishly. *I must have fed recently.*

She remembered waking up at sundown on the floor of her office, just one in a long string of identical awakenings. As on those other evenings, she'd felt an immediate chain of sensations: foggy awareness, crippling pain, and then desperate thirst. A memory coated in woolly fog told her she'd left the building and run off into the San Jose streets as the full force of the red thirst took her. From that moment on, she remembered just images and impulses: a scent on a street corner, cool pavement under her unshod soles, a mind-rattling scream, and a soothing warm gush flowing down her gullet.

I have killed and eaten. Where did I leave the remains? She shook her head but stopped abruptly when the swish of her matted coils past her ears deafened her. *I have fed*, she thought irritably, *but my senses are still too sensitive to function in a human world.* She looked at her hands and felt a powerful urge to suck the blood from her fingertips. *If I continue down this path, I will descend into savagery.*

"Descend into savagery." The phrase was from a lesson imparted by her maker.

Memories of those long-ago days had worn away under the friction of centuries. She no longer remembered the face of the Vampire who'd initiated her, but she remembered the things he had taught her. He'd called himself Silas—a name for one lifetime, though he had lived many.

Silas never explained why he had picked her of all those laboring in the fields of the Lowcountry, and she had never asked. She was simply overcome by the unique joy that came of knowing her life, heartbeat or no, belonged solely to her. She would never again be soaked in the putrid stench of indigo fermentation or collapse from the fatigue of churning the vats. She would never again try or fail to fend off the groping hands of the plantation's eldest son. No more sun-scorching harvests in the fields, no more chasing flies from the drying shed, no more lashings. Silas had advised her to walk away from it all and never look back. And she had . . . after burning down the indigo-processing buildings.

"Petty vandalism will be insufficient to sustain you," Silas had warned her as she watched them burn. "Without adequate mental stimulation, the Vampire part of you will begin to overpower what is left of your humanity, and you will descend into savagery."

Humans were never meant to be broken by Death and stitched up with threads of magic. Silas had explained that her body now existed in a delicate balance—too Fae to be human, too human to be Fae. The Vampire half was a feral creature, wild and vicious, so her human half had to be strong enough to balance it. That meant keeping her logical brain in a constant state of exercise; if her human mind was not fully engaged, the primal magic that held her undead body together would become too much for her to control, and she would become a raving beast.

Now, all these years later, she was stalking the city streets every night on bare feet, barely able to remember where she had been. Until recently, occasional sips from VIPs throughout the night had been enough to keep her functional; lately, she was draining multiple bodies every night and still struggling to control herself. She was killing indiscriminately and could not remember the faces, the voices, or even the taste of her victims. Those were the actions of a beast.

How long until blood no longer provides any lucidity at all?

A new sound battered her ears, exploding inside her skull. Kazimiera jumped to her feet, eyes closed and hands pressed to her ears. Nerve endings all over her body sparked and throbbed. She was about to sprint from the scene when the sound suddenly stopped. Eyes snapping open, she swung around and came face-to-face with a mass of muscle and fur.

"Kazimiera," Ishak's voice rumbled from within the huge hyena's throat. "You must return to Nocturne."

It took a moment for her to grasp his meaning, as every syllable burst through her head like machine-gun fire.

"I need blood." Though she barely whispered, the vibration of her own voice made her vision shake. She bared her teeth at Ishak. "Go away."

"People rely on you," he pressed. "Go back."

"Leave," she snapped.

Turning away from him, she stumbled toward the businesses, but quickly froze. There, reflected in the dark front windows of the nail salon, was a hunched figure with long, gangly arms. It stood before her with its hands outstretched, bony fingers extended like claws. The rags wrapped around its torso and shoulders implied a past life of vibrant color now lost to filth. The figure's skin was the purplish shade of a corpse, and its thick mess of hair, caked in mud and gore, infringed on its face like overgrown fungus.

Through the mess, Kazimiera clearly saw lips and a chin smeared with blood. Suspicion crept over her, and she brought one hand to her cheek. The figure did the same. She drew in a sharp breath.

"I have heard stories that Vampires lack reflections," Silas's voice echoed in her mind. "This is not the case. However, those who descend into savagery might wish it was true."

This is me. This is the result of relying on Nocturne for too long. The club has outlived its purpose. Only one thing helps my pain now.

The red thirst rose, and her lucidity began to fade. She swung around, putting her back to the glass, and gave the loitering hyena-man a snarl. "Blood," she hissed.

She crouched low to the ground, planting her feet and hands against the concrete in a lurking gargoyle stance. Then, in a slick, fluid motion, she launched herself over the Bultungin's head.

She landed on all fours at the far end of the parking lot, then took off at a sprint.

Blood. The thirst consumed her, swallowing all higher thought. *Seek. Kill. Feed.*

Senji

LIGHT COATED SENJI'S BLACK FEATHERS AS THE SUN CLIMBED the morning sky and crept past the bundles of clouds that sat low on the horizon. The growing heat of the day laid a haze over the land below Mount Umunhum, including San Jose. Standing atop the mountain's concrete block of a tower, Senji could see for miles. There was no sign of his partner.

Delia, can you hear me?

He repeated this search daily, sometimes staying on the tower for hours to stare out over their territory while mentally reaching for his partner. The routine was comforting, if fruitless.

The view from Mount Umunhum was quite extraordinary. Senji had always enjoyed seeing the world from a great height, even when he was young. He and his brothers had once skipped school to spend an afternoon climbing Inasayama, the small mountain just west of Nagasaki.

Inasayama was not nearly as tall as Mount Umunhum, but the view from its summit had been spectacular. That sweeping view of a thriving, industrial Nagasaki, not the devastated shell of a place he had glimpsed briefly after his death, was how he liked to remember the city.

A breeze brushed over his feathers, ruffling his folded wings. He recalled the happy expressions on his brothers' faces all those decades ago. Their parents had rarely taken a moment's rest from work, but Senji's boyhood mind had managed to capture some images of them smiling, even laughing. Those cozy moments snatched from time and kept snug inside his head like birds in a nest . . . it gave him a feeling without name. Nostalgia, longing, grief . . . something that lay somewhere in the cracks between those things. How strange it was to look back on one's own ended humanity.

Suddenly restless, Senji took flight. His wings caught an air current that lifted him over the mountain, high above the trees. Without thought, he dove toward the city.

The cars and pedestrians in the streets steadily swelled in size as Senji glided down from the heavens. Soaring over rooftops, he passed his gaze over the city below and then lifted his eyes to the sky. What he was waiting to see would come not from the ground but from above.

And today, he saw it.

Cloaked in a familiar magic that deflected the average eye, a dark spot dropped down from above. Descending out of the sky from realms unseen, his legs pedaling as if running down a steep hill, was a small wolf.

Yolotli.

Nicolás

NICO SPENT SEVERAL MINUTES IN DEEP SILENCE, ALIGNING with his spirit guides, before opening his eyes to see Yolotli in front of him, waiting patiently. The wolf was seated on Georgette's living room rug, just a couple of feet from where Nico sat in an armchair. To his right, Neil and Georgette sat together on the sofa, hand in hand. Senji was perched on an adjacent lamp, the nervous twitch of his feathers casting fluttery shadows on the wall. Mei-Xing stood a little ways off, gazing out the balcony door at her potted plants. Aside from the distracted Wood Nymph, everyone present was waiting for the *curandero* to begin relaying Yolotli's story.

With the assistance of his spirit guides, Nico could see Yolotli not just as an animal but as he really was: the flesh-and-blood vessel of a man's soul. When the wolf began to speak, Nico at first heard only growls and barks, but his spirit guides swiftly poured a translation into his brain.

"Do you understand what I say?" asked the wolf.

"Yeah, I can understand you," Nico said. "I'll do my best to translate."

Yolotli bowed his head in acknowledgment. "Certainly. I am most grateful for your assistance, *Noxhuiuhtze*."

Noxhuiuhtze. He heard the word in Nahuatl before his spirit guides belatedly translated it, as if they needed a moment's consideration before deciding on the word's meaning. Grandson. He smiled. Though the wolf did not mean the word literally, Nico's heart warmed to think of Yolotli as another ancestral spirit guiding his path.

"I arrived in Valhalla without incident," Yolotli began, Nico passing on his words to the rest of the room. "For a time, I hid from the guardian wolves who prowl the grounds, but I soon saw that they were not behaving normally. They moved mechanically, like sleepwalkers. I went closer to the Great Hall and spied the golden eagles on the roof. I am accustomed to seeing them alert and shining like torches, but now they are asleep, and emit only a dull glow."

"What does that mean?" asked Georgette.

"At the time," Yolotli replied, "I had no idea. I only knew that Valhalla's stalwart guardians paid no heed to me, an intruder on the grounds."

"Unheard of," muttered Senji, ruffling his wings.

"The front door had been left ajar," said Yolotli, "and the entrance hall was empty. Over the last few months, that hall has been consistently packed full of wounded and exhausted warriors, but I saw no one. The sounds of distant battle should have echoed through the hall, but I heard nothing of the war. What I did hear was the sound of a raucous celebration. Following my ears, I made my way through vacant hallways until I found the source of the noise." He licked his chops, a gesture Nico took for discomfort. "I was unprepared for the sight."

The wolf paused a moment, leaving his tense audience holding their collective breath.

The silence was broken by an impatient Senji snapping his beak. "Well?" the raven demanded.

"I saw," said Yolotli, "thousands of Valkyries. Far more than I have ever seen assembled, more than I knew existed.

Their garments stained, their skin smudged, and their hair in frightful tangles. They sang tuneless songs and laughed like madwomen. The stench of them," he growled, "the human stench! The room reeked of sweat and bodily fluids. Discarded weapons and armor pieces were strewn about, along with broken chalices and puddles of sacred mead. I saw more than one Valkyrie lying face down in the mess, toppled by drink or an angry punch. Those on their feet took no notice of their unconscious sisters. I heard bones break under stumbling feet."

"Fluids," Georgette repeated in a hush. "Bones. Spirits don't have either."

"I hid near the kitchen. From there, I could hear the singsong voices of the Idisi preparing drinks and roasted meat. Then I heard a voice say, 'I've run out, but I've sent for more. Ration the mead and food that you've already dosed until my messenger returns.' The Idisi chittered their reply: 'Yes, Gondol.'"

"Gondol!" Senji exclaimed, his sharp croak startling everyone in the room. "I knew this mess led back to her!"

"I followed Gondol at a distance," said Yolotli. "She was obviously the only Valkyrie not intoxicated. She gave off a faint but humanesque scent that exuded a sort of tempered excitement—the scent of someone who awaits a promotion, a gift, or a battle. In the front hall, I watched as she walked outside onto the steps and stood in the morning sunlight. Eventually, I saw a wolf land at Gondol's side."

"Was it her partner?" asked Senji. "Fernão?"

"I assumed so," said Yolotli. "However, she called him by a different name: Abelardo."

Senji blinked. "I don't believe I've ever heard that name among the partners."

"Nor have I," Yolotli said. "It was confusing."

Nico found himself in agreement. Everything Yolotli said struck him as confusing, in fact—but he resisted the urge to bombard him with questions. Instead, he focused on his role as translator and trusted that Georgette and Senji would know what to ask.

"The wolf carried something in his jaws," Yolotli continued, "a pouch of some kind, which he gave to Gondol. She inspected the contents and appeared satisfied. She said something to him, but rather than respond, he just stared at the ground and shuffled his feet. Gondol watched him for a moment, but then she seized him by the scruff and shook him."

Neil scrunched up his face. "Is that normal?" he asked. "I mean, I've only met Senji and Delia, but I can't imagine her treating him that way."

"A Valkyrie manhandling her partner is not unique," said Senji.

Yolotli waited for Nico to relay Senji's response to the group before adding, "Nor uncommon. However, it is odd that she would use her voice to command his attention rather than speak to him mentally. A word spoken aloud is far more easily ignored than one projected into the mind, and Gondol knows that."

Senji clacked his agreement.

"Regardless," said Yolotli, "Gondol maintained her grip on his scruff and snarled, 'Don't you dare ignore me. You're replaceable.'"

Nico saw the shock on Georgette's face several seconds before he absorbed the meaning of the words. Every Valkyrie was partnered with the man who killed her. Since Gondol was already dead, no other man could kill her. No

Valkyrie partner was replaceable. So what could Gondol mean by that?

"She checked the pouch again," said Yolotli. "She plucked out several small vials and held them up to the light, staring at them with great intensity. Then she said the words that have haunted me ever since: 'Get here faster next time. I can't afford to run out of Eitr.'"

Senji uttered a loud squawk as Georgette simultaneously caught her breath, her eyes growing wide behind her glasses. Neil squeezed her hand, but his blank expression betrayed his ignorance. He glanced at Nico, eyebrows raised—but Nico could only shake his head. He'd heard the word Eitr before, but he remembered nothing of what it meant.

"What's Eitr?" Neil asked.

"It's a . . ." Georgette fumbled with her words. "It's an ancient, elemental substance. It's basically the primordial ooze that all life comes from. It's also a poison."

Neil's brow furrowed. "It's both?"

"Yeah." She shoved one hand into her hair and tugged nervously at the curls. "It's like a medicine—life-giving in the right dose, life-threatening if used too much. Except Eitr is crazy potent. It gave the world life, but it's also capable of mass extermination."

Neil still looked perplexed, but having heard Georgette's explanation, Nico began to see the situation in Valhalla with greater clarity. Gondol was dosing the Valkyries' mead and food with Eitr, and it was gradually restoring them back to life. They had gained bones to break and fluids to leak.

Offering Yolotli a grim nod, Nico waited for him to continue.

"Eitr has weakened the Valkyries' bonds with their partners," said the wolf. "As an extension of this, Valhalla as a whole has grown weaker—the inhuman guardians of the grounds have lost their focus, the Idisi no longer care for the wounded, and the chosen who fight against Muspelheim are unable to replenish their strength."

"So as the Valkyries become human . . ." Senji trailed off.

"Valhalla diminishes," Yolotli finished, "and the enemy gains ground."

Senji flapped his wings hard, slapping them against his sides. "This is a catastrophe! Eitr, treason, the collapse of Valhalla's defenses—the situation is dire!"

Hanging his head, Yolotli sighed heavily. "There's more. There is to be a second Wild Hunt." He lifted his head and swept his amber eyes around the room. "Gondol planted the idea, and it spread through the party like a virus. I saw Valkyries beating their sisters bloody to win a spot in the Hunt."

"Why?" asked Senji, hopping from the lamp to the arm of the sofa. "What's the point of a second Hunt?"

"I asked myself that question." Yolotli sighed heavily. "Gondol has weakened Valhalla by restoring humanity to the Valkyries. By removing the strongest warriors from the premises, she can leave the realm utterly defenseless."

Senji stiffened. "If the second Hunt goes forward," he croaked, "Valhalla will be wide open to attack." He turned toward Georgette. "What do we do now?"

Georgette didn't respond. She just sat on the sofa, as pale and immobile as an ice sculpture but for the slight twitch of a muscle beneath her eye. Neil placed an arm around her, but Nico saw no indication that she felt comforted.

On the contrary, the young witch—Valhalla's one hope for rescue—looked absolutely terrified.

Georgette

GEORGETTE STARED AT YOLOTLI AS SHE FULLY ABSORBED what she had heard. Thousands of Valkyries wildly drunk. One Valkyrie poisoning the others with Eitr. A second Wild Hunt. As her brain incorporated each element of Yolotli's story into the bigger picture, she felt her hope for a simple resolution dim until it was entirely extinguished.

It's the worst-case scenario, she thought. *The world is literally coming to an end. What am I supposed to do?*

Neil squeezed her shoulder. It wasn't as reassuring as she knew he meant it to be, but it was, at least, a welcome reminder that she wasn't alone in the room. She looked at him. His expression was troubled but calm.

Most of Yolotli's story must sound like a fairy tale to him, she thought miserably.

Wanting to connect with someone who really understood, Georgette instinctively reached out for the best friend upon whom she had relied for emotional support for years. For one soul-warming moment, she locked eyes with Mei-Xing and felt the connection—the deep well of love and care—that she craved. But after giving Georgette a second's worth of comprehension, reassurance, and devotion, her gaze suddenly grew pained—then distant—and she turned her face away.

Please, Mei, Georgette thought, struggling to hold back tears, *I need you.*

But Mei-Xing stared out the balcony door without glancing back.

To her surprise, Georgette felt only a moment of despair at seeing her friend's detachment. Then she got angry.

Fine. She clenched her jaw, letting fury roll over her like wildfire. *If after everything we've been through together you can just look away, then to hell with you.*

The anger stampeding through her veins pumped raw energy into her body. The next breath she drew filled her with strength, and she sat up straighter in her seat.

"Okay," she announced to the room. The confidence in her own voice caught her off guard, but it felt good. "Senji, can you and Yolotli get back to Fólkvangr?"

"I believe so," said Senji. "Now that I've journeyed between there and here, I think I can retrace my steps. Why?"

"I'd like you both to question Fernão or Abelardo or whoever he is. I don't see Gondol discussing her plan with us, but maybe he will, especially if she's threatening to chuck him into Muspelheim. In fact"—she grew bolder—"maybe we should confine him. That would stop Gondol from getting more Eitr."

"And without Eitr," Senji eagerly broke in, "the Valkyries may regain reason without the need for drastic measures." Bobbing up and down, he squawked at Yolotli, and the wolf jumped to his feet. "We will detain Gondol's partner and learn what he knows."

"Cutting off the Eitr," Georgette continued, "might not prevent the second Wild Hunt." She nibbled her lip as she thought. "Last time, they came looking for a Werewolf. Who knows what, if anything, they'll be looking for this time." She pulled at a lock of hair, straightening it between her fingers and letting it bounce back into a tight curl. "I'll tell Audrey to spend her nights in the club, just in case." With a clear course of action falling into place, some of the anger boiling in Georgette's blood dissipated. She exhaled a tense breath, leaned her head against Neil's shoulder, and gave Nico a grim smile. "I need help coming up with a contingency plan."

"We'll work on it," Nico assured her.

Neil kissed the side of her head. "You've got this," he whispered.

"I hope so," she whispered back.

Warmed by his faith in her, she let his words soothe her doubts and fears. Then she saw Mei-Xing rise from the couch, open the glass door, and step out into the sunlight. To Georgette's eyes, her longtime friend looked ghostly and mechanical. On the Wood Nymph's heels, Senji and Yolotli hurried through the door onto the small balcony. They launched themselves over the railing and into the sky as Mei-Xing sank to her knees and began tending to her row of potted plants.

After weeks of emotional distance, her friend, though only just outside, seemed too far away for Georgette to reach.

Senji

THE NUMBER OF VALKYRIE ANIMAL PARTNERS IN FÓLKVANGR had vastly increased since Senji's departure. A few dozen beasts lounging about in the tall grass had swollen to entire herds of horses, packs of wolves, and flocks of birds. Senji swooped over the vast meadowland many times before he finally located an unoccupied branch on which to alight. From this spot, his eyes darted from one group of wolves to the next, struggling to locate Fernão . . . or Abelardo.

He easily spotted Yolotli moving among the crowd. Over the decades, Senji had seen a wide variety of wolves in Valhalla—from the small Arabian wolves with their big ears to huge white timber wolves—but Yolotli, a Mexican wolf, had a distinct yellowish-gray coat topped with cloudy black markings. To an experienced eye, he stood out like a butterfly among moths.

Is Fernão even here? Senji wondered as his eyes swept over the chattering crowds. *He may be running another errand for Gondol. What will we do then?*

A hoarse howl rang out above the general din, drawing Senji's gaze. At the southeast corner of the meadow, at the very edge of the tree line, was Yolotli. The dark hair that ran down his back stood at attention, a sharp blade ready for battle, and his four legs stood as rigid as pillars. Even from this far away, Senji could see he was baring his teeth at something in the windswept grass.

He launched himself into the air, soared directly toward the spot, and landed on Yolotli's back. He looked over the wolf's head—and saw a cowering ball of gray fur at his feet. Up close, he recognized the bony frame, the prickly fur, and the glazed expression. *Fernão.*

Yolotli snapped his jaws threateningly. "We know you have been bringing Eitr to Gondol," he snarled. "Explain yourself!"

Fernão stayed hunkered down with his chin pressed to the ground and his rounded back in the air, the breeze rustling through the fur along his spine. A few others—some wolves and a few horses—crept closer to the three of them with darting eyes and cocked ears.

When Fernão failed to respond to Yolotli's demand, Senji squawked in frustration. With a flap of his wings, he jumped to the grass and angrily pecked at the wolf's side. "Speak!" he commanded. "You are conspiring against Valhalla and endangering life everywhere! Speak, damn you!"

Concerned muttering rippled through the crowd gathering around them. From every side, Senji heard the gentle *swish-swish* of beasts walking through the tall grass. Though he kept his eyes locked on the silent wolf, he sensed dozens of eyes looking at him. *Gondol will not be able to keep this secret anymore,* he thought in triumph.

Fernão squirmed a bit and, very slowly, lifted himself a few inches off the ground—and attempted to army-crawl away from his captors.

Yolotli leapt forward and pinned him under his paws. "Stay where you are," he said, snapping his teeth next to the quivering wolf's ear. "Talk!"

Silent seconds ticked by. Senji leapt onto Fernão's back and pecked him again. Over the top of the long grass, he now saw that the circle of bystanders had grown. What had been just a handful of curious onlookers was now a group of at least one hundred Valkyrie partners, watching and murmuring. He clacked his beak in frustration. He had a mission to complete, a realm to protect, a partner to save. He dug his claws into Fernão's hide and once again commanded, "Speak!"

Fernão trembled but did not respond. Bounding forward, Senji scratched at the wolf's head and attempted to peck his eye. Fernão yipped and covered his eyes with his front paws.

Before Senji could attack again, he was surprised to feel Yolotli's paw on his chest, gently sweeping him off the target's head.

"Stop," his companion said.

Senji fluttered his wings, fluffed up his feathers, and squawked, "Why?"

Yolotli leaned in close to Fernão's head, eyes narrowed and nostrils undulating. "Something is amiss." Yolotli looked at Fernão again, his sniffing nose only inches from the cowering beast's shoulder, then stood tall. "This is," he said, projecting his voice over the bystanders' mutterings, "undoubtedly the same wolf I watched deliver Eitr to Gondol at Valhalla—Eitr she then used to poison the Valkyries."

Stunned silence swept through the animal partners. After a pregnant pause, Yolotli continued.

"The scent of this wolf is identical to the one I smelled then. However, I cannot say with conviction that this is Fernão. And I wonder . . ." He gave their captive a nudge with his foot. "Speak a word," he commanded. "Any word."

The wolf's fur bristled, but he did not move his forelegs from atop his head.

Yolotli nudged him again. "Your ears react to sound," he said. "You can hear me. Speak if you understand."

Holding his breath, Senji saw the wolf's upright ears twitch, but the beast spoke no word. He leaned in, trying to get a look at their captive's eyes through his paws. When he did catch a glimpse, he saw that they were wide and watery, darting from one animal to the next. *Like a bird with a broken wing watching predators inch closer.* Nowhere in those eyes did Senji see even a hint of comprehension.

"Nothing," he breathed. He raised his eyes to meet Yolotli's gaze. "Not a word."

"This wolf," Yolotli boomed at the crowd, "does not understand our speech!"

Murmuring swelled in the crowd, growing steadily louder until the air buzzed like the inside of a beehive. Senji sprang from the ground and alighted on Yolotli's back. He was about to ask his friend what their next step should be when a pale mustang shouldered his way to the front of the crowd and thrust his nose at the prisoner. It took Senji a moment to place him, but then the name materialized: Alonzo, partner of the Valkyrie Hlokk.

"This is not Fernão," he said. "I know Fernão well enough, have spoken with him many a time, and I tell you that this animal, though of similar stature and coloring, is not he."

Word sped rapidly through the gathered partners, bouncing from one ear to the next like an echo traveling down a long corridor:

"Fernão is gone."

"When was the last time you saw him?"

"This wolf is an imposter."

"Who is he?"

"Where is the real Fernão?"

The cacophony of voices boggled Senji's senses. Alongside those voices, his own internal voice reminded him that time was ticking away. *Delia needs me.* He hopped up Yolotli's spine until he stood on the wolf's neck.

"Can we take him, whoever he is, to the earthly plane?" Senji asked. "Maybe Georgette can communicate with him."

"Perhaps," Yolotli mused, "but I do not believe I can carry him alone, and you—forgive me, my friend—will be of limited aid in transporting a full-grown wolf through the air."

"Then we need assistance." Senji's gaze swept around the meadow. "Let's see who we can recruit."

Senji took to the air and, dipping one wing, flew in a tight circle around the babbling crowd. He let loose a wild and piercing shriek that cut through the talk like a cleaver. Countless eyes turned upward, locking on to him and tracking his movement as he swooped down and perched between the ears of the tallest horse in the crowd. The surprised Clydesdale jerked back his head, momentarily unbalancing Senji, but he righted himself quickly. Before his unwilling perch could object, he launched into a speech.

"The Valkyrie Gondol is poisoning your partners!" he bellowed. "This wolf knows her plan, but he cannot communicate with us. I have an ally who may be able to extract answers from him, but Yolotli and I cannot carry him to Earth alone. Who will help us?"

From atop the grumbling Clydesdale, Senji held his breath and scanned the crowd for any sign of a willing soul.

Fólkvangr was painfully still.

The partners stood frozen in place, their eyes glued to the ground. No one moved and no one spoke up. If not for the thump of his heart in his chest, Senji would have heard nothing at all. The surge of energy he'd felt just minutes earlier vanished and left him hollow.

When his Clydesdale perch snorted in annoyance and shook his head again, Senji jumped away, landing safely but heavily at Yolotli's side.

The wolf sighed. "Your loyalty to your partner is admirable," he said kindly, "but it is uncommon among our ilk. Do not forget that every Valkyrie in Valhalla received her commission because she died at the hands of someone here."

"You and Thrima seem to be on friendlier terms than most," Senji said.

"The *ixiptla* and I understand one another," Yolotli said. "I killed her, but I did not do so out of malice, like so many others here. She was chosen to serve as a proxy for the goddess Toci, to allow us to reenact Toci's apotheosis as a means of purifying and protecting our entire community. We were both playing our part, as our people's customs required." He looked around the field. "Most of these partners murdered their romantic partners in a jealous rage or killed their female relatives for the honor of their family name. Any man who disposes of a woman's life for such tawdry reasons must inevitably resent having to serve as her subordinate. He will not put himself on the line for the benefit of such a woman, even when the fate of the world is at stake."

Yolotli sniffed at their captive, still hunkered down in a prone position. "It would take a flock of ravens to take him to Earth," he said. "Conversely, just one more wolf, or a single horse, would do. So tell me, my friend, can you think of one?"

A thought flickered into Senji's mind. At first he rejected it as ridiculous, but the more he considered it, the more possible it seemed.

"Perhaps," he said. "Wait here."

He took flight and soared over the meadowlands and woods of Fólkvangr. The sweetness of the wind in his feathers and the lightness of his body in the air refreshed him and revived some measure of optimism in his heart. He could still save Delia. It wasn't too late.

After a sweep of the area, he zeroed in on his target. Alone beneath a tree, a painfully thin wolf sat hunched over in a crumpled position that Senji had never seen any other wolf assume.

He landed on the tree's lowest branch, just above the animal's head. As ever, the scrawny wolf stared vacantly at the ground while continuously muttering to himself.

"Giovanni," said Senji. "We need your help."

Giving no sign of having heard, Giovanni continued to feverishly recite prayers under his breath. With a sigh, Senji glided down to the ground and positioned himself directly under the wolf's nose.

"Perhaps you feel, as do the others here," he said, "that the Valkyrie you serve is not worth saving. However, in all the years I have known you, the only time I have ever heard you speak has been to pray. I hope that a man so devoted to his faith will do the right thing."

With a stuttering exhale, Giovanni fell silent. Slowly, his eyes gained focus, and for the first time, he seemed to genuinely look at Senji.

Pleased, the raven warbled softly. "Delia once told me that your partner, Rota, starved to death in your care during an exorcism—but there was no demon, only illness. So I believe I understand why you pray. It's because you failed her."

Pain flooded the wolf's watery eyes, and his ragged breaths made his prominent ribcage quake.

Senji offered a sympathetic nod. "You have another chance. Rota is in danger, along with the rest of the Valkyries. One of their own is corrupting them for unknown reasons. We have found one who can tell us her plan, but first we need to transport him to Earth. Will you help us?"

The wolf slowly straightened up until his shoulders no longer hunched. Sitting tall, his protruding ribs seemed less obvious and his scraggly fur looked fuller.

"Lucia," the wolf croaked in a rusty voice.

"Lucia?" Senji repeated. "Was that Rota's name?"

Giovanni nodded. "I can save her?"

"Yes," Senji replied, his optimism rising by the minute, "if you help us."

The last lingering fog vanished from Giovanni's eyes. With a grunt, he stood up and lifted his head high. "I will help. For Lucia."

Senji bobbed approval, grinning internally in a way his avian features could not express. *I'll save you, Delia. I promise.*

Georgette

"HI."

The cowering wolf lifted his head and looked up at her. They sat near each other in Georgette's living room on a shaggy area rug. Seated in front of him, her feet tucked back behind her and her long pink skirt spread out around her legs, she smiled politely.

"My name's Georgette," she said. "Can you understand me?"

He blinked, lifted his head a little bit into the air, and nodded.

"Can you speak?" she asked.

For a moment, he did nothing. Then, after taking a deep breath, he uttered a series of grunts and growls.

When he fell silent again, they looked at each other intently for several seconds.

After a beat, Georgette realized that he had just tried to speak, but she had not understood. She sighed and shook her head. The wolf whined, pinched his eyes shut, and hung his head low. His evident sadness pained her heart.

Senji leapt to Georgette's shoulder and peered down at the wolf. The other two Valkyrie partners, Yolotli and Giovanni, stood several feet away, conferring with each other in wolfish grumbles.

"I take it," Senji said in her ear, "that you do not understand him."

"No, I don't," she admitted.

Senji clicked his beak and shook his body into a feathery fluff. "Now what?"

Georgette looked down at the poor wolf. His belly was pressed to the floor, and his eyes were clamped shut as if he wanted to sink into the carpet and disappear. Gently, she placed her hands on the sides of his head and lifted his face. His eyes popped open and he met her gaze.

"I'm going to try to help you," she said. "I . . ." She trailed off, her lips parted and her eyes staring deep into his. Now that she was looking at him closely, she was realizing that something about this creature was not right. "You're not, like, one-hundred-percent *here*, right? I think—correct me if I'm wrong—that you might be . . . outside your body? I mean, I can touch you, so you have a body, but . . ." She searched for the right words. "I think you're a . . . ghost. Am I right?"

Slowly, the wide-eyed wolf nodded his head.

Senji warbled in surprise, and Georgette smiled at him as she rose to her feet.

"That clears up some of our questions," she said.

"But raises others," said the raven.

"So let's get some answers."

The wolf's eyes tracked her every movement as she glided to the sofa, picked up her phone, and scrolled through her contacts list until she found Nico's name. She pressed "call" and held the phone to her ear.

"Georgette!" he answered immediately. "Any news?"

"Yes, actually," she said. "Senji and Yolotli just showed up with Gondol's pretend partner."

"What?" Nico exclaimed. "So who is he?"

"I don't know yet. I need some help to figure it out. Tell me, does your aunt keep *ka* tea in stock?"

Georgette sat quietly with the three Valkyrie partners and their wolf-ghost captive as Nico carefully measured out herbs from his bag to add to the water. The teapot boiled and steamed, sending the aroma of *ka* tea floating through the apartment. Georgette inhaled the scent. It was bittersweet, with an underlying aroma of dairy and wax—rather like the stink of a cheese-scented candle.

"It's heavy on the valerian root," she said.

"Counterbalance for the mugwort," Nico said. He poured some tea into a mug and brought it to her. "Valerian root provides a grounding effect."

Georgette grimaced a bit as she took the cup, but she nodded. "I get it, but I don't need grounding."

Nico's eyebrows rose. "If your astral self drifts too far, you need something to pull you back to your body."

"I'm a witch," she reminded him before blowing the steam off the top of the mug. "A *bruja hereditaria*, remember? I don't need *ka* tea to give me magic for astral projection. I was born with magic. I just need the tea as a catalyst." She raised the mug a little until the steam misted her glasses. "I have gas in my tank. I just need a jump to get the car started."

"Right," Nico said with a nod. His expression suggested disappointment, perhaps with his own lack of knowledge. "Your magic is miles beyond mine, isn't it?"

A twang of guilt plucked at her heart. "No," she assured him. "Same neighborhood, just a different address."

Cradling the hot mug in her hands, she sipped the tea, letting its subtle energy build inside her. Nico took a seat in a nearby chair while Senji and the two wolves waited patiently across the room.

Minutes passed in tense silence before Georgette felt the shift in her power core she'd been waiting for. It was time; the necessary switch was ready to be flipped. She set down the half-empty cup and waved the strange wolf over to her.

"Stay close," she said. "I just need a minute."

Her breathing slowed and her vision went fuzzy. As she closed her eyes, the switch inside her flipped on command, and she separated into two halves. One part of her became unbearably heavy, sinking deep into the cushions of her seat. The other part grew light as a cloud and began to rise into the air.

She opened her eyes to see a silvery arm rise from her body, an ethereal twin of her living flesh. Following it, a ghostly double of her head, shoulders, hips, and legs slipped from her body as cleanly and smoothly as a dancer crossing a stage. Instead of the colorful tiered skirt and T-shirt her physical body wore, her soul body was covered only in vague clothing made of the same cloud-silk as the spirit itself. A thick silver thread, shimmery and luminous, connected her translucent soul to her unconscious body like an umbilical cord.

She knelt beside the wolf and cupped his furry face in her spirit hands for a second time as he gazed at her disembodied form in naked amazement.

"Let's try again," she said in a slightly fainter version of her voice. "What's your name?"

After a moment's hesitation, he said, "Juan Abelardo Perez."

She smiled. "Nice to meet you, Juan Abelardo."

Shock lit up his canine face, and he released his breath in a puff. His features brightened and his tail began to wag.

"Just Abelardo, Miss," he said, his voice thick with emotion. "Please."

Georgette's astral form settled into a sitting position on the rug before her guest, and she laid one hand on his shoulder.

"Tell me everything."

Words stampeded from Abelardo's mouth as if they had been lined up and waiting for exactly this moment.

"Twenty years ago," he said, "I worked as a driver for Mexico City Metrobús. One early morning, before dawn, when I went to collect my vehicle for the day, I was attacked by a stray dog. It was very big but bone-thin and staggering around like a newborn giraffe. It bit me on the arm—crunched right through my watch—and then it ran off. I went to the hospital and got the rabies shots. Everything seemed fine until one month later, when I changed for the first time."

"That must have been scary," said Georgette.

"Yes," he enthusiastically agreed. "But at the time I didn't understand what had happened. It seemed like a fever dream. I tried to forget about it and go on with my life."

"Until it happened again a month later."

"Yes. That time, I got loose in the city. I don't know how much damage I did, but I woke up the next morning with blood in my mouth. That's when the reps from Luna Gris contacted me."

"Luna Gris?" she said in surprise. "The Werewolf colony?"

He nodded. "They convinced me to move to their island. I lived there for twenty years—good, happy years."

Georgette's mind raced. Abelardo was a Werewolf. That explained why he looked like a wolf. But he was dead, right? Did Werewolf souls not regain human form after death?

Focus, she told herself. *Don't get off topic.* "How did you end up like this?"

"Like most Werewolves, I died on a full moon." Abelardo sighed, shaking his head. "No matter how healthy we try to be, our monthly transformations burn through life like a fire through kindling. When I died, I saw Santa Muerte standing over me—tall, skeletal, wearing a white robe. She pulled me out of my corpse, gestured for me to follow her . . . and then *that woman* appeared."

Though Georgette had a sneaking suspicion who he was referring to, she asked, "What woman?"

"Gondol."

Georgette felt her lips press together into a thin line and nodded. She glanced at their small audience—two wolves, one raven, and a man—before asking, "Gondol stopped Death from taking you?"

"She stepped in between my spirit and Santa Muerte and said something that sounded like gibberish to me. Holy Death faded away, leaving me behind. She cut the spirit thread that connected me to my body and led me away. When Gondol spoke again, somehow I could understand her."

"What did she say?"

"Only that I was exactly what she needed. I tried to ask what she meant, but she ignored me. Luckily for me, her partner asked the same question."

"Gondol's wolf partner?" she asked.

"Fernão," Senji interjected. "What happened to him? Where is he?"

Georgette held up a hand to stop his questions and kept her attention on Abelardo. "Fernão didn't know what she was planning?"

"Was Fernão his name?" A shiver went through Abelardo's

body, and he shook his head. "If he had known her intentions," he said in a low voice, "he would have run for his life." The fur on his back rose, and his ears flattened against his skull. "That creature's fate will haunt my dreams for eternity."

Georgette laid a spirit hand on his shoulder. "Tell me."

Abelardo took a deep breath. "She ignored pretty much everything he asked. It was clear that she held him in contempt. In fact, she never used his name. She said names are for the living and the loved, neither of which applies to him. She only called him '*bandeirante*.'"

"*Bandeirante?*" Georgette repeated. "What does that mean?"

Yolotli let out a short bark, drawing her attention. He made more noises that she didn't understand, but when he finished speaking, Senji translated.

"He says they were settlers in colonial Brazil," said the raven, "who expanded Portuguese borders and suppressed the indigenous people."

"Indigenous people like Gondol?" asked Georgette.

"I believe so," said Senji.

That tracks, she thought. To Abelardo, she said, "You said she led you away. Where did she take you?"

"At first we just flew through the air," he said. "I was confused, but there is nothing in the world like soaring through the sky! For that brief time, I was happy. When we landed . . ." His eyes widened and his lips curled back from his teeth. "When we landed, the world was on fire."

Another shiver sped along his spine, raising a line of fur from nape to tail. His eyes snapped shut and he flung his head back and forth, as if trying to shake himself free of the memory.

Georgette leaned in close and cupped his face in her hands again. "It's okay," she whispered. "You're safe. Tell me what you saw."

"Black ash," Abelardo moaned, "red flames, oozing oceans of lava. Not a speck of green or blue, no color of life. Fire as far as the eye could see. Rocks glowing from heat, a painful orange that scorched my eyes even though it didn't give off much light. The fire actually hurt." He peered deep into her eyes. "Do you know what it feels like when your soul burns? I do. There's nothing so painful as feeling the very essence of who and what you are burning away."

"That sounds terrifying," she said.

"It was." He paused, then said, "No, it *is*. She called the place Muspelheim, but . . . I know Hell when I see it."

"Muspelheim." Out of the corner of her eye, she saw her audience stiffen at the word. "Why did she take you there?"

"It wasn't for me," he said. "It was for her partner."

A knot twisted in Georgette's stomach. "What happened to Fernão in Muspelheim?"

"We landed on a tall, rocky crag, and Gondol drew her sword, raised it over her head, and waved it around. The hellfire reflected off its blade in white flashes. It lit up our location like a lighthouse. Gondol was smiling but Fernão was not. He was quiet at first but kept staring at her. Then he suddenly started shouting, furious that she wouldn't respond to his mental conversation, and demanding an explanation. She ignored him. Then"—he gulped—"the demons came."

"Demons," Georgette mumbled. "You mean Fire Giants?"

"I know what I saw!" Abelardo exclaimed. His legs shook, his teeth chattered, and his eyes filled with unwept tears. "Claws, horns, flames on their red skin. Hollow maws where their eyes should have been, as if they saw the world through darkness itself. *Madre de Dios*. I see them every time I close my eyes."

Georgette offered him gentle words and a comforting touch, but Abelardo's fear would not be soothed. His legs trembled so fiercely that he fell back on his haunches, gripping the rug beneath him with his claws.

"I was frozen," he continued. "I could do nothing but pray. Fernão was panicked and tried to run. Instead, she grabbed him and dragged him to the edge of the rock. He cried out, 'Gondol! Gondol, stop!' And she said, 'That's not my name.'"

"Not her name?" Georgette frowned. "But . . . it *was* Gondol, right?"

Abelardo hunkered down, belly to the floor, and drew deep, shaky breaths. "She said, 'That's the name Valhalla gave me after you killed me. After you destroyed my village, sold my family to sugar plantations, spent months using me for your pleasure, and then watched me die of the smallpox you gave me. You did all that to me. So tell me, *bandeirante*, what is my name?'" He closed his eyes, and pinprick tears leaked from their edges. "Fernão said nothing. And Gondol did not seem surprised."

After a moment of quiet, Georgette asked, "Did she kill him?"

"Worse," Abelardo replied. "She threw him to the demons, and they took him away." He opened his eyes and looked up at her. The bottomless well of fear in his eyes was deep enough to drown in. "I lost sight of him almost at once, but his screams . . . My God, his screams! I will never escape that sound. But Gondol . . . the smile never left her face."

"She threw Fernão into Muspelheim." Georgette spoke not just to relay the information to her horrified guests but also to make Abelardo's story real. Gondol had given her partner to Fire Giants—Valhalla's sworn enemies, the monstrous soldiers of Muspelheim that strove to conquer any realm they could reach. She refocused on Abelardo. "I'm sorry," she whispered.

"I wish I could take that memory away from you. If you were still a living human, I could use magic to do that but—"

"No," he interrupted. "No, I don't believe anything in Heaven or on Earth could remove that memory from my brain."

"I'm so sorry," she said.

With great effort, Abelardo slowed his breathing and pushed himself to a sitting position. "I don't remember much of what else happened that night. I was a mess of nerves. But I remember the demons giving something to Gondol, something small, before she grabbed me and flew us out of that hellscape. Soon, we were soaring through an empty gray expanse. I swear the gray mist was reaching for me with long, damp fingers, like it wanted to pull me into nothingness. It made my skin crawl."

"Where was this?"

"I don't know. It seemed impossibly vast, and we were the only ones traveling past it."

"An empty expanse with gray mist that tried to pull you in." Georgette glanced at Senji. "Does that mean something to you?"

"Niflheim," the raven replied. "The realm of the dead. The mist tries to pull in wayward spirits." He flapped his wings against his body and irritably clacked his beak. "Clever of Gondol to take that route to Muspelheim. Because Valkyries are spirits themselves, they avoid any route that passes Niflheim. Valhalla does not monitor that path."

Georgette returned her attention to Abelardo, asking, "Did she bring you past that mist every time?"

"She did not travel with me after that first time," said Abelardo. "She ordered me to mark the route we took so I could make the trip alone. If I refused, she said, she would toss me into Muspelheim with the *bandeirante*."

"So your choice was to obey Gondol or be sent to Hell?"

He nodded, a fresh tear trickling down his snout. "I begged her to let me go, but she paid me no more mind than she had her discarded partner. As we flew, she pulled a white vial from her robes, popped off the stopper, and splashed a drop of something into my mouth. The liquid was so cold it burned all the way down my throat. In seconds, my dead heart started beating. I gasped and my lungs filled with air. Gondol tossed another drop into my open mouth, and my spirit grew skin, fur, muscle, and bone. That liquid—the Eitr—brought me back to life. But . . . it wasn't just me."

A long-missing puzzle piece suddenly clicked into place in Georgette's mind. "The Eitr she gave you brought back your body but also the Werewolf infection," she deduced. "And you said you died on a full moon night." She turned toward Nico, who was staring at her in rapt attention. "That must have been the night Audrey was bitten. By him." She snapped her eyes back to Abelardo. "She dropped you on Earth that night? Why?"

Abelardo cringed, his expression full of shame. "At some point, Gondol flew us close to Earth. It was the first time in twenty years that I had smelled uninfected humans, and when that scent hit my nose, the virus inside me went crazy. My memory fades after that, but I think I started thrashing around and Gondol lost her grip on me. I think I fell out of the sky. The next thing I remember was wandering unfamiliar streets after sunrise, covered in blood. That's when Gondol found me." He turned his face away, ears laid back. "I'm ashamed that I infected someone. I removed myself from human society for twenty years to avoid that very thing. If my apology would mean anything to this Audrey, please tell her how sorry I am."

Georgette nodded and promised that she would. She didn't think Audrey would accept such an apology, but Abelardo probably knew that. He had once been in her shoes and knew how it felt to be in her position.

"Gondol was furious about my escape," he continued, "but as it turned out, my rampage gave her the opportunity she had been waiting for."

"Valhalla ordered a Wild Hunt," said Georgette, "and that led to the never-ending party."

"Since then, I've fetched Eitr for her many times."

"Well, not anymore," Georgette told him. "Gondol's not getting any more Eitr from you. You're free of her."

Now, at last, some of the tension began to melt out of Abelardo's body. His fur lay flat, and his limbs no longer shook. A smile briefly crossed Georgette's face but was dashed when Senji squawked loudly, shattering the silence in the room.

"Ask him what Gondol wants," he urged her. "We need to know why she's doing this."

Though reluctant to disrupt Abelardo's newfound peace, Georgette asked him, "Do you know what Gondol hopes to get out of all this?"

"Oh yes," he muttered. "She has ranted about it many times. She feels she was cheated. She wants the human life she was robbed of by Fernão. She knows that what she's doing could end with Muspelheim eventually razing the Earth, but she doesn't care. She wants those stolen years so badly she's willing to sacrifice everything to get them. Even all of humanity."

A shudder rippled through Abelardo. With a heavy sigh, he closed his eyes, sank to the floor, and flopped onto his side. With his story finally told, all energy and fear seemed to leave his body. Within seconds, he was asleep.

Georgette gathered her astral form above her sleeping body and allowed her silvery spirit to pour back into her flesh. Her two halves reunited, her eyes slowly fluttered open and scanned the room. Her gaze came to rest on Nico, who was nervously tapping his fingers against his knees, and then on the Valkyrie partners, who stood staring back at her in worried expectation. She had no idea what she could say to them that would improve the situation. They now knew what Gondol was doing and why she was doing it, but how much help did that information provide? They still didn't know how to stop her or how to bring the Valkyries to their senses. Despite everything they had learned, they were really no closer to saving the world than they had been yesterday.

Before the witch could think of anything to say, Senji and the two partner wolves jolted as if electrified. As one, their heads swung toward the window, and they leapt to their feet with fur and feathers bristled. Georgette squinted in confusion—but then she felt it. The air had grown thick with power, as if a storm was seconds away from cloudburst. Nico looked confused, but Georgette locked her eyes on the window; this could mean only one thing.

The sky outside had grown dark in the blink of an eye. Black clouds swirled like soup in a cauldron above the city. Thunder rumbled in time with lightning, flickering between the clouds, and a rough wind rattled the window glass. Electricity crackled through the hairs on Georgette's arms.

Nico strode across the room and peered out into the dark city. "Is that what I think it is?"

"Yeah," said Georgette. She joined him at the window, her voice trembling with unease and despair. "It's the Wild Hunt."

Mei-Xing

FROM THE MOMENT SHE SAT DOWN IN THE SILVER OAKS Country Club restaurant, Mei-Xing dissociated herself from the situation. Jin was seated next to her, a drink in his hand and a smile on his face as his parents glared at him from across the table. Mr. Li had said very little throughout dinner aside from grumbling about pain in his neck and jaw, but Mrs. Li had been quite vocal with her opinions. A steady flow of wine kept Mei-Xing separated from the drama, wrapping her in a cloud of dull disinterest that blotted out the world. Nothing the Lis said could claim her attention.

Until her phone buzzed.

When Mei-Xing pulled out the phone, she heard Mrs. Li huff a harsh breath. "This one ignores us all evening," she sniped, "and now she's looking at her phone."

Mei-Xing didn't recognize the number, but that was not surprising. The only number saved in the contacts was Jin's. She was about to hit the decline button, but then she heard Jin chortling under his breath. Shooting him a quick glance, she saw that he was grinning from ear to ear at the sight of his mother's scathing fury—and the sight brought her crashing back to reality. No one here liked her or desired her company. Without a grove to embrace her, she was a lonely weed growing through a concrete crack.

Standing up, she said, "I have to take this." Before any of the Li family could react, she trotted out of the club's dining hall, weaving her way around the waitstaff and other patrons. She didn't stop until she ducked through an outer door and the wind hit her face. The warm, blustery breath of nature sobered her a bit, and she leaned against a nearby wall with a sigh of relief, then pressed the accept button and held the phone to her ear. "Hello?"

"Mei!"

The sound of Georgette's voice triggered a series of emotions that quickly collapsed into each other. Love, confusion, annoyance, anger, sadness, despair . . . Within seconds, the feelings rose, fell, and settled over her like frost on the morning field. Numb once again, she flatly replied, "Yes?"

"Mei, look at the sky! That's not a storm, it's the second Wild Hunt. Please, please, find a safe place to hunker down until the Valkyries pass."

She lifted her gaze. Overhead, dark, churning thunderheads expanded across the sky, and blazes of lightning flamed out from behind the blackness. Curious, she slipped off one shoe and placed her bare foot on the manicured lawn. A slight charge sizzled up from her toes, warning her of the electrical buildup. Through her drunkenness, she managed to register that the storm was a serious threat. If she needed to "hunker down," she definitely did not want to do so at this damn country club.

"Where?" she asked, her voice flatter than she meant it to be.

"Can you get home?"

"Are you home?"

"No. I have to get to Nocturne. We don't know if the Valkyries are still looking for a Werewolf or not. I need to be close to Audrey just in case they're hunting for her."

You want me to go home but you're going to Nocturne. Mei-Xing's already muted mood dimmed. *My grove should never isolate me in a storm.*

"Mei? Are you there?" Georgette's voice crackled through the phone, half of the syllables swallowed by static. "Please . . . home, it's . . . Hunt. I don't . . . maybe . . . Mei? Mei-Xing? Where—"

With a sharp click, the line went dead. Mei-Xing listened to the silence until the wind began to howl and whip the loose material of her dress all around. She paused and gauged the situation. *The storm isn't as close as it appears, but it's gearing up to be a monster.* She slid her foot back into her shoe and pondered her next move.

"Well," a voice as smooth and noxious as oil poured into her ear, "my father just told my mother that his chest hurts, so they're going home." Jin Li stepped up beside her and, as usual, flopped an uninvited arm around her shoulders. "I guess we're all finished here."

"Fine," she said, shrugging off his arm. "Take me home."

"Home? Nah, it's still early." He returned his arm to her shoulders and gave her a squeeze. "Let's go out!"

The too-big smile on his face told her that he still expected to be entertained and had no intention of taking her home until that expectation was met. Mei-Xing had no car and no money to pay for a ride, and Silver Oaks was too far from downtown for her to walk. She ought to call Georgette back, ask her friend to send an Uber . . . but no. *My grove no longer embraces me, so I must stop reaching for them.*

"There's a storm coming," she said, pointing upward. "It is a bad night to be out."

"At home or at a club, we'll be inside either way." He leaned his head toward hers and teased, "I won't let the big bad storm get you."

"Don't touch me!" She pushed him away. "I don't like you."

He laughed as he always did when she rebuked him, as if her words were a joke and her boundaries mere suggestions that he was free to ignore. Mei-Xing hated that laugh even more than she hated the man himself.

"I'll get the valet to bring my car around front," he told her. "We'll hit the city, check out some clubs."

A venomous retort sprang to her tongue, but then she had a sudden thought. "Nocturne," she said abruptly. "Club Nocturne."

Surprise lit up his features. "Why there?"

"I have friends . . . I know people who work there."

He shrugged. "Okay. I haven't been there since the manager wouldn't approve me for a VIP room"—he scowled at the memory—"but we can pop in there before jumping to the next place."

Jin walked off a few steps to flag down a country club employee, briefly leaving Mei-Xing alone to question the workings of her own mind.

Why did I suggest Nocturne? Why . . . I know why. I don't want to leave my grove. Georgette cared enough to warn me about the Wild Hunt. Maybe my bond with my grove can be saved. Maybe I don't have to leave. Or . . . maybe I'm just craving interaction with my own kind. Maybe I need to re-immerse myself in the Fae world.

Maybe I'm just lonely.

Kazimiera

BLOOD DRIBBLED DOWN KAZIMIERA'S CHIN AS SHE RIPPED fistfuls of meat from her latest catch and shoved them into her maw. As her stomach filled, her feral self grew still, retreating to the recesses of her mind like a caged animal dragging its meal into the corner to growl over it in peace. A familiar calm came over her, one she knew would be short-lived and unsatisfying.

Swallowing the flesh and blood, Kazimiera rubbed her eyes and took her first clear look at her kill. A young woman, maybe twenty-five, with dyed red hair, acrylic nails, and a tattoo of a green heart between her breasts. Her blood was tart on Kazi's tongue, suggestive of long-term substance abuse. The obsessive quest for a fix certainly explained why she would wander around lonely areas of a city at night with such a storm brewing.

Storm?

The Vampire raised her cat-like eyes to the sky and confirmed that a thick blanket of black clouds hung low over the city. Suspicious, she squinted. Her powerful night vision pierced the darkness and broke through layers of magic. Valkyries, too many to count. Astride their crazed, horse-like beasts, they stampeded across the sky, waving their weapons and screaming wildly. It should have been terrifying, but Kazi found the sight of it all no more than a pesky annoyance. Though a Wild Hunt posed a serious threat to most, for her it meant nothing more than the end of her hunt.

Nocturne, she thought, her human consciousness asserting itself over its monstrous other half. *Wait out the storm at Nocturne.*

She irritably scooped up the remains of her kill and began trotting back to the club. Raindrops, fat and heavy, began to fall from the embattled heavens, quickly evolving from a light splattering to a rampant downpour. Within seconds, Kazimiera was drenched. The flaccid limbs in her arms jiggled against her body as she picked up the pace. At a full-out run, she had to grip the corpse tightly to keep loose organs from bouncing out of the gaping hole in the torso.

I can finish eating this in my office, she told herself as her bare feet splashed through freshly formed puddles. *It's less than I usually eat in a night these days, but if I eat it slowly, maybe it will keep me sated until the storm passes.*

If it didn't . . . well, surely there was someone in her club who could disappear and not be missed.

Ishak

ISHAK WAS RELAXING IN BED, AN OPEN BOOK IN HIS HANDS, when he received the dreaded text from Georgette: *Second Wild Hunt incoming.* His eyes immediately darted to Ziya, asleep in her crib next to him. They had known another Hunt was coming, and he had felt prepared for it, but seeing the words now sent a jolt of paternal fear through his racing heart. Until he became a father, Ishak had no idea what a frightful place the world was.

A knock on his apartment's front door forced him out of bed. After slipping quietly around Ziya and closing the bedroom door, he walked toward the entrance. Before even opening the door, he identified the person on the other side of the door by their scent. *Erskine.*

The Selkie, shirtless and shoeless as he often was, stood in the hallway sporting a nervous expression. Shoving his long hair back over his shoulder, he peered at Ishak through watery blue eyes.

"We have a problem," he said. "One of the customers has been . . . too forward with the female staff."

Ishak sighed. "Where?"

"Third floor."

"A VIP?"

"No." Erskine drummed his fingers against his thigh. "In fact," he said with a grimace, "he's on Kazi's blacklist."

Ishak was surprised that the Nocturne Fae would admit a banned person into a VIP room. But more to the point, he was deeply confused as to why Erskine was coming to him with this issue. "Have you spoken to Georgette?"

"Ah," Erskine said. "No. Georgette is doing a lot already. And now the Wild Hunt is starting again. We're sorry to ask you, but perhaps you could step in? Aside from Kazi and Georgette, you are the one in the best position to assert authority."

Ishak's eyebrows leapt up his forehead. Authority? That was not a word he would apply to himself within Nocturne. However, upon reflection, it made sense. He was not beholden to the building's spells or to Kazi herself. And it filled him with pride that his new community trusted him. He wanted to be worthy of their confidence.

"Why was a blacklisted guest allowed into a VIP room?" he asked.

"Well, only one of them is blacklisted. The other . . . that's complicated."

"What do you mean?"

"It's just . . ." Erskine's face scrunched up in frustration, and he gestured with both hands like a young child trying to snatch flies out of the air. Knowing how scatterbrained Erskine could be, Ishak wondered if the Selkie was trying to grab and hold on to a single thought. "If we kick him out, we'll have to kick her out too, and no one wants to do that."

"Her?"

Erskine offered Ishak a smile that came across as both feeble and confused.

"Mei-Xing."

Neil

UPON ENTERING NOCTURNE, NEIL RAKED BACK HIS rain-drenched hair and began working his way through the tight crowd. Nocturne was hopping tonight, pulsating with live music and a hundred human voices all wrapped up in perfectly balanced darkness and artificial glow. It took him a few minutes to elbow his way through the noisy crowd, but before long he made his way to the stairwell at the back of the room.

Neil shot off a text to Georgette to ask where she was as he started to climb the stairs. When he was halfway between the second and third floors, the door just above him opened and Ishak stepped through. Pleasantly surprised, Neil raised a hand in greeting.

"Hey," he called out, coming to a stop on the mid-floor landing. "Nice to see you."

Ishak met his gaze and nodded in a friendly but distracted sort of way. "And you," he said, slowly descending the steps. Several times, he turned his head to cast worried glances at the third-floor door before coming to a stop on the landing by Neil and offering him a hand.

As Neil returned the handshake, he asked, "Have you seen Georgette?"

"She is here, there, and everywhere," Ishak told him with a brief smile. "Although she has already checked the strength of the magic that protects this building many times, she is going from floor to floor checking it again. When it comes to the well-being of those living here, your woman is tireless."

My woman. Neil loved the sound of that.

"Something on your mind?" he asked when the Bultungin glanced back at the door yet again. "You look worried."

"Not for Georgette," Ishak quickly assured him. "It's . . . I've just seen Mei-Xing."

"Really?" Georgette hadn't said Mei-Xing would be here tonight. It struck Neil as the sort of thing she would mention. "Where is she?"

"In a VIP room with a man." Ishak's lip rippled slightly and his nostrils flared. "The man had an arm around her and was pushing drinks on her. She seemed unhappy."

Understanding sank into Neil's gut. "Asian guy?" he asked, already knowing the answer. "Kinda skinny, expensive clothes, low-key acts like he's better than everyone in the room?"

Ishak raised an eyebrow. "Yes. You know him?"

"I work with him."

"Then you can vouch for him?"

Neil only stared back blankly in response.

"The employees told me that he's blacklisted, but they decided to let him in tonight because Mei-Xing is with him," Ishak said. "He has been a bit inappropriate with the staff, and now they are trying to decide if they should blacklist him again. But if you can vouch for him—"

"No," Neil said firmly. "I won't vouch for the guy. He's a jackass. But," he reluctantly added, "I don't want to kick anyone out in the storm. And Georgette won't want to stir up any drama for Mei-Xing. They haven't been on the best of terms lately."

Ishak exhaled slowly. "Well," he said, "as long as they are in the VIP room, the employees will keep the jackass under control." He nodded at the descending stairs. "The VIP Fae have asked me to relay some food orders to the restaurant kitchen and also to visit Miss Collins. Apparently, Georgette warned the Werewolf to stay in the basement until the danger of the Wild Hunt has passed, and none of the staff have had time to check on her."

"Sounds like they've put you to work," said Neil. "Do you need a hand?"

"No, thank you," Ishak replied with a polite smile. "I'm happy to help my neighbors. However, I have told them that once I've completed these chores, I will be returning to my apartment to be with my daughter. Erskine was kind enough to offer to watch her for a while, but he has a short attention span and I want to relieve him soon." He started to step away, then stopped and looked at Neil. "If you see Georgette before I do, please tell her that Mei-Xing is here."

Ishak trotted off down the steps and soon disappeared from sight, but Neil stayed on the landing. It had never sat well with him that Mei-Xing was spending so much time with Jin when she so clearly disliked him. Georgette, whose attention had been pulled in too many directions to count in recent weeks, chalked it up to Nymph hormones, seasonal depression, and other excuses—but he didn't know what to make of it all. He only knew that the woman he loved was under an immense amount of stress and her best friend wasn't helping.

A text message alert dinged, startling him. He fished his phone out of his pocket and read Georgette's text. *Sorry, crazy busy! I'm in the security office. Come see me?*

He smiled at the invitation. Thoughts of his girlfriend filled his mind, burying his vague misgivings, and he began to climb the steps.

Mei-Xing

ENTANGLED IN AN UNEASY SLEEP, MEI-XING DRIFTED through strange dreams—a discordant medley of fantasy, memory, and distant sounds. Her awareness rose and fell in waves like a stormy ocean; one moment, she was deeply submerged in sleep, only to bob to the surface a moment later, tantalizingly close to consciousness. In those short seconds when her mind approached the waking world, she could feel her body—the heaviness of her limbs, the itchiness of the buds on her chest, and . . .

Pain.

She sank into a sleepy half memory of cuddling in her mother's lap during a summer thunderstorm and felt the atmospheric weight of warm mist on her skin. Rising close to consciousness again, she heard a thunderstorm, just like in her dream. Worse, the pressure on her chest and torso remained.

Pain.

Unmeasured time passed as her consciousness seesawed up and down, but throughout it all the pain continued—tearing, pushing, burning. Mei-Xing fought to open her eyes but found her eyelids would not obey. Her body was much too heavy; it was as if she had been buried in sand.

Pain.

With an effort, she pulled on her *Hathiya* brand. Immediately, a rush of energy flowed into her body, banishing sleep at last. As her senses cleared, she finally managed to open her eyes but saw only darkness.

And the pain—splitting her in half—didn't stop.

She finally understood that something was on top of her, pinning her down. She tried to lift a hand to push it away but her arm wouldn't move. There was a hand clamped over her wrist. She tried to shout, but all that came out was a groan. The pain was unbearable.

Stop! Stop!

In a whoosh, the pressure holding her down vanished, and the pain instantly diminished to an ache. Mei-Xing sat up and discovered she was not on the floor but rather a desk. The room was still dark, but she could see that her glamour was intact. Her dress, on the other hand, had a rip in the skirt and was bunched up over her thighs. As she shifted her weight, she felt the pain again radiating through her body from between her legs. Now nursing an alarming suspicion, she stared across the dark room and managed to make out two shadowy figures against the far wall.

Mei-Xing's trembling fingers found a lamp on the desktop and flipped it on. The moment the lamp's dim light filled the room, one of the dark figures jerked its head upward, swung around, and locked on to her with a sickly green glow in its eyes.

Mei-Xing recoiled. Fresh blood dripped from the jagged rows of teeth in the Vampire's unhinged jaw. Kazimiera turned and lowered her hungry mouth to the second figure on the floor. Just before the Vampire's head obscured her view, Mei-Xing saw the other figure's pallid face: Jin.

He didn't move or make a sound as Kazimiera drank his blood; his hands lay limp at his sides, and his legs were stretched out before him. His pants were down around his ankles.

As the Vampire continued to feed, Mei-Xing slid backward, inching away from them, and scanned her surroundings. This was Kazimiera's office. She didn't remember coming in here; her sober memories faded out while they were still in the VIP room. Jin had handed her glass after glass of alcohol, his laughing demands of "Try this!" growing progressively slurred as the night wore on. After that, she could recall nothing until waking up on Kazimiera's desk . . . pinned beneath Jin.

Revulsion wormed through her skin and burrowed into her core. She swiped at her arms and legs, but she couldn't wipe away his touch. The ache between her legs flared up as she moved. Feeling exposed, she hurriedly pulled her dress down to cover her thighs, slid off Kazimiera's desk, and darted toward the office door.

Before she could exit, pink-and-white petals suddenly fluttered down around her.

Startled, she stopped in her tracks and put a hand to her chest, feeling through her glamour to find her buds. They had blossomed into star-shaped flowers that were already beginning to wilt. The implications of this twisted in Mei-Xing's stomach. The strength left her knees and she sank to the floor.

You dragged me out so many times, she silently cursed Jin. *So many nights, so much wine . . . why tonight? Why did you have to do this appalling thing right at the moment I bloomed?*

The office door suddenly flew open, casting a ray of bright light into the room. Georgette rushed inside, out of breath.

"What happened?!" she exclaimed, dropping to her knees beside Mei-Xing. "I felt you pull on the brand." She cupped Mei-Xing's cheeks in her hands. "Are you okay?"

Before Mei-Xing could speak, Neil burst into the room. His gaze darted first to the two girls on the floor and then to the grisly activity taking place deeper in the office. The light from the hallway did little to illuminate the truth of what was happening as the Vampire and Jin were still mostly in the shadows.

Neil reached for the overhead light switch.

When the room lit up, Kazimiera reared back from Jin with her hands over her eyes, her fang-filled jaw still unhinged and dripping fresh blood down her chest. Neil yelped at the sight and froze where he stood, staring at the Vampire in primal horror.

Jin groaned; then a frail breath rattled through his bloody throat.

Mei-Xing's eyes were riveted by the scene until she heard Georgette let out a soft gasp. Glancing at the witch, Mei-Xing saw her fingers outstretched toward the petals on the floor.

"Oh, Mei," her friend whispered, "what happened?" Her hands flew to Mei-Xing's face again, and this time, Mei-Xing met her gaze. Years of sisterly friendship asserted themselves in that moment, and an unspoken explanation passed between them. Georgette's eyes filled with comprehension and tears. "That bastard," she muttered, throwing her arms around her friend.

Mei-Xing stiffened for a moment but then, quite unexpectedly, melted. Hot tears leaked from her eyes as she embraced her best friend. For a short minute that felt like a long night, they cried together while wrapped in each other's arms.

"Holy crap," she heard Neil exclaim. "That's Jin."

Through blurry vision, Mei-Xing saw Neil snap out of his shock and hurry toward the bleeding man. Kazimiera hissed and with a casual swipe of her arm hurled Neil across the room. He struck the far wall with a grunt before landing in a heap on the floor.

Still gripping Mei-Xing with one arm, Georgette reached toward her boyfriend, but he held up a hand.

"I'm fine," he panted. "Jin's alive. Stop her!"

The urgency in his voice was galvanizing—even to Mei-Xing, who had no desire to help Jin see another day. Georgette jumped to her feet, but then, to Mei-Xing's relief and delight, she bent down to hug her friend once more.

"Don't move," she said. "I'll be right back."

As Kazimiera lowered her jaws toward Jin's bleeding throat once again, Georgette lunged and shoved her, pushing her backward onto the floor. "Odhran!" the witch shrieked toward the hallway. "Louis!"

Down on all fours, Kazimiera snarled and crept toward Georgette, her reflective eyes all afire with hunger and rage. Mei-Xing felt a subtle shift in the air as her friend summoned ethereal power for a spell.

"Odhran! Louis!" Georgette screamed again as her fingers performed a series of distinct movements.

Mei-Xing felt a hand on her shoulder. She glanced over to see Neil crouched next to her.

"You okay?" he asked.

She shook her head and made no attempt to wipe the tears from her face.

Neil's expression tightened and he looked away. "Sorry," he said. "Stupid question." He ran a hand over his face and mumbled, "I knew Jin was an asshole but I didn't think . . . God, I'm so sorry."

With a roar, Kazimiera sprang at Georgette with horrifying speed—then froze in the air mid-leap, perfectly still, with jaws agape and claw-like nails extended, as if she had become a photographic image captured by a camera lens.

Georgette held her hands in the air, muscles trembling

with sustained effort, as if the Vampire's lack of movement was directly tied to her own.

Odhran the Dullahan bolted into the room clutching his severed head under his arm, followed shortly by Louis the Blemmye, who panted heavily through the large mouth in his stomach. Georgette breathed a sigh of relief, though she took great care not to move her hands.

"Him," she said, nodding at Jin Li. "Take him out of here and try to help him."

"Take him . . . where?" asked Louis, his large eyes, positioned just in front of his shoulders, wide at the sight of blood.

"I don't know!" Georgette shouted. "Please, just get him away from Kazi!"

Louis hurried to obey. Jin—his face pale and drawn above his oozing red throat—moaned as the Blemmye scooped him up and carried him away.

The sight of Jin's blood gave Mei-Xing some satisfaction, but then she glanced down at herself with a look of disgust. The glamour that hid her true form, the false appearance that had appealed to such an odious man—she couldn't stand it a moment longer. She dropped the glamour. Bark instead of skin, grass instead of hair . . . and clearly visible pink-and-white blossoms spread across her chest and shoulders. Pressing one mossy hand over them, she felt the petals dropping away through her fingers.

"Odhran," Georgette said, her words growing strained, "is there anywhere we can put Kazi where she won't be a danger to anyone until she calms down?"

"Possibly the basement," the Dullahan rumbled. "The same room we outfitted for the Werewolf. But," he added, "Audrey is currently in there. Also, that room is three floors down and we have a packed house."

"Okay." Georgette sighed. "Get someone to clear the stairwell, and send someone else to tell Audrey that she'll have to move."

"What about the Hunt?"

"One crisis at a time!" she said through clenched teeth. "Hurry! I can't hold her forever!"

Odhran vanished into the hallway. Mei-Xing vaguely heard him calling out to various employees for assistance, but she didn't pay much attention. While her eyes tracked Georgette's struggle to maintain the freezing spell, her mind forcefully took her back to the last time her buds had bloomed. To her final days with her birth grove. To the tiny sprout she was unable—unwilling—to nurture. Could she go through that again? Could she be a parent to another child created against her will? Did she want to be? The thought made her lightheaded.

"Not alone," she whispered. Still clutching at her chest, she subconsciously began to rock back and forth. "I can't do it alone."

"Shh, take it easy," said Neil. He placed his hands on her shoulders and squeezed gently. "You're not alone."

"Who do I have?" she moaned. "Georgette was my grove, but now she's with you."

For a moment Neil fell silent, his hands still resting on her shoulders. Then, to her surprise, he chuckled. "You're not alone," he repeated. "I know I've taken up a lot of Georgette's time lately, but I promise, she's still your grove. She's told me all about how you two met and what being a part of a grove means. She said it's more than best friends, even more than family in some ways." He smiled kindly at her, and Mei-Xing suddenly realized that he was looking at her unglamoured, inhuman form without a hint of fear.

"I knew early on that the two of you were a package deal. Georgette's said multiple times that you and she are"—he paused, seeming to search for the right words—"connected by roots and rain."

Mei-Xing stared at him, stunned. The correct phrase was "bound by root and rain," but Neil clearly understood the meaning. Georgette had held true to their grove bonds all this time.

"In fact," he broke into her thoughts, "I really should have spoken to you sooner. I'm the newcomer, so I'm supposed to ask your permission to join the grove, right? I'm supposed to . . ." After a moment's thought, he gave a decisive nod, held out an open hand to her, and said, "I want to live among you. May I drink from your water?"

"I . . ." she trailed off. She didn't know how to respond or even how to feel. The request wasn't quite right and was meant to be said as part of a ceremony, but she saw the sincerity behind it. It could have come from the mouth of a Nymph or Spirit wishing to settle among any established grove. Neil was human. This was distinctly unhuman-like behavior. And it filled her with hope.

When she opened her mouth again, the whisper that left her lips seemed to do so of its own free will. "You won't take her away?"

He grinned, eyes sparkling. "I don't think there's anyone in the world with the power to take Georgette away from you."

New tears welled up in Mei-Xing's eyes as the weight of weeks and months lifted from her tired shoulders. She slipped her hand into Neil's, bark on flesh, and gave it a squeeze.

"We have water to share," she said, "and we invite you to partake."

Georgette

THE MAGIC HOLDING KAZIMIERA IN PLACE WAS RATHER slipshod, hastily constructed from some loose ethereal threads Georgette had yanked from the larger fabric of spells woven throughout the building. When Kazi sprang at her, she had instinctively summoned a handful of structural threads, linked them to the ends of her fingers, and propelled them at the Vampire. The threads had slid smoothly into Kazimiera's body, hardened, and locked her muscles in place.

Finding the threads had been easy, given that Georgette was the one who'd cast the spells in the first place. She knew what each otherworldly strand did, where it connected to the building itself, and how it interlocked with the larger tapestry of magic. But the ligatures keeping Kazi still were linked directly to Georgette's fingertips, feeding off of her own energy. It was exhausting. And Kazi, though unable to move, fought against the magic like a vicious dog at the end of a leash. Through their forced connection, Georgette could feel the Vampire clenching every muscle. And though she tried not to look at them, she could feel her eyes blazing into her.

Hurry, Odhran, she silently urged the Dullahan as she felt her magic reserves trickling away. *I can't hold her much longer!*

Kazi's body jerked, her outstretched arms twitching and her claw-like fingers flexed. The sudden movement made

Georgette gasp, but she surged more of her dwindling strength into her spell and froze the Vampire again.

Georgette's heart thumped in her chest, driven to painful exertion by fear. To her horror, she saw Kazi's unhinged jaw draw upward—her face was contorting into a primal snarl. The strand connected to Georgette's left pinky finger trembled and snapped, the magic from which it had been formed dissolving into nothing as the Vampire's right leg lurched forward.

Odhran! she screamed inside her head. *Where are you?!*

Two more threads broke, loosing one of Kazi's arms. She swiped at Georgette with so much force that had Georgette not been just beyond the reach of those pointed nails, she would have been ripped to shreds.

Her hands shaking, Georgette fought the urge to leap backward as her control of Kazi's movements waned. *I'm out of time!*

Another strand broke. With her mouth freed, a red-eyed Kazi opened her jaw to its full extension and shrieked like a madwoman. The stench of blood and rot on the Vampire's breath assailed Georgette's nose as the inhuman scream shook her ears. In that moment, she felt herself face-to-face with Death itself.

She reacted instinctively. She reached through her *Hathiya* brand—and pulled a huge amount of magic into her body.

Immediately reinvigorated, she effortlessly expanded her spell to bind Kazi's limbs and slam her to the blood-stained ground. Summoning more power from both her newly refilled core and the interwoven spells surrounding her, she froze up the Vampire's muscles again and this time bound the ends of the threads to the floor. Now, instead of straining against Georgette's bodily reserves of energy, Kazi would have to fight the hundreds of interlocked spells that held the building together—leaving Georgette's hands free to help move her to a secure place.

Georgette shook the tension out of her arms. She felt better than she had all evening, maybe all week. Her entire body felt energized, like her muscles were so juiced with magic that she might float up to the ceiling. She looked down at her hands—and saw a silvery glow coating her skin. She stared, puzzled. Eerie, pale light surrounded her as if it was leaking from her very pores. "The hell?" she murmured.

Turning around, she saw Mei-Xing—human glamour gone—holding tight to Neil. The Nymph, cradled in Neil's arms, looked half asleep and quite peaceful, considering the horror she had endured that night. Looking at Georgette with a quizzical expression on his face, Neil opened his mouth to speak—but before he could, the room suddenly fell deathly still.

The hair on Georgette's arms stood on end. It took her a moment to realize that the silence stemmed from the fact that the thunderstorm had abruptly stopped. At first she thought the Wild Hunt must have moved on, but then the truth struck her head-on. She looked at her silvery hands again with wide, horror-stricken eyes.

"Oh no," she whispered.

The power surging through her body, the energy she had drawn through the brand, was Valkyrie magic. In her moment of panic, Georgette had stolen a massive amount of power from Delia.

The Wild Hunt had not ended. It had found a target.

The Eitr-crazed Valkyries had sensed the presence of Valhalla magic in a place where it should not be, and now they were on their way to seize it.

Delia

THE NUCKELAVEE THAT CARRIED DELIA THROUGH THE sky, rolling over thunderheads on lightning-laced hooves, tossed its head and kicked out its hind feet every few steps. Its muscles, linked to Delia's legs by its yellow veins, were tense and twitching. Every Nuckelavee on this Wild Hunt was bucking, gnashing its teeth, or shrieking as if wounded. But Delia felt only a vague unease about the Nuckelavees' uncharacteristic behavior. All she cared about was the Wild Hunt.

The storm they rode over the Bay Area pulsed with feral power. The clouds that suffocated the sky were pure black, so loaded with rain and rage that they seemed ready to explode. Delia's fellow Valkyries wailed wordless screams that sounded to her more like the cheers of Mardi Gras revelers than the battle cries of warriors.

As the fierce wind carried them ever closer to the city lights below, Delia's Nuckelavee slowed and fell behind the others. From the back of the group, she saw how sloppy the others appeared, flailing their arms about like children on a carnival ride. Some part of her mind noticed that she and her sisters had ridden into the storm without their armor, but the heady intoxication of the Wild Hunt dowsed her worry. She urged her beast forward to catch up with the group.

A dark flutter zipped past her eyes, whisked away by the swirling wind as quickly as it appeared. She ignored it, but the flutter soon returned, and this time it grabbed on to her, seizing some of her unbound hair in its talons.

"Delia!" the raven shrieked, his voice nearly swallowed by the storm. "What are you doing?"

She swung her arm at the bird, but her aim was poor. With irritation, she noticed that the pack of Valkyries had pulled even farther ahead of her.

"Delia!" the raven screamed again. He had somehow gotten to her shoulder and was digging his claws into her skin. "Delia, you have to stop this!" he bellowed into her ear. "Turn back!" She swiped at him, but he snapped at her fingers to ward away her hand. His sharp beak drew blood. "Stop, Delia! Don't you know me?"

"Stupid bird!" she sputtered as she tried to shake him off. "Go away!"

The razor-point claws clinging to Delia's shoulder tightened, and he let out a strangled warble that sounded like annoyance but also pain. "Delia!" he cried. "Gondol has poisoned you! She has poisoned you all with Eitr! Where is Gondol now?"

Gondol. The name slipped through the haze that kept her apart from reality, and she felt memories ooze across her consciousness. Gondol gave her drinks. Gondol called for more food. Gondol proposed another Wild Hunt. Gondol. Clear-eyed Gondol who didn't partake of the refreshments but who made sure there was plenty for everyone else. Smiling Gondol who never once tried to join the second Hunt she championed.

"Where is Gondol now?" the raven repeated.

"Valhalla," she replied.

The bird cursed but Delia barely heard. The momentary

clarity she had experienced faded, and her muddled thoughts returned to the Wild Hunt. Her sister Valkyries were still far ahead, but her Nuckelavee was closing the distance. In less than a minute she would be side by side with them again, just in time to charge into San Jose.

"Turn around, Delia!" the raven urged. "You have to—"

A shudder went through the bird's body, rendering him silent. The twitching raven sprang into the air with a shriek and was immediately caught and carried away by the furious wind. At the same time, Delia felt something happen inside of her: a powerful hand invaded her core, forcefully seized hold of her very essence, and squeezed it. What power remained in her body suddenly drained out of it like water emptying down an unplugged drain.

All of the otherworldly fabric that made up her clothing shimmered out of reality, replaced by the rough material of the white nurse's uniform she had died in. The silver Valhallan magic that made up her ethereal being disappeared, leaving her dull and heavy. Within seconds, her magic was almost entirely gone. From the drunken and crazed Valkyrie warrior Svanhild she devolved into the ghost of the Navy nurse Delia, except her spirit was weighed down by the Eitr that had brought her to the very brink of life.

The Nuckelavee stopped dead and reared up. With a yelp of surprise, Delia felt the beast's veins rip free of her legs as she slid off its back. When she grabbed at its slick sides and tried to pull herself back up, she found she had no strength in her limbs to do so. Her almost-alive spirit body felt so obscenely heavy that raising even one arm was a painfully difficult endeavor. She fell into the clouds, and the Nuckelavee bolted off into the darkness, following the Wild Hunt and leaving her alone.

As black blood dripped out of her skin where the Nuckelavee's veins had been, the craze of the Wild Hunt gradually left Delia, though the haze of mead remained. There in the turbulent clouds, her transformed body buoyed by the black squall, her mood began to stabilize.

Staring up at the sky, she saw the raven circling.

"It's Georgette!" he yelled. "She took your magic!"

The Valkyries rode farther and farther ahead, and the storm traveled with them, leaving her behind. The clouds beneath Delia thinned until the diminishing storm could no longer support her heavy ghost body and she started to sink. Fumbling with hands that felt as dexterous as slabs of meat, she tried to grab fistfuls of cloud to steady herself, but the vapor passed through her fingers and her descent picked up speed. A rush of adrenaline momentarily cleared her brain, and her frantic eyes locked on to the raven flapping frantically above her. She flung out an arm.

"Senji!" she screamed.

He tucked his wings and plummeted after her.

Georgette

WHAT DO I DO? WHAT DO I DO?

Georgette's mind reeled. It was too late to return Delia's power. The Wild Hunt was on its way. She could feel its approach like animals could feel a coming earthquake. Nothing would stop them from finding her.

If I'm in Nocturne when they get here, everyone in this building will be in danger.

Georgette's frantic eyes darted to Neil and Mei-Xing. The Nymph was asleep. The horrific night she had experienced and her ill-timed blossoming meant there would be future issues to address, but for now she was out of danger. Neil, meanwhile, stared at Georgette with the wide-eyed intensity of someone who didn't understand what was happening but knew it was bad.

They're coming.

Explosive footsteps thundering down the hallway drew her gaze to the doorway. Ishak burst into the room. His eyes blazed with a predator's skillful observation as he took in the scene. Then he locked gazes with Georgette and held up his left arm. The brand. He had felt her draw on the brand for power and come running when he correctly guessed it was an emergency.

They're coming.

Georgette pointed to Kazimiera. "The spell won't hold forever," she said to Ishak. "Lock her up in Audrey's room."

She swung her attention to Neil. "Please take care of Mei-Xing."

"Georgette," he said, his voice low and serious. "What's happening?"

"I have to go," she said. She stared deep into his worried eyes. "I love you."

Neil blanched. Holding out a hand to her, he opened his mouth but was interrupted by a vicious crack of lightning. The flash of it momentarily filled the window with an overpowering golden light and cast a spotlight over Neil's alarmed expression.

They're here!

Tearing her gaze away from her boyfriend, Georgette ran across the office, threw open the window, and jumped. As her body passed through the spells that blanketed the building, she fully embraced the magic she had stolen from Delia and let it flood her veins. The silver glow that glossed her skin blazed into a lustrous white radiance and lifted her into the air. She took flight and soared upward into the blackened, crackling sky.

It was not the first time Georgette had flown. "Borrowing" magic from a flight-capable Fae species was a standard part of a witch's magic instruction. Most young witches looked forward to learning how to fly, but Georgette had not enjoyed the lesson. Being suspended in midair using power that wasn't her own sent her anxiety spinning. Soaring above San Jose now, steadily climbing into the sky, made her stomach clench, but she didn't give herself the luxury of being afraid. There was no time for fear.

Entering the thick storm clouds, her hair became so

drenched that her curls deflated to half their volume. Her lavender cocktail dress plastered itself against her skin as it became water-laden. When one shoe fell off her foot, she felt a moment of panic, followed quickly by the realization that her panic was ridiculous. She kicked off the other shoe and let it fall.

Bursting into the black heart of the storm, she found herself exactly where she wanted to be: face-to-face with the Wild Hunt.

The sight of one-eyed, skinless horses unsettled her, but not nearly as much as the crazed expressions of the Valkyries riding them. The warrior women were all dressed in stained used-to-be-white shifts, some of which were ripped in places that left their legs and breasts exposed. They clung to their kicking beasts while their unbound hair streamed wildly in the turbulent wind, their bloodshot eyes rolling back in their heads. Most alarmingly, Georgette noticed that many of the women sported large bruises and cuts that wept blood.

Floating in front of the pack, Georgette swept her wet hair out of her eyes, clenched her jaw, and spread her arms wide. The Nuckelavee herd came to an abrupt stop mere feet from her.

She drew a deep breath and let her voice ring out loud and clear: "I'm the one you came to find! I surrender!"

The ethereal eyes of the Valkyries stared at her blankly, as if she had spoken gibberish. No obvious signs of thought showed in their eyes. In those eyes, Georgette saw nothing but bloodlust. A few Valkyries at the edges of the group started to tug at their mounts, trying to veer away toward the city below. Georgette thought of Neil and Mei-Xing, of the dozens of Fae in Nocturne, and of the hundreds of thousands of innocent people in San Jose—and she made a choice.

Flexing her stolen power, she let Valhalla's magic shine through her skin and light up the dark cloud that encased them all.

Every Valkyrie's face snapped in her direction; their savage eyes zeroed in on her and her alone.

"Valhalla sent you on a Wild Hunt to find something unusual!" she bellowed, silver-white light rippling across her body. "You found me! Obey your orders, end the Hunt, and take me with you to Valhalla!"

The Valkyries cast uncertain glances at each other and muttered amongst themselves. Georgette began to worry that they were too far gone mentally to appreciate the significance of seeing a witch wield a Valkyrie's power, and her mind raced to think of what else she could do to drive the point home. But then a Nuckelavee with no rider trotted up from the rear of the group and made its way to the front line.

A dim sort of light came into the eyes of a tall woman at the front of the pack, and she gestured at the riderless creature with a hand that was missing two fingers. "Where's Svanhild?" she slurred to no one in particular. "Wasn't she with us?"

"I took her power!" Georgette quickly shouted. "I branded her and drained her magic!"

The Valkyries' attention returned to Georgette in an instant, their eyes blazing. The three-fingered woman waved two of her sisters forward, and all three urged their mounts toward Georgette, blades drawn and ready. The others began to turn their Nuckelavees around, causing the darkness of the Wild Hunt storm to lighten into a less threatening gray. Despite the hard expressions of the three Valkyries taking

Georgette into custody, the overall air of the group at least felt calmer now.

Georgette tried to focus on that success instead of what might happen next.

Nicolás

FROM THE WINDOW OF THE BOTANICA, NICO STARED IN astonishment as the downpour stopped in the blink of an eye and the black sky swiftly faded to gray. He watched as the clouds seemed to turn on their heels and retreat the way they had come. *The Wild Hunt is leaving*, he realized. *But why?*

"*Mijo!*" Mariana's authoritative voice broke into his thoughts with the force of an airhorn. "You cannot clean the window with your eyes!"

"Sorry, *Tía*." He began spraying and wiping the glass. "I just noticed that the storm is breaking up."

"Oh?" With her arms full of prayer candles, she stepped up beside him and peered up at the sky. After a moment's examination, she nodded smartly and said, "Good. There was more than enough damage the first time. May Valhalla never darken our skies again."

She shot an accusatory glare at the clouds before carrying the candles back to the shelves. Nico proceeded to clean the window while keeping one eye on the receding storm. This turn of events was strange but ultimately it was good news. The Wild Hunt had ended quickly and the Valkyries were going home. That meant Valhalla would not be vulnerable and Gondol's plan would, at the very least, be postponed. *Georgette will be relieved.*

Out of the corner of his eye, outside the window, Nico thought he saw movement. He turned toward it, looking out at the nearby intersection, where the light of a streetlamp flickered across the watery sheen covering everything. At first he saw nothing—but then he caught the motion again and narrowed his eyes at it.

There. On the far side of a parked car, a bird was flapping its wings in an agitated manner, like it was trying to fly but couldn't get airborne. For a moment, he assumed it was a pigeon, maybe recovering from being knocked into a building by the storm, but the feathers looked too dark. *Like*—his heart skipped—*a raven.*

He dropped the spray bottle and sprinted out the front door, his aunt's startled shout following him into the street. Splashing through puddles, he rounded the parked cars and raced into the intersection.

It was indeed a raven, one that was strenuously flapping its wings but unable to take flight due to what was gripped in his talons. It was the wrist of a woman—a woman who was badly bruised, soaked to the bone, and lying unconscious on the pavement.

Wide-eyed, Nico caught his breath.

Delia.

The moment he saw her, he felt his spirit guides flood his mind, urging him forward and opening his ears to the cries of the frantic raven.

"I cannot lift her!" Senji shouted over the wind. "I managed to slow her fall from the clouds and steer her toward your shop, but she is too solid for me to carry! Please," he squawked frantically, "help me!"

Nico stared at the pair, his brain too rattled to issue orders to his body.

Suddenly, Mariana's hand clamped over his arm. She gasped and exclaimed, "*Madre de Dios!*" before rushing to Delia's side. She had already grabbed the fallen Valkyrie's wrist from Senji and begun to check for a pulse by the time Nico finally snapped back to his senses.

"She's a Valkyrie, Tía," he said, stepping forward. "She doesn't have a heartbeat."

Mariana squinted, first at him and then at the unconscious woman.

"But . . . she does," she said. "It's not a normal heartbeat but . . . here!" She took his hand and yanked it to Delia's chest, pressing his sweaty palm to the rough fabric of her old-timey nurse's uniform. "Feel that?"

Despite his own heart racing from the contact with her, Nico could feel a very faint, very irregular heartbeat through Delia's skin. It had no rhythm and no vigor, like it was being played by a distracted drummer with only one drumstick, but it was there. Furthermore, her body gave off heat—not much, but far more than a dead woman should possess.

Nico steeled his resolve and reached down to scoop her up. He fully expected to have trouble lifting her, but she was uncannily light. He pulled her close against his chest, her head lilting softly against one shoulder as Senji perched on the other.

"Thank you," the bird panted.

With Delia in his arms, Nico hurried back to the Botanica, Mariana rushing ahead to open the door for them. Once inside, she locked the door and flipped the sign to CLOSED. Meanwhile, Nico took the Valkyrie to the back room and set her down in the old armchair that his aunt kept forgetting to dispose of.

Delia slumped into the threadbare cushions, mumbling

softly in her sleep, and Senji hopped onto the back of the chair to watch her. Mariana swept the Valkyrie's tangled hair out of her face and gingerly brushed her fingertips over the large purple bruise on her cheek. Then she began bustling about the room, tutting like an old woman. Within seconds, she was returning to their guest's side to cover her with a blanket and begin drying her soaked hair with a towel.

"I don't think she's 'alive' enough to sustain life-threatening injuries," Senji said, "but the bruises are real, and I think I heard a bone snap when we landed." He stared down at his partner while shaking the rain from his feathers. "I think the Eitr has brought the Valkyries to a semi-living state. They are gradually growing new living bodies a little bit at a time. They must still be spirits for now, or they would not be capable of harnessing a storm for the Wild Hunt. Delia fell from the sky slowly because her body is now solid but still incomplete. Given enough time and enough Eitr, she will grow a new, entirely human body for her spirit to occupy and cease to be a Valkyrie at all. I believe in Delia's case the process has been propelled along due to Georgette draining away her power. Had she not done so, I might have—"

"Wait!" Nico interrupted. "Georgette did what?"

"Drained Delia's power," Senji repeated. "That's why I brought her here when she fell. I can only assume that something has happened at Nocturne."

Nico bolted from the room with his heart in his throat. He grabbed his phone from the countertop and immediately called Georgette. It went straight to voicemail. Pacing the floor, he dialed Neil instead.

"What the hell's going on?" Nico exclaimed before his friend could utter a word.

Neil took a deep, ragged breath and said, "Jin brought Mei-Xing to Nocturne, got her drunk, and . . . assaulted her. Kazimiera grabbed him and started drinking his blood but she wouldn't let him go so Georgette used magic to stop her. Then Georgette started to . . . I don't know, glow. Then she jumped out the window and flew away."

In the background, Nico could hear many voices, one of which sounded like Ishak, talking over each other in worried tones.

"I-I don't know what's going on," Neil sputtered. "Kazimiera's locked up in the basement and Jin's still alive, I guess, but no one knows what happened to Georgette."

"I think I do," said Nico. He spun out a quick explanation of how he found Delia and what Senji had told him. "I think," he finished, "that Georgette drew on Delia's power out of desperation, in order to subdue Kazimiera. And I think she realized too late that by doing so she was basically broadcasting her position to the Wild Hunt. She flew away to protect everyone in the building. I think she either led the Valkyries away or gave herself up to them so they would take her back to Valhalla instead of attacking the city."

"Shit," Neil groaned. Ishak's muffled voice said something to Neil, who replied in kind before returning to the call. "Everyone here is freaked out that Kazimiera's gone nuts and that Georgette's gone AWOL." He exhaled in a puff and then sniffed loudly. "How do we get her back? I don't want Georgette out there alone."

"Yeah," Nico mumbled. Running his fingers through his hair, he made his way to the back room, the phone still at his ear. Mariana was hard at work cleaning Delia's wounds and making her comfortable. He saw her glance nervously at Senji a few times, but as long as the raven remained perched on the back of the chair, she seemed inclined to let him be.

Nico thought of Georgette when he had first met her: anxious, tearful, deeply traumatized. Since then, he had seen her grow in confidence, progressing in leaps and bounds. He knew she was stronger than she thought she was, both in her mind and her magic, but Valhalla was no place to put that strength to the test, particularly when it was full of crazed Valkyries. His friend was in very real danger.

"Stay at Nocturne and keep everyone calm," Nico told Neil. "I'll get back to you soon."

He ended the call before Neil could respond. Refusing to second-guess his intentions, he pocketed his phone, turned toward Senji, and blurted out, "Can you get me to Valhalla?"

Mariana's eyes, full of alarm, snapped in his direction. Nico ignored her and kept his gaze on Senji, who seemed to be pondering the question.

"Valhalla is a realm of the dead," he finally answered. "The living cannot enter."

"Does that mean," Nico asked hopefully, "that the Valkyries can't take Georgette there?"

"No," he said after a pause. "I am alive too, and the bond between me and Delia makes it possible for me to enter Valhalla. Georgette is connected to Delia through me, and she has absorbed a vast amount of Valkyrie magic. She will be able to enter. You, however . . ." He fluffed out his feathers and snapped his beak. "Even if I could carry you, your living body cannot cross into that realm."

"My living body," Nico mumbled.

"Nico," Mariana said in a warning tone. "You can't go to Valhalla." She enunciated each word while poking him in the chest. "What do you think you're doing?"

He met her probing gaze. "I'm being who you taught me to be, Tía. This is what you've devoted years of your life training me for. What's happening in Valhalla is too huge to ignore. Thanks to you, I may have the skills to help stop it."

Mariana emitted an annoyed *tsk!* and then let loose a barrage of Spanish. Nico didn't try to follow what she said, but he understood her meaning nonetheless. If their positions were reversed, he would be just as skeptical—but that didn't change what he had to do. Smiling in the face of his aunt's tirade, he calmly put his arms around her and hugged her.

She went silent and stood stiffly in his embrace.

"I'm doing this, Mariana," he said gently, "and you can't scold me out of it."

A few seconds passed before she untensed and reluctantly embraced him back. "*Tonto,*" she whispered.

"Yeah." He chuckled. "You'll need to take care of Delia while I'm gone. And me, too." He smiled, nervous but grateful for her in that moment. "Do we have any more *ka* tea?"

Georgette

THE GREAT HALL OF VALHALLA WAS AS MAJESTIC AS THE legends claimed, but Georgette's focus was on the unconscious women littering the massive steps leading to its entrance. As the members of the Wild Hunt marched her up the steps, her eyes moved from one passed-out Valkyrie to the next, taking note of their vivid purple bruises and the puddles of vomit dribbling over the stair edges. The Valkyries flanking her seemed to barely notice their fallen sisters—even trod on their hair and fingers as they walked.

Even more concerning to Georgette was the fact that her captors were so shaky on their feet that they were actually using *her* to steady themselves during the climb.

What am I hoping will happen? she asked herself. *What am I supposed to do?*

No answers came to her. Her sole intention when she surrendered to the Hunt had been to protect Nocturne and everyone inside. She had done that. Now what? *Should I run? Should I fight? Should I try to reason with them?* She just didn't know.

Their group came to a stop at the top of the steps. Georgette gazed up at the huge front doors towering before them and swallowed hard, trying and failing to moisten her dry throat.

She took in a deep breath and exhaled slowly, and with that she felt her nerves settle into a grim resolve. *I never had purpose in my life until I became part of the Nocturne community. If giving myself up to Valhalla will keep everyone safe, I would do it a hundred times.* She watched Valhalla's doors swing wide and let the Valkyries lead her inside. *Let's do this.*

She was prepared for the riders of the Wild Hunt to take her before an arbitrator of some kind, or maybe to lock her up, but when they were only about halfway across the enormous entrance hall, her Valkyrie handlers seemed to run out of steam. The one to her left wobbled, briefly regained her balance, and then slid to the floor with a thump. Startled, Georgette looked down at her; the three-fingered woman seemed to be fast asleep, already snoring with her cheek against the stone floor. Georgette turned to her right only to discover that the other guard, a woman with a scar across her throat, had wandered away.

Swaying drunkenly with each step she took, the scarred Valkyrie held one hand to her head, fingers rubbing her frizzled braids, as she made her way toward the far end of the room.

"Mead!" she bellowed, echoes of her hoarse voice booming through the high rafters. "Idisi! Bring me mead!"

The scarred Valkyrie disappeared around a corner, still shouting for a drink.

Dumbfounded, Georgette stood alone in the middle of the room, rainwater dribbling from her hair and dress. When no one else appeared, she brought her bound wrists up to her face and began whispering a simple spell that dissolved the fetters on her wrists into dust.

Shaking the stiffness out of her arms, she tried to decide if being abandoned in Valhalla was a good thing. It drastically increased her chances of getting out of the situation alive, yes—but, on the other hand, if this was the state of the Valkyries, then Valhalla was completely undefended.

Unable to think of what else to do, Georgette followed the Valkyrie who had gone in search of mead. She hadn't walked far when she heard a mob of female voices fill the air, along with the sound of clattering dishes. Hugging the wall, she moved closer to the buzzing central area until the party came into view.

Her heart skipped. The tightly packed sea of Valkyrie heads stretched into the far corners of the gigantic room.

My God! She broke out in a cold sweat and scurried backward. *There's so many!* A mix of dread and wonder filled her. *I'm probably the first witch in history to see this many Valkyries in one place.*

"Skogul!" Georgette heard someone shout. "What are you doing here? The Hunt can't be finished already."

"Mead!" demanded the voice of the scarred Valkyrie. "Give me mead!"

Over the hubbub of the party, Georgette heard the smack of skin on skin. "Not until you answer my questions!"

Georgette crept forward again and peered around the hallway corner into the big room. Skogul, the arresting officer with the grotesque scar, was leaning against a wall with one hand on her cheek. Before her stood another Valkyrie—a small young woman with straight, dark hair and black and red bands painted across her heart-shaped face.

"You can't slap me," Skogul slurred, her tone lost between disgust and indignation. "I'm in charge, Gondol."

Gondol. Georgette stared, her brow furrowing. The traitor, the mastermind, the architect of the apocalypse . . . was a short, snippy-voiced girl with a sour expression?

"Oh, you're doing a great job," scoffed Gondol, waving a hand at the party taking place around them. She leaned forward and poked the much taller woman in the chest. "If you want more mead, you will answer me. Why did the Wild Hunt end so soon?"

The question seemed to baffle Skogul, who stared into space while Gondol glared at her.

Seconds ticked by. Finally, Skogul dropped her hand from her cheek and smiled at her scowling sister.

"We found a witch," she said. "Brought her back."

A flash of pure shock crossed Gondol's painted face. She looked so ridiculous that Georgette had to stop herself from chuckling. *This is who everyone's afraid of?*

"Was the witch dead?" Gondol managed to ask.

"No," Skogul replied. She held out her hand like a child demanding candy. "Mead!"

Gondol slapped her hand away. "How could you bring a *live witch* to Valhalla?"

"Because," Georgette said loudly, "I siphoned Valhalla's power from one of your sisters."

Gondol's dark eyes snapped in her direction, and in an instant Georgette realized how unimposing she must look—a young witch in a cocktail dress, soaked to the bone, with no weapons or shoes. Gondol scoffed, sidled past Skogul, and slowly walked toward Georgette, one foot in front of the other, with her shoulders squared.

"Stealing power from a Valkyrie is a crime against Valhalla," she said, low and solemn. "So is trespassing." With one hand, she seized her sword by the hilt and pulled it free of its scabbard. A reflection of firelight danced across the silver blade and cast an unearthly glimmer over Gondol's face. "Both are punishable by death."

The sight of an armed Valkyrie approaching with murder in her eyes robbed Georgette of air. This was a childhood fear incarnate, a literal boogeyman of her youth. Every witch parent taught their children that if you messed with Valhalla, no one would save you. Georgette had known the danger when she struck a bargain with Delia and Senji, and now the bill had come due.

But then a powerful thought brought back Georgette's breath and steadied her heart. This was not Valhalla itself. This was one young woman with the power of a Valkyrie. Georgette was also a young woman with the power of a Valkyrie.

She leveled her gaze at Gondol and said in as loud a voice as she could muster, "What's the punishment for treason?"

Gondol froze. The sword in her hand shook slightly. A short distance behind her, Skogul tilted her head, her eyes bobbing between the two women. Other nearby Valkyries turned and stared, glassy-eyed, at the strange commotion.

Keep their attention, Georgette urged herself. *This is basically the world's biggest, craziest, longest-running frat party full of people whose biggest ambition is to get their next drink. To get through to them, you've gotta be the flashiest, loudest thing in the room.*

"You've betrayed Valhalla," she shouted, stepping forward and pointing at Gondol. Using Delia's magic, she lifted herself off the floor and floated upward until her knees were the height of the Valkyries' heads. "You've been spiking the food and drinks with Eitr!" She projected her voice. "You made a deal with Muspelheim!" She saw more faces turn her way as the color drained from Gondol's face. Georgette let the Valkyrie magic inside her shine through her skin, sending out a silver glow that drew even more eyes. "You weakened Valhalla to make it vulnerable to the enemy! You, Gondol," she bellowed at the top of her lungs, "are a traitor!"

A sizable chunk of the Valkyries were now focused on Georgette. Though her back was to them, Gondol clearly heard the reduction of chatter; her sword arm lowered as she cast nervous glances over her shoulder. Georgette maintained her midair position and angelic glow as she eagerly waited for the crowd to rise against the rogue Valkyrie.

But then Skogul's head snapped in the opposite direction. "Mead!" she shouted at an attendant with a tray of cups. Others also called for drinks. Soon, the Valkyries' drunken babbling continued as if it had never stopped, and all eyes turned away from the witch floating at the edge of their gathering.

Gondol smirked, and Georgette felt her blood run cold.

"Did you think that would be enough?" the Valkyrie mocked her. "I've given them their first taste of real life since their partners robbed them of it. You don't know what that feels like. You could never imagine the sweet, miraculous intoxication of regaining true sensation." She stalked forward, her sword gripped in her hand. "The feeling of wind on your skin that makes those tiny arm hairs flutter. The taste of food in your mouth, the movement of it going down your throat, the fresh weight of it in your gut. A heart that beats and blood that flows. And to feel yourself age—oh!" she cooed in a dreamy voice. "I had no idea how much I'd missed growing older! To be dead is to be forever static, reduced to a frozen moment in time. To feel my body undergoing change for the first time in hundreds of years . . . ah!" With a girlish grin, she twirled in a circle and laughed. "It's bliss!"

Still floating, Georgette desperately searched the crowd for the eyes of someone, anyone, who was paying attention.

But there was no one. Every Valkyrie had a drink in her hand and an oblivious smile on her face. The witch felt her silver glow dim as her confidence began to fade.

Sticking the point of her sword into the wooden floor, Gondol leaned on the hilt, resting her hands on the pommel, and smiled up at Georgette.

"Once Muspelheim takes Valhalla," she said, "they will give me enough Eitr to make me fully human again. Then I will finally get to live the life that bastard Fernão stole from me. I will travel. I will find love." Her smile widened and her dark eyes twinkled with anticipation. "I will be happy." With a contented sigh, she let her head drop to the side, her long, straight hair swishing over her shoulder. "Muspelheim might invade Earth eventually but . . ." She gave an exaggerated shrug. "The Fire Giants have given me revenge against my murderer and the chance for a new life. Even if I only get to live that life for a few years, I will die happy."

"And everyone else?" Georgette finally found her voice. "You don't care if the whole world burns so long as you get what you want?"

Gondol's smile slipped and her expression hardened. Eyes gleaming with a dark inner fire, she straightened up and yanked her sword out of the wood plank holding it in place. "You do not get to judge me," she hissed. "You have never been dead." Her boots slowly lifted off the floor as she floated up to be eye to eye with Georgette. She lowered her chin and curled her lips away from her clenched teeth. "But I can fix that."

A bolt of terror shot through Georgette, but it passed quickly. Like a long-forgotten muscle memory, the stolen Valkyrie power inside her pushed outward from her core and enveloped her body like liquid armor. She extended her arm, flexed her fingers, and, though she couldn't explain how, summoned Delia's sword into her hand. It was as if Delia's magic, flowing through her veins, extended outward through her palm and shaped itself into a long silver blade, weightless as a cloud and thrumming with power.

She glared at Gondol. "You can try, bitch."

Shrieking a wild battle cry, Gondol flew at Georgette, her sword poised for the kill.

Nicolás

THE FRESHLY BREWED KA TEA FILLED THE SHOP WITH A sage-like aroma. Nico held up a piping-hot cup in his hand, allowing the steam to lick his face. His aunt stood over him, mumbling under her breath. Though he didn't bother trying to discern her words, with one glance he could see the motherly combo of anger and worry blazing through her eyes.

"It's too much mugwort," she snapped for the fourth time in minutes. "Your astral form will drift too far without more valerian root to anchor you."

"Tía," he said on an exhale, "we've been over this. If I'm too weighed down by my body, my spirit won't be able to pass into Valhalla. I have to be as close to dead as possible in order for this to work. That's why you'll monitor my body while I'm gone."

Senji squawked.

Nico nodded at him. "And Delia, too, right?"

Mariana tsked and waved a dismissive hand in the air. Then her eyes drifted to Delia, and she gently reached out to adjust the still-unconscious Valkyrie's bandages. "I'll watch her," she said, brushing Delia's damp hair out of her face. "But"—she pointed a sharp-nailed finger at Senji—"if she wakes up and wants to leave, I can't stop her. Even in her condition, a Valkyrie can easily overpower my *brujería*."

Senji clicked his beak and bobbed his head, which Mariana seemed to take as agreement. She replied with a curt nod of her own before returning her attention to Nico.

"Well?" she said irritably. "Drink if you're going to drink."

The uncommon tone of fear in her voice came over Nico like an ill-fitting shirt—scratchy, distracting, and tight in the wrong places. He wanted to smile and tell her that he would be fine, but he knew she wouldn't buy it. She understood perfectly well the risk they were taking, perhaps even better than he did. Instead, he raised his cup to her.

"*Salud*," he said, and gulped down the tea. The taste was bitter, but he forced the entire draught down his throat before handing the empty cup to Mariana.

"How long until it kicks in?" he asked.

"Lie down," she replied. "If you fall out of that chair, you might hurt yourself."

He complied, lowering his body to the area rug and stretching out his legs as best he could in the Botanica's cramped back room. Very soon, he felt his eyelids grow heavy.

"Tía," he mumbled, "give the pouch to Senji and open the back door."

The sound of his aunt moving around was fuzzy and distant, as though it was taking place several rooms away. For a moment, Nico felt insufferably heavy, his body a stone statue sinking deep into a floor not solid enough to bear its weight. Then a switch flipped inside him and the weight was gone. Suddenly he was climbing, slow but steady, like a helium balloon. A sense of calm cradled him as he floated upward.

He opened his eyes and glanced down. Several feet below him lay his unconscious body, flat on his back, eyes closed, a tiny line of dribble at the corner of his mouth. A silver sinew rose out of the body's chest and up to his astral form, now floating halfway between floor and ceiling. He reached out his spectral hands to touch the umbilical thread. Through it, he felt the faint beat of his heart and sensed the flow of breath through his lungs.

Mariana bent over his sleeping form and checked his pulse. She nodded and sighed, giving his shoulder an affectionate rub. "*Buena suerte, mijo,*" she murmured.

"Thanks, Tía," he said, knowing she couldn't hear him.

Nico turned his astral body in a barrel roll until he came face-to-face with Senji. Still perched on Delia's chair, the raven was leaning in close to his partner's face as if searching for some sign of consciousness. A faded green pouch the size of a baseball was tied to Senji's left leg, and he clutched at the soft leather with his talons.

"Ready?" asked Nico.

Senji looked up. "Yes," he said, his words now crystal clear. "Give me your hand."

Nico reached out to him. In one fluid motion, Senji took flight, seized him by the hand, and carried his spirit out the back door, over the streets, and high into the night sky.

During his *curandero* training, Nico had astral projected on multiple occasions and traveled to many strange, otherworldly places. Each of those forays into another realm had always felt like an intense dream wrapped up in gauzy fog that kept him physically detached from whatever he might encounter.

This time, as Senji soared into the upper atmosphere and across ethereal boundaries, Nico felt sharp and alert, as if he had somehow brought his bodily senses along with him.

The transition to Valhalla's realm was both sudden and subtle—one moment they were flying up through clouds and then, abruptly, they were descending upon a grand estate with red-gold trees and an endless, roaring river. At no point did Nico feel that Senji had altered his course; they flew in only one direction, and yet at some point, up had become down.

Moonlight shone over the Great Hall's shield-thatched roof, and huge eagles slept on the highest points with their heads tucked into their wings. Behind the hall, an old-growth forest stretched into the distance, vanishing into a dark horizon.

The vast marble stairs leading up to the building were covered by a number of unconscious women. Nico swung his leg wide to avoid stepping on one of them as Senji deposited him at the top of the stairs, just outside the enormous open doors of the main entrance.

"So far so good," he said. He looked at his hands and saw that his astral skin was now opaque, like true living flesh. "I look real."

"You are," Senji said. As if to emphasize the point, he perched on Nico's shoulder and gripped him with his sharp claws. "There are no ghosts in Valhalla. You exist here essentially as a duplicate of yourself, just like the chosen who become whole here after dying."

Nico's *curandero* brain immediately catalogued this information and stored it away for future consideration. Right now, Georgette needed help.

He untied the green pouch from Senji's foot. "Where's the kitchen?"

Valhalla's kitchen was smoky and dark, lit only by a central hearth and a few torches in the corners. The Idisi flitted about the soot-covered floors with platters and cups in their hands, none of them giving Nico more than a passing glance. Looking at them filled him with an uncanny-valley sensation. Though they appeared human on first glance, they were a little too thin, a little too smooth, and a little too similar to one another for his comfort.

One Idis turned a spit over the great fire, occasionally brushing a liquid glaze onto the half-consumed carcass impaled on it. The roast was a large, muscular animal that, despite its webbed feet and finned tail, Nico's nose insisted was pork. Not far from the hearth stood a pen that hemmed in an abnormally large goat with long, silky white fur and twisty horns. The creature happily munched away on a trough full of budding branches while an Idis milked it. The goat's udder produced not milk but clear golden mead that the Idisi were busily pouring into empty goblets and carrying out a swinging door at the far end of the kitchen.

On Nico's shoulder, Senji bobbed his head. "Look!" he commanded.

Next to the swinging door stood an Idis with a tiny bottle in one hand and a dropper in the other. As each tray of mead goblets approached, she swiftly deposited a drop of liquid in each cup before the Idis carrying the tray proceeded through the doors.

"Eitr," Nico deduced. He turned to look again at the glaze the Idis was painting over the roast. "That too," he said. He tried to count the Idisi, only to realize that they were too alike for him to tell apart, given their constant movement. "How do we fend them off long enough to take it?"

"Fend them off?" Senji said in surprise. "No need." With a shriek that split Nico's eardrum, he launched himself at the Idis holding the Eitr bottle and began slapping her elfish face with his wings. The creature screamed, dropped the bottle, and bolted for the exit with her arms covering her head. Her companions immediately echoed her screams and likewise threw their arms over their faces and ran for the closest door.

Nico watched, slack-jawed, as the sinewy women ricocheted off each other in their rush to escape. Within seconds, the kitchen was empty.

"Idisi are harebrained ninnies," Senji explained as he hopped across a table strewn with dirty dishes. "They share a handful of brain cells among them, and they all act on the strongest emotion any one of them is having in the moment. If you influence one, you influence them all. I imagine," he added in a grumble, "that is how Gondol roped them into her service. They will be back in a minute to resume their work, probably with no memory of what just happened."

"Got it," said Nico. He made a beeline for the goat, the green pouch in his hand. "Let's get this done."

He lifted the nearly full bucket of mead from beneath the goat's udder and moved it closer to the fire in short, shuffling steps. After setting it down, he opened the pouch and shook some ground-up herbs into the bucket. He stirred the mead until the herbs were dissolved. *Lobelia*, he thought, *bayberry, ipecacuanha, and probably some others Mariana thought of on the fly. Hope this works.*

Across the room, Senji grabbed up the bottle of Eitr, flew to the ceiling, and let it fall. The glass vial shattered on impact. Nico kicked over the bowl holding the glaze for the meat and used his foot to smear the liquid over the stone floor. Grabbing a similar bowl from the table of used dishes, he scooped up some of the seasoned mead and set the newly full bowl near the roast. Then he started grabbing any goblet he could find and filling it with mead.

He had filled a tray's worth of cups when the doors swung open and the Idisi filed back into the kitchen, their expressions calm. They walked right past him and, as Senji had predicted, resumed their duties without skipping a beat.

The raven flew to Nico's shoulder, and together they watched as one Valhallan attendant brushed the meat with the herbed mead as if it was the same glaze from before. Other Idisi filled cups from the herbed bucket and carried them out of the kitchen to serve to the Valkyries. Nico sighed with relief. Everything was proceeding smoothly.

The Idis who had previously been dosing the drinks knelt on the floor next to the shattered Eitr vial. Her multi-jointed fingers reached tenderly for the broken shards like a mother bird discovering the cracked remains of her egg.

Nico leaned down, took the forlorn woman by the arms, and raised her up. "Hey," he said to her cheerfully. "I have a new job for you." He placed the green pouch in her open hand and gently closed her too-long fingers around it. "Every time the bucket is full"—he pointed at the goat—"sprinkle some of these herbs and stir them into the mead before you fill the cups." He flashed his best customer service smile. "Okay?"

The elvish woman smiled back. Nico struggled not to show his discomfort. Her smile, like the rest of her, was just slightly inhuman, stretching a little too far on her cheeks and showing a little too much of her teeth.

The Idis happily trotted off to stand next to the goat.

"Things are going well," Senji said.

"So far," Nico agreed. He watched as an attendant carried a tray full of herbed mead toward the party. "I hope Gondol doesn't bring them more Eitr."

"She won't," said Senji. "Abelardo was her delivery boy, and he will never set foot in Valhalla again. Yolotli is taking him home."

"Home? What do you mean?"

The raven warbled deep in his throat, an unusual but contented sort of noise that eased Nico's concern. "Abelardo's spirit," he said, "is leaving this world at long last to find peace beyond the veil."

Georgette

THE CLANG OF SWORD ON SWORD STARTLED GEORGETTE and made her freeze. Her muscles tensed and her wide eyes locked on Gondol's snarling face, now just inches from her own. Then Gondol lashed out her free arm, grabbed the front of Georgette's dress, and flung her out of the air.

Georgette crashed shoulder-first into the floor, knocking down several drunk Valkyries. As they sputtered complaints, she hissed in pain and grabbed her shoulder. Before she could fully process her injury, she saw Gondol flying straight toward her, sword outstretched to inflict a killing blow.

With a frightened yip, Georgette hurled her body out of the way. Gondol's sword-point plunged into the wooden floor, cleaving a plank in half.

She's so fast! Georgette flew upward, panting. Despite the fall and the pain in her shoulder, she had managed to hold on to Delia's sword. She tightened her grip around the hilt. *She may look like a kid but she's a lot older than me, and a helluva lot more experienced.*

Gondol yanked her sword free and flew into the air again, rising above the heads of the Valkyries. The two combatants hovered just below the rafters of the cathedral-high ceiling, each holding a silver sword and staring at each other. Below them, Valkyries laughed in drunken obliviousness.

Gondol dashed in Georgette's direction. Instinctively, Georgette relied on the Valhallan power coursing through her veins to guide her reflexes, and she darted out of the way in the instant before Gondol swung her sword. Whipping around, she made a chopping motion with her own sword as Gondol came close, but the move was sloppy and didn't land.

Before Georgette could recover, Gondol attacked again. This time, her sword sliced into Georgette's leg, leaving a bloodless, searing pain in her calf.

Heart racing and hands shaking, Georgette bolted to the far side of the ceiling. Catching herself before full-blown panic could set in, she forced herself not to flee. *If I run, then there's no one to stop Muspelheim.* She looked across the open space at Gondol's slow approach, at her battle-ready expression, and felt the blood drain from her head. *I need to be smarter about this. In a fair fight, she's got me beat, so—her eyes darted to the party below—to hell with fighting fair.*

Reabsorbing the sword into her body, Georgette folded her arms and dove into the crowd. She plunged in between clusters of Valkyries and landed roughly but safely on the sticky floor. Gritting her teeth against the pain in her calf, she began to army-crawl as fast as she could, zigzagging back and forth among the legs of the Valkyries, changing her direction at random to disguise her location. The Valkyries' total lack of interest in anything not mead related finally worked in her favor: not one of them moved out of her way or even glanced down at her. In no time at all, she was effectively lost beneath the sea of packed-in bodies.

Somewhere overhead, she heard Gondol cursing as she flew from one side of the room to another. *She can't see me,* she thought in triumph.

Working quickly, she cast a healing spell over her leg. It

was a soul-wound—no injury to her flesh but instead a cut into her very essence—but even so her magic managed to dull the pain. *Now what do I do?* Huddled low on the floor, tightly shielded from view by laughing drunks, she couldn't see Gondol through the sea of knees and elbows.

She might only get one shot at catching her opponent off guard, so whatever she did had to work on the first try. *How can I be faster or slow Gondol down?*

Several yards away, a loud clatter rang out over the general din, and a woman's voice bellowed an incoherent yowl. What followed was a horrible strangling sort of noise, like someone gagging up a colossal ball of phlegm. Georgette heard the overlapping conversations around her slowly die down as the gagging sound spread to multiple places. Then a rancid stench assaulted her nose, making her wince.

The hell? she thought, pinching her nostrils shut. *Smells like . . . rotten eggs? Ugh!* Her eyes flew open wide. *It's puke.*

The retching sounds spread deeper into the room, and simultaneously the stench intensified. Two of the Valkyries nearest to her groaned and doubled over. Their cups of mead dropped to the floor, the contents splashing over Georgette's arms as she crawled backward to avoid the impending vomit storm.

More Valkyries began to gag and bend down, leaving Georgette exposed. She continued to shuffle about, trying her best to stay hidden, but she quickly realized that the wave of vomiting was moving through the crowd faster than she was. Gondol would inevitably spot her soon.

Anxiously wiping the spilled mead from her arm, Georgette saw tiny speckles of dried herbs on her skin. Curious, she brought her forearm to her nose and sniffed. There was a faint but familiar mix of scents underneath the mead:

tobacco, mildew, and pine. *Lobelia, ipecacuanha, and bayberry*. Emetic herbs to induce vomiting and force the women to purge the Eitr. Herbs that would be known to a witch . . . or a *curandero.*

Nico? she wondered. *How?* But she didn't care. She sighed with relief and smiled. She had help. She wasn't alone.

The *Hathiya* brand under the spilled mead stared up at her, and suddenly she had an idea. She reached out for a cup someone had dropped and scooped it up, careful not to spill the spoonful of mead lingering in the bottom.

By now the fetid stink of the Valkyries' vomit was making every breath she took deeply unpleasant. Holding the cup to her chest, she pulled herself into a crouching position and drew in slow, deep breaths. As the crowd around her thinned out, she focused on drawing more power through her brand.

The last of the partygoers shielding her from view moaned and fell to their knees. Georgette's gaze whipped around the room before locking on to Gondol. Still flying high enough to be out of anyone's reach, the Valkyrie was watching her sisters through an expression both bewildered and alarmed. Georgette couldn't help but smirk. Clearly, Gondol had not been prepared for this development.

Drawing the nearly empty cup to her lips, Georgette whispered a spell into the few drops of mead remaining. The liquid readily absorbed her craft and began to hum with magical energy.

One last breath. And then, when Gondol's back was turned to her, Georgette launched herself into the air and barreled toward her target.

When she was within striking distance of Gondol, Georgette drew back the cup and flung it at her. By the time the Valkyrie swung around, sword at the ready, it was too late to dodge. The cup struck her square in the chest, the mead droplets splattering across her neck and cheek and mussing her painted color bands. Unfazed, Gondol raised her weapon to strike, but Georgette spun away and dashed out of her reach. Before Gondol could catch up to her, she activated the spell she had woven with Mei-Xing's power.

The remains of the plants in the mead flared to life and sprouted directly out of Gondol's skin. The Valkyrie gasped in shock and swiped at the rapidly lengthening shoots, but she couldn't tear them away fast enough to slow their growth. She screamed, soared backward, and rammed herself into the wall as the sprouts extended outward, thickened, and hardened into branches. In mere seconds, the spilled mead had transformed into a thick, bristly shrub that thoroughly engulfed Gondol from head to toe.

Trapped within the bush, the Valkyrie screamed, bashed herself against the wall, and, just as Georgette had hoped, dropped her sword. The silver blade toppled to the vomit-soaked floor with a clatter as its owner tried to fight her way out of the plants.

Shifting her source of internal magic from Mei-Xing to Ishak, Georgette flung herself at the shrub, arms outstretched, and transformed her body. With the speed of a lightning strike, her limbs lengthened, her skin sprouted yellow fur, and her face twisted and grew. When she reached the shrub, Georgette was a fully transformed Bultungin. She locked her arms around the bundle of branches and pulled Gondol out of the air, taking her to the floor. Her captive continued to scream and thrash, but Georgette held the shrieking bush tight against her chest, ignoring the scratches the branches inflicted on her arms.

Navigating her way around more vomiting women than she cared to count, Georgette located the dropped sword and pinned it under one hairy foot. "Nico!" she howled in a voice she barely recognized as her own. "If you're here, come take Gondol's weapon!"

Gondol screamed again, and one of her flailing arms shot out of the bush. Georgette tightened her embrace until the branches dug deep into her arms, but Gondol continued to break one branch after another.

"Hurry!" she shouted. "I can't hold her forever, and Muspelheim is on its way!"

Neil

NOCTURNE'S THIRD-FLOOR EMPLOYEE LOUNGE WAS A HUB of nonstop activity. Neil watched one Fae after another scurry about the breakroom for a wardrobe change or a quick bite to eat before dashing to a VIP room for their next booking. Arms crossed over his chest, he clutched handfuls of his shirtsleeves and held on so tight that his knuckles turned white. He wanted to be angry at the Nocturne Fae for working while Georgette was missing, but truthfully, he envied them. No one knew where Georgette was, if she was safe, or how to help her, but at least the Fae had jobs to keep them busy. All Neil could do was wait and worry.

He shifted his weight in his chair. Every few minutes, his eyes darted to the black screen of his phone where it sat on his knee, hoping but not expecting. After their initial conversation, Nico had stopped responding to texts, and Georgette hadn't even had her phone on her when she'd flown out the window. Still, he couldn't stop himself from hoping someone would contact him. Magic could make a woman fly; it could stop a crazed Vampire in mid-attack. Surely it could also make a phone ring.

The deer-in-headlights look on Georgette's face just before she flew out the window into the storm kept materializing into his thoughts. The memory of her voice saying, "I love you," clawed its way through his brain until he had to clamp his eyes shut to stop tears from leaking onto his face.

You gotta come home, babe. You gotta be okay.

On an adjacent loveseat, Jin slept like the dead, legs draped over one arm and head pressed against the other. Someone had bandaged his throat and bundled him up in a blanket before leaving him in the break room to either die of blood loss or find his way back to consciousness alone. It wasn't until after Neil had carried Mei-Xing—so deep asleep that no amount of motion or noise could wake her—to an empty VIP room for the night that he'd happened across Jin. It had been difficult to look at him—just the thought of the man had soured his stomach—but he'd forced himself to perform a cursory scan to assess his condition. Jin's face had been pale and his breathing painfully shallow, but he had seemed stable. Regardless, Neil had freely admitted to himself then that he wasn't going to rush the bastard to a hospital, and he hadn't changed his mind in the ensuing hours.

Out of the corner of his eye, Neil saw several more figures enter the room, but he didn't turn to face them until he recognized Ishak's voice. The Bultungin was ushering a young woman into the break room. Laptop under her arm, she cast a curious glance around the room, her eyes quickly but thoroughly scanning each Fae present.

"You will be safe in here, Miss Collins," said Ishak as he politely gestured her inside. "Again, I apologize for the inconvenience."

"I don't think 'inconvenience' is the right word," she said with a shake of her head. "I mean, this room looks more comfortable than the basement. It was just a little weird to be shut down there for my protection only to be ordered out so Vampire Whatshername could be locked up in my place. But"—she shrugged—"I'm getting used to my life being weird."

"Indeed," Ishak replied. "Please, make yourself comfortable."

She walked across the room and took a seat in a cushy chair next to a row of vanity tables where two Fae were using the lighted mirrors to adjust their makeup. They both greeted Miss Collins politely, shaking her hand and introducing themselves, and she responded in kind. They returned to their reflections, and she folded herself into a crisscross position within the chair. She silently opened up her laptop, popped in her earbuds, and resumed watching whatever was on the screen, not giving her fantastical surroundings another glance.

Ishak approached Neil, giving Jin only a cursory, disgusted look before half sitting on the far arm of the sofa. The Bultungin sighed and rubbed his eyes. "The Vampire is . . . deeply unhappy about being locked in the basement. Fortunately, no one was hurt getting her in there, and she appears to be successfully contained."

Neil nodded but didn't respond. He didn't care what condition Kazimiera was in.

Ishak seemed to share his opinion, because he did not mention her again. Instead, he held up his left arm and inclined his head at the *Hathiya* brand on the underside of his wrist. "She's alive."

It took Neil a moment to grasp his meaning, but when he did, he sat bolt upright in his chair. "Georgette? You can sense her?"

"She has siphoned off a great deal of my power and is using it, though I cannot say for what purpose." Ishak flexed his fingers, his dark eyes fixed on the intricate interlocking designs of the brand. "She is very active, physically and magically."

"But she's okay?" Neil leapt up from his chair and took a step toward Ishak. "You're sure about that?"

"Yes."

"Is there . . ." Neil swallowed to wet his dry throat, and started again. "Is there any way we can help her?"

"I am helping," Ishak said. "I am allowing Georgette unrestricted access to my power."

"But there must be more!" Neil exclaimed. Teeth gritted in frustration, he jammed his palms into his forehead. "There must be something—"

"No." Ishak locked him in a stern gaze and shook his head. "Waiting under these circumstances is painfully difficult, but it really is the best option." He placed a firm, steadying hand on Neil's shoulder, at which point Neil realized that he was trembling. "Your woman would never siphon my power on a whim. That she now uses my power without my permission tells me that she finds herself in . . . exceptional circumstances. Whatever she faces, she will triumph and she will return. I have faith in her. So must you."

Neil let his hands drop to his sides and exhaled. "I believe in her," he murmured. "I just . . . I just want to know she's safe."

"Of course you do." Ishak flashed a kind, weary smile. "Everyone here wants to know she's safe. But what Georgette would want is for me to look after the residents of this building, whom she sacrificed herself to protect. And I believe she would want you to protect Mei-Xing in her absence rather than stand guard over this"—he gestured at Jin—"failure of a man."

"Oh, I'm not guarding him," Neil said, shooting Jin a sharp glare. "I'm making sure he doesn't wake up and wander off without being held accountable for his actions."

Ishak nodded approvingly. "Georgette would want that. And, I imagine, so would Mei-Xing." Ishak rose from his perch. "Even so, check on Mei-Xing now and then. She will almost certainly sleep until dawn, but I will be too occupied with other matters to attend to her if she awakens sooner."

Once Ishak left, Neil returned to his chair—but he was seated for less than a minute before he was startled by a buzzing sound. He automatically snatched up his phone, eager to answer the incoming call, only to discover that it was quiet.

The buzzing continued. After a few seconds, he finally realized it was coming from Jin.

He rose from his chair and made a quick search of the unconscious man before locating a buzzing smartphone in the pocket of his jacket, which had been crammed between the cushions. On the screen, he saw one word: *Mom*.

His first instinct was to let it ring until the call went to voicemail, but then he saw that Jin had eleven missed calls, all from his mother. However much he hated Jin, he didn't have the heart to let Mrs. Li worry about her son.

Accepting the call, he held the phone to his ear and said, "Hello, Mrs. Li."

The familiar voice of his boss's wife burst through the phone in an explosive string of Mandarin that rattled his skull. He yanked the phone away from his head as she shouted, and then slowly inched it closer again, repeatedly trying and failing to interrupt her tirade. It took a minute for him to force his words into the split second when Mrs. Li drew breath.

"PLEASE STOP!" he finally bellowed, and her voice fell silent at last. Relieved, he sank back into his chair and, running his free hand through his hair, said, "Mrs. Li, this is Neil. Can I help you?"

She sighed a deep, ragged breath. "Where is my son?"

"He . . ." *He forced himself on a Wood Nymph, lost a lot of blood to a Vampire, and no one's taking him to a doctor.* "He's asleep."

There was a long pause, during which the Nocturne Fae walked in and out of the room while chattering amongst themselves. Neil knew some of the noise must be traveling through the phone, betraying that they were in a busy location.

"He's passed out at a club," Mrs. Li said flatly.

"Yes, ma'am."

She muttered something but then cut herself off and cleared her throat. When she spoke again, she had resumed the usual tone he associated with her: stiff, chilled, and faultlessly polite.

"My husband," she said, "has been complaining of pain for days. It got worse earlier this evening, and I insisted he go to the hospital. Well . . ." She coughed once and sniffled. "He's suffered a heart attack. He needs surgery."

Neil's blood pressure dropped so quickly that the room around him began to spin. Grabbing the edge of his chair for support, he stared down at the floor and struggled to focus. Mr. Li? The man who'd taken Neil under his wing and nurtured his talent for sales? His mentor had suffered a heart attack?

He put a shaky hand to his forehead. His skin was clammy and uncomforting.

Mrs. Li's sharp inhale snapped him back to attention, and he raised his head. His pulse was thundering in his ears, but he still heard her loud and clear as she said, "My husband needs his son."

"I'm sorry," Neil said. The words felt thick and alien on his tongue. "Mr. Li is . . . I'm so sorry."

"Can you wake Jin up?"

Neil looked at Jin. The bandage on his throat appeared dry, and the red stain on it had not spread, suggesting that the bleeding had stopped. However, his skin was pale, his eyes were sunken, and his breath was shallow. Neil reached over and pinched Jin's leg as hard as he could. Aside from a soft moan, there was no response.

"No, ma'am," he said with a sigh. "He's out cold."

"Then let him sleep," Mrs. Li snapped. "Better that my husband thinks I couldn't reach Jin than to tell him his son is a selfish drunk right before he goes into surgery."

He's worse than a drunk, Neil thought, but aloud he said, "I understand."

"When he wakes up, instruct him to call me."

Mrs. Li abruptly ended the call. Neil briefly considered calling her back to ask which hospital they were in but quickly discarded the idea. This wasn't the time to send flowers. "Bastard," he snarled in Jin's direction.

His concern for Mr. Li mingled with his worries about Georgette, leaving his brain a jumbled, anxious mess. Too tired to sleep, he leaned forward, put his elbows on his knees and his face in his hands, and waited.

Nicolás

EMERGING FROM VALHALLA'S KITCHEN, NICO IMMEDIATELY gagged and slapped a hand over his nose. The pungent stink of digestive acid hung thick in the air. Every Valkyrie was on the floor, and each one appeared to be surrounded by a pool of regurgitated booze and stomach juices. The amount of vomit was impressive; it formed a chunky liquid layer over the wood planks that covered the room almost wall to wall.

"Well," said Senji as he alighted on Nico's shoulder, "I'd say the herbs were effective."

"Yeah," Nico agreed. "Let's just hope emptying their stomachs makes the Valkyries snap out of their daze."

"Nico!" shouted a gravelly voice.

He turned and saw a large bipedal animal, standing tall above the sea of vomiting Valkyries, clutching a writhing bush. At first he assumed it was a Werewolf, but he soon dismissed the idea. The beast's fur was a sunny yellow with swirly patterns of light brown stripes and dots—nothing like a wolf's pelt. Furthermore, its snout was blunter than a wolf's, its upright ears were rounder, and its tail was shorter.

At the moment when he locked eyes with the animal—bright blue eyes—Nico finally understood. Breaking into a jog, he hurtled over the Valkyries in his path to get to Georgette.

When he got close, the bush in Georgette's grasp let out a horrific scream, and a flailing arm burst through the leaves and branches in his direction. Senji squawked and leapt away as Nico exclaimed, "Shit!" and jumped back, only to stumble over a vomiting woman and fall to the wet floor. "What is that?" he asked.

"Gondol," said Bultungin Georgette. "Here!" She kicked out one leg, sending a sword sliding through lumps of partially digested meat in his direction. "Get her sword out of here."

Trying to ignore the smell and texture of what he had fallen on, Nico climbed to his feet and took the sword. The blade was light in his hand, much lighter than it looked, but he didn't have time to think about it. The bush began to thrash about in Georgette's arms, causing the witch to flinch and tighten her embrace even as the sharp points of the branches drew blood from her skin.

"Hurry!" she said. "My spell is wearing off."

An atonal caw broke the air as Senji swooped low over Nico's head and flew toward the nearest hallway. "Follow me!" he cried.

With a curt nod, Nico took off after him.

Senji led Nico through a seemingly endless tangle of hallways before finally bringing him to a half-open door. Nico burst through it—and suddenly found himself in the open air.

He was at the top of the colossal front steps. Under a cloud-streaked moon, Valhalla's fields stretched far into the night, disappearing into ancient forests thick with shadows. Small oases of trees and shrubs dotted the grassy expanse here and there, and a river, black in the darkness, flowed steadily in soft twists and turns across the land.

The immensity of his surroundings left Nico momentarily frozen, but a flash of black feathers cut in front of his vision and he blinked with a gasp. Senji swooped over the steps, uttering a throaty caw. "Keep moving!" he cried.

Gripping the sword, Nico headed downward. He had to keep dodging left and right to avoid treading on the passed-out Valkyries sprawled over the steps.

The moment his feet touched grass at the bottom of the stairs, he broke into a run—but he didn't get far before Senji flew low over his head.

"Give me your hand!" shouted the raven.

Nico obeyed. Senji seized him by the wrist and lifted him into the air, sword and all. Together, they ascended at an angle, climbing gradually higher while simultaneously flying in the direction of the dark forest. Then, suddenly, Senji squawked loudly and drew back, flapping his wings wildly to slow his speed.

Following the raven's gaze, Nico stared in shock at the sudden appearance of a great black cloud that was descending out of the sky—and heading straight for them.

Clapping his wings to his side, Senji dropped out of the air, dragging Nico along with him. They fell toward the ground so fast that Nico's stomach launched into his throat. Had he been in his physical body rather than his astral form, he was sure he would have puked. He yelped and started to pedal his legs out of terror, but Senji dug his talons into his wrist.

"Look!" the raven commanded as he leveled out again.

The black cloud shot over their heads, narrowly missing them and blacking out the moonlight. Only then did Nico see that the cloud was composed of large black birds, all headed for the Great Hall.

"It's the Valkyrie partners," Senji said. "They've returned from Fólkvangr. Look!"

Nico saw many figures emerging from the line of dark

trees below them: a herd of Valkyrie partners. Horses and wolves ran at a fast clip, all headed for the Great Hall—led by a thin wolf with his head hung low.

"Giovanni," Senji said approvingly. "He did it!"

Nico didn't need to know the whole story to understand that this was good news. "If the partners can sense the Valkyries, it means they're sobering up, right?"

"Yes," the raven agreed, heaving a sigh far deeper than his small body should have been able to hold. "Come! Let's fly on. If we keep Gondol separated from this piece of her power, maybe Georgette can—"

A deafening explosion suddenly boomed through the air. Nico craned his neck to look back at the Great Hall. What he saw made his jaw drop. Just above the hall, golden roof tiles and shards of wood flew through the night sky. The flock of birds that had just passed by scattered in all directions, many of them shrieking in pain as chunks of debris rained down upon them.

A lone woman draped in rags rose into the air with her arms outstretched to either side. Her long, dark hair whipped wildly around her head, partially obscuring her face, but in the rays of moonlight Nico caught glimpses of the painted bands across her eyes and cheeks.

Gondol.

The enraged Valkyrie shrieked so loudly that despite the distance between them, Nico instinctively dropped her sword and clapped his free hand over his ear.

Gondol's scream grew rapidly louder, like the whistle of a train barreling toward him. Before Nico could utter a word, she struck him head-on. All breath fled his lungs as the enraged Valkyrie drove him into the ground with such force that his body violently displaced the dirt beneath him.

Gasping, Nico threw his arms up to defend himself, but Senji hurled himself at Gondol's twisted face before she could strike. He beat the screaming Valkyrie about the head with his wings, tearing at her face with his claws, until with one quick swat she sent him spiraling out of sight. Senji disposed of, she leveled a vicious glare at Nico that shot ice through his veins before she leapt forward, snatched up her sword, and took flight back toward the Great Hall.

Frozen to the spot, Nico watched Gondol grow smaller as she flew. A sense of dread spread through him. Gondol was armed . . . and angry.

Georgette

GRITTING HER TEETH IN PAIN, GEORGETTE STARED DOWN at the deep, crisscrossing scratches on her empty arms, then up at the jagged hole smashed open by her escaped captive. Gondol was gone.

Why didn't I hold on? she scolded herself. *How could I let her go?*

A groan drifted to her ears, and she turned her head. A Valkyrie was rising from the floor on unsteady legs, one hand on her stomach and another pressed to her head. The woman's long braids were frizzy and unkempt, and those on her right side were crusty with half-dried vomit.

It wasn't until Georgette spotted the scar on her throat that she recognized the Valkyrie as Skogul.

After vigorously rubbing her face, Skogul opened her eyes and looked at Georgette, her brow furrowed. "Who are you?"

"I . . ." Georgette said before snapping her mouth shut. The deep, hoarse tone of her voice startled her. For a moment, she had forgotten that she was still in Bultungin form. She released Ishak's power through the *Hathiya* brand and let her body become human again. "I'm the witch you arrested tonight."

Skogul squinted and shook her head. "Arrested? What are you talking about?" She scanned the room with a bewildered expression. "What happened here? I . . ."

Her gaze sank to the floor, and a strange light came into her eyes. The silence stretched out and haunted the space between them.

"My God," the Valkyrie captain finally muttered. "We've been in here for weeks, haven't we? Why did we—"

"Gondol," Georgette interrupted. "Gondol's been drugging you all with Eitr."

"Eitr?" Skogul paused and then nodded. "I remember," she said in a louder, clearer voice. "I remember talking to Gondol. She . . . she sent us on another Wild Hunt. And," she declared after another pause, "she was angry when we returned so soon." Her eyes grew sharp as they locked on to Georgette again. "Why did she do this?"

"She made a deal with Muspelheim," Georgette hurriedly explained. "She gets a second chance at life in exchange for selling out Valhalla. I can tell you more later, but right now there's no time. Muspelheim's coming."

A flurry of noise in an adjoining hallway suddenly filled the air. The Valkyrie captain instantly snapped to attention and, with a forceful gesture, summoned her sword. When the silver weapon appeared in her hand, she gripped it tight, her eyes trained on the hallway entrance.

The noise intensified, growing into the pulsing roar of a ruptured dam. Skogul's face twisted into a scowl, and she shifted her weight back and forth, ready for battle.

Georgette quickly moved out of her way.

A large black wolf burst into the room first; a stream of horses and other wolves followed. Skogul lowered her sword as hundreds more stampeded into view and began to spread out among the Valkyries—who, Georgette realized with elation, were starting to rise.

One by one, the women climbed to their feet, groaning

and looking a bit dazed but clearly sober. Each animal laced his way through the stirring crowd until he located his partner, at which point he took his station at her side, offering assistance as she pushed herself up from the vomit-coated floor. From overhead, a squawking flock of birds descended through the hole in the ceiling as ravens and crows sought out their partners. Soon, the room was abuzz with voices, human and animal.

A large pied crow swooped past Georgette's head, making her gasp in surprise. It circled Skogul twice before she gave a nod and allowed the bird to land on her shoulder.

"Nsaku," she said to the crow, "what did you see outside?"

"A Valkyrie erupted through the ceiling of the Great Hall, Kimboti," the crow replied. "Many were injured by the falling pieces of roof."

Skogul's eyes darted to Georgette. "Gondol?"

Georgette nodded.

Returning her gaze to her partner, Skogul asked, "Where is the traitor now?"

"She attacked a man, a spirit, carrying a sword. That was the last I saw."

"Nico!" Georgette exclaimed in a flush of panic. Muspelheim instantly forgotten, she used Delia's power to fly toward the ceiling. As she approached the gaping hole Gondol had left in her wake, she summoned Delia's sword into her hand and wrapped her fingers around the hilt so tightly that her arm trembled.

Below, she heard Skogul barking orders at the Valkyries—but as she passed through the hole in the roof and into the open air, the captain appeared in front of her, sword at the ready.

Georgette's heart skipped a beat as deep-rooted childhood lessons about the dangers of Valkyries flooded her brain. "Please don't stop me," she said. "I don't want to cause a problem with Valhalla, but I have to help my friend."

"Go," Skogul replied. "There will come a time for questions, but right now"—she set her jaw as she scanned the land that surrounded the Great Hall—"I have bigger concerns."

Gondol

GONDOL SWIPED AT HER CHEEKS AS SHE FLEW BACK TOWARD the Great Hall, trying to erase the feel of the raven's claws. When she glanced at her hand, she saw face paint. She had smeared her tribal makeup. She growled with anger and grief.

Years of planning, ruined in the blink of an eye. She had thrown that bastard Fernão into the fire and cheated Death of the Werewolf she'd used to replace him. She had gotten the Idisi to drug the food and drink with Eitr to disrupt the Valkyries' power. She had kept the party going for weeks and even convinced the Sisterhood to engage in an unnecessary Wild Hunt . . . All for the purpose of weakening Valhalla to the point that the chosen could no longer recover from battle. And it had worked. She had singlehandedly disarmed the ethereal military force and thrown open the gates for invasion.

All for nothing.

Gondol had died before ever really getting to live, and her short life had been infused with hardship and violence. While still in the rosy flush of adolescence, she had witnessed the invasion of her home and the capture and sale of her family. Fernão, one of the foreign attackers, had kept her for himself until a dormant disease hitchhiking in his body struck her down. As a spirit, Valhalla had given her a purpose: defend the world against Fire Giants who razed all in their path. Though initially reluctant, she soon embraced her new identity. But this laudable occupation came with a dark side that slowly whittled away at her soul.

For hundreds of years, she'd watched millions delight in every happiness she had been denied: security, education, love, children, old age, legacy. She'd gone through the motions of fetching souls for the war, but with each delivery she'd grown more bitter. Why defend a world full of people living the life she was denied? What was her reward for such altruistic service? More years of an afterlife spent side by side with her killer?

So when agents of Muspelheim had approached her and offered her a deal, she'd agreed.

Gondol reached the front of the Great Hall, and there she saw her last hope: a smattering of Valkyries passed out on the front steps. These women had never made it to the party after the Wild Hunt, which meant they hadn't vomited up the Eitr. If she could get them riled up, they might be convinced to fight the sober sisters—stall for time long enough for Muspelheim to arrive.

Gondol grabbed the Valkyrie nearest to the top step and yanked her into a sitting position. "We're under attack!" she shouted in her face. "Muspelheim has infected the sisters inside the Great Hall! Wake the others on the steps! We must hold them off!"

Without waiting for the groggy woman to respond, Gondol grabbed another drunk woman and shook her awake. One Valkyrie at a time, she worked her way down the stairs.

Near the bottom of the steps, Gondol took hold of a woman who lay face down on the stone with her arms half buried in her long, curly brown hair. She roughly flipped the woman over and recognized her drool-covered face.

"Wake up, Rota!" she said, slapping her. "We're under attack!"

Rota's eyes opened, but Gondol saw no light of consciousness in them. Snarling, Gondol punched her right between the eyes. Rota's head recoiled and bounced forward again, and focus finally entered her eyes.

"Get up!" Gondol commanded. "The other Valkyries have been infected by Muspelheim! We have to defend Valhalla!"

"Lies!"

Startled, Gondol turned to see a thin wolf with his teeth bared racing across the grass toward them. He drew himself to an abrupt stop at Rota's side but kept his intense gaze locked on Gondol.

"Do not listen to this woman, Lucia," he said to Rota. "She is the cause of Valhalla's troubles."

"What?" Rota mumbled as she pressed a hand to her head. "Troubles?"

"The drunkenness, the battle losses, all of it!" the wolf shouted. "This woman, Gondol, she is—"

In a whip-quick motion, Gondol materialized her sword into her hand and thrust the blade into the wolf's chest all the way up to the hilt. The wolf's eyes went wide and his mouth hung open in frozen silence as Gondol yanked back her arm to retract the blade. Rota gasped in unison with her partner as the spirit sword left his chest without leaving a visible wound.

Gondol threw out her arm to stop Rota from rushing to him. "Don't! He's been compromised! He's a danger to us all!"

With a gurgling cry, the wolf collapsed. His ochre eyes looked up at her, but to Gondol's surprise, there was not a hint of malice in their depths. Instead, she saw sadness. And the sight of it made her skin crawl.

Rota began to claw at her head, raking her fingers through her thick hair. Gondol understood what was happening. As the wolf died, the bond between him and his Valkyrie was growing thin and fading into oblivion; Rota was being drained of his consciousness and memory. Gondol had experienced something similar when she cast Fernão into Muspelheim. Rota's bond was disappearing, erasing her partner from her entirely.

"My God," Rota muttered. She crouched by the wolf, her hands hovering above his body; a lone tear trickled down her cheek. "Don Giovanni."

The sorrow in Rota's voice sent a bolt of fury through Gondol. She seized her by the hair and shook her. "That is your murderer!" she snapped. "Why do you cry?!"

Rota did nothing to defend herself against Gondol's attack. She just wept and murmured the wolf's name again and again.

Every tear from Rota's eyes enraged Gondol. Every Valkyrie was like her, after all—every one a murdered woman supernaturally bonded to her killer and charged with protecting a world she was no longer allowed to enjoy. Witnessing Rota's grief, she felt bile rise into her throat. "Why are you crying?!" she shouted again, shoving Rota to the ground.

The wolf's eyes glazed over and his chest ceased to rise. Rota lay crying at his side, her outstretched fingers floating inches from his face.

Gondol stared at the nonsensical scene with her teeth bared. "Why do you care?! What did he ever do for you except steal your life?!"

A crow swooped across the front steps, calling out to one of the Valkyries Gondol had awakened. Suddenly overwhelmed by the fury she had nursed for centuries, Gondol screamed and launched herself at the bird with her sword held aloft. Caught by surprise, the crow squawked only once before her silver blade sliced through him and he dropped to the ground in a heap of lifeless feathers.

"Murderers!" Gondol roared. "Woman killers! You should have all stayed dead!"

The main door of Valhalla swung open for a crowd of emerging Valkyries, partners by their sides. Gondol's Eitr-infected troop seemed to have grasped that a battle was at hand and were struggling to summon their weapons. It was a pitiable sight: a few dozen drunks preparing to fight a battalion. Unless Muspelheim arrived within minutes, there was little chance of salvaging her plans.

Now secure in the knowledge that she was well and truly done for, Gondol felt a powerful shift in her emotional state. No more panic, no more anger, no more hope. All she wanted now was to take her pound of flesh before the end came.

Gripping her sword, she set her sights on the nearest group of animal partners and hurled herself, weapon ready, straight at them.

Georgette

GEORGETTE FLEW OVER VALHALLA'S SWEEPING GROUNDS, trying to find Nico. A faint golden sunrise glow peeked over the treetops, but the sky above remained dark; she could barely make out where the fields that surrounded the Great Hall transitioned into thick forest. The wind plastered Georgette's damp curls flat against her skull and stabbed through her tattered dress, chilling her. She shouted for Nico as she flew but got no response.

Wrapping her shivering arms around herself, she flew higher in the sky. Looking back toward the Great Hall, she saw Valkyries stream out of the open doors of the Great Hall on horseback, alongside wolves, or with birds on their shoulders. A much smaller group of warrior women had grouped together on the steps with their swords drawn, waiting to meet their approaching sisters, but even from a distance they looked off-kilter, teetering on unsteady legs.

She yanked her gaze away. She had to find Nico.

She felt a tug on her *Hathiya* brand. Recognizing the sensation as a summons from Senji, she allowed the magical brand to guide her. She soon spotted a lone man kneeling in the grass and quickly descended to the ground next to him.

"Nico!" She exhaled in relief. "You okay?"

The *curandero* looked at her but didn't rise to his feet. A faint, wispy silver cord, tethered to his spirit at one end, floated lazily in the ether, disappearing in the distance. That it was there told Georgette that Nico's body, wherever it might be at the moment, was still alive.

"Gondol took back her sword," he said, sounding despondent.

"We did our best." Senji's voice rose out of the tall grass. The raven hopped into view in a flutter of black feathers and landed by Nico's leg. He peered anxiously in the direction of the Great Hall. "What now?"

After offering an arm for Senji to perch on, Georgette stood up, and Nico did the same. "Thanks to you two, most of the Valkyries are sober and functional. The Sisterhood will get control of this situation, find Gondol, and repel Muspelheim." Hearing herself say the words aloud released a knot of tension so deep that Georgette felt she must have been carrying it in her soul. She smiled. "I think everything's okay."

Nico closed his eyes and exhaled a long breath as Senji warbled appreciatively.

The raven leapt into the air, making the short flight from Georgette's arm to Nico's shoulder. "We have completed our mission," he said with a satisfied snap of his beak. "I will fly us back to the shop so we can look after Delia. Perhaps," he added after a brief pause, "if we purge the Eitr from her as well, her injuries will heal."

Nico stared up at the brightening sky with a soft smile on his face. "I can't believe we pulled it off. It felt like such a long shot."

"Yes," Senji agreed. "But we triumphed!" He let out a series of ebullient clicks while puffing out his throat feathers like an Elizabethan ruff. "Victory, my friend!"

Nico's laugh made Georgette grin. It was joyous, full-hearted, like he had never felt such relief before. A warm affection for both him and Senji filled her chest. *These guys are heroes*, she thought, *and I'll never let them forget it.*

Suddenly, something traveling at great speed crashed into Georgette—slamming the air out of her lungs and sending her head whipping violently forward, rattling her brain and boggling her vision. Grabbing her around the midsection in a crushing grip, it drove her off her feet, sped her along the tree line in a blur of motion, and flung her into the sky.

Georgette spun and tumbled helplessly through the air until her lungs finally unclenched and allowed her to breathe. Gasping, she managed to slow her flight only for an instant before she was struck again, this time from behind. Her attacker grabbed her around the waist and drove her straight toward a cluster of trees. Panic electrified Georgette, and she instinctively summoned Delia's sword into her hand. Quickly, she spun the hilt in her palm and stabbed the blade downward, slashing at the arms holding her. The moment the sword sliced into them, a wounded scream filled the air and the arms vanished.

Georgette pulled up just in time to avoid the trees and whirled around to face her assailant.

Gondol hovered in midair a few yards away, clutching her arm to her stomach. Her black and red makeup was badly smeared into a brownish smudge across her eyes, and long rivulets of tears ran down her cheeks. Her flashing eyes narrowed at Georgette, and her lips parted in a vicious snarl.

"You," she said, "ruined EVERYTHING."

Georgette gripped Delia's sword tightly. From the Great Hall, she could hear Valkyrie voices calling out for Gondol, demanding that the traitor show herself. Gondol either did not hear or chose to ignore them. Her hate-filled, teary eyes stayed fixed on Georgette.

"You," she growled. "YOU BITCH."

Before Georgette could blink, the Valkyrie charged with her sword held high, ready to strike.

Gondol

THE WITCH HAD DESTROYED GONDOL'S HOPES AND DREAMS. If she could not have the new life she deserved, she would have revenge. She'd already cut down as many of her sisters' animal partners as she could before fleeing the Great Hall. Now she would do the same to this meddling bitch.

She slammed into the witch as hard as she could and hurled her into the sky.

As they fought in midair, she had a desperate thought—one that she latched on to like a mountain climber clinging to a frayed rope. But she would have to get control of the witch first.

Flying at her opponent again, she succeeded in disarming her enemy—but dropped her own weapon in the process. The two blades fell, glittering silver in the rising sunlight as they dropped to the ground.

Undeterred, Gondol grabbed the witch by the front of her dress and held her fast.

"Sister!" she yelled—not at the astonished witch but through her, to the one whose magic she wielded. "My sister Valkyrie! This witch has stolen your power! If you can hear me, fight her!" Hot tears rolled down Gondol's cheeks and past her lips, salting her tongue. "Sister! Take back your power! Don't let her win!"

The witch tried to pull away, confusion and fear swimming in her eyes, but Gondol yanked her close.

"Fight!" she yelled. "Fight!"

The witch kicked and pulled her hair, but Gondol refused to budge. She leaned in and shrieked at the top of her lungs, "FIGHT!"

Delia

DRAWN BY A DISTANT VOICE CALLING HER "SISTER," DELIA stirred to consciousness and cracked open her eyes. She found herself reclining in a cushy chair with a blanket draped over most of her body.

A room took shape around her, lit by an unseen lamp that propelled shadows toward the far wall. She inhaled and caught her breath in surprise when an overwhelming assortment of aromas—dusty and herbal—filled her nose. She turned her head and winced as the touch of rough fabric against her cheek shot electric pain through her. She lifted her hand to touch the spot, but the movement set off a series of new aches in her arm.

Slowly, gingerly, she held up her hand. Two of her fingers were bandaged together, and her palm was covered with well-cleaned scrapes. As her gaze traveled along her arm and clocked the many cuts and bruises in her skin, she gradually began to remember what had happened: the Wild Hunt, the loss of her power, the fall from the clouds, Senji struggling to slow their descent.

"Senji?" she mumbled, looking around the cluttered room.

She didn't see her partner, but she did notice a woman—middle-aged, dark hair in a bun, muttering to herself—on the floor nearby. Pushing herself up a bit, Delia saw that the woman was kneeling next to a young man who was lying on his back with his eyes closed. She seemed to be checking his vitals, and appeared oblivious to Delia's presence.

Delia squinted at the man's face. He looked familiar, but she couldn't place him.

Sister!

The voice intruded on her thoughts again, clearer but still distant. Bit by bit, Delia gathered fragments of the voice's message and pieced them together.

Sister. Witch. Stolen power. Take back. Fight!

Now suspicious, Delia swept the blanket off of her body. She saw that she was wearing her Navy nurse's uniform—the one she wore the day she died, the one that only reappeared on her when Georgette drained her power.

I fell because of Georgette! she realized. Anger flushed through her as her eyes darted to every bloody scrape and colorful bruise on her skin. *Who the hell does that witch think she is?*

Furious, she reached inside herself, seized the tether that bound her to Georgette, and started to pull her magic back. She encountered resistance, but she yanked hard on the brand and felt Georgette give ground. Soon, the nurse's uniform faded and Delia's Valhallan-spun shift dress returned. Though the pain of her injuries diminished, the wounds themselves were not closing, so Delia reeled in her power faster in an effort to make her body whole.

Delia!

Senji's voice reappearing inside her mind caught her off guard. Pausing, she momentarily allowed him to engage her attention.

Where are you? she demanded. *I have bruises—*

Delia, stop this instant!

The urgency in his tone startled her. *What?*

Let Georgette use your power!

After a moment of muddled thought, she suddenly felt Senji's internal presence wrench control of the *Hathiya* away from her. Valhalla's magic began to drain out of her again.

Raging, Delia pushed back against his consciousness. *Stop!* she shrieked.

Delia, he responded in a calm voice, *this is an emergency. Georgette—*

The witch is a thief! Gritting her teeth, Delia dug her nails into the arms of the chair as she fought within their shared mental space. *Let go!*

Gondol poisoned you with Eitr, said Senji.

Let go! Delia screamed again. *Georgette's stealing from me and you're helping her!*

He sighed, a sound of sadness and great frustration, but she felt his determination hold firm. *I cannot let you do this. You will understand when you sober up.*

Like a pair of wrestlers, they grappled in close combat within their shared mind, each fumbling for a hold but unable to gain an advantage. Delia shouted disjointed threats and insults at her partner, but Senji never said a word. His silence enraged her more than his defiance did.

Unexpectedly, a childhood memory flashed through Delia's mind. She and her sisters were playing tug-of-war with the neighbor's sons. The boys knew they were stronger than the three Beauregard sisters, and they smirked obnoxiously at the girls from the far end of the rope. Delia shared a knowing look with her sisters, and they gave the rope one big yank before dropping it completely. The neighbor boys flew backward and landed in a heap while the girls laughed. They lost the game, but it was a victory.

Delia gave Senji's mental presence one last shove and then fully released her hold on the *Hathiya*. Power roared out of her, emptying her battered body of magic but also removing her link with Senji. The moment she felt him vanish, she seized control of the *Hathiya* again. This time, she pulled her power back into herself so fast that the room around her seemed to spin.

Finally, her limbs, though still bruised, felt light enough to float out of the scruffy armchair. With a gesture, she summoned her sword into her hand and held it up before her eyes. The sight of its glittering silver blade brought a grin to her face, and she laughed aloud with the joy of victory.

Georgette

TO ESCAPE FROM GONDOL'S GRASP, GEORGETTE HAD TO rip the front of her already torn dress, leaving shreds of lavender cloth in her attacker's hands. Finally free, she flew away as fast as she could while anxiously tying together loose strips of the remaining cloth to cover her exposed chest. The crazed Valkyrie's shouts followed her as she gave chase.

What the hell? Georgette thought, her mind spinning. *Why was she shouting at me about—*

The truth struck her hard. *She was talking to Delia* through me. *Did Delia hear her?*

She received her answer when she felt the stolen Valkyrie power draining out of her body and returning to its source. Pure terror shot through her veins; she was high above the ground and rapidly losing the magic that allowed her to fly. Despite her frantic efforts to keep the magic, she suddenly found herself losing altitude at an alarming rate.

As the wind pummeled her face and wailed in her ears, she flailed her limbs and screamed, her gaze locked on the ground that was quickly rising to meet her.

A flutter of black feathers whizzed past her head. Something caught the back of her dress, yanking it upward, and her fall slowed.

Still crying in fear, she looked back over her shoulder and saw Senji gripping her dress in his talons. His wings beat the air as wildly as her heart beat in her chest.

"Senji—"

"Wait!" he snapped.

Obediently, she closed her mouth and glanced down. They were still falling, albeit not as fast as before; Senji's efforts to keep her airborne were not having much effect. She tried to think of a spell that would help the situation, but knowing that she was ten seconds from impact made concentration impossible. With a yelp, she threw her arms around her head.

Valkyrie energy suddenly flowed into her through the *Hathiya*, and Georgette grasped at it eagerly. In a split second, her body was light enough for Senji to bring their fall to a stop. As she touched ground, she took a shallow breath and cracked open one eye. She exhaled the breath in a gasp. Tears leaked from her eyes as she extended her arms and placed her fingers in the grass. Senji released his grip and she flopped onto her side, panting, her pulse sputtering.

"Delia is still drunk from Eitr," Senji said, his beady eyes twitching. "I'm trying to funnel the power to you, but she's fighting me." He squawked loudly as he shook his head. "She's not listening!"

"Because she heard *me*." Gondol hovered a few yards away from them, sword in hand and a victorious grin on her face. "So it's Svanhild's power you stole." She floated toward them slowly, her bloodshot eyes narrowed. "She heard me, and now she's taking it back."

Georgette saw Senji's small body tensing beneath his feathers. Her *Hathiya* brand hummed, feeding her a hint of the back-and-forth struggle taking place between Senji and Delia. From what she could sense, neither had a clear advantage.

She looked at Gondol inching closer, at the sword in her hand. Watching the Valkyrie's slow approach, she realized, *She's waiting to see who ends up with the magic before she attacks.* She remembered watching Delia cut the soul from a man's body, leaving him at once comatose and a homeless spirit. A shudder ran down her spine. *If I don't have Valkyrie magic, I can't summon Delia's sword to protect myself from the same fate!*

A violent jolt went through the raven's body, and he suddenly collapsed to the ground, unconscious. Simultaneously, Georgette felt the last remnants of Valkyrie power vanish from her body. She trembled. Delia had won.

She scooped up Senji and jumped to her feet, only to see Gondol flying at her. She froze in fear, unable to do anything but watch the seconds of her life tick away.

"Georgette!"

Nico's shout rang out across the field. Gondol faltered, her eyes darting over Georgette's shoulder, and Georgette snapped out of her trance. With Senji limp under her arm, she took off running. Behind her, she heard Gondol bellow in anger and knew the pissed-off Valkyrie would give chase.

She looked ahead. Nico was hurrying toward her from only a short distance away. Panting, she veered in his direction, put her head down, and pumped her legs as fast as she could. Though she was at an all-out sprint, she sensed Gondol growing closer.

"Run, Nico!" she shouted. "RUN!"

Nicolás

NICO RAN TOWARD GEORGETTE AS FAST AS HE COULD, BUT with each step, his legs inexplicably grew heavier. Georgette was obviously running at top speed, and yet the distance between them wasn't shrinking. Much to his astonishment, her every move seemed deliberate and pronounced, as if she were running in slow motion. The snarling Valkyrie flying after her, meanwhile, was raising her sword in such sedate movement that Nico could see the light of the rising sun inching across its blade.

Gondol was so close to Georgette that when that sword finally swung, it would definitely cut the witch down. But the blow did not come. The world had slowed to a crawl—except for Nico's racing mind.

What the hell's going on?

Nico commanded his astral body to move faster, but it did not respond. Panic briefly overwhelmed him, but years of his aunt's lessons swiftly asserted themselves. *This is happening for a reason*, he told himself. *I need to accept it, assess it, and abide by it.*

Obeying his training, Nico pulled his focus away from his surroundings and turned inward. *Speak to me*, he called to his spirit allies as, across vast expanses of inner space, he projected his thoughts to them. He closed his mind to all else in the world, opened himself on every level to their guidance, and forced himself to be patient as he waited for their response.

He didn't wait long. The familiar sensation of their emerging presence filled him like warm coffee poured to the brim of a cup. From realms unseen, the voices of his spirit guides began to whisper into his brain.

Nico returned his senses to the immediate scene with the understanding that regardless of anything he did, Georgette could not outrun Gondol's sword. *Because*—he embraced the thought—*I'm in the wrong place.*

There was only one other place he could be.

He reached for the silver cord that bound his disembodied soul to his body, seized it, and snapped his consciousness to its far end.

Opening his eyes, Nico saw that Mariana was bent over him in a protective stance. He couldn't see what she was shielding him from, but he did see that time was once again moving at a proper speed. That meant he had only seconds to save Georgette.

Help me! he called out to his spirit guides.

They responded by flooding his muscles with electricity. He knocked Mariana aside and jolted to his feet. He spotted Delia in the armchair, holding her sword aloft with a silly, drunken grin on her bruised face. A powerful impulse pushed away every other thought in his brain, and in that moment, Nico made the sudden but conscious decision to obey. He flung himself at the Valkyrie.

Delia's gaze shifted to him, but she had no time to react. Nico grabbed the weightless sword from her hand, swung it around, and plunged it into her chest.

Delia gasped and, with a puzzled expression, looked down at the sword buried to half its length between her breasts. "But I'm already dead," she muttered, confused.

A wave of dizziness swept through Nico, and he stumbled backward.

What have I done?

Before he could collapse, Mariana caught him under his arms and gripped him around the chest in a vise-like hold. Limbs quaking, unable to move, Nico could do nothing but stare in pure horror at the woman he had once idealized—the woman he had just stabbed.

The color began to drain from Delia's face. She lifted her head and looked at Nico through dull eyes. Her body slumped back in the chair and her arms slid down until they dangled over the sides.

She continued to stare at Nico as the light left her eyes.

Gondol

AS GONDOL CLOSED THE SHORT DISTANCE BETWEEN HER and her victim, she felt a smile spread over her face. Her eyes were locked on the back of the witch's head—a mop of springy yellow curls that the Valkyrie was moments away from splitting in half with her blade. She had lost so much that day—her Sisterhood, the second life she had been promised—but at least she would have vengeance against the witch who had brought all her plans tumbling down.

With a shriek of victory, she swung her sword with all her might.

The blade slashed through empty air.

Shocked, she abruptly drew herself to a stop. She whirled around, whipping her head back and forth, but she saw no one. The witch, the man, and the raven were gone.

Awash in confusion and fury, she screamed.

I had her! Dammit, where did she go?

She was flying higher into the air, planning to search the area from above, when something grabbed her foot. She looked down to see a thin green vine snaking up out of the grass and actively wrapping itself again and again around her ankle. More vines suddenly sprang up and stretched in her direction, snagging her legs in their tendrils. Cursing, she launched herself into the air with force, ripping the plants up by the root, but new vines fired out of the dirt and took their place, winding their way around her limbs and dragging her back to Earth.

Within seconds, the vines grew thick and robust. They twined themselves around her thighs, waist, and wrists, tightening their hold until she lost feeling in her hands and feet. Her fingers went numb, incapable of gripping her sword; rather than drop it, she reabsorbed the blade.

Though she fought against her restraints, Gondol found that she could hardly move. All she could think in her impotent rage was, *This is the witch's doing.*

"Bitch!" she bellowed. "Where are you?!"

As the vines holding her combined into a big, writhing knot, her eyes at last spotted a figure floating high above her. A crown of golden curls, flowing Valkyrie robes, one silvery finger pointing at Gondol. The witch.

A lump hardened in her throat. Somehow, this skinny blonde interloper had once again robbed Svanhild of her power and was using it to constrain her. Gondol thrashed with all her strength, fighting against the vines in a desperate last attempt to get free and throw herself at her captor, but in vain. In the end she could do nothing but glare at the witch, even as her vision blurred with tears.

Soon the little witch's raven friend soared into view and alighted on her shoulder. Following him, there came a great wave of Valkyries and their partners, flying in such tight formation across the sky that they blocked out the light of the morning sun. It was an entire brigade of Valhalla's shieldmaidens, armed and alert, charging into battle.

Gondol pinched her eyes shut. Her sisters were on their way to repel Muspelheim's invasion.

Half a dozen Valkyries broke away from the group and formed a circle in the air above Gondol. Though their clothes were all stained with blood and vomit, their fiery eyes betrayed no hint of intoxication, just fierce determination.

"Sister Gondol!" Skogul shouted down, pointing her sword at the bound woman. "I place you under arrest for high treason!"

The six women descended to the ground and tightened the circle around their prisoner.

"Your status as a warrior of Valhalla is rescinded forthwith," said Skogul. "You will be stripped of your power pending a thorough investigation—"

"Save your lies, Skogul," Gondol croaked. She leveled her gaze at the commander. "There won't be an investigation. You already have a mountain of evidence. All you needed was the identity of the AWOL Valkyrie. And now, thanks to *her*"—she snarled up at the witch—"you know it was me." Swallowing her tears, Gondol met Skogul's impassive expression without flinching. "Let's get it over with."

Skogul calmly nodded to the witch, who made a gesture with her outstretched hand. The squirming mass of vines surrounding Gondol's body briefly stiffened, then turned brown, and then withered away into a pile of decaying leaves and stems. Gondol looked up at the witch, still hovering over the scene, and felt one last twist of righteous indignation.

You ruined EVERYTHING.

The five Valkyries with Skogul simultaneously unsheathed their swords and pointed them at Gondol.

"Surrender your weapon," Skogul ordered.

Gondol silently raised her arm and opened her palm. Each of the five Valkyries took half a step forward, bringing their sword-points to just beyond Gondol's reach while staring at her down the length of their blades. Skogul's intense eyes tracked Gondol's every move. With theatrical deliberation, Gondol began to summon her weapon from the Valhallan power within herself. Then, with more speed than she had ever employed before, she drew back her arm, materialized the blade into her hand, and hurled it like a spear directly at the floating witch's heart.

Senji

AFTER LOSING THE STRUGGLE WITH DELIA FOR CONTROL of their shared powers, Senji had passed out. The drain of magic was so sudden that his brain immediately dropped into darkness. He had no sense of himself—no thoughts or dreams—but then the power surged back into his tiny body, and he exploded back into consciousness.

"You okay?" Georgette whispered to him, holding him close.

"Yes," he replied, relieved.

While Georgette used Mei-Xing's powers to capture Gondol, he went to fetch the other Valkyries. An easy task, as it turned out, since the entire brigade was already headed in their direction. Senji led Skogul and five others back to Georgette and then perched on the witch's shoulder to watch them take the traitor into custody. The victory felt hollow without Delia there to see it.

From several yards above the ground, he tried to reestablish his link with Delia, but without success. Not only did his partner not respond to his calls, the space within him that she normally occupied felt eerily empty. He scanned his mind for her familiar echoes, but Delia's memories—the memories Valhalla had poured into his brain when they were bonded after their deaths—were elusive. They were there, he was sure, but they seemed too slippery to hold. This was unlike anything he had ever experienced before during their decades-long partnership.

Delia? Please answer me.

A sudden movement on the ground below them brought his focus outward. His heart stopped when he saw Gondol's blade hurtling in Georgette's direction.

On the day of Senji's kamikaze flight, he had hesitated upon spotting the ship he was meant to hit. He didn't want to die—but he did want to make his family proud. Putting his plane into a nosedive, he kept his thoughts on his loved ones as he completed his mission.

Now, more than seventy years later, Senji did not hesitate. He instantly dove between Georgette and the blade.

Though tiny, his body's impact was enough to divert the sword's flight, ensuring it wouldn't touch Georgette. But in the process, it pierced his chest and passed through his body from tip to hilt.

Georgette's scream rent the morning as she snatched his falling body out of midair and pulled him to her chest. But the Valkyrie blade had already done its damage: Senji's spirit had been separated from his flesh.

He was floating upward, watching Georgette cradle his body. After an initial flash of panic, Senji grew calm. He experienced no pain or fear, just a pleasant sort of numbness that whisked away all his worries. An incandescent blue mist sprayed out of both his body and soul as his astral self flew unchecked through the air. The star-like sparkle of that mist mesmerized him, and he reached out to touch it as he soared farther away. He was surprised to see that his incorporeal soul had human hands, not wings or talons, and he stared at them in childlike wonder.

The flow of blue mist slowed and then ceased, but his soul continued to sail away, the sobbing Georgette getting smaller and smaller by the second. Through it all, Senji felt at peace.

Just before Georgette disappeared from view, the glow of Valkyrie magic suddenly left her and she plummeted, shrieking, out of the sky. *Of course*, Senji thought after a moment of drowsy reflection. Without his and Delia's magic, she must be falling to Earth. The thought momentarily upset him, but then he again became calm. She would be okay. They all would. His part in their lives was over.

Senji's vision became fuzzy, gradually erasing all of Valhalla from his sight, as the morning sky shifted into a midnight-blue blanket of stars. He looked down at himself. His spirit was in human form, dressed in the uniform he had worn on the day of his kamikaze flight. One hand drifted to an inner pocket of his flight suit and withdrew the photo he'd always carried of his parents and brothers. Their serene faces gazed out at him from that moment frozen in time. And then they smiled. Their voices called to him, happily urging him to join them. They had missed him. They loved him. He had completed his mission and it was time to come home.

Senji smiled. He closed his eyes. He let go.

"*Lâche pas la patate*, Delia."

Georgette

GEORGETTE SAW THE SWORD LEAVE GONDOL'S HAND. BEFORE she could react, Senji dove between her and the weapon. It ran him through and then sailed noiselessly away. And all she could do was scream.

When she caught his limp body, she could feel a fluttering heartbeat within his chest, but it grew weaker with every second. She rushed to cast a healing spell, but since Senji was physically uninjured, it was ineffective. And yet his life was draining away, turning to mist that slipped between her fingers, along with the magic he shared with her. Georgette's hands trembled and helpless tears burned her eyes.

"Senji!"

A final breath leaked from the bird's beak, and his heart went still. Simultaneously, the last trace of Valkyrie power left Georgette's body and she dropped from the sky. She fell not to the ground of Valhalla but through it—across a cloudlike ethereal boundary, and down toward Earth.

Wild wind sent her tumbling as it roared in her ears and drowned out every other sound. Sudden, biting cold penetrated the pitiful remnants of her cocktail dress and crusted her skin in an arctic freeze as she tumbled uncontrollably through the sky. Instinctively, she called upon Ishak's power and sprouted thick yellow fur all over her body for warmth.

Then she controlled her spin, faced herself downward, spread her limbs for stability, and squinted into the wind.

To her own surprise, she did not feel overwhelmed by fear. She was falling, but the ground was so far away that it didn't really seem to be getting closer. In fact, if not for the air stinging her eyes, she might have called the experience fun. It felt like flying.

But I'm not flying, she reminded herself. *I'm falling. And I've probably got less than a minute before I hit the ground.*

She steeled her resolve to find a solution before she wound up a bloody smear on the pavement. Her access to Valkyrie power was gone. She couldn't sense Delia, and Senji was . . . She tearfully shoved her grief aside. *Focus.*

Mei-Xing's powers wouldn't be any use in the air, and Ishak's shape-shifting abilities did not include wings. And . . . that was it. Those four were the only beings Georgette had access to via her *Hathiya* brand. If she were a true Nichols witch, she would have the magic of dozens, maybe even hundreds, of Fae creatures available to her—but Georgette, as her mother so often pointed out, was a disappointment to her family. Since she lacked familiars to steal from, she would have to rely on her own limited magical energy.

She suddenly remembered a spell Aunt Laurel had taught her, one Georgette's sisters and cousins had shown no interest in learning. It was a cute trick, they'd all said, but not actually good for anything. *We'll see about that,* she thought now.

Working from memory, she recited the incantation, summoned the appropriate energy, and sent it throughout her limbs and torso. The spell took effect and altered the composition of her body, hollowing out her bones and withering her muscles until they were a fraction of their previous weight. Then, as the winds tossed her much lighter body about like a cork in river rapids, she used another spell to expand what was left of her tattered dress, creating dual stretches of fabric between her arms and her sides.

With great effort, she extended her spindly arms and legs until her makeshift gliding wings caught the wind and buoyed her up. The minimal muscle in her limbs made holding herself steady a challenge, but she felt that it was working. Her descent was slowing. While she had bought herself some time, however, she hadn't saved herself from the inevitable: a likely fatal landing.

What else can I do? she thought frantically. *I've got a few more minutes to work with. What's the best way to use them?*

Unprompted, images of Neil popped into her head. His warm, good-humored smile lit up her mind and nearly made her sob out loud. She tried to swallow the hard lump in her throat, but then an image of Mei-Xing appeared, and the lump grew larger. She might never see either of them again. Ishak, Ziya, Rue, Poppy, Nico, and all the Nocturne Fae . . . Without realizing it, she had seen them for the last time. There was so much she still wanted to say to everyone. The lump sprang from her throat as a loud sob that was immediately snatched into oblivion by the wind.

Another lump started to form, fed by misery and panic, but Georgette gulped it down.

I will not die like this! Not! Like! This!

With seconds ticking away and her strength rapidly depleting, Georgette settled on a final, desperate strategy. She threw open her senses to every thread of magic within her reach: ley lines, spiritual avenues, ethereal energy veins running between realms, absolutely anything she could access, even if only for a microsecond. She shot a powerful vibration through every string and strand she managed to touch to convey an urgent message: *HELP!*

The ground still looked far away, but she knew it was getting closer. *HELP!* She wanted to hug Mei-Xing and help her recover from what that bastard Jin had done. *PLEASE!* She wanted to make long-term plans with Neil—marriage, kids, the whole nine yards. *HELP ME!* She wanted to send Ishak and Ziya home, no matter what it took. *ANYONE!* She wanted to meet with Nico for another therapy session. *PLEASE!* She wanted to get Kazimiera's problem under control. She wanted to give Rue a place to escape to once she turned eighteen. She wanted to find Delia and grieve Senji. She wanted so much more. *HELP ME, PLEASE!*

A dot appeared in her distant vision, zipping through the sky along the horizon at a shocking speed. Blinking rapidly against the constant wind assault, Georgette saw the dot shift its direction and fly toward her, growing larger as it got closer. Now a large blur to her squinting eyes, whatever was coming toward her suddenly shot up, passing her by and disappearing from her sight. Before she could do more than gasp, it dropped down next to her and paralleled her fall.

"Yolotli!"

Ears flapping and fur rippling in the wind, the small wolf gestured with his head. Georgette lunged for him, threw her wasted arms around his neck, and clung to him fiercely. With stomach-dropping swiftness, he halted her fall and began a slow, controlled descent. The musky smell of his body filled Georgette's nose as his confident movements calmed her fried nerves.

"Thank you!" she shouted into the wolf's ear. "You saved my life!"

Yolotli bobbed his head in response and continued to carry her toward Earth.

Georgette considered asking him to return her to Valhalla—she had promised Skogul an explanation, after all—but then she realized he couldn't take her there. The only reason she'd been able to enter Valhalla in the first place was because her body had been inundated with Delia's power, and she couldn't draw on that power anymore—not with Senji gone.

Senji.

Grief took hold and drove out all else until, burying her face in Yolotli's fur, she quaked with tears.

Yolotli dropped Georgette on Nocturne's roof and immediately hurried off, racing away up into the brightening sky. Once the building was solidly beneath her feet, she released her spell and Ishak's power, which left her feeling weak and empty.

The sounds of traffic and chattering pedestrians gradually rose from the street below and filled the air. Minutes ticked by, and all Georgette could do was gaze up at the clear, beautiful sky through tear-filled eyes.

Delia & Senji

Delia skirted the border of existence, toeing the line of oblivion. It was not life, it was not death. It was and it was not. She had no sense of herself, no memory, no feeling. She had no senses, no surroundings, and virtually no grasp of her own existence. She was something less than a soul. She was . . . a spark. A dwindling ember destined to be extinguished in the absence of kindling upon which to grow.

Then she heard a voice. Faint. Kind. Wistful.

Lâche pas la patate, *Delia*.

Delia. Yes. That was her name. The spark alit upon the name, caught, and blazed like the sun. She was Delia. She remembered. Consciousness formed around her growing light and molded itself into a familiar shape from memory—thoughts, feelings, knowledge, sensation.

The spirit of Delia Beauregard, the Valkyrie Svanhild, became whole and reemerged from nothingness.

Instinctively, her revived soul sought its body, but the Eitr-spawned flesh was gone. Clearheaded for the first time in weeks, she now understood why. That body had only ever been an incomplete construct—a poisonous, drunken dream. Once her soul was severed from it by a Valhallan blade, the body could not last. It dissolved and was gone forever.

Delia's consciousness strove toward reality. With each step, she sensed the magic of Valhalla returning, strengthening her and lighting her way. As a fully empowered Valkyrie, she reached for her partner, wanting his comfort and guidance.

Senji.

The silence that followed upset her in a way she couldn't explain. She hurtled onward, her spirit approaching the real world, and yet she did not hear his voice.

Senji?

She heard nothing but the echo of her own voice in the silence. Though she was whole again, she felt a profound emptiness clinging to her soul.

Senji . . .

Delia

DELIA AWOKE AND SPRANG FROM THE BOTANICA ARMCHAIR robed in full armor. The sword that had dealt her a second death was now in her hand, clutched in ghostly fingers that pulsed with Valhallan magic. Delia examined it, along with her reflection in its silver blade. There was her face, just as young and statically timeless as the day she died on the deck of that ship.

Lowering the sword, Delia's gaze fell upon two mortals staring at her. The woman with dark hair in a bun stood at the far end of the small room. Her face was an impassive mask—one carefully crafted to disguise her emotions, Delia sensed—but her eyes danced tirelessly over Delia as if searching for the one inch of her that made sense. The young man clung to her in a fierce embrace, but his bloodshot, waterlogged eyes were on Delia. Everything in his expression and posture said that what he was witnessing was shocking. When Delia looked into his eyes, she experienced a powerful magnetic pull that she had not felt since . . .

Tearing her gaze away from the pair, Delia launched herself upward, through the ceiling, and into the sky. Not once did she glance back as she barreled upward, onward to Valhalla.

The place in her mind that usually housed Senji's voice was empty. The part of her senses that she shared with him was untouched, unused. The memories of his life Valhalla had poured into her upon their mutual death felt distant and vague, like a dream hours after waking. Senji's very presence, once an essential aspect of her afterlife existence, was now nothing but footprints in the snow.

Descending out of the skies above Valhalla, the rising sun blanching the last of the dawn colors to blue, Delia made straight for the Great Hall. Near the front steps, she saw a cluster of sleeping Valkyries bound and under guard. Though this sight was peculiar, she quickly directed her attention to the other side of the steps, where a few Valkyries had laid out the bodies of horses, wolves, and, to her horror, a number of ravens and crows.

She made an abrupt landing nearby and ran full tilt toward the lifeless partners.

"Stop!" shouted a Valkyrie with just one eye. She stepped in Delia's path with a hand held up. "Identify yourself!"

"Svanhild," Delia replied. "I fell from the Wild Hunt." Her eyes swept over the line of dead animals. "Who did this?"

"Gondol," said another warrior woman. She dropped a dead crow with grayish feathers next to the body of a large white wolf. "She got them"—she pointed at the group of sleeping captives—"to attack us while she killed all of these partners."

Scanning the dozens of fallen beasts, Delia felt nauseous. "No one stopped her?"

The other Valkyrie huffed and tossed a tuft of frizzy red hair out of her eyes. "The bitch got us drunk on Eitr so Valhalla would be unguarded when Muspelheim attacked."

"Muspelheim?" Delia's mind reeled. "Are the Fire Giants attacking?"

"No," the redhead said. "Some witch got us all to puke up the Eitr, and the Sisterhood went out in force to push back the enemy. Early reports say Muspelheim decimated the front lines but retreated when they saw hundreds of Valkyries approaching."

"I think . . ." Delia paused, digging deep into her memory to get through past intoxication. "I think she wanted to be mortal again so she could enjoy the life she never got to live."

"Seriously?" scoffed the redhead. "All this because she's butthurt about dying young?"

"A lot of us died young," said the one-eyed Valkyrie. She dropped a wolf corpse next to the others and then pointed to her eyepatch. "I got a bullet to the head when I was seventeen, working my after-school job. The twitchy a-hole just wanted money, but when I popped open the register, the noise startled him and he pulled the trigger." She nodded down at the wolf carcass she had just added to the row. "That's him. Can't say I didn't resent him for killing me, but I wouldn't destroy the whole world because of it. And," she added with a sigh, "I didn't want this for him. We liked protecting the world, y'know? I kinda thought that was the whole reason behind partnering Valkyries with their killers—to overcome personal feelings for a greater good." She shook her head. "What happens to Valkyries without partners, anyway?"

"They get 'retired,'" said the redhead. "A Valkyrie without a partner—without an enduring tie to the living—is like a gun without a safety. Too dangerous to keep around. She's relieved of duty and shuffled off to the next life, and her official name gets reassigned to a new recruit."

A sour look crossed the one-eyed woman's face as she shifted her gaze to her deceased partner. "You killing me started this little adventure, and her killing you ended it. Under other circumstances, I might appreciate the irony."

A pair of Valkyries approached. The first unslung a wolf from her shoulders, while the second deposited an armful of dead birds. When the last bird fell, Delia's eyes widened and her gut clenched. Every other bird had been a slightly off shade of black, or had a not-quite-right beak or too-long wing feathers. But this final raven was so intimately familiar to Delia that at the sight of him she felt the excruciating twist of all her fears coming to pass. The miniature *Hathiya* brand on his leg, the final nail in the coffin, extinguished her last flicker of hope.

A strangled cry burst from her throat as she lunged past the other Valkyries, her hands outstretched toward Senji's lifeless body.

Georgette

GEORGETTE AND MEI-XING SAT TOGETHER QUIETLY, THEIR arms around each other and their heads together, their tears and words finally run dry. The rough bark of Mei-Xing's hand in hers and the leafy aroma of the Nymph's grass hair filled Georgette with contradicting emotions. Though she still felt heavy with grief, she also felt renewed. Sharing her misery with her best friend had not eliminated the heartache, but it had mended their bond—and regaining that connection had filled a bleeding hole in her heart.

"Ladies." Ishak's voice broke into their commiseration.

The pair raised their eyes to see their Bultungin friend standing over them with Ziya in his arms. He wore such a somber expression that Georgette realized he must have overheard their unhappy conversation. "I do not wish to interrupt," he said kindly, "but Neil is still in the lounge, waiting to hear from you."

"Oh God!" Georgette exclaimed. She swiped her bare arm across her face, wiping the tears from her puffy eyes. "He must be so worried!"

"He knows you have returned," Ishak reassured her. Ziya fussed as her father shifted her to one arm and used his free hand to retrieve Georgette's phone from his pocket. "I messaged him while the two of you talked."

Mei-Xing's fingers tightened around Georgette's hand. "Then why didn't he come up here?" asked the Nymph.

"Because he is guarding the . . ." Ishak's lip curled. "Offender."

Mei-Xing's petal lips shriveled and her iridescent eyes darkened. "He's still here," she hissed. "He's still alive."

Ishak stepped around the two girls and picked up a sweatshirt from the sofa. He held it out to Georgette, who accepted. While she slipped it over her head, covering the tattered remains of her dress, Ishak leaned toward Mei-Xing and said, "That can change, if you wish."

Georgette opened her mouth to protest but then chose not to speak. Though she'd seen more than enough violence that night, she didn't particularly care if Jin lived or died. And it would not be a hard sell to the Nocturne Fae that Jin should be thrown into the basement as food for Kazimiera.

A sob burst from Mei-Xing's throat. Startled, Georgette forgot her thoughts of Jin and pulled her friend into a hug.

Her cheek pressed into Georgette's shoulder, Mei-Xing shook her head. "I just want him to leave me alone!" she croaked. "I never want to see him again!" She lifted her head to look at Georgette with a hopeful expression. "Please," she pleaded, "I want him to go away. I want him to forget me. I want . . ." She clamped her mouth shut as she lowered one hand to her stomach. "I want any seedling I grow to be mine alone."

Fresh tears filled Mei-Xing's eyes, and Georgette felt a rush of both compassion and comprehension. In the madness of all that had happened, she had forgotten that this was not the first time Mei-Xing had blossomed. Years ago, back in China, Mei-Xing had made the difficult decision not to nourish her only sprout. Regardless of the circumstances that had led to her friend having a second chance, Georgette meant to throw her full support behind her.

"I'll take care of it," Georgette promised. "He will *never* bother you again. And"—she blinked back tears—"I swear I'm going to be the best auntie ever."

One step into the employee lounge, Georgette locked eyes with Neil—and relief flooded her body. He leapt to his feet and darted toward her, and she met him halfway, throwing her arms around his neck with a sigh so deep it hurt her lungs.

Neil planted kisses on her neck, his arms trembling as he crushed her against his body. For the first time in weeks—perhaps far longer—Georgette felt safe. She felt that she had come home.

"I'm sorry," she whispered in his ear.

"No," he whispered back. "You don't owe anyone an apology, least of all me." He pulled back from her a little, just enough to kiss her lips and then press their foreheads together. "You made the best decisions you could with the information available to you. And you were so brave!" he said with a smile. "I'm proud of you."

Smiling and weary, Georgette stared into his eyes and held him close, letting his body heat warm her inside and out. "Thank you," she murmured. "I love you."

"I love you, too." He squeezed her even tighter. "I'm in this thing for the long haul. Don't ever doubt it."

"Same." She planted a firm kiss on his lips and lingered there for a moment. When she finally ended the kiss, she said, "I need to do something. Can you help me?"

"Whatever you need."

Georgette followed a few steps behind Erskine and Crispin as they carried a weak and groggy Jin toward Nocturne's main entrance. After casting a basic healing spell over Jin to make him fit for travel, Georgette had grabbed the first two Fae she saw who could pass for human and enlisted their help.

Neil led the way through the building, opening doors as the Incubus and Selkie carried Jin between them along hallways and down stairs. As they went, Georgette used the last of her strength to prepare a spell. She had made a promise to Mei-Xing, and she meant to keep it.

Jin finally roused himself out of his stupor when Neil opened the front door and the fresh morning air gusted over them. Groaning, he rolled his head back and forth until his gaze came to rest on Neil.

"What's going on?" he muttered.

"You're leaving," Neil firmly replied.

Erskine and Crispin stopped before reaching the door—the spells that kept them safe stopped at the boundaries of the building—and shifted Jin's weight to Neil. Neil held Jin up by one arm and dragged him over the threshold, Georgette just a step behind. All three emerged into a sunlight-drenched city that was blissfully unaware of how close it had just come to disaster.

"Man," Jin moaned, eyes closed against the sun, "I feel like shit." He started to rub his neck but stopped when his fingers touched the bandage wrapped around it. Confused, he asked, "What's this?"

Taking a deep breath, Georgette reached out and planted both hands on Jin's head.

Brow furrowed, Jin squinted at her through bloodshot eyes. "What're you—"

"You drank way too much." Georgette laced her voice into her spell, passing the words via magic directly into Jin's brain to construct new memories over those she wanted to erase. "You inappropriately touched a bunch of women. One man confronted you, you hit him, he injured your neck." Fixing him in an unblinking stare, Georgette blazed her spell deep into Jin's mind and pushed hard to overwrite the previous night. "You are done with Mei-Xing," she enunciated. "You got bored of her, told her to get lost, and threw away the phone you gave her. She left the club with another man." She leaned in close and put every last ounce of her remaining energy into one final push: "You will never speak to her again."

As the spell wrapped up and Georgette let her hands drop to her sides, she sensed the magic taking hold. Though she was worn out from her night in Valhalla, Jin was too hungover and weak from blood loss to resist her influence. She was sure the spell had worked. *You're safe, Mei.*

"What'd you say?" Jin mumbled as he rubbed his eyes.

"I said," Georgette said in a loud, clear voice, "that you've been permanently banned from Nocturne. If you come back here again, we will call the police."

Jin rolled his eyes and huffed. "Whatever. Where's my coat?"

"Here." Neil shoved the coat into Jin's hands and proceeded to drag him toward the street. "I got you an Uber. It'll take you to the hospital."

"I'm fine!" Jin shoved Neil away; he staggered for a few steps before finding his balance. "I don't need a hospital."

"Not for you," Neil told him. "The hospital where your dad is having surgery."

Jin stopped in his tracks and slowly turned his head to give Neil a puzzled look. "What?"

A red sedan rounded the corner and, in response to Neil's wave, pulled up to the curb. Georgette opened the car door as Neil grabbed Jin's arm once again and yanked him toward the Uber.

"Your dad had a heart attack last night while you were drunk off your ass and assaulting women." Neil flung a slack-jawed Jin into the back seat. "He's having open-heart surgery right now. Your phone's in your coat pocket. Call your mom." He slammed the car door shut.

A glaze of shock and disbelief stayed on Jin's face as the Uber drove off and disappeared into traffic. Jaw clenched, Neil ran his fingers through his hair and exhaled through flared nostrils. Georgette slipped an arm around his waist and rested her head on his shoulder. He put an arm over her shoulders and kissed her frizzy blonde curls.

"That's been my night," he said with a sigh. "Tell me about yours."

A million memories of the past night flooded Georgette's mind, but one asserted itself above all others. Silent tears streamed down her cheeks.

"Senji."

Georgette

THE WEEK FOLLOWING SENJI'S DEATH PASSED IN A STRANGE off-kilter tempo wherein days would fly by in a jumble but for the occasional mournful hour that limped and dragged. Georgette lost count of how many times she related the tale of what she'd experienced in Valhalla. Each time she did, she had to repeat aloud that Senji was dead, and the words broke her heart all over again.

Eventually, once everyone had heard the story, she was able to go about her work at Nocturne without interruption. Neil had urged her to take time off to grieve, but with Kazimiera confined to the basement Georgette felt she had to step up. At least her heavy workload kept her occupied.

Of all those she spoke to during that week, Nico was the only one who never asked for her story. At first, she assumed this was because he had been there to witness most of what had taken place—but soon she began to suspect that he was intentionally avoiding the subject. Curiosity nibbled at her, but she was too busy and too tired to ask him directly. She figured that if he had something to tell her, he would come to her in his own time.

But at the end of the week, it wasn't Nico who came for Georgette. It was Delia.

She arrived at Georgette's apartment early one morning with Yolotli and his partner, a Valkyrie named Thrima, at her side. Mei-Xing let them in through the balcony door and then stood and watched as the small Valhallan contingent approached Georgette, a stiff air of formality clinging to every step.

"Georgette Delaney, previously Ivy Nichols O'Reilly," stated Thrima, "you are summoned to Valhalla to explain your actions in regard to the traitor Gondol, as well as to give an account of your prior dealings with the Valkyrie Svanhild."

Mei-Xing cast a worried stare at Georgette. Heart racing, Georgette shot a glance at Delia's face, but the Valkyrie's morose, downturned expression did not change.

Georgette desperately wanted to know how bad this situation was—she had trespassed in Valhalla and she had branded a Valkyrie with her *Hathiya* mark, both of which were death penalty offenses. If not for Thrima's presence, she would have pounced on Delia and shaken her until the answers she wanted spilled from her mouth. Instead, she swallowed hard and made a quick assessment of the situation.

Delia's clearly not under arrest, she observed. *If I was in trouble for making a deal with her and Senji, then she'd be in trouble, too. And if they meant to kill me, they could just do it. That they've come here like this is . . . polite.*

Mei-Xing muttered dark, vengeful utterances under her breath until Thrima, eyes narrowed with annoyance, turned her head to look at the Nymph. In that moment, Delia met Georgette's gaze. Though their *Hathiya* bond was broken, Georgette immediately sensed her friend's pain. *Senji.* But this wasn't the time. She raised her eyebrows and inclined her chin in Thrima's direction. A glimmer of understanding crossed Delia's eyes, and she offered a tiny nod.

With that reassurance, some of Georgette's anxiety retreated, and when Thrima turned to face her again, she nodded. "If you can get me there without killing me," she said, "I'll go with you."

"We've made special arrangements," said Thrima, "that should allow you to pass through the barrier into Valhalla's realm."

"'Should' allow me to pass?"

"Well, yes." Mildly flustered, Thrima licked her lips and glanced down at Yolotli. The wolf made a soft grumble. "This situation is unprecedented." She held out her hand to Georgette. "Come. They are waiting."

With her hand in Thrima's, Georgette passed into the realm of Valhalla without difficulty, and they proceeded toward the Great Hall. Considering that the last time she had been there, the building had been stuffed with drunken warrior women, it seemed to be in excellent shape. But they didn't stop there; Thrima flew them past the Great Hall and over the expansive fields that surrounded it.

Georgette's anxiety began to trickle back in.

Thrima led them over the dense forest of ancient trees with no obvious destination in sight. Georgette nervously looked askance at Thrima's and Delia's grave expressions and wondered if she had made a mistake. If nothing else, she should have asked more questions about Valhalla's intentions.

Eventually, Thrima plunged out of the sky, taking the others with her in a nosedive toward an especially dark patch of trees. Georgette gasped and then held her breath as their small group dropped below the treetops and continued, to her surprise, into a skinny crevasse that zigzagged through the forest. The crack in the forest floor looked miles long, and yet it was barely wide enough for each of them to fit into single file as they dropped below ground.

Wide-eyed in amazement, Georgette scanned the rock walls on either side of her. The deeper they went, the smoother, shinier, and more crystal-like they became.

Thrima gradually slowed the group's flight before landing on a thin ledge. Georgette set her grateful feet on the firm surface, dropped Thrima's hand, and wiped her sweaty palm on her pant leg, hazarding only one glance over the edge into the crevasse's seemingly bottomless depths before turning away. A few steps in from the ledge, they came to a narrow gap in the rocks and slipped through one at a time.

The space they entered was a glittering crystal cave nearly as large as Georgette's apartment. The milky rock walls emitted a soft white glow—faint, but bright enough to light up the space. A slightly acrid scent in the air stung Georgette's nose and made her eyes water, but she was so dazzled by her surroundings that she found it easy to ignore.

From an adjacent hallway, Skogul stepped into the room. The Valkyrie captain was impeccably dressed in her official regalia, and her previously chaotic black hair had been neatly plaited into tight braids that lay flat against her scalp and draped over her shoulders. She greeted Georgette with a nod before instructing Thrima to wait where she was and stand guard.

Georgette felt a moment of concern until she caught a glance from Yolotli—a kindly look that seemed to say, "All is well"—before he dropped down on his haunches at his partner's side.

Without a word, Skogul turned and headed back down the

hallway she had come from. Georgette hesitated to follow, but when Delia gave her a gentle nudge forward, she obeyed.

The three women walked down a hallway of glowing crystal—Skogul, then Georgette, with Delia bringing up the rear. Each step Georgette took bounced back at her not as echoes through the air but as vibrations through her skin. Unnerved, she repeatedly pulled one of her curls straight and then let it go to spring up against her cheek. The repetitive motion kept her buzzing nerves in check.

"I have spent this week," Skogul said, "collecting evidence and interrogating the prisoner." Every word bounced off the crystal walls and against Georgette's skin, as tangible as a raindrop. "I am confident that I have as clear a picture of this travesty of a situation as I am likely to get."

Still walking, she tipped her head to the side just far enough to reveal one dark eye. Skogul's gaze was sharp but, as far as Georgette could discern, not malicious.

"The Valkyrie formerly known as Gondol gave a full confession. She is unrepentant. The only regret she has expressed is that her plan failed." Skogul stopped, turned around, and, with her back straight, fully faced Georgette. "We have you to thank for the traitor's failure."

Skogul's unblinking stare gave Georgette the urge to fidget. She felt a need to fill the silence stretching between them but didn't know what to say. She made a noncommittal half shrug, half nod she hoped would serve as an answer.

Skogul shifted her gaze to Delia. "Svanhild has explained the deal she made with you," she said, her tone hardening. "It is an unforgivable crime and calls for the highest punishment."

Georgette's heart skipped and her eyes darted over her shoulder, searching for an ally in that moment of fear, but her friend stood perfectly still and maintained a stoic, almost glazed expression.

"Svanhild," Skogul continued, "has been adamant that Valhalla hold her solely responsible. She explained why she allied with you and . . . I understand." The Valkyrie captain looked at Delia again, and a peculiar light glittered in her eyes. She swallowed heavily, and the jagged scar across her throat rippled. "The chance to see an earthly loved one again is a temptation every Valkyrie knows intimately . . . myself included."

Delia nodded without a hint of emotion.

Skogul sighed and raised one hand to her forehead, gently rubbing her temples. "Svanhild's interactions with you," she said to Georgette, "make quite a story. But where I lose the plot"—she lowered her hand—"is when you took it upon yourself to infiltrate Valhalla and, at great risk to yourself, expose Gondol's treason." For the first time, her expression shifted into one of curiosity. "Why did you do it? What did you expect to gain?"

Georgette licked her lips. "I-I didn't expect to gain anything," she stammered. "Senji asked for my help and . . ." She balled up her fists against her thighs and drew a deep breath. "There was no one else who could help, and it was the right thing to do."

"I see," Skogul said after a pause. She turned and continued to walk down the hallway. "That completes my investigation."

Brow furrowed, Georgette fell into step behind her. "It does?"

"Yes. Here is my official conclusion." Without missing a step, Skogul drew herself up straight and cleared her throat. "Valhalla knew that a Valkyrie was leaving her assigned area and that this unsanctioned activity might be linked to our losses on the battlefield. I had long suspected Gondol of being the Valkyrie we were looking for but could not prove it. I secretly enlisted Svanhild's aid as an undercover operative. Following my orders, Svanhild allied herself with a witch, and the two of them set up a reason for me to call for a Wild Hunt. Unfortunately, following the Hunt, Gondol unexpectedly began her systematic Eitr poisoning. Svanhild's raven then activated my contingency plan and made contact with the witch, who came to Valhalla and helped set the matter right. The traitor was apprehended and Muspelheim's invasion was thoroughly repelled, though at great cost: we lost many in the battle, and before her arrest, Gondol murdered dozens of animal partners, forcing us to retire many additional Valkyries."

Georgette felt the blood drain from her cheeks. She whipped her head around, but Delia continued to look straight ahead, the soft glow of the crystal walls barely catching her eyes.

"Will Valhalla accept that?" Georgette asked the captain. "I mean, I really appreciate what you're doing—but your 'conclusion' has some holes in it, not to mention that it throws you under the bus."

"By allying Valhalla with a witch, I exposed a highly dangerous criminal," Skogul replied. "Valhalla will accept and forgive that." She glanced back, overlooking Georgette to nod at Delia. "You will have to keep that brand on your ankle to maintain appearances."

Georgette stared at the captain. "Does that mean Delia is not being 'retired' like the others?"

"Correct," said Skogul.

A faint hope fluttered in Georgette's chest. "Then, can Senji . . . ?"

Skogul shook her head, rekindling Georgette's grief. "He was the final victim of Gondol's treachery. However, Valhalla has future plans for Sister Svanhild. Until it is time for those plans to unfold, she will be on leave." The captain's face softened slightly as she looked at Delia. "I will keep tabs on you, but I see no reason why you shouldn't be allowed to visit your sister when her time comes."

For the first time, Delia's lips curled into a soft smile. "Thank you, Sister Skogul."

The captain shrugged. "After all this, it seems like a small thing."

With a wave of her hand, Skogul led them a few more steps to a place where the passage suddenly opened up. The light of the crystal walls ended at the threshold, leaving the space before them dark and uninviting. The slightly bitter air that Georgette had managed to ignore since their arrival becamc harsher here, so severely acidic that every breath burned her lungs.

Wiping tears from her eyes, she lifted the neck of her shirt over her nose and mouth as a makeshift mask. It wasn't much help. "Thank you," she said through her shirt. "And I'm sorry for trespassing. I never wanted to come to Valhalla."

Skogul, who seemed unbothered by the air quality, let out a low chuckle. "I believe you. To the best of my knowledge, you are the first witch ever to come here." The smile dropped from her face as she got toe to toe with Georgette. "Make no mistake: this is your last visit. The brand you put on Svanhild must remain to give weight to the official story, but you cannot use her power to pass Valhalla's borders again."

"I couldn't if I wanted to," Georgette quickly explained. "I'm not connected to Delia anymore. I can't even sense the brand on her."

"Regardless, I have brought you here not just to conclude my investigation but also as a warning," the captain said sternly.

"A warning?" Georgette shuffled back a step, glancing around at the murky darkness. "Where are we?"

Skogul's face hardened even further, and a cold fire shone from her eyes. She summoned her sword into her hand and struck it against the nearest wall with a strange twang. A spark leapt off the blade and, to Georgette's shock, ignited the air above them. A painfully bright blaze spread along the ceiling of the cavern like flame following a dribbled trail of gasoline. It lit up the area for only a moment before burning itself out—but in that brief second, what Georgette saw turned her knees to jelly.

The cavern was made not of crystal, like the entrance, but of mirror-like obsidian that reflected the airborne fire as dim and ghostly glimmers. Black stalactites as sharp and jagged as knives hung down from the ceiling, and sizzling moisture dripped from their points. Underneath the highest concentration of stalactites, directly in the path of the acid drops, a naked female figure was bound to the floor with silver chains. In the instant before the flames burned out and returned the cave to darkness, Georgette saw the face of the writhing victim. All of her muscles were clenched, her gritted teeth were fully bared, and her eyes were pinched shut, as if she was using every fiber of her being to stop herself from screaming. Even without red and black face paint, the young woman's identity was clear.

Georgette gasped. "Gondol."

"Aracê!" a defiant voice screamed through the black cavern. "Aracê!"

"What's she saying?" asked Delia. Her tone struck Georgette as inappropriately calm in the face of the horror they'd just witnessed.

"It's all she says now," Skogul told her. "Even before we stripped her of her Valkyrie name, she refused to answer to anything but her human name: Aracê."

"What is this?" Georgette asked even as she edged her way backward, heading for the light of the hallway. "What's happening to her?"

"About a mile under our feet," said Skogul, "lives a colony of Hydras. This cave is one of the only places in existence where their poisonous fumes condense and drip from the stalactites." The captain glared into the dark, her lips pulling away from her teeth in a sneer. "Hydra poison has many unique properties. Right now, it's burning away our treasonous sister's Eitr-grown flesh. Once her body is gone, it will burn her spirit. But her spirit won't burn away. It will just *burn*." She cast a razor-sharp glare at the witch. "Do we understand each other?"

"Yes, ma'am," Georgette whispered.

With a brisk nod, Skogul turned her back on the unseen prisoner and marched toward the crystal passage. "That will be all," she announced. "Valhalla thanks you for your service."

Thrima took Georgette to the border of Valhalla, whereupon she handed the witch off to Delia and instructed her sister Valkyrie to escort their guest back to Earth.

As his partner flew away, Yolotli lingered at the border.

"Thank you for everything," Georgette said.

He offered a courtly head bow, smiled as only a wolf could, and trotted off.

Delia took Georgette's hand without speaking, and they began their descent through the cloudy boundary between realms. The image of Gondol's pain-stricken face haunted

Georgette as they descended out of the sky above San Jose, yet she couldn't summon much sympathy for the disgraced Valkyrie. She knew what Gondol had intended to do—what she would probably try to do again if allowed her freedom. Moreover, Georgette had been warned all her life never to cross Valhalla. Gondol had surely received the warning as well, and had chosen to ignore it. Georgette was mostly just relieved not to share Gondol's fate.

The feel of Delia's hand in hers—a temporary sensation made possible by Valhalla's "day pass"—brought Georgette's thoughts back to the present. As they soared over the city together, she suddenly realized she had one last question for her Valkyrie friend.

"Did they bury him?"

The question made Delia close her eyes and lower her head. Altering their flight path, she swooped down to the nearest building and landed on the roof. She dropped Georgette's hand and wandered to the edge of the building, running her fingers through her long hair.

Georgette followed her but kept a respectful space between them.

"They allowed each Valkyrie to choose for herself what would happen to her partner's body," Delia replied with a sigh. "I asked for Senji to be cremated. I have his ashes stowed in a safe place for now." Tears leaked from her eyes, and she made no attempt to wipe them away. Each fat droplet rolled down her cheek and dripped from her chin. "I want to take the urn with me when I visit my sister in her death hour. Senji promised he would go with me. I know he would be insulted if I left him behind."

"I'm so sorry," Georgette blurted out. "Gondol was aiming at me. Senji—"

"Not another word," Delia interrupted. "Gondol threw that sword at you because she's a snake. Senji took the hit because that's who he is . . . was. And you were there in the first place because you put your life in danger to protect everyone else. Senji would never regret the choice he made. Don't dishonor his memory by wallowing in guilt." Putting her hands on Georgette's shoulders, Delia fixed her in an intense gaze that seemed to make the entire world around them slow to a crawl. "Promise me."

Staring into Delia's eyes, Georgette felt her lip tremble as she recognized what she was seeing. The Valkyrie was mourning her partner, but underneath the grief she was proud. Senji had died a hero, and nothing else mattered to her.

Tears stinging her eyes, Georgette nodded. "I promise."

A strained smile spread over Delia's face, and she nodded in return. Impulsively, Georgette jumped forward and, before Valhalla's temporary magic could wear off, threw her arms around the Valkyrie and hugged her tight.

At first, Delia stiffened, but then she relaxed and returned Georgette's embrace. Locked together, the pair quietly wept for their fallen friend.

Nicolás

AFTER DELIA RESURRECTED AND FLED THE BOTANICA, NICO had stared wide-eyed at the empty chair she'd left behind. Minutes passed, during which he felt eerily detached from his body. He had a deep-seated sense that something monumental had happened here—something so much bigger than the death and rebirth of a Valkyrie—and knowing that he was an integral part of it made him lightheaded.

Once he confirmed that Georgette had arrived home safely and their mission had succeeded, he put all thought of that night out of his mind and threw himself into his work. By splitting his time between the Botanica and his internship, keeping his gaze forward and his mind focused on whatever task was at hand, he could pretend that nothing had changed. He could pretend that he had not been to Valhalla, that Senji was fine, that he had not stabbed a Valkyrie. Any hint of his crush on Delia vanished; whereas the mental image of her stately beauty used to stir up butterflies in his stomach, now the only feeling he associated with her was the fear of what having murdered her, even if only temporarily, meant for his future.

One evening, as he sat alone in his apartment, he drowned out his intrusive thoughts by watching Netflix on his laptop while eating a hastily assembled sandwich. Suddenly, he had the sensation of being watched. He brushed it off, assuming it was Neil grabbing something from his room in between visits to Georgette. But then . . .

"How odd."

The voice startled him so badly that he dropped the last bit of bread crust and turkey as he whirled around.

Behind him, within arm's reach, stood Delia. Seeing her so close, draped in her signature flowy white cloth, threw his carefully regulated emotions into a tailspin.

Delia's expression was contemplative as she looked down at him. "I remember meeting you," she said, "but I can't seem to recall your name."

Silence stretched between them as the chatter of the show on his laptop filled the air. Delia raised an eyebrow, and blood rushed to Nico's head, making his cheeks burn. "Sorry," he blurted out. He snapped the laptop closed, silencing it, and then jumped to his feet. "I'm Nicolás García." He held out his hand toward her but quickly retracted it when he remembered that she was a spirit. "Nico."

She nodded. "Delia Beauregard."

"I know. I mean," he quickly backtracked, feeling the flush on his cheeks, "I remember."

Casually turning aside, she began to amble about the apartment, her opaque form touching nothing while her gaze swept over everything. Nico watched her, unsure of what to do or say. Though no longer infatuated, he still felt a pull toward the Valkyrie, as if a string that connected them was gradually tightening, growing shorter and drawing them together.

"It shouldn't have happened, you know," she said at last.

"What?"

"You wielding my sword."

He winced. "I'm so sorry. I just . . . with Georgette in Valhalla and—"

"Not that." She turned to face him. "You acted justly and I don't fault you for it. But it should have been impossible for you to physically touch a Valkyrie weapon. Unless infused with Valhallan magic, mortal flesh should be incapable of touching it. And yet"—she glided in his direction—"you seized it easily and without hesitation." She tilted her head and squinted. "How did you know that you would be able to do so?"

Nico had no idea. He had so actively avoided thinking about that night that it had never occurred to him that he had done something impossible. Shaking his head, he said honestly, "I wasn't thinking about it. I wanted to help and my spirit allies guided me."

A light of understanding glistened in Delia's eyes. "Your allies were the agents of fate," she said. "Have they told you why they guided you as they did?"

"I haven't been able to connect with them since that night."

Delia winced. "Like my connection to Senji."

Nico's breath caught in his throat. "Georgette told me that Senji . . . that he passed. I'm sorry." He swallowed hard. "If what I did contributed to his death—"

"It didn't," she interrupted. "The only blood on your hands is mine."

Nico opened his mouth to apologize again, but Delia waved him off.

"Your actions are the reason I've come here today." She pressed her lips tight together, forming a thin line, before asking, "Do you know how Valkyrie partnerships are formed?"

"I . . . think," he said carefully, "that a woman chosen to be a Valkyrie is partnered with the soul of the man who killed her."

"Exactly right. Furthermore, a Valkyrie whose partner dies is 'retired' from service. By that I mean her soul is sent beyond the veil and her Valhallan name is passed on to her replacement. My partner"—her voice hitched slightly—"has died. But Valhalla has not ordered my retirement. I am . . . on sabbatical, I suppose you could call it, until my next partner becomes available."

Nico stood quietly, waiting for her to finish her explanation, but she said nothing more. He shook his head. "Next partner?"

"The man who killed me."

He understood. Everything that had happened to him suddenly made sense, as if he had only been looking at snapshots of his life until now, when he had finally been given a view of the entire landscape. From the moment he saw Delia, he had been drawn to her . . . because they were fated to be joined by Valhalla. His spirit guides had compelled him to grab her sword knowing full well that he, as her future partner, was the only one who could touch it. It was even possible that the latent potential Aunt Mariana had sensed in him as a child—the potential that had led to her teaching him *brujería*—was just another step in the preordained journey designed to bring him to this moment.

"How . . ." He rasped his words through a dry mouth. "How long until . . . ?"

"Until you die?" Delia sighed. "I don't know. It could be tomorrow, it could be seventy years from now. Valkyries are given no more than a few days' notice before we're sent to collect the slain." After a long minute of scanning every inch of his face, a small, kind smile lifted her lips. "When the time comes, whenever it may be, I will be there to fetch your soul. Once our two spirits make contact, our memories will pour into each other, and we will be bonded for the duration of our service to Valhalla." She inclined her head slightly. "Unless you refuse."

"No," he replied quickly. "I've always believed that things happen for a reason. I was chosen for this." Jaw set with newfound resolve, he pulled himself up tall. "I'll see it through."

She smiled. "Senji used to say that he was glad to have a purpose, even if he had to meet Death before finding it."

The edges of her lips sank. Her gaze drifted away, and she stared into thin air as though she was listening to distant music. Behind her obscure expression, Nico thought he saw an intertwining helix of exhaustion and expectation. It was the face of a sleepless woman waiting for the sun to rise.

"*Ganbatte kudasai*, Senji," she whispered into the ether.

"'Do your best,'" Nico automatically translated. When Delia turned to him with a quizzical look, he shrugged. "I watched a lot of anime in college."

To his surprise, she chuckled. "I would say it to Senji and he would respond with, '*Lâche pas la patate*.' It's an idiom I learned growing up in New Orleans that means 'Don't give up.' It was a mark of trust between us, our way of encouraging each other."

Nico nodded. "*Échale ganas*," he murmured.

"What's that?" asked Delia.

"It's something my aunt used to say when she first started training me. *Échale ganas*. It's like . . . 'Give it all you've got.' You just reminded me of it."

"*Échale ganas*," Delia repeated. She spoke the words slowly as if tasting them, trying them out. Then she turned around and glided toward the nearest wall. "I'll remember that."

Before even reaching the wall, she had vanished. Nico continued to stand in place, staring into space for several minutes as he replayed their conversation in his head.

Deep within his core, he felt the slightest whisper of encouragement from his spirit allies; hearing it, he let the last trace of worry melt away. His greater purpose in the universe had been revealed. There was nothing else to worry him now.

Kazimiera

KAZIMIERA SAT HUNCHED ON THE FLOOR OF THE EMPTY stockroom with her back wedged into a corner and her cracked, jagged fingernails perfectly still atop her bent knees. Black, bloodshot eyes, half covered by her matted hair, stared unblinkingly at the bolted door opposite her position. Her entire body was as still as stone with one exception: the razor-sharp incisors of her upper jaw continuously chewed on her lower lip. Rhythmic and incessant, the chewing had become a self-soothing behavior akin to the pacing of a caged animal between barred walls. After days of this behavior, her lower lip was nothing but a clump of bloody flesh.

There was a celebration taking place upstairs in her club. Due to the witch's noise-muffling spells, Kazimiera couldn't hear it, but she could feel the sound through the walls. Each footstep, each voice, each popped cork was a painful vibration that worked its way through her bones and into her skull until it resounded with the force of a sonic boom. Every fiber of her being screamed for blood to drown out the pain, but since the only available blood in the room was her own, she could do nothing but chew her lip.

Her gaze darted to the left; the minute sound of her eyeballs moving in their sockets sent a bolt of pain through her head. To her left, there sat a stack of plastic containers licked so clean they could have been fresh out of the package. Once a day, the hyena-man brought her a new one full of "blood tofu"—a somehow even less appetizing name for pig-blood curd. Despite finding pig's blood repulsive, Kazimiera consumed every batch as it arrived. Her pointed teeth sliced apart the spongy blocks like knives through jelly, and the chunks slid down her throat to the taste of gelatinous metal. It filled her stomach and kept her functional, but it provided poor nourishment and certainly didn't sate her hunger.

The first time the hyena-man opened the door—the morning after she was thrown in the basement—Kazimiera hurled herself at him, jaw unhinged and claw-like fingers poised to strike. Before she could land a blow, he whipped out a spray bottle and spritzed her in the face. Initially just startled, she fell back, shook her head, and blinked rapidly to clear her eyes. Only then did she feel the intense burn. With a yelp, she frantically tried to rub her face clean, only to then feel the burn on her hands as well.

"Garlic water," said Ishak. She heard him place something on the floor—a container of blood tofu—and then he stepped back to the threshold. "I'm leaving you a damp towel to wipe away the spray and clean yourself of your grime."

"How dare you!" she shrieked, swiping wildly at her blistering eyes. "This is my building! You live here on my charity!"

"I live here through Georgette's generosity," he corrected in a vexingly calm voice. "Everyone else who lives here is a victim of circumstance, as well as your predatory nature." She heard the schlump of a towel dropping to the floor nearby. "For the time being, you are confined to this room, just as your staff are confined to the building. However, whereas they are trapped in here due to being refugees, you are being held because you are a danger to those around you."

Hissing through her teeth, Kazi said in a low voice, "I am not a wild animal. I am experiencing sensory overload."

"A condition for which you have willfully refused treatment," he replied. "Georgette offered you a spell that would improve your symptoms, but the only solution you will accept is murder. Not only are you killing innocent people, in doing so you risk drawing attention from authorities to yourself and those in your care." She heard the squeak of hinges as Ishak began to swing the door shut. "You will get no sympathy from me."

She shrieked, but he closed and bolted the door without another word.

No sympathy from him. That, she realized, was exactly why he was the only one delivering her food. Her staff would bend to her wishes, and the witch, faced with enough aggression, would be cowed. But Ishak had never seen her as anything more than an enslaver; he probably savored the chance to imprison her. The hyena-man was the perfect jailor.

Days passed in a sickening delirium. Without human blood, Kazimiera's muscles began to waste away. Hour after pointless hour, she sat in the corner, staring straight ahead and re-devouring her lower lip. Several times, she heard the witch outside her prison cell using magic. Each new spell improved the sound insulation but never blocked the noise completely. Even when all else was silent, Kazimiera's hypersensitive hearing was subjected to the sounds of her own creaking joints, shifting muscles, and stomach digesting pitifully inadequate meals. Her own body had become as much a torture chamber as the room's four walls.

Kazimiera counted the empty plastic cartons and then tried to apply that number to her foggy memory. What night was it that the witch had tossed her into this room? Taking her best guess, she counted forward, marking the days of the week. Was this a Monday night? The club was closed on Mondays. Why was there a party upstairs? She cast about for a reason, but her nutrient-deprived brain soon sank into a stupor.

Eventually, she was jolted out of her lethargic state by the sound of the door unlocking.

Feeding time at the Vampire zoo.

The door slowly swung open to reveal Ishak and, to Kazi's surprise, Georgette. The witch inched into the basement room on bare feet, her blue eyes wide and alert. Clad in a loose green dress, her hair was decked out in colorful fresh flowers and her arms were wrapped in stringy vines.

Though the witch's attire was bizarre, the thing that drew Kazimiera's attention was the tiny clay pot cupped in her hands. The little flowerpot itself—an earthy orange—looked ordinary enough, but from within leaked tendrils of glowing mist. Kazimiera didn't know what the witch was up to, but she knew magic when she saw it.

"Whazzat?" she growled.

"A spell," Georgette whispered. She stepped inside, never taking her eyes off Kazimiera. "It should help with your problem."

"Don't want," said Kazimiera.

The witch sighed. "Right now, what you *want* isn't as important as what you *need*." She tipped over the pot and poured out its luminous contents.

The mist tumbled down, touched the cold floor, and spread outward. The mist rapidly grew in volume until its soft shine coated every inch of the floor. It continued to spread, climbing the walls and rolling across the ceiling, until it knitted together overhead, completely enclosing the room. For a moment the shine intensified, lighting up the basement with the glow of a dawn sun; then it vanished, leaving the room illuminated only by its usual dull artificial light.

Before she could demand an explanation, Kazimiera felt the rumbling in the walls diminish. The thundering in her skull fell silent as the sound vibrations from the building faded away and the concrete room became perfectly still. The worst of her pain floated away, leaving her with just a faint ache.

Though her level of pain was immensely relieved, consequently reducing her hunger, Kazimiera felt a rush of fury. The basement was no longer a prison cell for a killer, it was a padded room for a mental patient. She jumped to her feet and charged at the witch, bellowing, "HOW DARE YOU!"

Georgette gasped and stumbled backward. Ishak lunged, grabbed the witch, and yanked her into the hall. Kazimiera saw a sliver of opportunity. All she had to do was push past those two to get into the hallway. After that, it was a straight shot to the stairwell, which would take her to the nearest exit. Days of eating nothing but pig's blood had left her weak, but she should be strong enough to—

She slammed face-first into an invisible barrier and, with a yelp, fell to the floor, hands flying to her throbbing brow and cheeks.

"*Rosa canina*," said Ishak. He sounded entirely too pleased for Kazimiera's liking.

"What?" she snapped.

"Wild rose," Georgette explained. "I've read European accounts of using wild rose plants to keep Vampires confined.

I wasn't sure California's native species would have the same effect; luckily, my best friend is a Wood Nymph who can grow just about anything." She gestured at the walls. "I included some *rosa canina* in the spell."

"And," Ishak added, "I convinced Mei-Xing to grow some climbing roses along the outside of the doorframe just in case." Amusement twinkled in his dark eyes. "It seems effective."

"Was this always your plan?" Kazimiera snarled at the witch as she got to her feet. "To imprison me in my own building? To force-feed me your magic? To take my place?"

Instead of the meekness and self-reproach Kazimiera had grown to associate with Georgette, the witch looked annoyed. "Kazi," she said with a huff, "my only plan right now is to get back to the party."

"Celebrating your takeover?"

"No," the witch replied irritably. "The resident Fae threw a party to celebrate Mei-Xing and I officially bringing Neil into our grove. It's a really big deal for us."

"And yet"—Ishak turned his attention to the Vampire—"she stepped away from this momentous occasion to cast a spell for your benefit . . . a spell she has been working on for days." He looked down his nose at Kazimiera. "Kind of her, is it not?"

"Shut up!" Kazimiera roared, glaring at Georgette. "I order you to remove this magic at once!"

After a tense silence, the witch tightened her lips and shook her head.

Full of impotent rage, Kazimiera screamed at the top of her lungs, sending bolts of pain through her own head, and threw herself at the door for a second time. Once again, she bounced off the invisible barrier and crumpled. This time, she curled into a ball with her back to her jailors.

Georgette exhaled sharply. "This may come as a shock to you, Kazi, but locking you up in here wasn't planned."

Kazimiera whipped her head around. "You expect me to believe that?"

"Well, yes. You know this room was supposed to be for Audrey."

"Who," the hyena jumped in, "no longer needs it. Thanks to Georgette, her Werewolf transformations are already easier. In fact, Georgette's spells and tattoos are so effective that the Luna Gris Werewolf colony is interested in hiring her to replicate them."

The witch's cheeks turned pink, making her splotchy freckles stand out. "I'm happy that it worked out. And," she said with a deep breath, "I'll be happy when you're doing better. But for now, staying here is the best thing for you."

"Who are you to decide what's best?" Kazimiera snarled. "Nothing in this building belongs to you, least of all me."

"I know," said Georgette. "But people depend on you. The Fae need your building and the system you've built around it to survive. You hired me to protect this building and the residents from threats. Right now, the biggest threat to the Nocturne community is you."

"Community?" scoffed Kazimiera. "Is that what we're calling this building full of ingrates?"

"We *are* a community," said Ishak in a low, level voice. "These Fae have embraced my family, and despite their understandable fear of witches, they have welcomed Georgette."

"I have a duty and a moral obligation to keep them safe," said the witch. "Right now, that means keeping you here."

"You self-righteous bitch," Kazimiera spat. "I built this business from the ground up. I run every damn aspect of it. If a Pixie farts on the fifth floor, I know about it. Do you seriously think you can last a month in my shoes?"

"Well," Georgette said with a shrug, "I guess we'll find out." She moved a couple of steps aside to make room for Ishak, who stepped forward and placed a full food container on the floor. "I promise to let you out of here once you're in control of yourself. I'll find better food and treatments for you as soon as I can. Please just focus on getting well."

She swung the door shut; the heavy locks bolted into place, and the spells encasing the room cut Kazimiera off from any hint of the outside world.

Still seated on the floor, a quiet she had not known for weeks settled upon her and soothed the ache in her head. Nevertheless, isolated in the basement of her own building, Kazimiera couldn't remember ever having felt so helpless and outraged.

Neil

NEIL FINISHED SHUTTING DOWN THE COMPANY COMPUTER and made one last sweep of his desk. Everything belonging to him was packed up in a cardboard box. All that was left was the computer and a small stack of completed paperwork bringing him up to date with his clients. Any work that accumulated after today was no longer his responsibility.

The office was eerily quiet for a Thursday morning, but that didn't surprise him. Ever since Jin had announced the news of his father's heart attack via company mass email, Neil was the only employee who'd been showing up for regular hours. Work was still getting done, but whereas it had once flowed at regular intervals, it was now trickling in just hours before deadline, often full of careless errors. Neil had done his best to pick up the slack out of respect for the Li family's circumstances, but as of now, he was finished. All that remained was to make it official.

As if on cue, the main door opened, and a familiar set of footsteps strode into the office.

Steeling himself, Neil quietly cleared his throat before turning to face the newcomer.

"Jin," he said, nodding politely despite the rush of anger and disgust the other man inspired.

He had not seen the boss's son since putting him in the Uber in front of Nocturne. The intervening time had clearly been rough. Jin's usually immaculate hair was mussed, and he was dressed in a faded tracksuit that Neil knew he normally wouldn't be caught dead in. A frayed bandage around his neck hid any sign of the Vampire's bite, but he still looked as pale as he had the night he received the wound.

"Listen," said Neil, "I need to talk to—"

"Glad you're here," Jin interrupted, his voice raspy. Gesturing around the empty office, he demanded, "Where the hell is everyone? My father's phone has been blowing up with calls from clients, and I can't get ahold of anybody who works for me."

Out of habit, Neil started to bite his tongue—but then he realized he didn't have to hold back. A weight lifted from his shoulders as he prepared to unload all the things he'd kept quiet about for years.

"They don't work for you," he said. "They work for your father. You taking over for your dad means they're done putting up with your crap."

Jin's already pale face drained of its residual color as he pulled back in surprise. He opened his mouth but couldn't seem to find a word of response. Instead, he just shook his head as his face scrunched up into a mask of disbelief. "The hell did you just say?" he croaked.

"This is your dad's company," said Neil. Now that the ice was broken, he felt years of pent-up annoyance barreling out of him with the force of an avalanche. "Your dad made Li International what it is through a lifetime of hard work, and he kept it all running smoothly day-to-day. People respect him, and their hard work was a reflection of that respect. All you've ever done is nod off in meetings, pawn off your paperwork on employees, run off to the country club, and"—he added with a glare—"put your hands on unconsenting women."

Jin's eye twitched. Neil knew that Georgette's magic had wiped Jin's memory of the sexual assault; still, it wouldn't prevent him from recalling all the times he'd put an unwelcome arm around Mei-Xing or all the female Nocturne personnel he'd inappropriately touched.

After pausing a moment to let his words sink in, Neil pressed on. "You've had years to learn how to run this company, but you couldn't be bothered. No one here is going to teach you now. They know full well that you aren't up to it. This"—he spread his arms wide and conspicuously swept his gaze over the unoccupied desks—"is what they think of you." Letting his arms flop to his sides, he looked Jin square in the face. "This is the result of you being an entitled little shit."

Jin's mouth opened and closed, making him look like a gasping fish. Neil stood there for a long moment, meeting his shocked gaze and enjoying his well-earned sense of satisfaction. Then he scooped up the box containing his few personal possessions, gave the office one last wistful glance, and looked at Jin with a smile. "I quit."

Jin jolted like he'd been jabbed with a cattle prod. "What?" he exclaimed. "No! You can't!"

"I'll visit your dad when he's feeling better and give him a face-to-face goodbye," Neil said. "I owe him that. I'm grateful for all the time and effort he spent teaching me the business. But"—he shook his head—"I won't work for you. I never want to see your sorry ass again."

With a curt final nod, he breezed past Jin and strode toward the door. The thump of his steps on the floor, uncommonly loud in the empty office, sounded like a hammer driving nails into the coffin of his career. *I can't think that way*, he told himself firmly. *I've gained a lot of valuable experience working for Mr. Li. And if I stay here and work for Jin, my career will be over anyway. At least this way, I'm not compromising my principles.*

"You can't quit," Jin shouted after him. "How the hell am I supposed to run this place without your help?"

Without looking back, Neil replied, "That's not my problem."

He marched through the door and down the hall, heading to the elevator for the last time. Part of him felt a deep sadness at walking away from something he'd devoted years of his life to, but the rest of him had already accepted that this was the clear path forward.

I'll find another job, he told himself, confidence growing with every step. *A better job. In the meantime, I'll have a great few weeks with Danny next month. I'll spend some more time with Georgette and help Mei-Xing with the seeds she keeps talking about. I'll give the apartment a deep clean and maybe finally learn to cook.* Pushing through his lingering doubts, he centered his mind in that positivity. He thought of Georgette's sweet face and felt a smile on his lips. *I've got nothing but good things ahead of me.*

Mei-Xing

ALONE IN THE BATHROOM, MEI-XING SAT ON THE EDGE OF the bathtub and looked down at her unglamoured body. With one hand, she ran her fingers down her throat and chest. After weeks of chafing from the buds, her woody chest was once again smooth. Her belly, on the other hand, had grown a new stalk topped with a rapidly swelling green orb. It had begun no bigger than a marble but was now almost the size of a golf ball, and its color had shifted to a sunny yellow. Mei-Xing had felt a change within herself and knew it was almost time. In a few minutes, the orb would fade to brown, the stalk would shrivel, and the seedpod would detach from her body.

As she waited for her womb to finish transferring seeds to the pod, she leaned her head against the wall and closed her eyes. Jin's smirking face was there, waiting behind her eyelids. Vague memories of him touching her, groping her, pushing inside her made her feel like her bark was infested with termites. She pushed his image away. Thanks to Georgette's magic, he would not remember what had happened that night. That meant he wouldn't face justice for assaulting her—but it also meant he would never know about these seeds. If there was a child, it would be Mei-Xing's alone. She would finally raise a child in a happy, loving grove with no abusive influence, just as she had always wished. It was the kind of chance her first sprout had not had.

For so many years, she had stubbornly refused to remember that little sprout. Now, though, as she felt the first flutterings of motherly connection to her seeds, she also felt the first twist of true grief. It had been within her power to save the seedling, to nurture it as a mother should, but she'd chosen not to. She still felt it was the right decision, but the loss had been a painful one, and until now she had never allowed herself to mourn it.

I'm so sorry you never got to live, my little one, she thought. *If I had thought I could provide you with a healthy, happy family, things might have gone differently, but that wasn't the case. Had you lived, you would have suffered. I didn't want that for you. For us. I hope you found peace in the Great Mother's embrace.*

A cramp in her stomach made her open her eyes and glance down at the pod. The outer casing had gone brown, and it was slowly rotating clockwise as its stem dried up. She watched as the connective fibers turned black and the orb broke from her torso. Cradling it in one hand, she used the other to carefully pinch away the last little bit of the stem, drop it to the floor, and then rub her thumb over the circular scar it had left behind. It was identical to another scar just a tad higher on her stomach.

She stripped away the pod's casing as if peeling a piece of fruit and then gently poured the seeds into one palm. One by one, she placed her seeds on the vanity countertop while recalling the most important lesson about seeds that her birth grove had always preached, the "rule of three halves": a Wood Nymph was only considered a successful mother if at least half of the seeds she produced were fertilized, if at least half of the fertilized seeds eventually sprouted, and if at least half of the sprouts survived their first transplant. In her long life, Mei-Xing's mother had achieved this distinction all four times she had reproduced. During her most recent fertile period, her mother had produced forty-one seeds in total. Twenty-six of those had sprouted over the course of a decade. Eighteen of the twenty-six survived transplant, of which Mei-Xing had been the fourteenth.

Fourteen. What a strange omen that number had turned out to be. Her eyes lingered heavily on the row of seeds she had placed on the bathroom vanity just now. Fourteen seeds.

So few, she thought. *My mother and aunties would be disgusted. My sisters and cousins would whisper and laugh behind my back. But*, she reassured herself, *it doesn't matter. They have no claim over these seeds. My new grove provides the healthy, loving environment I always wanted to raise a child in. I have no partner but I also have no abuser. I'm free.*

She smiled and began to examine each seed in minute detail.

She quickly discarded five. They were puny and brittle, obviously unfertilized. The sixth gave her pause, but after some thought she included it in the discard pile. It looked fertilized but the shell was too pliable; a gummy seed had no chance of maturing. She pushed all six to the far end of the vanity, planning to reabsorb their nutrients back into her body later.

Three of the eight remaining seeds were abnormally small. Mei-Xing didn't like their odds of sprouting, but she would give them a chance. Two others were a bit larger but misshapen, their surfaces puckered by little dents, but Mei-Xing had seen plants grow from similar seeds in the past. The last three seeds all looked auspicious; plump and coffee-brown, they were the type of seeds any Wood Nymph would hope for. But one of the three seeds was especially large and had a robust sheen that seemed to sing to her of the eager life within.

Affection filled Mei-Xing's heart as she brought it close to her lips. "Hello, my child," she whispered. "I expect you will be the first to break the surface of the soil. Grow quickly, little one. I'm waiting to meet you."

She smiled at her eight seeds. Eight out of fourteen. More than half.

Georgette

GEORGETTE UNLOCKED THE DOOR AND WALKED INTO HER apartment with her keys in one hand and her phone in the other, held to her ear. Darkness greeted her within, along with the eerie stillness that was the usual accompaniment of 3:00 a.m. Out of habit, she glanced at the glass balcony door and the mini-jungle of potted plants outside. She felt Mei-Xing's presence there, deep asleep in the grasses and flowers.

Also nestled among those roots, safe in the warm, damp soil, were Mei-Xing's eight seeds. Georgette smiled. She couldn't wait to be an auntie!

The moment she closed and locked the door behind her, she kicked off her shoes and, with a sigh of relief, continued barefoot into the living room. She had been wearing heels for almost twelve hours, and her feet were screaming.

Her handbag slid off her shoulder onto the floor, and she dropped her keys into its open top. "Okay," she said into her phone, speaking softly though she knew she was alone in the room. "I'll take a look at the staff assignments tomorrow—sorry, I mean *tonight*—when I come in. Since Louis will be set to leave by the end of the year, we should start making decisions about how to shuffle everyone so that all the posts are covered."

Through the phone, Odhran talked on about Nocturne's various needs: fresh ingredients for Ailill's new July menu, replacement speakers for the club, and additional personnel for security. Georgette let him talk but her mind wandered. She was exhausted, and all she wanted was to peel herself out of her dress and collapse into bed. What she did *not* want was be on the phone when Odhran inevitably brought the conversation around to Kazimiera.

Everyone in the building was deeply concerned about Kazi. The Fae seemed to understand that she was not well and was a danger to them all in her current state, but having her locked up in the basement was bad for morale. The Vampire was their savior, their protector; they all held her in high regard. The sooner Georgette could improve her condition, the better for everyone. But progress had been slow, due in large part to Kazi's refusal to cooperate in her own treatment.

Odhran rumbled on, and Georgette reached the end of her ability to listen. "I hear you," she interrupted him as she headed for her bedroom, "but I can't do any ordering or budgeting at this hour. Some of us need to sleep."

The Dullahan fell silent for a moment, and then his deep voice emitted a sort of half chuckle, half grumble. "I keep forgetting," he said. "Witches are human, after all."

This struck Georgette as a backhanded way of pointing out that he should be having this conversation with Kazimiera rather than her, but she chose to brush it off. She was tired and might be reading too much into things.

"Tell you what." She smooshed the phone between her ear and her shoulder while she shimmied out of her dress. "You take a look at the employee roster and see if you can find someone who's a good fit for your security team. If you find someone and they're willing, I'll sign off on it when I come in later."

"Just like that?" Odhran sounded skeptical. "You don't want to make the final decision?"

Because, Georgette thought, *Kazi would never let anyone else make the call on anything having to do with Nocturne.* She pressed the speaker button and set down the phone on her dresser, freeing her hands to pull one of Neil's old T-shirts over her head. *Kazi wants things done her way or no way. She needs to be involved in every decision. That's what they're used to.* She yanked the clip out of her hair and shook out her curls.

"Is there anyone who knows more about Nocturne's security than you?" she asked.

After a pause, Odhran replied, "No.""Then you should make the decision." She scooped up the phone and headed into the bathroom, where she set the phone on the counter and flipped the light switch. The light was blinding; she slammed her eyes shut, wincing against the sudden brightness. "Just let me know who you pick." She cracked open her eyes to see her weary, makeup-smeared face looking back at her in the mirror. After weeks of long hours, she had gotten used to looking this way after work and no longer cringed at the sight. "I trust your judgment."

A long silence flowed from the phone, during which Georgette plucked out her earrings and started scrubbing away her makeup.

"I . . ." Odhran rumbled. "I will do that." Another pause and then, "Thank you."

With that, he ended the call.

Georgette wondered if he was pleased that she had given him free rein or if he was annoyed that she was deviating from the established routine. Either way, it could wait until after she had gotten some sleep.

She glanced into the mirror to confirm that her face was clean before wrapping her curls in a satin bonnet. All signs of her workplace getup were gone. She smiled. The prospect of a long sleep genuinely made her fatigued body feel lighter.

Phone in hand, she flipped off the bathroom light and stepped into the hallway.

She stopped before reaching her bedroom. A soft glow lit up the far end of the hallway, drawing her eye. *I must have left a light on.*

With an annoyed sigh, she walked toward the living room, her mind already drifting into sleep. But the moment she stepped into the light, an all-too-familiar voice shocked the fatigue out of her.

"Well," said Hazel. She was sitting on the sofa, dressed in one of her designer pantsuits, her arms and legs crossed. Her expertly dyed brown hair—straight, smooth, glossy—reflected the light from the table lamp as a dull shine. Her dark eyes simmered with hostility. "Well, well, well," she repeated while drumming her long red nails on her sleeve. She raised one perfectly arched eyebrow. "And?"

An avalanche of adrenaline made Georgette dizzy. Instinctively, she reached inside herself to tug on her *Hathiya* brand, wanting to summon her friends for help—but she forced herself to stop. She drew a deep breath and centered herself in the moment. She straightened up and narrowed her eyes at her mother.

"Did you break into my home?" she snapped. "Using magic doesn't make it any less illegal, Mom."

Hazel pursed her lips. "Where's my apology?"

The words made Georgette's anger skyrocket. She couldn't

count how many times throughout her childhood she had heard her mother ask for—no, demand—an apology without explanation. Oftentimes, she used this tactic to gather intel—walking up to a family member at random, insisting on an apology, and waiting to see what that person would confess to. If no apology was forthcoming, Hazel made her target's life miserable by ordering the rest of the family to shun them.

But I'm already shunned, Georgette thought with bitter satisfaction, *so there's not much she can do to me.*

"I don't know, Mom," Georgette snarked, surprising herself with her boldness. "Have you tried looking up your ass, since you spend so much time there?"

Pure rage contorted Hazel's features as she leapt to her feet. "DON'T YOU DARE!" she thundered. "I am your mother—"

"Blah blah blah!" Georgette shouted back. "What the hell do you want?"

Hazel balled her fists at her sides. "You," she hissed, "owe me an apology for skipping the Fourth of July."

It took Georgette several seconds to process her mother's words. Had she really magically transported herself all the way across the country to demand an apology from Georgette for failing to attend their family's party? *Today's July sixth*, she realized. *I worked right through July fourth and never once thought about the party.* With a grin, she thought, *I completely forgot about it.*

Hazel's eyes blazed with fury, and her entire body trembled from her clenched muscles. "You're smiling?! I sent you a plane ticket. I paid for a hotel room. I spent all that money just so you could be part of the family for ONE DAY."

"I told you I wasn't coming." Georgette couldn't help but chuckle.

"You ungrateful brat!" said Hazel. "I gave up my body for nine months to give you life. I provided you with a home, I put clothes on your back, and I never let you go hungry. Your childhood was full of comforts, unlike mine!" She took another step forward, and Georgette caught a whiff of the peach candies that her mother used to hide wine on her breath. "I gave you—"

"Gave me what? Food? Clothes? Shelter?" Georgette gave an exaggerated shrug. "That's literally the bare minimum that parents are supposed to do for their children." She offered her mother a pitying smile. "I think you're just upset that I'm not willing to do what you want me to do anymore."

"Shut your disrespectful mouth!" Hazel snarled. Georgette could see the tiny wrinkles on her mother's face that even magic and Botox together couldn't quite hide. "I am the head of this family," she said through her teeth. "Without me, you will never amount to anything!"

"I helped avert an apocalypse without you," said Georgette. In the stunned silence that followed, she smiled at her mother. "I saved Earth from a Fire Giant invasion. I got an official thanks from Valhalla. So . . ." She laughed. "Yeah. I didn't amount to much when I was stuck with you, but now that I've gotten away from the family, I think I'm doing pretty good."

Hazel's mouth opened and closed several times before she clenched her jaw and flashed a calculated look of disgust. "I'm disappointed in you, Ivy."

"I'm disappointed in you too, Mom."

Hazel's eyes blazed. "What did you say?"

Georgette lifted one hand to her face, lit a spark of magic, and illuminated the clan signet that had been magically imprinted on her cheek at birth. "As the head of the family, you can sense every witch who has this mark. You're like the hub of a wheel. These marks are spokes connecting all of us to you." Her face hardened. "Not too long ago, I was in serious trouble and I reached out for help in every way I knew how. You must have heard me." She glared at her mother. "But you didn't come to help me."

With a pompous sniff, Hazel lifted her chin and looked down the length of her nose. "You stopped answering my calls," she retorted, "so why should I answer yours?"

Though Georgette had expected just such an answer, the smug look on her mother's face seemed to be daring her to find fault in that logic. She shook her head and pointed at the door. "Leave," she said. "This is my home and you are not welcome here. I never want to see or hear from you again."

Hazel scoffed and sauntered forward, the lamplight casting her shadow over Georgette. "You are a part of this family whether you like it or not. You belong with us." She planted her feet and put her hands on her hips. "You will unblock every member of the family on your phone and you will write to them, apologizing for your behavior."

As a child, that look and that voice were enough to bully Georgette into submission. Now, after everything she had been through, she felt nothing but exhaustion. This back-and-forth with her mother would go on forever unless she put a definitive end to it.

With a weary sigh, she closed her eyes and put a hand to her forehead. "How about this, Mom?" she mumbled. "I'll unblock them and send a group message."

"Good," replied Hazel with a cluck of her tongue. "I knew you would see reason."

"I'm not apologizing." Georgette opened her eyes again and leveled a stony glare at her mother. "I'll write a group message listing all the secrets I've learned by virtue of being part of this 'family.'"

Hazel frowned. "Secrets?"

"Funny thing about being raised by people who think you don't matter—nobody's careful about what they say around you." Georgette flashed a joyless smile. "I know where all the skeletons are. I know you use magic to hide Dad's financial crimes from the authorities. I know you got Aunt Laurel to make each of Dad's mistresses miscarry. I know Lily's already shopping around for her next affair partner. I know Daphne tracked down her deadbeat father a couple of years ago so she could set fire to his house. I know Clove has been reaching out to other witch families on the sly to see if she can build support for a possible coup against you. I know she tried to find support in the extended Nichols family, but most of them still think no one on our side of the family should ever have become matriarch in the first place. Did you know"—she leaned forward—"that a lot of your cousins suspect you poisoned your own mother to steal the headship? According to them, Grandma Rose died so soon after she first got sick that Great-Aunt Iris, who should have been next in line to be matriarch, didn't have time to make the trip before you snatched the headship runes off Grandma's body. Your cousins seem to think that you panicked when you heard Iris was on her way and gave Grandma a double dose."

Georgette paused and tried to gauge her mother's reaction but found Hazel's expression difficult to read. Undaunted, she pushed ahead.

"I could send all of that and more in a group text to absolutely everyone," she said. "How do you think the family will respond? Because I'm not sure they'll stay civil once all the secrets are out in the open."

Knowing her mother, she was making a risk assessment of the situation. If everyone's dirty laundry, crimes, and suspicions were brought to light, it could lead to all-out Nichols civil war. All it would take was a disgruntled cousin (of which there were many) calling the IRS to get Michael O'Reilly's bank accounts frozen. Without his money, Hazel would have to rely on magic alone to maintain control. She had a fearsome reputation in the magic community, but could she really hold the line if she was attacked by her own family? Could she hold on to her power without backup?

Hazel stayed silent and stock-still. Georgette gave her a minute to think and then leveled another cold glare in her direction.

"All I want," she said, "is to be left alone. I don't care what anyone back East thinks of me. I don't care about your reputation with Boston's high society or with the witches of the world. I am happy where I am. I do not need you. Tell the family, all of them, to stop trying to contact me." Scowling, she slid forward into her mother's space. "Call off your dogs," she whispered, "or I'll take them to the pound."

At last, Hazel snapped out of her reverie. Looking Georgette up and down, she hmphed. "You will regret this," she snarled. "You have no idea what it means to turn against the family. You are not prepared for what's coming."

Georgette pointed at the door again. "Get out."

Curled up on the sofa, Georgette hugged her legs to her chest, rested her chin on her knees, and stared out through the balcony door. Her mother had long since gone and she was exhausted, but she could not quiet her mind long enough to fall asleep. Try as she might, she couldn't pin down what she was feeling. It was almost an absence of emotion. Like she was trying to feel something that just wasn't there. It was . . . odd. And for some reason she needed to sit with the feeling, awake and contemplative, until she grew accustomed to its presence.

The sky slowly became colorful as the dawn crept over the city. On the balcony, Mei-Xing's garden began to perk up as the Nymph slowly roused from her night's slumber. As sunlight hit the balcony railing, Georgette had the fleeting thought that Senji might come by today. Then she remembered, and her heart ached all over again.

Through unfocused eyes, she saw the balcony door slide open. "Why are you still awake?" asked Mei-Xing as she stepped inside.

"Hazel was here," Georgette mumbled.

"Oh." Mei-Xing tensed, and her eyes darted around the living room. "Is she . . . ?"

"I kicked her out."

The Nymph's body relaxed and she smiled. "Good. What did she want?"

Jumbled memories of the conversation whizzed around her head, but Georgette made no attempt to put them in order. "Some pointless crap that only matters to her."

Mei-Xing nodded. "Maybe you should talk to Neil about it later. He likes being part of those conversations, and he needs to know what Hazel is really like."

Georgette smiled. It was amazing how quickly Mei-Xing's attitude had changed from avoiding her and Neil to joyfully embracing them both as equal members of her grove. In such a short time, they had become a family of three. *A real family*, she thought. *For all Hazel's big talk, she'll never really understand what family means.*

"Tell me about the seeds," she said, patting the seat beside her. "How are they?"

Mei-Xing's face lit up. She plopped down on the sofa next to her friend and rested her head against her shoulder. "I can sense them all," she whispered in a tone far happier than Georgette had heard from her in months. "They are sleeping in the warm soil, nestled among my roots and dreaming of the day they will sprout."

"When will that be?"

"I cannot be sure, but . . ." She giggled. "I think soon."

Closing her eyes, Georgette pressed her cheek against the crown of Mei-Xing's head. All the troublesome thoughts and feelings brought on by her mother seemed so much smaller now. She had a real family, built on love; a job that had become her calling; and a network of people who respected her. Whatever else might happen in her life, she had come a long, long way.

"I can't wait," she said.

Acknowledgments

THANK YOU TO MY HUSBAND, MATT. I AM THE BEST VERSION of myself when I'm with you.

Thank you to my son, Eric. You are an inspiration to me.

Thank you to my mom. You're always there for me.

Thank you to Eileen McFalls, Barbara Levin, and the Women Writers of the Triad critique group. I continue to grow as a writer because of your time and effort.

Thank you to the staff of SparkPress for polishing this book into its final form.

Thank you.

About the Author

ALISON LEVY has been writing since childhood as a means of coping with undiagnosed anxiety and ADHD. She earned a BA in Anthropology from the University of Virginia and moved to the Washington DC area after graduating. Two years later, she moved to Pennsylvania, where she attended the University of Pittsburgh Law School and met her now husband. She is currently a stay-at-home mom and lives with her husband and son in Greensboro, North Carolina.

Author photo © Ivan Saul Cutler

Looking for your next great read?

We can help!

Visit www.gosparkpress.com/next-read
or scan the QR code below for a list
of our recommended titles.

SparkPress is an independent boutique publisher delivering high-quality, entertaining, and engaging content that enhances readers' lives, with a special focus on commercial and genre fiction.